Shattered Crowns:

The Scapegoats

Christina Croft

© Christina Croft 2011

"... Aaron shall lay his hands upon the head of the live goat, and confess all the faults of the sons of Israel and all their transgressions and all their sins...and the goat shall bear all their sins." (Leviticus 16: 21-22)

List of Characters

Royalties

ADALBERT (1884-1948) 3rd son of Kaiser Wilhelm II
ALBERT I (1875-1934) King of the Belgians
ALEXANDER (1888-1943) Prince Regent and later King of Serbia
ALEXEI (1904-1918) Tsarevich of Russia; only son of Tsar Nicholas II
ALIX (1872-1918) Empress Alexandra of Russia; wife of Tsar Nicholas II; first cousin of Kaiser Wilhelm II
AUGUST-WILHELM 'Auwi' (1887-1949) 4th son of Kaiser Wilhelm II
CAROL I (1839-1914) King of Roumania – born Prince Karl Eitel of Hohenzollern
CAROL (1893-1953) Prince – later King – of Roumania
DONA See 'Victoria Augusta'
EDWARD VII 'Uncle Bertie' (1841-1910) King of Great Britain; uncle of Kaiser Wilhelm II
EITEL-FRIEDRICH (1883-1942) 2nd son of Kaiser Wilhelm
ELIZABETH 'Sissi' (1837-1898) Empress of Austria-Hungary; wife of Emperor Franz Josef
ELIZABETH (1843-1916) Queen of Roumania; wife of King Carol I
ELIZABETH (1876-1965) Queen of the Belgians
ERNST (1904-1954) Younger son of Archduke Franz Ferdinand
FERDINAND (1841-1928) King ('Tsar') of Bulgaria – Austrian born Prince of Saxe-Coburg-Kohary
FERDINAND 'Nando' (1865-1927) – Crown Prince, later King of Roumania

FRANZ FERDINAND (1863 -1914) Archduke of Austria-Este; heir to the throne of Austria-Hungary
FRANZ JOSEF (1830 -1916) Emperor of Austria-Hungary
GEORGE (1865-1936) King George V of Great Britain; first cousin of Kaiser Wilhelm II
JOACHIM (1890-1920) 6th son of Kaiser Wilhelm II
KARL (1887-1922) Archduke and later Emperor of Austria-Hungary
MARIE 'Missy' (1875-1938) Crown Princess, later Queen of Roumania
MAXIMILIAN (1832-1867) Emperor of Mexico; brother of Emperor Franz Josef I of Austria
MAXIMILIAN (1902-1962) Elder son of Archduke Franz Ferdinand
MAY (1867-1953) Queen Mary of Great Britain; wife of George V
NANDO See 'Ferdinand'
NICHOLAS 'Nicky' (1867-1918) Tsar Nicholas II of Russia
OSKAR (1888-1958) 5th son of Kaiser Wilhelm II
OTTO (1865-1906) Archduke of Austria-Hungary; brother of Archduke Franz Ferdinand; father of Archduke Karl
OTTO (born 1912) Archduke of Austria-Hungary; eldest son of Archduke Karl
PIUS X, (Giuseppe Sarto) (1834-1914) Pope
RUDOLF (1858-1888) Crown Prince of Austria; son of Emperor Franz Josef and Empress Elizabeth
'SISSI' See Elizabeth
SOPHIE CHOTEK (1868-1914), Duchess of Hohenberg; morganatic wife of Archduke Franz Ferdinand
SOPHIE (1901-1990) Only daughter of Archduke Franz Ferdinand

VICTORIA AUGUSTA (1858-1921) German Empress; wife of Kaiser Wilhelm II
VIKTORIA LUISE (1892-1980) Princess of Prussia; only daughter of Kaiser Wilhelm II
WILHELM II 'Willy' (1857-1941) German Emperor
WILHELM (1882-1951) Crown Prince of Prussia; eldest son of Wilhelm II
ZITA (1892-1989) Archduchess and later Empress of Austria-Hungary; wife of Archduke Karl

Politicians, Court Officials and Military Leaders

BERCHTOLD, Leopold 'Poldi' von (1863-1942) Austria Foreign Miister
BILINSKI, Leon (1846-1923) Governor of Bosnia-Herzegovina
BISMARCK, Otto von (1815-1898) Former Chancellor of Germany
BETHMANN-HOLLWEG, Theobald (1856-1921) Chancellor of Germany
CLAM-MARTINIC, Heinrich (1863-1932) Austrian statesman; close friend of Archduke Franz Ferdinand
EULENBURG, Philipp von (1847-1921) close friend of Kaiser Wilhelm II
FREDERICKS, Vladimir Borisovich (1838-1927) Minister of the Imperial Court of Russia
GIESL, Wladimir (1860-1936) Austrian Foreign Ministry official
HARRACH. Franz von (1870-1934) Bodyguard to Franz Ferdinand in Sarajevo
HÖTZENDORF, Franz Conrad von (1852-1925) Austrian General and Chief of Staff
HOYOS, Alexander von (1876-1937) Austrian Foreign Ministry Official; adjutant to Berchtold
JAGOW, Gottlieb von (1863-1935) German Foreign Minister

JAROSLAV von Thun & Hohenstein brother-in-law of Franz Ferdinand

KROBATIN, Alexander von (1849-1933) Austrian Minister of War

MOLTKE, Helmuth von (1848-1916) German Chief of Staff

MONTECUCCOLI, Rudolf (1843-1942) Chief of the Austrian Navy

MONTENUOVO, Prince Alfred von (1854-1927) – Chamberlain to Emperor Franz Josef of Austria-Hungary

POINCARÉ, Raymond (1860-1934) French President

POTIOREK, Oskar (1853-1933) – Austrian Military Governor of Bosnia-Herzegovina

POURTALÈS, Friedrich (1853-1928) German Ambassador to St. Petersburg

REDL, Alfred (1864-1913) Head of the Austrian Counter-Intelligence Service.

REID, Sir James (1849-1923) Personal Physician to Queen Victoria; medical advisor to King Edward VII and King George V

RUMERSKIRCH, Karl (1867-1947) Adjutant to Archduke Franz Ferdinand

SAZONOV, Sergei (1860-1927) Russian Foreign Minister

STÜRGKH, Karl von, (1869-1916) Austrian Prime Minister

SZÀPÀRY, Friedrich (1869-1935) Austrian Ambassador to St. Petersburg

TIRPITZ, Alfred von (1849-1930) Admiral and Secretary of State for the German Navy

TISZA, Istvan (1861-1918) Hungarian Prime Minister

TSCHIRSCHKY, Heinrich von (1868-1916) German Ambassador to Vienna

WIESNER, Friedrich (1871-1951) Austrian Foreign Ministry official

Prologue

On 28th June 1914, Archduke Franz Ferdinand and his morganatic wife, Sophie Chotek, were shot dead in broad daylight on a crowded street in Sarajevo. The murder of a relatively unknown archduke in a remote Bosnian city might well have been quickly forgotten were it not for the fact that this seemingly minor event ignited a spark that would explode into one of the bloodiest and most pointless conflicts in history. Within four years, over sixteen million people from one hundred countries would lie dead on the battlefields of the First World War.

By 1914, through a series of alliances, Europe was largely divided into two separate camps: the Triple Alliance of the Central Powers of Germany, Austria-Hungary and Italy, and the Triple Entente of Russia, Britain and France. The clashing of these empires has often led to the First World War being described as an Imperial War and their emperors have provided a convenient scapegoat on which to pin the blame for the consequent slaughter. In reality, however, not one of these monarchs – who were close friends and cousins – had any desire for war and each of them struggled desperately to maintain peace.

"All our cousins," wrote Princess Marie Louise of Schleswig-Holstein, *"were more like brothers and sisters than mere blood relations."*

This novel – the first in a trilogy following the royalties of Europe from 1913 to 1918 – tells the story of the very human tragedy that befell those cousins and friends; a tragedy which may have been deliberately engineered to lead to the destruction of the Russian, Austrian and German monarchies.

Chapter 1 – The Schloss Artstetten, Austria – April 1913

The dazzling reflection of the sun did nothing to lighten Archduke Franz Ferdinand's mood as he viewed himself in the full-length mirror. Rather than raising his spirits, the light served only to accentuate the deepening furrows in his brow and the wisps of grey sprouting through his stiffly waxed moustache. He peered at the image in the glass and saw in every line and wrinkle the scars of the humiliation heaped upon him by those whose hearts were too narrow to understand love. In the crevices around his eyes he saw, too, the deep-rooted anger that those bigots at court had dared to snub and shame the woman who meant more to him than life.

He leaned closer to the mirror, adjusting his medals and rubbing his cuff over the lustrous buttons of his blue jacket, determined that not one speck of dust would sully his uniform on his return to Vienna. No matter what insults they whispered behind their hands, he would stand erect and dignified, proudly displaying the confidence acquired through his forty-nine well-spent years until all those sneering ministers and sycophantic courtiers would have no choice but to treat their future emperor with the respect he deserved.

His boots clicked over the parquet floor as he turned from the mirror and strode onto the balcony to inhale the fresh mountain air and the scents of roses emanating from the trellis. Radiant in its summer splendour, the sun poured over the onion-domed towers and white walls of the castle and gleamed on the limbs of three children running happily over the lawns below. Their laughter immediately dispelled Franz Ferdinand's irritation and their smiles brought such a rush of delight to his heart that it suddenly dawned on him that the intransigence of his uncle, Emperor Franz Josef, might not have been such a cruel blow after all. Perhaps, by insisting, even before they were born, that these little ones would be excluded from the succession and could never inherit the throne, the Emperor had unwittingly granted them more freedom than he had ever known.

Power had cost the aged Franz Josef dearly and even a cursory glance at the recent past showed that the Habsburg monarchs had been handed more of a crown of thorns than a crown of roses. What benefits, Franz Ferdinand wondered, had kingship brought his uncle? None whatsoever; only the alienation of those closest to him, sorrow within his family and the ceaseless strain of trying to hold this fragmented empire together.

Of course, thought Franz Ferdinand, these problems were mostly of the Emperor's own making. With a little more understanding and a lot less reliance on his self-seeking ministers, he could have made his own life and the lives of those around him far happier. Had he opened his eyes towards the future instead of fixing his gaze on the past, he might have averted the tragedies that had beset the latter part of his reign and even found some means of appeasing the many different factions in his empire. If Uncle Franz Josef suffered, his obstinacy and refusal to break with tradition were largely to blame.

As Franz Ferdinand's eyes moved beyond the park to the rooftops of distant villages, he couldn't help but envy the ordinary folk going about their business, free of the constant scrutiny that plagued archdukes and kings. Like a child lying in the long grass, peering into the miniature world of tiny creatures, he had often stared out intrigued by lives that seemed so different from his own. It wasn't simply a matter of wealth or power that separated the Habsburgs from the ordinary Austro-Hungarian people; it was rather as though an invisible wall separated those of royal blood from the rest of humanity – a wall as substantial as a fortress and equally impossible to breach.

On one side of the wall, extended royal families stretched across Europe like a spider's web of intricately woven and delicately balanced relationships: siblings and cousins, aunts and uncles, all manner of kinship, protected by titles and a lineage that could be traced back through centuries. It had sometimes fascinated Franz Ferdinand to think that the balance of power was maintained by such hereditary threads but it puzzled him to see that so many members of this elite clan had sacrificed love, happiness and passion for the sake of sustaining the bloodline through suitable dynastic marriages.

On the other side of the invisible wall was a world as impenetrable to the Habsburgs as theirs was to the majority of their countrymen. It irked Franz Ferdinand to think that so many of his siblings and cousins remained cocooned in the immutable Viennese court with neither the desire nor the perspicacity to so much as glance at the changing world outside. Through the extensive travels of his younger years he had come face-to-face with cultures and lives so different from his own that the Emperor's highly-prized traditions and petty protocols, which dominated so much of life in Vienna, had begun to appear as little more than flimsy anachronisms, obsolete and out-of-place in this new and progressive century.

The further he had travelled, the more clearly he had begun to understand something of life beyond the narrow confines his upbringing but only through Sophie had he been able to delve more deeply into that world. Through her he had begun to pierce the shroud of imperial mystique to a reality quite as spectacular in its way as the glittering world of royalty. At the other side of the wall, people married for love; they pursued dreams and followed their hearts, unrestricted by appearances, titles or bonds of duty. At the other side of the wall, people were free.

At the sound of approaching footsteps he turned to see Sophie stepping onto the balcony with a smile no less enchanting than that with which she had first captured his heart.

"You're ready to leave?"

He took both her hands in his, "I wish you were coming with me. I hate these separations from you and the children."

"I *will* come with you, if that is what you want."

"No," he shook his head adamantly, "I won't let them subject you to any more humiliations."

"It doesn't bother me. As long as we have each other, nothing they say or do can hurt me."

"It bothers me..." he began but she placed a finger on his lips to silence him.

"Don't let it upset you, Franz. Just think that it's only a couple of weeks until the Kaiser's daughter's wedding. Won't it be wonderful for us to appear together in public there?"

She smiled but the sorrow in her eyes re-ignited his anger.

"It's absurd that the German Kaiser acknowledges you but here, among our own people – among members of my own family! – you are treated with such disdain! Who do they think they are? They're not worthy to brush the dust from your feet. They're like ostriches with their heads stuck in the sand, refusing to see that if they opened their eyes and their petty little minds they would recognise among them a brilliant and beautiful woman who is every inch worthy of becoming Empress."

"Oh Franz," she ran her hand over his cheek, "we knew before we married that this is how it would be. We accepted it, and never once in these thirteen years have I regretted my decision."

"Nor have I, but I *do* regret what you have suffered on my account."

"Suffered?" she laughed. "Suffered the company of the most loving and attentive husband in the world; suffered the delight of our beautiful children and the enduring love of a man who means more to me than life itself! Franz, do you honestly think I care a jot for those silly slights or for titles and rights when I am the most blessed woman in Austria?"

He leaned across the balcony and, plucking a single red rose from the trellis, handed it to her. "It's not about the titles or even the way they've barred our children from the succession. What really hurts and angers me, is that I want them to appreciate and love you as much as I do."

She inhaled the scent of the petals, "I don't need their love, Franz. Yours and the children's is more than enough for me."

He reached for her hand and the rose's thorn caught his finger, piecing the skin until a thin stream of blood trickled towards his wrist. She pulled out a handkerchief and pressed it to the wound as tenderly as if he were a small child, "It wouldn't do for the heir to the throne to enter Vienna with blood stains on his uniform."

He shook his head, "Look at it. Being *of the blood* is all that separates us. You would think from the way they speak of it that the Habsburg blood is quite different from everyone else's. But look at it, Sophie! Mine is the same colour, the same texture and serves the same function as yours. When the Mexicans shot Uncle Max, was his gore more regal than that of a factory worker mangled in his own machinery? When the anarchist drove his knife into Aunt Sissi, or when Cousin Rudolf blew out his brains, did their blood look any different from the blood that poured from the soldiers' wounds on the Balkan battlefields? Look closely and tell me if you can see anything in it that makes it superior to yours."

She laughed and the ludicrousness of their arguments made him smile too. "It is nonsense, isn't it? But for such a ridiculous reason, whole lives are spent in misery. Out of all the millions of people in the world, do you know how many families are considered worthy of producing brides for the Habsburg archdukes?"

She carelessly shook her head as she held the handkerchief to his scratch.

"Somewhere between fourteen and twenty," he said. "The scope is limited enough for the royalties of other countries but for the Habsburgs there's the added restriction of finding not only a royal bride but a Catholic royal bride. Is it any wonder that there are so many unhappy archdukes and archduchesses in Austria when the criterion for marriage has nothing whatsoever to do with love or even compatibility?"

She appeared too engrossed in ensuring that the cut had stopped bleeding to pay a great deal of attention to his words.

"And they don't realise," he continued, "that their damned obsession with maintaining the bloodline is the very thing that is destroying it. The same families always marrying each other, weakens rather than strengthens the dynasty. I read somewhere once that a contributing factor to the downfall of so many Roman Emperors was the fact that half of them were quite insane due to generation after generation of interbreeding. Anyone with a half a brain can see that the same is true in *this* family."

"Oh Franz," she smiled, "you're clutching at straws."

"Am I?" he raised his eyebrows. "Franz Josef only became Emperor because his uncle and predecessor, Emperor Ferdinand, was a complete imbecile. The poor fellow was pleasant enough from all accounts but absolutely incapable of ruling. He could hardly sign his own name and behaved more like a child than a grown man. No wonder they deposed him. His sister was even more sorely afflicted – insane and so disfigured that she spent her entire life confined to a room where no one was allowed to see her."

"Poor things," Sophie said sincerely.

"Poor things indeed, but I'll tell you the cause of their affliction: their parents were *double* first cousins. That's where their obsession with marrying into the blood leads them! "

"Perhaps," Sophie said, "they were just unfortunate. I have never heard of any other members of your family suffering in that way."

He smiled cynically, "You haven't heard because they keep these things quiet. Reputation is everything to them. The Emperor's own brother, who was whisked away from Vienna to avoid further scandals in the bathhouses, found his greatest pleasure in wearing women's clothes!"

Sophie laughed and shook her head.

"And what of Uncle Max's widow: quite insane, refusing to believe that her husband is dead, and confined by her brother in some Belgian palace? And," he lowered his voice to a whisper, "what of Aunt Sissi?"

"The late Empress?" she frowned.

"Her behaviour was hardly rational: galloping about on fast horses; being sewn into her riding habit each morning; half-starving herself and tight-lacing to the extent that she had only a nineteen inch waist after bearing four children. Rumour has it that she once had herself strapped to the mast of a ship during a storm! And, of course, let's not forget that she was a second cousin of poor mad King Ludwig of Bavaria who lived in a fantasy world until he drowned both himself and his doctor. These are the families that are deemed suitable and *of the blood* but the perfectly rational Choteks are unworthy of the heir to the throne. If I had married a mad Bavarian princess, it would have been perfectly proper to treat her as the future Empress, whereas the beautiful, intelligent and sane Sophie Chotek is denied such respect simply because she hasn't a regal lineage dating back centuries!"

"The Empress," said Sophie tactfully, "was greatly loved by the people."

"She was beautiful – which always makes a difference – and it's true that she had their best intentions at heart. Without her, I doubt the Emperor could have held on to Hungary. All the same, there was an instability about her, which was greatly exacerbated by the Emperor and his mother compelling her to fit into all their ridiculously rigid and out-dated traditions." He looked up at the sky in exasperation, "There again Uncle Franz Josef and Aunt Sissi were first cousins – no wonder Cousin Rudolf turned out as he did."

"You told me," she said quietly, "that the Crown Prince's mind was affected by addictions to alcohol and medications."

"And unspeakable diseases picked up from his numerous lovers."

She blushed, "His parentage wasn't responsible for that."

"His parents were – or at least his father was. His upbringing was brutal and they married him off to a Belgian princess whom he did not love and who I doubt loved him. What a waste of a life! He was as stifled in these traditions as his mother was. The Emperor never gave him the opportunity to express his opinions or implement any changes. Everything always had to be the way it has always been. The boy was utterly crushed by it – it's not surprising he sought an outlet in all those addictions; and then, when he killed himself in that mad suicide pact with his mistress, what was the Emperor's immediate reaction? Not remorse, not unbearable sorrow that his only son had been driven to despair, but a desperate need to keep the whole sordid business quiet so as not to cause a scandal. Do you know how they did that?"

She shook her head, unwilling to hear more, but he was so incensed that he could not restrain himself, "They propped up the dead mistress in a carriage and drove her through the town so it would appear that she was still alive when she left Mayerling. Then they asked her mother to announce that the poor girl had died somewhere else some time later." He glanced over the balcony to where his children were playing and, with more than a hint of bitterness, sighed, "They are the people deemed worthy of respect and fit to rule this country, while our children…"

"…will be spared all that pretence and all those horrendous restrictions," Sophie smiled.

"Yes, you're right," he sighed and for several minutes gazed at her lovingly.

"Well," Sophie said eventually, "I suppose you had better be going."

He nodded reluctantly.

"And no matter what the Emperor says, please try to restrain your temper."

He raised his eyebrows in feigned innocence, "I *always* keep my temper."

"You know what I mean," she smiled fondly. "Even though you don't agree with him, try to be tactful. Remember that he has had more than his share of suffering. A brother killed by revolutionaries, his wife murdered by an anarchist, his only son dying in such dreadful circumstances – life cannot be easy for him."

He kissed her, tenderly, "For *your* sake, Sophie, not for his, I will be a model of tact and understanding."

Chapter 2 – The Schönbrunn Palace, Vienna –April 1913

Behind a desk covered with papers in neatly ordered piles, Emperor Franz Josef sat like a relic of a bygone age. The whiteness of his walrus moustache and the tufts of hair sprouting at either side of his bald head gave him such an ancient appearance that it seemed to Franz Ferdinand that he might have lived since time began.

"Sixty-five years on the throne;" he thought as the attendant announced his arrival. *"He has outlived so many other monarchs; witnessed the unifications of Italy and Germany; has had so much time to create harmony..."*

The Emperor raised his head and the severity of his deeply-lined features suggested that all he had gained from experience was a determined resistance to change. Judging by the portrait hanging on the wall beside him, he had once been a handsome man whose youthful features and upright bearing epitomised the vibrancy of his powerful and cultured empire, but now only the glistening medals pinned to his uniform bore any trace of that former glory.

"...He has lost our Italian possessions, alienated Russia, compromised with Hungary, led us into an inferior position with Germany and has done nothing whatsoever to unify the many different cultures in the empire."

In spite of his mounting antipathy, Franz Ferdinand bowed respectfully and the Emperor, putting down his pen and raising his soulful blue eyes, beckoned him closer.

"Franz," he said warmly, "thank you for coming. I trust you're well."

"Very well, thank you."

"And your family?"

"They're well, too," he replied brusquely, resisting the impulse to suggest that if his uncle had cared to extend the invitation to Sophie and the children, the question would have been unnecessary.

"I'm pleased to hear it."

Franz Ferdinand could not resist, "Are you, really?"

"Come now, Franz," the Emperor gesticulated towards a chair. "I know that you consider me heartless in this matter but you must understand my position."

If he hoped for a nod of agreement to assuage his guilt, he was to be disappointed. Franz Ferdinand sat down, his face as rigid as flint.

"You might be unaware that I, too, married for love."

Franz Ferdinand glanced at him.

"My mother arranged for my aunt and her daughters to visit Bad Ischl with the intention that I should propose to my cousin, Hélène. I was on the point of doing so when Hélène's younger sister escaped from her governess and ran into the room." The soulful blue eyes took on a misty appearance, "She was only fifteen years old but so full of life and eagerness that from my first glimpse of her, I knew that *she* was the one I would marry."

Reluctant to show any interest, Franz Ferdinand drummed his fingers on the arm of the chair but the Emperor, absorbed in his memories, continued, "Our mothers were not at all happy about it but I was adamant. I said – just as you did when you insisted on marrying Sophie – I would marry Sissi or I would remain a bachelor forever. The following day our engagement was announced. So you see, Franz, I *do* understand your feelings."

The Archduke, unable to contain his bitterness, shook his head, "With respect, sir, I don't think you do. Before your wedding, you were not compelled to suffer the humiliation of standing in front of sneering ministers to publicly renounce all rights for any children born of your marriage. Your wife was not barred from using the Imperial Box at the theatre or from taking part in state processions. The late Empress did not have to take the lowest place in the line of precedence, nor was she was prevented from sitting beside you at formal dinners. Was she ever refused an invitation or treated as though she didn't exist? No, sir, I don't think you have any idea how I feel."

The Emperor inhaled sharply and for a moment Franz Ferdinand anticipated a fierce rebuke but his uncle merely exhaled in a low hum and murmured, "The Empress was of the blood."

Franz Ferdinand huffed and shook his head, "It is amazing and shocking to me that other royal houses are willing to welcome my wife whereas here, in her own homeland, she is treated with such disdain."

"*Other* royal houses?" the Emperor frowned.

"When we visited Roumania two years ago, Queen Elizabeth was more than welcoming."

Franz Josef almost laughed, "The Queen of Roumania would welcome anyone who has a romantic story to tell. Not long ago her husband banished her from the court because of her undue attachment to some little poetess whom she was trying to marry off to the heir. Being accepted in Roumania is of no significance."

"But it *is* significant to be accepted in Germany. The invitation to the wedding of Kaiser Wilhelm's daughter is a triumph for us. In Berlin, if not in Vienna, Sophie will receive the respect that is due to the wife of your heir."

The Emperor's frown deepened and his voice came out in a low growl, "You must have misunderstood, Franz. You were not invited; you were simply informed about the wedding."

As though a bolt of lightning had struck him, every muscle in Franz Ferdinand's body stiffened, "What?"

"It was a courtesy to notify you but it should have been clear that it was not and never could be an invitation to your wife. It would be insulting to the Kaiser and demeaning for us to have a former lady-in-waiting representing the Austro-Hungarian Empire."

Fearing he would explode with rage, Franz Ferdinand jumped to his feet and paced to and fro across the room, clenching his fist and hammering it into his opposite palm. The Emperor, determinedly oblivious of his fury, reached across his desk and flicked through a pile of papers.

"In your position it is one thing to marry for love but quite another to expect the world to accept it. As my heir you must be aware of your duty to maintain standards and uphold the traditions that have helped the Habsburgs to survive through so many centuries."

"I did not choose my position," Franz Ferdinand snorted. "I never expected to become your heir."

"None of us chooses our role. Some call it fate; I believe it is God's will. Do you think *I* chose this? I was only eighteen years old when I came to the throne. They were dangerous times; revolutions were breaking out all over Europe but, had I refused to accept my responsibility when my uncle abdicated, the empire would have fallen into the hands of republicans and anarchists."

Franz Ferdinand shook his head bitterly.

"It's the same for everyone born into royal families. Look at Tsar Nicholas. He never expected his father to die so young, leaving him to rule the vast Russian Empire at only twenty-six years old. The same is true of Kaiser Wilhelm in Germany. Who would have imagined that his father would die after only a couple of months on the throne? But did Wilhelm shirk his duty? Did Nicholas? No, they did not. They accepted responsibility as the times demanded. In Britain, too, were it not for the death of his elder brother, George would never have been king, but when the time came he didn't object and say he had not expected it. He rose to his responsibilities and that is what you must do instead of behaving like a truculent schoolboy. My son's tragic death altered everything for all of us and sulking and complaining is not going to change anything."

Like a reprimanded child, Franz Ferdinand subserviently lowered his head but inwardly he seethed and only the recollection of his promise to Sophie restrained him from venting his anger.

"Besides," said the Emperor, "we have compromised in your situation. In spite of the strength of opposition from my ministers and the rest of the family, I gave you permission to marry the woman of your choice. I even granted her a title and raised her to the position of Highness. The least you can do in return is to accept the conditions of your marriage graciously and without complaint."

For a few minutes there was silence and the atmosphere was so charged with Franz Ferdinand's smouldering anger that it seemed that even the Emperor dared not continue.

"Is this why you summoned me here?" he eventually muttered. "You wished to inform me that we are not invited to the wedding?"

The Emperor shook his head, "There are far more important things to discuss. Sit down; I have a proposition for you."

Still seething, Franz Ferdinand returned to the chair as his uncle picked up a pen and tapped at the desk for several seconds before explaining, "In spite of our differences, don't think that I underestimate your commitment to our armed forces and to the empire. I'm aware that your fellow officers have the utmost respect for you and I know that you have strong views about the necessity of modernising our military and naval resources."

He looked up, and Franz Ferdinand nodded, "The navy is in a desperate state. Britain and Germany have put so much effort into expanding their fleets while your ministers are reluctant to spend anything to improve ours. Even with your support, Admiral Montecucolli had to fight tooth and nail to prevent them from cutting his budget by half, and even then he had to press ahead and order the construction of dreadnoughts without ratification from the Treasury."

The Emperor frowned attentively but said nothing.

"The situation in the army is even worse. Your Imperial and Royal Army, and the Austrian and Hungarian armies work independently of one another, creating a serious lack of cohesion. The recruits of different ethnic groups – Bosnians, Magyars, Poles and Czechs – speak different languages and are not educated sufficiently to understand their officers' orders. In peacetime this is ludicrously inefficient but in war time it would be catastrophic. On top of that, the scandals of recent years have left us with a shortage of highly-trained officers who are capable of commanding respect. Should some unforeseen event occur demanding a military response, I doubt we would have enough sufficiently trained and available troops to meet any opposing forces."

"Which is why," said the Emperor, passing his pen from one hand to the other, "it is so important to maintain our firm alliance with Germany."

"And to do that it's vital that we keep pace with other European powers. Kaiser Wilhelm sees it as a necessity that we improve our military capability so that, if the unthinkable were to happen, we would be able to mobilise sufficient troops to stand up to the combined forces of France, Britain and Russia."

"The unthinkable?" the Emperor's eyes widened. "You seem to be taking a pessimistic view of our ability to maintain peace."

Franz Ferdinand dramatically clasped his hands together, "More fervently than ever, I pray for peace. Austria is not equipped to involve herself in an unnecessary war but it's obvious that in order to maintain peace we need to be strong. Germany and Britain are arming at such a rate that they neutralise each other's potential as a threat; but Britain's allies in the Entente are strong and if we are seen as a weak ally of Germany we upset the whole balance of power. Weakness invariably leads to disaster. The present conflict in the Balkans came about only because of the weakness of the Ottoman Empire."

"Fortunately," said the Emperor, "that situation appears to have been resolved. Greece, Bulgaria and Serbia have succeeded in driving the Ottomans out of Europe, and the Ottomans too weak to retaliate or try to win back their territories."

Franz Ferdinand's frown deepened, "I fear it is only a temporary truce. From all accounts, King Ferdinand of Bulgaria is not at all satisfied with his spoils and there's a suggestion that he is about to turn on his former allies and re-ignite the whole situation."

"Well," the Emperor sighed, "if these little Balkan states continue wrangling and warring among themselves, they will simply become worn out and lose all appetite for causing any more trouble along our borders."

Franz Ferdinand, shaking his head in amazement at such naïveté, leaned further across the desk, "This isn't merely a petty dispute between minor states! It is a highly dangerous situation. You must see that any conflict in the Balkans leads to further unrest within your own empire."

The Emperor blinked and shook his head slightly as though reluctant to hear more, but Franz Ferdinand persisted. "What will happen if Bulgaria turns on the rest of the Balkan League? The Roumanians have many long-standing disagreements with Bulgaria so they will probably seize the opportunity of joining with Greece and Serbia to settle old scores. The Bulgarians will be defeated in no time and the Serbs will be so puffed up with victory that they will become even more vociferous in demanding a separate Slav Kingdom, including *your* territories of Bosnia and Herzegovina."

"No," the Emperor said as though he were trying to convince himself. "Their demands are nothing more than hot air. The Serbs would not dare to try to take Bosnia-Herzegovina from us. They know that, against the might of Austria-Hungary, they would be decimated."

Franz Ferdinand's exasperation welled like a torrent in his chest. He stood up again and paced to and fro, "Every victory that the Serbs gain in the Balkans increases their confidence in their dream of uniting the whole of the region into one kingdom. Every inch of soil that they take from Bulgaria will fuel that dream and they will not be satisfied until they see it fulfilled."

The Emperor looked up at him, "So you're in accord with my ministers who constantly urge me to send troops to take a pre-emptive strike at Serbia to prevent her from becoming too powerful?"

"On the contrary, I couldn't disagree more!" Franz Ferdinand flew back to his chair. "In their obsession with crushing Serbia, they forget that the Serbs have strong cultural and religious ties with Russia. If we were to launch an unprovoked attack on Belgrade, the Tsar would feel duty-bound to defend his little ally."

"Berchtold assures me that the Tsar will never intervene as long as…"

"Berchtold!" Franz Ferdinand spluttered, as though the name were an oath. "What does he know of the Tsar's intentions? Is he a mind-reader now?"

The Emperor permitted himself a brief smile. "Don't forget that for five years he was our ambassador to Russia, and now as Foreign Minister he is in frequent contact with his counterparts in St. Petersburg. He is convinced that it will take at least four more years for the Russian army to recover from their disastrous war with Japan, and that the Tsar has too many problems at home to interest himself in Serbian affairs."

Franz Ferdinand pressed his hand to his forehead, trying to stem his mounting agitation.

"Berchtold is not alone in his thinking," the Emperor continued. "So many of my ministers and ambassadors – Giesl, Sturgkh, Krobatin, and others – believe that at some point war with Serbia will be inevitable and that the sooner we strike the better, before the Serbs gain any more ground and before the Tsar's army is brought back up to strength."

Franz Ferdinand clenched his fists so tightly that his nails dug into the skin of his palms.

"They assure me that we would have the full support of Kaiser Wilhelm, and the Tsar would not be willing to stand up to both Austria-Hungary and Germany."

Franz Ferdinand could remain silent no longer.

"Damn their narrow-mindedness..." he began, and his exasperation exploded in such a torrent of anger that his words ran senselessly together, coming out as nothing more than a series of curses and expletives, punctuated by gasps of frustration. The room swirled before his eyes – the red walls, the furnishings and carpets merging in a mass of distorted shape and colour. Tension, gripping his shoulders like a vice, spread down his arms, causing his hands to shake so violently that only by clinging to edge of the desk was he able to retain any semblance of self-control. He tried to breathe more deeply and, half-closing his eyes, envisaged Sophie before him, whispering gently to calm him, "*Franz...Franz...*"

Only then did his rage subside sufficiently to allow him to become aware of his surroundings once more and aware too, that the Emperor was staring at him with an expression of confused concern. Without a word, the old man moved across the room to a side-table where he poured a glass of water from a jug and placed it on the desk in front of his nephew. As though gradually waking from a nightmare, Franz Ferdinand rubbed his eyes and, pulling Sophie's handkerchief from his pocket, dabbed at the sweat on his brow.

The Emperor pointed to the glass, "Take a drink, Franz. Calm yourself."

Muttering an almost inaudible apology, the Archduke obeyed and, as the water cooled his tongue, the atmosphere of the study eased a little.

The Emperor returned to his chair and stared across the room as though he were staring into a distant memory.

"It might interest you to know," he murmured, "I do not share my ministers' opinion in this matter. Someday, perhaps, war with Serbia will be inevitable but at the moment we have neither the right nor the need to carry out an unprovoked attack."

Relieved as much by the regaining of his self-control as by the Emperor's soothing tone, Franz Ferdinand nodded, "The Balkan situation is far more serious than many of your ministers realise. The consequences of the decisions taken now, will affect the world for good or for ill for years, decades, even centuries to come. In their blind obsession with crushing Serbia, these ministers fail to understand that this isn't simply a matter of removing an inconvenient annoyance; nor is it about anything as simple as one state or another gaining a little more land. This is about dreams and aspirations and honour – all of which are far more powerful than any army. The Serbs passionately believe in their right to create their Slav Kingdom and any attempt to destroy that dream will only strengthen it. You cannot fight an idea or a dream with military strength; you might suppress it or silence it for a while but the more you try to crush it by force, the more martyrs are created on whose blood the dream feeds, and the stronger it becomes. Sending our troops into Belgrade would increase rather than decrease the threat to your empire."

The Emperor hummed pensively.

"Five years ago," Franz Ferdinand said, "I warned against the annexation of Bosnia-Herzegovina, knowing that it would inspire great antipathy towards us from the Serbs, but I was ignored."

"As I recall," the Emperor said quietly, "you also warned that the Russians would intervene to prevent the annexation but, in fact, apart from a few complaints, they did nothing."

"That was only because the Russian Foreign Minister was duped into an agreement that we failed to honour; but now there is far more at stake. The alliances between France, Britain and Russia have been strengthened and every country is arming so quickly that that the slightest friction between the major powers could spark an explosion the like of which the world has never seen. Much as I mistrust Russia, I do not doubt that the Tsar is an honourable man who sees himself as the Serbs' protector. If we were to send an army against them, he would come to their assistance at whatever cost. If your ministers are correct, Germany would then come to our assistance; and the French, who have been waiting over forty years to regain the territories lost in the Franco-Prussian War, would be quick to seize the opportunity of taking revenge on Germany. Before we know it, the whole of Europe will be tearing itself apart."

The Emperor leaned back, shaking his head. "You *are* a pessimist, Franz. Such an outcome is impossible. An autocracy like Russia cannot possibly maintain a firm alliance with republican France. What's more, Kaiser Wilhelm is a first cousin of both the Russian Tsarina and King George of Britain. Their family ties are strong enough to ensure lasting peace throughout Europe."

Franz Ferdinand raised his eyebrows doubtfully, "The British king has little influence over what his Parliament does; and I seriously doubt that the family ties between the Tsarina and the Kaiser would be strong enough to keep their ministers and generals in check. In such circumstances, it's more vital than ever that we strengthen our own military force and do all we can to unite all the different factions within the empire so that we maintain the balance of power across Europe because as soon as it tips one way or the other an unimaginable horror will explode."

He paused in the hope of a response but the Emperor remained silent for several minutes before asking, "So what do you suggest? We ignore the Serbian threat but in the meantime strengthen our army and navy to match those of our neighbours?"

"That is where I would start but a great deal more needs to be done. The problem with Serbia is merely a symptom of a far deeper canker at the very heart of your empire. The lack of cohesion in the different armies is symptomatic, too, of the lack of cohesion between all the different groups and provinces that fall under the banner of Austria-Hungary. Unless something is done to unite these many different groups, each with their own culture, language and aspirations, the whole empire is in danger of disintegration and collapse."

The Emperor inhaled sharply but Franz Ferdinand continued undaunted. "Since the people of these provinces feel that they are ruled from Vienna by ministers who have no understanding of their culture and traditions, it is no wonder that they dream of independence. If they feel that their views are not represented or understood within the empire, they naturally look elsewhere for liberation, which is why the Serbs' call for a separate Slav Kingdom is so appealing to many of them. If, however, the people of these different provinces felt that they had some form of autonomy under your rule, the Serbs' dream would appear less attractive to them and in time it would become obsolete."

He paused for a moment before continuing more tentatively, "Ten years ago, when I visited the United States of America, I observed a form a government which I know would work well here."

The Emperor's jaw dropped in disbelief but Franz Ferdinand persevered, "Although united under one central government, each state makes its own laws and maintains its own customs. Since the Austro-Hungarian Empire comprises so many different cultures and languages, there are always going to be tensions but there are ways of easing those tensions. Granting some form of federal autonomy to the Slavs, the Czechs and other groups would create a sense of independence and remove any unrest or dissatisfaction."

"I have never heard such a preposterous suggestion! You would have me carve up Austria-Hungary into so many self-governing states that there would be no empire at all!"

"No, no," Franz Ferdinand shook his head quickly, "on the contrary. It works perfectly in America and…"

"A young nation that was founded as a republic has nothing to offer an autonomy whose traditions go back centuries! We have already made enough concessions in granting the Hungarians the dual monarchy. I have no intention of creating further divisions, which would only lead to anarchy."

Franz Ferdinand opened his mouth to protest but the Emperor silenced him with a raised hand. "Your political views lean far too much towards republicanism and I trust that before you inherit this throne you gain a clearer understanding of what it means to be Emperor."

Franz Ferdinand, desperate to restrain himself from another angry outburst, bit his lip and clenched his hands by his sides.

"On the other hand, I share your opinion about the need for improvements in our armed forces, which brings me to the reason why I asked you here. I am creating you Inspector of the Austro-Hungarian Army so that you can make further investigations into what needs to be done and, after reporting to me, implement whatever improvements are necessary. I will include an Admiralship in the appointment, authorising you to make similar inspections of the navy."

So pleased was he at the unexpected announcement, that for a few moment Franz Ferdinand quite forgot his fury and almost smiled.

"Regarding the army, you will work in close contact with Franz Conrad von Hőtzendorf."

"Hőtzendorf?" Franz Ferdinand frowned, "I thought you dismissed him over his calls for the invasion of Italy."

"I took your advice and reinstated him."
Not wishing to show his elation, Franz Ferdinand, nodded, "In spite of his belligerence, I believe he's a courageous man who has the best interests of the army at heart."
"Then, as long as you keep his more aggressive tendencies in check, I am sure you and he will work well together."

The Archduke murmured his gratitude and made a trite remark about being honoured to do his duty in the service of the empire but, when the Emperor signified that the meeting was concluded, he could not resist a final jibe.

"Since this appointment will require me to spend more time in Vienna, I must telegraph Sophie at once and ask her to come here with the children."

The Emperor didn't respond but, with a far lighter heart than when he arrived, Franz Ferdinand walked briskly from the room. Deliberately ignoring the courtiers who lined the corridors, he pushed open the giant door separating the Emperor's apartments from the rest of the palace and, as he hurried down the Blue Staircase and out into the courtyard, he prayed that the news of his promotion might soften Sophie's disappointment about the German wedding.

Chapter 3

When the Archduke had gone, Emperor Franz Josef moved to the window and looked up at the ominous clouds shrouding the sunlight and plunging the study into a shadowy gloom. The early morning brightness had given way to oppressive heat and now, in the late afternoon, it seemed to Franz Josef that there was something curiously apt about Franz Ferdinand's visit coinciding with the gathering storm.

As the first raindrops fell on the courtyard below, he pressed his head to the glass, wondering why his nephew's company always left him feeling so unsettled. Perhaps it was simply that it was difficult to take to a man of such a stormy temperament, particularly one who made not the slightest effort to be agreeable. On the contrary, Franz Ferdinand didn't care what people thought of him but had very few qualms in making known his low opinion of them. Such frankness might have been refreshing, the Emperor thought, in a court that was filled with sycophants and flatterers but there was something unnerving about Franz Ferdinand's bluntness and the sense that his simmering temper might explode at any moment.

He turned from the window and, as the shadows spread over the walnut desk to the deep red walls and furnishings, a flash of lightning illuminated the portrait of the late Empress, whose sad eyes gazed dreamily towards the opposite door as though seeking some means of escape. In the boom of thunder that followed, Franz Josef's mind ran back through the decades and a series of vivid images passed before his cloudy eyes. Sixty years had passed since their first meeting but he recalled with complete clarity the wild young girl who flew into the room at his summer residence, Bad Ischl, and darted about like a butterfly. Who would have thought that so fragile a creature could shatter his reserve and send his emotions, normally so stoically held in check, spinning and whirling into chaos? So slim, she was, and so delicate and yet in those laughing eyes he had seen something more powerful than the strength of the whole Imperial Army – in one single smile and one flash from those eyes he saw *freedom*.

For a few brief days, over half a century ago, he had dared to step out of the rigid routine that had dominated his childhood and youth. He had dared to allow himself to laugh and express emotion, to follow his heart, not his head or convention, and for the first and only time in his life he had dared to stand up to his mother.

"I will marry Sissi or I will remain a bachelor forever."

Even now, he smiled with pride at that singular moment of triumph and the heady rush of exhilaration that surged through him when she accepted his proposal!

"So beautiful, you were," he murmured, drawing nearer to the portrait. Her long chestnut hair flowed over her shoulders, falling all the way to her ankles; her very soul shone through those expressive eyes; and her youthful complexion and perfect figure were so exquisite that she might have been crafted in marble by the hands of angels. Franz Josef's eyes moved over the portrait and his smile slowly faded at the realisation that all that most attracted him to her – her freedom, her youthful zeal and vivacity – he himself had destroyed.

"You *were* like a butterfly," he murmured, "and I, like an ignorant schoolboy, trapped you in a jar, stifled your *joie de vivre* and crushed your pretty wings until you found death preferable to life."

His eyes drifted to his desk where the orderly piles of papers awaited his attention, and he tried to console himself with excuses. Life for Sissi would, of course, have been different if he hadn't been Emperor. Had he not been fettered by the constraints of the court and centuries-old Habsburg traditions, he could have given her the liberty she treasured more dearly than life itself. She would have been free to run barefoot, to laugh aloud and to dance in her child-like reveries, to ride her fast horses and to fraternise with whomsoever she chose. If he hadn't been Emperor, he would have been free to love her as she needed to be loved.

He shuffled the papers. With hindsight it was easy to see his mistakes but as a young man, raised in that atmosphere of duty, how could he have known that she was slowly suffocating in the rigid court etiquette? Perhaps, at the time, had he been more aware of all that she suffered, he could have learned from his mistakes but instead, he thought, glancing at the miniatures on his desk, he simply repeated those errors with his son.

He picked up a portrait in an oval frame: a fine young man, so smart and dashing in his braided blue military jacket, the Order of the Golden Fleece dangling around his neck. Franz Josef ran his hand over the pale cheeks and reddish hair, recalling his joy when he first placed the Order in the baby's cradle and proudly whispered, *'This is my son.'*

"Poor Rudolf," he sighed remorsefully. "If only I had realised that you'd inherited your mother's free spirit, I could have been much more understanding. I could have helped you find outlets for your dreams instead of crushing and confining you, trying to force you to conform to what the court expected."

And yet, he thought wearily as he replaced the portrait, *all I did, I did with the highest intention. It was not my choice to be Emperor. God called me to this,*

*and my duty is and always has been to uphold tradition.
For this I have sacrificed those dearest to me and for
this I would lay down my life.*

He reverently blessed himself and was about to
sit down at the desk when a knock at the door distracted
him.

The attendant's announcement: "His Imperial
Highness Archduke Karl von Habsburg-Lothingren,"
heralded the entrance of a tall young man who walked
into the study with a smile as cheery as if he were
taking a Sunday stroll by the sea.

Franz Josef's weariness lifted instantly.

"Karl, dear boy, good to see you!" he said,
opening his arms to embrace his great-nephew with
genuine affection.

"I hope I am not disturbing you, Uncle. I know
how busy you are…"

"Not at all, not at all! I'm glad you're here. I
had intended to take my usual walk but," he waved
vaguely in the direction of the window, "when the
storm began I resigned myself to an afternoon of paper
work."

"Always so much to do," Karl glanced at the
papers. "You put us to shame, Uncle. In Vienna they
say that they could set their clocks by you – every
morning at your desk at five o'clock sharp, before the
rest of the city is awake."

"Why break the habit of a lifetime?" Franz Josef
smiled. "Besides, if I stay in bed late, I might dream
and dreams turn so quickly to nightmares."

"Surely not," Karl's innocent eyes shone like a
child's. "A clear conscience such as yours must enjoy
perfectly undisturbed sleep."

"My conscience?" Franz Josef glanced at the
portrait of his son before shaking away unwelcome
thoughts and nodding towards the door. "The storm

might keep us indoors but it shouldn't prevent us from taking a walk. Come, let's stroll through the palace and you can tell me all your news."

"You are not too busy?"

"I am never too busy for a daily walk. Believe me, Karl, the older you get the more important it is to keep up with physical exercise. I've seen too many old men seize up with stiff joints due to sitting too long and walking too infrequently and I'm determined that that won't happen to me. What a poor impression Austria would make on the rest on the world if her Emperor shuffled around like a clockwork toy!"

They walked along the corridor, commenting on the sudden change in the weather and the general warmth of the season and with every step the Emperor felt increasingly refreshed by the joy emanated from his great-nephew.

"How is Zita?" he asked.

"Very well, indeed, thank you!" Karl's eyes shone with delight. "She sends you her warmest love and hopes to see you soon. Oh and..." he paused and fumbled into an inside pocket, "she asked me to give you this."

Into the Emperor's hand he placed a small photograph of a bright-eyed baby, lying peacefully in a cradle.

"What a splendid little fellow!" Franz Josef's gnarled fingers stroked the infant cheeks. "How old is he now?"

"Almost six months. He's so sturdy and strong and he has such an interested and intelligent air about him. Little Otto..."

"Named after your father," the Emperor said. "I trust they will have only the name and handsome features in common."

Karl looked at him through naïve eyes and the Emperor shook his head, unwilling to offend his innocence. It was strange, he thought, that one generation could differ so starkly from the next. Here was Karl, so pious and devoted to his wife, the son of a philanderer whose early death had undoubtedly been the result of his decadent lifestyle; and whose reputation had sunk to the depths when he was caught wandering through a hotel lobby, drunk out of his wits and wearing nothing but his sword and his Orders. The longer the Emperor looked at the photograph of the baby, the more he thought, too, of the disparity between himself and his own son. Abstemious, physically fit and devoted to duty, how could he have fathered and raised a child who at such an early age had become so dependent on drink, medications and mistresses that by the time of his death at only thirty-one years old both his mind and his body were in ruins.

Feeling Karl's eyes upon him, Franz Josef smiled, "Otto – the name of the first Holy Roman Emperor. Your son has a great tradition behind him."

They had reached the top of the Blue Staircase, where Karl offered an arm to steady him as he reached for the banister.

"Take good care of this little one," the Emperor said, tucking the photograph into his pocket.

"We will!"

"And Zita, too – take care of her, Karl. A loving wife is the greatest gift a man can have – a lesson that I, alas, learned too late."

Karl's brow creased into a brief frown, "I'm so sorry, Uncle. I was so absorbed in our joy that I quite forgot you…"

"No, no, no," Franz Josef patted his hand. "It does me good to see you looking so well and so happy. So much of the time I am surrounded by long faces and miserable ministers who talk of nothing but unrest and dissention. It restores my faith in the good God to see that someone is blessed with happiness."

As they neared the foot of the staircase, Karl said, "I met Uncle Franz on my way in. He seemed unusually cheerful today."

The Emperor grunted and Karl smiled.

"I know you and he don't always see eye-to-eye and some people speak badly of him, but he has always been very kind to me. He was affability itself at our wedding and he couldn't have been more congenial than when he stood proxy for you as godfather at Otto's christening."

The Emperor mumbled unconvinced, and Karl's smile widened, "I think many people misjudge him because he isn't given to small talk but, when he does engage in conversation, he shows himself to be one of the most interesting and learned men I have ever met. He has so many interests and, through his travels, he has gained such a vast knowledge of different countries and cultures that he is able to speak with authority on so many subjects."

"Perhaps if he had travelled less and concentrated more on studying the history of his own family, he wouldn't have been so eager to break with the traditions that have preserved the monarchy for centuries."

Karl shrugged awkwardly, "It *is* unfortunate that he fell in love with someone deemed unsuitable but you have to admit that he is utterly devoted to his children and he must love his wife very deeply to be willing to endure all the snubs and criticisms he has suffered on her account."

"Franz Ferdinand was unpopular long before he married that woman." The Emperor's eyes narrowed as he thought back through the years. "He was a shy, little child, self-absorbed and introverted and so puny that we hardly expected him to survive; and now he is a clumsy, lumbering man, who makes no attempt to charm or to endear himself to people. He is so obtuse that it wouldn't surprise me in the least to discover that he had deliberately set out to marry a lady-in-waiting simply to cock a snoop at us all."

Karl laughed and, in spite of himself, the Emperor laughed too.

The attendants in the entrance pushed open the doors to the Great Gallery where the rain beat against the windows like the sound of a thousand dancers tapping their shoes on the polished floor. Even on so dull an afternoon, the radiance of the crystal mirrors and gold stucco decoration created such brightness that the echoes of a Strauss waltz rang through Franz Josef's ears until he felt almost young again – the dashing Emperor elegantly swirling through the ballroom, holding his beloved Sissi in his arms.

He nodded towards a chair, which Karl brought to him, and when he had sat down he craned his neck to look up at the magnificence of frescoes adorning the ceiling.

"Gugliemi captured it all so perfectly."

Karl followed his finger as he pointed out the details of the painting. "It's a tribute to our family and all that made our empire great. Do you see Emperor Franz and Empress Maria Theresa there in the centre?"

Karl nodded.

"Around them are the symbols of the wealth and resources from the different provinces of the empire. I come here sometimes to remind myself of the importance of maintaining all those traditions." His neck began to ache and he lowered his head. "Tradition, Karl. It's more important now than ever. The world is moving so quickly that we are in danger of losing any sense of order or stability. The spread of the railways, the arrival of motor cars, the abundance of printed materials and the advances in technology are driving everything forwards at such a pace that there is barely time to settle to one thing before something new emerges."

"Like a great river gaining momentum," Karl smiled.

Franz Josef nodded, "That's why we must maintain tradition as an anchor in the midst of change. You see, dear boy, we are more blessed than many other rulers but we also have a greater responsibility. Our duty isn't only to our people but also to God and the Church. Austria, the successor of the Holy Roman Empire, doesn't that say it all?"

Karl nodded as attentively as a disciple at the feet of a charismatic teacher.

"The heritage of our empire and that of the Church are interlinked. The Church is blessed with the sacred tradition handed down to us from the apostles, and we have an equally sacred duty to uphold and preserve all the traditions that made Austria-Hungary great."

"Your Imperial and *Apostolic* Majesty," Karl smiled.

"Exactly." The Emperor put out a hand and let Karl help him to his feet. "This is why we had to take such harsh measures regarding Franz Ferdinand's marriage. Of course, I understand the power of a young man's passion and I am not so old as to have forgotten how it feels to be in love."

"Uncle Franz was not so young when he married. He was well into his thirties, was he not?"

"Old enough to know better than to be swayed by his heart! His *duty*, Karl, his *duty* should have come first. In our position personal feeling must always be secondary to duty and the good of the country. Even if I had wanted to, I could never have allowed a lady-in-waiting to become Empress. It would have destroyed the traditions that have kept this family together for almost a thousand years."

"I am sure Uncle Franz understands that. He must appreciate your graciousness in granting Sophie a title."

The Emperor frowned, "I went further, Karl. I raised her from Serene Highness to Highness and from Princess to Duchess of Hohenberg but it wasn't enough for him and his bitterness knows no bounds. Good heavens," he shook his head in exasperation, "he has no idea how fortunate he is! When the Tsar of Russia's brother married a commoner, the Tsar had no option but to strike him from the succession and banish him from the country. The same was true of his uncle and all the other Russian Grand Dukes who insisted on unsuitable matches. Franz Ferdinand has kept his titles, his lands, his position and, in spite of his waywardness, he is still my heir. He considers himself hard-done-by when he has been given *everything* he ever wanted – the wife of his choice, children who love him, the freedom to raise them as he pleases…all of that and one day he will succeed to the throne. You would think he might show a little gratitude for his blessings but instead he shows us nothing but antipathy, believing himself to be an innocent victim whom we have wronged."

It was clear from Karl's troubled expression that he had no desire to be drawn into the dispute between Franz Ferdinand and the court, and the Emperor felt a pang of guilt for having spoken so bluntly in front of him.

"Perhaps," he said, by way of an apology, "I am too old and too steeped in tradition to understand the way that the world is moving these days."

Karl shook his head, "No, Uncle, you are like an anchor for the whole of the country; a sure anchor that we can rely on in these changing times."

An almighty boom of thunder rattled the windows and caused the chandeliers to tremble and tinkle above them.

And when this anchor can no longer hold, Franz Josef thought, *the ship of the empire will be cast adrift on the ocean to be dashed against the rocks and be seen no more...*

He squeezed Karl's arm, "When I am gone," he said, "you will be Franz Ferdinand's heir. Promise me, Karl, that when your time comes, you will do everything in your power to preserve the traditions of the Habsburgs."

"I promise," he nodded solemnly.

Franz Josef turned to the window and stared pensively into the storm.

Chapter 4 – Potsdam, Germany – 24th May 1913

Music and laughter echoed from the wedding party as Kaiser Wilhelm stepped into the gallery of the White Room and, lighting a cigarette, caught sight of his reflection in the mirror. He smiled at the ostentatious display of medals and Orders pinned to his chest and, raising his head, observed with pride that his face bore no trace of his father's ineffectual liberalism. On the contrary, the strength of his features – high cheekbones, strong chin and perfectly waxed moustache – displayed the ideal expression of a German Emperor. Not a whisker out of place, not a speck to mar the sheen of his uniform, the image looking back at him from the glass was every inch worthy of a Prussian Kaiser descended from Frederick the Great.

He smiled at the reflection. It pleased him immensely that, today of all days, this was the image that he had presented to the world: Germany, personified in her Emperor – robust and confident, powerful yet benevolent, no longer a stripling nation or weaker relation but a mature and dominant force which would, with a firm hand, control and maintain peace throughout the whole of Europe.

He turned to view his profile when suddenly, like Icarus falling from the sky, he plunged from the heights of pride to the depths of shame.

"Damn this arm! Damn it!" he growled at the glass.

No matter how aligned the rest of his proportions or how successfully the tailored pocket disguised that withered limb, the knowledge of its weakness had brought a lifetime of anger and grief.

Aristotle was correct, he sighed: every great hero had one fatal flaw but the tragedy in his case was that the flaw was so obtrusive and there was nothing he could do to correct it.

A series of painful recollections hurled him into the familiar morass of self-pity: the humiliation of being nine-years-old and unable to use a knife and fork; the shame of repeatedly falling from his pony; the pain of his bruises as he was forced back into the saddle; and hour upon agonising hour of standing in the doctors' useless contraptions with weights and pulleys that stretched and drew on his shoulder, half-wrenching it from its socket in a fruitless attempt to make the wretched limb grow. The physical suffering was harsh enough but nothing could compare with the excruciation of the overheard whisper, "*a one-armed man can never be king.*"

"A weaker man than I," he snarled at the mirror, "would have been crushed by this deformity..." and suddenly his self-pity seared into anger. "*She* could not love me because of it. She was ashamed of me and yet she was to blame! She dominated my father; emasculating him with her liberal ideas and English ways, but she – for all her learning – wasn't even capable of bearing a healthy heir!"

The memory of his mother's face appeared so vividly before him that she might have been there in the gallery with him. How he had longed for her affection – hadn't he dreamed about her and written effusive letters, telling her how much he adored her and how he loved her beautiful hands? But she never responded and it angered him even now to think he had demeaned himself by expressing such feelings. All he had ever wanted was to please her and earn her admiration but she thought him slow-witted, unnatural and ungrateful and no matter what his achievements he could not recall her ever uttering one word of praise.

He stretched to full height, "Look at me now! I can steer a horse without reins and outride the finest cavalrymen in Prussia. I can converse with kings on any subject, and I command far more respect than my father ever did! But you," he shook his head, "you're still not here to see it."

For a moment his heart softened at the recollection of happier times. He felt her gentle eyes upon him as he ran on the beach on the Isle of Wight, and he saw her smile as she showed him around her childhood homes: the nurseries at Buckingham Palace; the ancient halls of Windsor Castle and the roaring log fires in secluded Balmoral. Mama never seemed so remote on those holidays; she spoke softly to him and enjoyed his company. With a vague sense of confusion, he recalled overhearing her whispering to her mother, Queen Victoria,

"If I were allowed to spend more time with him and play a greater role in his upbringing, it would be so much easier but the court fears that my influence is too English so I have no say in what he is taught or what ideas are presented to him. That abominable Bismarck flatters him and fills his head with militaristic ideas of Prussian superiority so that whenever Fritz and I try to try to reason with him, we appear weak or unpatriotic."

He looked again at his face in the mirror and a pang of guilt ruffled his conscience. Had he judged her too hastily and treated her too harshly? Had he rushed in too quickly when Papa was on his deathbed? Had it really been necessary to send in his troops to seal off the palace and ransack the death chamber to teach his sobbing mother that *he* was now Kaiser and her influence was at an end?

Unable to bear the guilt, he shook his head. If she had listened to him, it wouldn't have been necessary. The German doctors were far more competent to treat Papa's cancer but she had insisted on seeking diagnoses and treatments from England, regardless of what an insult that was to her adopted home.

"You see," he murmured, trying to ease his conscience, "that was why, when you succumbed to the same illness, I ensured that German doctors were responsible for your care. That was why I denied you the English funeral that you craved and why I *could* not allow you to have the British flag on your coffin! You were the German Empress, for heaven's sake, not the English princess of your childhood!"

He pressed his hand to his ear, trying to silence the demons that had taunted him for so long. If only Mama had been more like Queen Victoria, things could have been very different. Grandmama did not see him as weak – she recognised his potential as a noble German Emperor. While she lived, the two nations could stand side-by-side, their combined heritage bringing peace and culture to the world. With Grandmama's passing, and the accession of Uncle Bertie as Britain's King Edward VII, that seemingly unbreakable bond had been severed. For almost a decade an aggressive rivalry had replaced the former cooperation between the two countries, and the mutual respect they had once shared had been twisted into antipathy.

Wilhelm peered more closely at the mirror and, as he stared intently at his own face, that of his late uncle, lying in state, floated through his mind. Along with the rest of the family, he had paid his respects to the corpse of the British king but, while others struggled to contain their grief, it had taken Wilhelm even greater self-control to conceal his relief and elation. Looking down at that lifeless body, lying like a great oak felled by a storm, it had dawned on him that the death of King Edward VII marked the dawn of a new age for Germany and for her Emperor.

Huge, bronchitic and bloated by his own excesses, Uncle Bertie, no less than Wilhelm himself, had come to personify his empire. Like her king, quaffing and gluttonising at his table, Britain's appetites had become insatiable, ravenously gobbling up so much of the world. Like her king, too, flirting and sprawling with his Parisian whores, Britain had abandoned her rightful partner, Germany, choosing instead an adulterous alliance with France. This was all Uncle Bertie's doing, Wilhelm thought. With his patronising attitude and his lack of respect for his Kaiser-nephew, the nine years of his reign had brought nothing but tension between two great nations whose union had been sealed seventy years earlier in the marriage of Wilhelm's grandparents, Queen Victoria and Prince Albert of Saxe-Coburg-Gotha.

Three years had passed since Uncle Bertie's death but still that union remained unrestored. Britain continued her liaison with France and had even extended her alliances to create a comfortable ménage-a-trois with Russia, leaving Germany – the young and virile nation – to seek dubious comfort in the arms of the aged and decrepit old crone, Austria-Hungary.

"Now, though," Wilhelm murmured, adopting the pose of a hero, "it is time for the restoration of the true order. When Britain realises that her era of domination is over and it is Germany's hour to take the lead, she will abandon her flirtation with France and return to me, begging for an alliance like an unfaithful wife pleading for her husband's forgiveness."

He smiled at his own magnanimity, "I will take her back. I will overlook these past thirteen years and, in her gratitude, she will treat me with respect and devotion. Germany is in the ascendancy. Our military prowess, our growing navy, our social welfare programmes and advances in industry, outclass those of any other nation, and I, as her Kaiser, the All-Highest, am the most influential ruler of the age!"

Footsteps along the gallery drew his attention from the mirror and he turned to see Count zu Eulenberg striding towards him, wreathed in smiles.

"If I may say so, Your Majesty, everyone appears to be thoroughly enjoying your daughter's wedding and, as the eyes of the world are fixed on Berlin, we are surely making an excellent impression."

Wilhelm rested his hand on his shoulder, "Remember, Philipp, this is above all a family occasion. We have assured King George and Tsar Nicholas that it will not be seen as a state visit."

"Of course, sir, but it's gratifying to know that when your guests return home, having experienced true German hospitality, they will have only friendly feelings towards us and understand that we have no desire to make enemies of them."

"That's right," Wilhelm nodded enthusiastically. "Our greatest desire is to see a peaceful Europe in which Germany plays the most prominent role."

"With you at the helm," Eulenburg smiled.

He twitched his moustache in sham humility and, looking down into the White Room, observed the familiar faces of his many relations – sons, sisters, cousins and aunts. There was May, Queen of Britain, resplendent in her cloth-of-gold gown as the flickering lights of candles glistened on her diamond collar. In the opposite corner, her husband, King George, stood talking with Tsar Nicholas of Russia while snakes of smoke from their cigarettes intertwined above their heads.

"The royal mob," he said, smiling.

"I beg your pardon, sir?"

"The royal mob – my late grandmother's epithet for these family gatherings."

Eulenburg looked down at the guests, "It's small wonder that Queen Victoria was known as the grandmother of Europe."

Wilhelm nodded. The web of family ties stretched through so many ruling houses – from Russia to Denmark and from Sweden to Spain, through Germany, Greece, Norway, Roumania and Britain – that it was clear that whoever ruled this family was master of the continent and, through their empires, master of the world.

Eulenburg, as though reading his thoughts, said, "It must be a great responsibility to be the head of such an illustrious family."

Wilhelm smiled and again his thoughts drifted back through many memories. The first twenty-two years of his reign had been overshadowed by the charismatic characters who sat on the British throne. Queen Victoria's longevity and Edward VII's powerful personality had stamped themselves so deeply on the minds of the people of Europe that there was little room for the new German Kaiser to shine. What was more, it was they who pulled all the strings within the family – their children, grandchildren, nephews and nieces stood in awe of their wisdom and almost invariably yielded to their advice.

"You are right, Philipp," he said, as his eyes moved towards the British king. "My cousin, George, has neither the character of our grandmother nor the charisma of his father. I *am* the natural head of this huge extended family."

"And," Eulenburg enthused, "the most influential ruler in Europe. As a constitutional monarch, King George little control over his government so his influence on the world stage is negligible. It requires far greater strength of character to be in your position, where everything depends on your judgement."

Wilhelm basked in his admiration.

Eulenburg looked around the room, "I suppose it's the same for the Emperors of Russia and Austria. They, too, are autocratic rulers with responsibility for all the decisions which affect their people."

Reluctant to share the praise, Wilhelm shook his head. "Nicky hasn't the stomach of a Russian Tsar. He would rather retire to the country to live like an English squire than rule his Empire. In spite of his alliances with Britain and France, the boy is malleable and eager to maintain friendly relations with us."

"The *boy*?" Eulenburg laughed. "The Tsar is well over forty."

"His age is irrelevant. To me he always appears as a young boy who needs guidance and advice." He smiled in satisfaction. "As for Austria-Hungary, the Empire is so fragmented that Franz Josef depends upon us for support. The poor old Emperor is quite out of touch with the changing times and I think we would do far better to concentrate our attention on his heir."

"Archduke Franz Ferdinand?"

Wilhelm nodded and walked towards the staircase, "It's a pity he couldn't be here today. I like him. He speaks his mind and doesn't care a jot for what people think of him."

"That's just as well since, from what I hear, people have a very low opinion of him."

Wilhelm laughed, "I respect a man who isn't swayed by public opinion. Besides, he made a very good impression on the King and Queen of Roumania and his support for the Magyars could help create an alliance with the Roumanians if ever that should be necessary."

"Necessary?"

"The more influence we have in the Balkans the better to counteract Russian interference in the region." He looked over the banister towards George and Nicholas, laughing together like brothers. "Yes," he continued, more to himself than to Eulenburg, "I could do business with Franz Ferdinand; and a man who is so out of favour at home is grateful for all the support he receives from abroad. A few words of flattery to his wife and I'll have him eating out of my hand."

Eulenburg glanced at him, mildly surprised.

"There's more to being an Emperor than commanding armies or giving orders to ministers," he laughed. "If you wish to win the friendship of a king, you first must flatter his wife." He clicked his heels and smiled at his own brilliance. "So you see, Philipp, with George powerless, Nicky malleable, Franz Josef dependent upon us and Franz Ferdinand desperate for my friendship, I am the only one with any real influence." He glanced at his arm and smiled at the irony of the situation, "The whole future of Europe rests in my hands."

Eulenburg gazed at him and it pleased Wilhelm to know that the Count's devotion went far deeper than flattery.

"Well, if you will excuse me, sir, I was on my way to inform Prince zu Furstenberg that everything is ready for the Fackeltanz."

"Yes, yes, you go ahead," Wilhelm dismissed him with a wave of his arm. "Oh, and by the way, Philipp, the Empress and I are very grateful for your meticulous planning of all the ceremonies today. Everything has gone perfectly."

"In true Prussian fashion," Eulenburg smiled and, with a slight bow, hurried down the stairs and along the corridor.

Wilhelm put out his cigarette and was about to return to the festivities when the sound of English voices distracted him. Instantly he threw back his shoulders and, adopting a more imperial stance, turned to see several members of George's suite approaching. He smiled and they bowed in unison and when pleasantries had been exchanged they began to walk on but, by reflex, Wilhelm reached out to Sir James Reid.

"Sir James, a word before you go…"

"Of course, Your Majesty," he replied in a soft, Scottish accent as his companions disappeared along the corridor.

"You have been in the service of the British Crown for a long time now. I like to see that. Loyalty is an admirable quality."

Reid's face melted into an avuncular smile, "Thirty-two years, sir. I am honoured to have been physician to three monarchs: Queen Victoria, King Edward VII and now King George V – though, I am here today as part of Queen Mary's suite, not the King's."

Wilhelm nodded distractedly, his thoughts returning to an earlier meeting with Reid on a corridor at Osborne House, twelve and half years before.

"My grandmother held you in very high regard."

Reid lowered his eyes modestly.

"She was a woman of great discernment," Wilhelm continued. "The world has been much poorer for her passing."

"Indeed, sir," said Sir James in a manner typical of a courtier, "Queen Victoria was greatly loved."

"You know that today is her birthday? She would have been ninety-four had she lived. A rather apt day for my daughter's wedding, don't you think?"

A mischievous glint danced in Reid's eye, "As I recall, sir, Her Majesty was never very fond of weddings."

Wilhelm laughed too loudly, "It never stopped her from trying to arrange them!"

Reid smiled gently in reply and Wilhelm's laughter faded.

"I was very devoted to my grandmother – *very* devoted. I valued her support and she respected my position as Emperor even though many other members of my family failed to appreciate it." A hint of bitterness had crept into his tone but he quickly tried to correct it, "It mattered a great deal to me to be present at her death but, were it not for your assistance, I doubt that it would have been possible. Several of my aunts and cousins were…" he broke off, humiliated even now by the memory of their unkindness to him.

Reid, seeming to sense his unease, intervened softly, "Sorrow and fatigue can often affect one's judgement. In my experience, when people are witnessing the death of someone they love, they sometimes behave in ways which later they might regret."

"Yes," Wilhelm said. "*You* understood that the Queen wanted me there and that, even though the others misinterpreted my motives, I wished only to pay my respects as a grandson."

Reid nodded.

"It is entirely thanks to you that I was the one in whose arms she died. That memory will remain with me always."

For a moment, lost in the recollection, Wilhelm was oblivious of his companion and it was only when

Reid coughed pointedly that he shook himself from the reverie.

"Sir James, I would like to show my gratitude by bestowing on you one of our greatest honours: the Order of the Eagle, First Class."

Reid's eyes opened widely with delight and it pleased Wilhelm not only to have been able to compensate the doctor for his kindness but also to display his own benevolence.

"I hope you will accept it," he prompted.

"I am more than honoured, sir."

"Good! Jolly good! I will see that it is organised forthwith. I'm sure you appreciate that such an Order is a mark of our esteem." He glanced towards the White Room and his laughter echoed along the corridor, "The Tsar hands out Orders as freely as if he were throwing farthings to beggars. Russian Orders are ten a penny, as they say in England, but our German Orders are far harder to come by."

With his usual tact, Reid smiled and seemed relieved when the conversation was disturbed by a posse of footmen hurrying towards the White Room carrying candelabra.

"Ah," said the Kaiser, "it must be time for the Fackeltanz."

Reid raised his eyebrows questioningly.

"You haven't experienced the Torch Dance?"

"No, sir."

"It is a Hohenzollern tradition – one not to be missed. Come…"

He stepped closer to the door when a sudden overpowering sense of foreboding caused him to halt and stand rigid. Above the laughter, the felicitations and merriment, a dark spectre seemed to hang over the proceedings, so mysterious and ominous that it rooted him to the spot.

Reid glanced at him in confusion but for several seconds Wilhelm was unable to react, as a story he had heard in childhood rushed through his mind.

"Belshazzar's feast," he eventually murmured. "Sir James, are you a religious man?"

Obviously taken aback by the question, Reid shrugged, "I was raised as a Presbyterian, sir."

"Then you will be familiar with the Old Testament. Do you recall the story of King Belshazzar's feast?"

Reid nodded.

"I forget the details," Wilhelm said, his eyes fixed on the guests, "would you recount them for me."

Reid cleared his throat as though disconcerted by the request, "If I remember correctly, King Belshazzar held a lavish feast on the eve of an important battle. He and his guests became increasingly intoxicated as the evening wore on, drinking toasts to their gods from the sacred vessels taken from the Israelites' Temple."

"That's right, that's right," Wilhelm whispered, as the details began to return to him.

"Suddenly a human hand appeared to be writing on the wall: *Mene, Mene, Tekel, Parsin.*"

"What language is that, Aramaic or Babylonian?"

"I don't know, sir, but when King Belshazzar read those words he turned white and shook with terror. None of his soothsayers or sages could make sense of them so he summoned the prophet Daniel who interpreted them for him."

"And his interpretation?" Wilhelm said without looking at him.

"I'm afraid I don't remember, sir."

"No?" Wilhelm raised his eyebrows. "*'The days of your kingship are numbered...You have been measured and found wanting. Your kingdom has been divided and taken from you.'* And that very night King Belshazzar was murdered in his sleep." He peered across the room, imagining a hand writing those very words on the wall.

Could it be, he wondered, raising his hand to his chest, that something terrible was about to happen; something that would change the world forever and hurl all that was safe and familiar towards doom? He shook his head to dislodge the fear and assured himself that such dark imaginings were merely the effect of fatigue, wine and his unexpressed grief at his beloved daughter's imminent departure. Even though the political climate was precarious, family ties were strong enough to secure lasting peace with his neighbours. Conflict with Britain was unimaginable; and Nicky was too close a friend to ever become a foe.

He suddenly became aware that Reid was staring at him and, as much to distract from his embarrassment as to dispel his own dark thoughts, he laughed loudly, "The Old Testament is filled with fairy tales and gory stories, is it not? But now is not the right time for theological debate. The Fackeltanz is about to begin. Come, Sir James."

Brushing aside the footmen, who hovered like flies in the entrance, he strode into the White Room with a smile as bright as a jester's.

Chapter 5

Wilhelm stood on the dais, staring over the heads of the guests, who waited in the semi-darkness for the start of the Fackeltanz. A thrill of anticipation ran through the room as a series of silhouettes appeared in the doorway: a pageant of pages, carrying glowing candelabra, leading Princess Viktoria Luise into the hall. As the light of the glimmering candle flames speckled the neo-baroque walls and shimmered on the golden ceiling, colours swirled kaleidoscope-like before Wilhelm's eyes. With the same joyful wonder as when he had first seen himself captured on the flickering images of a moving film, his heart pounded at the sight of the green and black marble pillars and pedestals, the myriad of shades of silks and chiffon, and the iridescent jewels dangling from ears and wrists as the wedding party turned to applaud the bride. An awe-struck child enclosed in the body of a German Emperor, Wilhelm glanced at the faces of his guests and almost giggled with proud delight at the thought of how impressed they must be by so stately a spectacle in such magnificent surroundings.

What foresight he had shown in transforming this room from a typical eighteenth century Prussian hall into a majestic symbol of the glory and power of the mighty unified Germany! It had been well worth the thirteen years and six million marks spent on the renovation, for – from the glorious staircase and niched arches commemorating his ancestors, to the double throne representing his dual role as King of Prussia and German Emperor – this place more than any other embodied and demonstrated to the world Wilhelm's image of his role in uniting the victories of the past with the vision of a glorious future.

It was hard to believe that throughout his early childhood the idea of a unified Germany had seemed little more than a dream. What a miracle of organisation and diplomacy had been required to amalgamate into one nation twenty-six separate kingdoms, grand duchies and principalities, each with its own ruler and traditions, from quintessentially German Anhalt to British-ruled Hanover; and from dreamy, Catholic Bavaria, to the military might of Protestant Prussia! It was only natural, Wilhelm thought, that the King of Prussia should take precedence over all the other German rulers. His childhood had been littered with reports of Prussian conquests; he recalled the ease with which his grandfather's army had taken Schleswig-Holstein from the Danes, and his father's triumphant return from Könnigrätz, following the swift defeat of Austria in the Seven Weeks War. Most clearly of all, though, he remembered the resounding success of the Franco-Prussian War and the glorious moment, forty-two years ago, when his grandfather stood in the Hall of Mirrors at Versailles to be proclaimed the first German Emperor.

The pages approached and the light of their candles illuminated the innocent face of the bride. In an instant, all thoughts of past victories and present glories vanished as a wave of sadness welled in Wilhelm's chest. The sight of his daughter's beautiful smile brought home to him the realisation that she was no longer the little girl who adored him and whom he loved so dearly, but a grown woman whose life would now be devoted to another man. Unexpected tears burned his eyes, distorting the candle flames until shafts of light shot in all directions like stars in the pages' hands. Viktoria Luise stepped closer and he took her arm in his, smiling to conceal his grief as they stepped into the dance.

According to the traditional rites, he must lead the bride around the room, inviting other guests, in order of precedence, to join the choreographed procession. Though normally he would have relished the opportunity of remaining the centre of attention, in that moment he longed only to hide away, to nurse his sorrow at Viktoria Louise's impending departure. He threw back his head and, adopting his most majestic bearing, clung to his daughter's hand, wishing he could keep her close by his side forever.

Round and round the room they strolled, weaving through the clusters of guests and gathering more and more participants in the dance: the Tsar of Russia, the King of Britain, the Duke of Brunswick, the Kaiser's brother and sons...For over an hour the pageant continued until the faces blended into one, and Wilhelm, exhausted by days of festivities, felt almost fit to drop. Yet now he did not want the dance to end for with every step came the growing sense that this was no longer a lively celebration but rather a trek along the Via Dolorosa that would culminate in the excruciating Calvary of parting with his innocent child. Even more harrowing than his personal sorrow was the increasing awareness that an emperor personifies his empire and the events of his life are reflections of events unfolding on a larger scale. Could it be, he wondered, that, as these royalties danced and sang to mark the end of Viktoria Luise's childhood, they were also unwittingly participating in the swansong of an age of innocence – an idyll of peace and beauty that was rapidly slipping from their hands?

His eyes darted around the room, desperately seeking any means of prolonging the dance to postpone the moment of separation but all too soon it was over. As custom demanded, Viktoria Luise raised her garter aloft and hurled it into the throng of guests who, with cheers and cries and squeals, fell upon it like ravenous vultures squabbling over a carcass. In the midst of the commotion, the Tsar turned to the bride and said softly,

"I hope that you will be as happy in your marriage as I am in mine."

If his daughter answered, Wilhelm, suddenly aware of the tears rolling down his wife's face, did not hear. Desperate to contain his own grief, he turned his back on the Kaiserin and clung to Viktoria Luise's hand for several seconds before placing it in that of the bridegroom.

"Come," he said, leading them from the Hall, "it's time for you to change before your journey."

As they moved swiftly along the corridors, the cheering, chattering and applause from the White Room faded until the only sound was the Kaiserin's uncontrollable sobbing. Unable to face her sorrow and fearful that he, too, might succumb to his emotions, Wilhelm blurted out several over-jovial remarks and slapped his new son-in-law heartily on the back but, as they neared the door of the state apartments, he could no longer maintain the façade.

"When you are ready," he said, backing away, "I will accompany you to the station. For now, I must return to the guests."

When the door had closed behind them, he stood for some minutes, pressing his hand to his eyes to stem his rising tears. Slowly he drifted back along the corridors, trying to adopt a more cheerful pose but laughter echoing from the White Room only increased his sense of desolation. He stepped towards an ante-room and, leaning against the door, closed his eyes and breathed deeply when suddenly he felt the weight of a hand on his shoulder.

"Willy?"

Like a guard caught napping at his post, he jumped to attention and found himself looking directly into the violet-blue eyes of the Tsar.

"Nicky," he murmured.

Nicholas' eyes brimmed with sympathy, "I can imagine what a wrench it must be to part with your daughter."

Too tired to deny it, Wilhelm nodded, "It's strange; I felt only joy and pride at my sons' weddings but today parting with Viktoria Luise is…" He broke off and sniffed, determinedly quelling his emotion. "That's the way of it, I suppose – sons grow into men but, whatever their age, daughters remain our little girls forever."

Nicholas smiled gently, "When the time comes, I am sure that Alix and I will find it terribly difficult to part with our girls."

"I should count my blessings," Wilhelm shrugged and, as often happened when his emotions were heightened, he heard himself talking too quickly, "You will have to go through this four times, whereas once is enough for me. You know, my grandmother used to say there are too many princes in Prussia. I think she was right. Viktoria Luise has always been such a ray of light in our family and there have been times when I have wished that at least *some* of her brothers had been girls, too. Six boys in a household can lead to so much tension." An image of his eldest son and namesake flitted through his head, "In no time at all they grow from docile children into rivals who go out of their way to contradict their fathers. We'd be happy to keep our daughters beside us forever, eh, Nicky? But the sooner sons grow up and fend for themselves the better!"

A melancholic sadness clouded the Tsar's eyes and Wilhelm winced, suddenly realising the tactlessness of his comment. Absorbed in his grief, he had quite forgotten the rumours surrounding the health of Nicholas' only son. Little Alexei, the pride of his parents, was, it was said, frequently confined to bed, gripped by an agony so intense that his cries could be heard all over the palace. No one ever spoke openly of his illness but Wilhelm had little doubt that the boy had inherited the terrible bleeding disease, haemophilia, which had already caused so much heartache in Queen Victoria's family. Wilhelm had seen an uncle bruised and contorted in pain as internal bleeding caused his joints to swell; and a cousin and nephew, afflicted by the same condition, had not even reached their fifth birthdays. As he looked into Nicholas' eyes, he saw the unbearable sorrow of a father who stands helpless in the face of his beloved child's agony; and he knew that in Nicholas' case that sorrow was compounded by the fact that this child – so long-awaited by his country and so loved by his parents – was heir to the Romanov throne.

In any other country, Wilhelm thought, knowledge of the boy's condition would surely have evoked sympathy, but the Russians, with their mystical view of the world, saw their Tsars as little less than gods and, if word of the heir's illness got out, the consequences for the dynasty could be devastating. So, Nicholas suffered in silence, while his wife, Wilhelm's German-born cousin, Alix, tortured herself with guilt that the incurable condition had been passed to the child through her blood.

Awkward and discomfited by such thoughts, Wilhelm reacted as always with over-ebullience. "Well," he said, punching Nicholas' arm, "my guests will think me a very poor host if I abandon them for too long. Let's go back to the party."

He gesticulated towards the White Room but Nicholas remained still.

"I'm sorry, Willy, but it's time I was leaving. It's been a wonderful day and I should like to stay longer but there is so much to do back at home and..."

"Yes, yes, of course," Wilhelm nodded quickly. "In all the excitement, I'd quite forgotten your plans to leave tonight. No rest for an emperor, eh?"

Nicholas smiled and Wilhelm suddenly had a desperate desire to delay his departure. As long as the guests remained and the party continued, the distraction of entertaining could keep his inner demons at bay.

"Surely you have time to take a drink with me before you leave? I have hardly had a moment to speak with you since you arrived."

Nicholas hesitated but Wilhelm, determined to accept no refusal, strode past him into the ante-room and, before Nicholas had time to protest, poured two glasses of Asbach brandy.

"I haven't even asked how your family are. All well, I hope?"

Nicholas nodded and took the glass from his hand.

"It's a pity that Alix couldn't have come with you. We would have loved to have seen her. I always relish the opportunity of meeting with my cousins."

"She would have liked to have come but the journey would have been too tiring for her in the middle of all the tercentenary celebrations."

"Ah yes," Wilhelm nodded, "three hundred years of Romanov rule. May I drink a toast to three hundred more! Prost!"

Nicholas smiled and took a sip of brandy, "Then allow me to return your good wishes by drinking to *your* jubilee. I understand you have many celebrations planned for next month."

"Yes, indeed," Wilhelm nodded enthusiastically. "Twenty-five years on the throne is worth a pageant or two!" No sooner had he said it than his spirits sank. A Silver Jubilee seemed so paltry compared to the Romanov tercentenary; and even the forty years of the German Empire paled into insignificance beside a monarchy that had lasted for three centuries.

"You know," he said, struggling to overcome his sense of inadequacy, "it might sound arrogant to admit it, but I am proud of what I have achieved since my accession and even more proud of what my country has achieved since unification."

The violet blue eyes washed over him in a gentle gaze.

"After all the wars and battles that were necessary to unite us into one nation, we have now had forty years of peace. We have not sought to extend our borders and have had no desire to provoke antipathy in our neighbours. Instead we have generated prosperity at home, and improved trade, working conditions, transport, education and culture. I know that the British are suspicious of our growing naval power but it is not, and never has been, our intention to create friction or a sense of rivalry."

He was aware that Nicholas was staring into his glass as though reluctant to be drawn into such a conversation.

"The fact is, Nicky, you know that the prosperity of a country depends on its overseas trade. Britain thrives on her exports and imports from colonies all over the world. Good grief! Canada, Australia, India, Africa....is there anywhere that the British haven't planted their flag?"

"Willy," Nicholas began tentatively, "I really don't think this is the time for..."

"No, no," Wilhelm interrupted earnestly, "don't misunderstand me. I am not criticising their success. On the contrary," he raised his glass, "good luck to them!" He gulped the brandy and licked his lips thoughtfully before continuing, "All I am saying is that Germany, too, has a right to her place in the sun. If we are to enjoy overseas trade, we need a strong navy to protect our merchant fleets and to demonstrate to the world that we are also a great nation, worthy of the respect that is shown to the other major powers."

Nicholas, refusing to be drawn, glanced at his watch several times and edged towards the door.

Wilhelm stepped past him, "I know you need to leave but there is something else I'd like to say before you go." With no attempt at subtlety, he closed the door, preventing Nicholas' escape and the intrusion of eavesdroppers.

"Our families are so closely connected. We have known each other all our lives; spent holidays together, attended the same family gatherings, funerals, weddings – wasn't I the one who persuaded Alix to overcome her scruples and convert to Orthodoxy in order to accept your proposal?"

Nicholas smiled but Wilhelm observed a wariness in his expression as though he wondered where this monologue would lead.

He put down his glass and opened his palm in gesture of sincerity, "May we speak plainly – not as Emperor to Emperor or Kaiser to Tsar, but as friends, cousins even?"

Nicholas nodded, "Of course."

"I mentioned the tensions that can occur in a household of six sons. As children, they are compliant and submissive but as they grow up they need to expand, to express their individuality and take responsibility for their own lives. Isn't that natural?"

"Perfectly natural."

"And wouldn't it be wrong to deny a boy the right to grow and to develop into the man he was born to be?"

Nicholas, clearly bemused, nodded.

"If an overbearing parent were to attempt to stifle that growth, or to keep the man as a child forever, never allowing him his own opinions..." an image of his mother flashed through his mind, "...denying him the right to build friendships, treating him with disdain as though he were unnatural, and accusing him of ingratitude simply because he did not agree with his parents..." He heard the tension in his own voice and was suddenly, excruciatingly aware that, as he spoke, his right hand had taken hold of his withered left arm and was clinging to it violently as though trying to tear it from its socket.

He laughed to conceal his embarrassment and reached into his pocket for a cigarette case.

"As I see it," he said, clicking open the case and holding it out to Nicholas, "the nations of Europe are in exactly the same position. We are like one family but within that family there are many different characters, all of whom have the right to follow their own course and become the countries they were created to be."

Without a word, Nicholas took a cigarette and held out a lighter. Buying time to regain his composure, Wilhelm rested the cigarette in the flame but did not inhale for several seconds.

"For too long," he eventually continued, "Britain behaved as an overbearing parent, denying other nations the right to expand. In my grandmother's time, Germany was still in her formative years and we were more concerned with establishing our borders than expansion but, by the time of Grandmama's death and my uncle's accession, we had grown into manhood yet Britain continued to treat us as a child."

Seeing that the wariness had not lifted from Nicholas' brow, Wilhelm smiled and adopted a more convivial tone.

"The truth is, Nicky, as I look around, it's clear that the old vision of Europe is no longer valid. The world has changed beyond recognition in the past forty years. Once, Britain, France and Austria dominated the continent. Russia – forgive me – was seen as remote and insignificant; and Germany nothing but a collection of minor states. Yet here we are today, you and I – Russian Tsar and German Kaiser – the only monarchs who have any real authority or influence in the whole of Europe."

Nicholas' eyebrow flickered, and Wilhelm, sitting down on the arm of a chair, drew on his cigarette and exhaled the smoke in one long breath.

"Three years ago I attended the funeral of King Edward VII and, as I followed the coffin through the streets of London, it was clear that his death marked the end of an era. I cannot pretend that I was fond of the man but I must admit that he had a powerful personality and presence enough to influence international affairs. George, we both know, is an entirely different character from his father. He'd rather stay at home with his stamp collections than play any part in foreign affairs. For all his grandiose titles – King of the United Kingdom and her dominions, Emperor of India – he is nothing more than a cypher. His government decides a course of action and he simply adds his signature to a document."

Nicholas flicked the ash from his cigarette, "There are times when I envy the freedom of constitutional monarchs. Given the choice, most people in our position would prefer to spend more time with our families than shouldering the responsibility for every aspect of our people's lives."

"Indeed," Wilhelm said impatiently, "but as autocrats you and I do not have that choice." His thoughts returned to his uncle's death. "Apart from George and I, six other kings walked in that funeral procession and it occurred to me that not one of them had any real power whatsoever. There was the Danish contingent: King Frederick of Denmark, his brother, King George of the Hellenes – both of whom, God rest their souls, have since followed my uncle to the grave – and Frederick's son, Carl, King of Norway." He paused to recapture the scene more clearly. "Carl looked so young and inexperienced; not an autocrat, nor even a king by right, but one who was *chosen* and elected by a foreign people. The same was true, of course, of King George of the Hellenes – Danish princes on foreign thrones. Mere puppets! A nation that chooses to install a foreign king can equally easily depose him."

Nicholas said quietly, "German princes, too, have been elected to foreign thrones. King Carol of Roumania, King Ferdinand of Bulgaria…"

"Ferdinand, the self-styled *Tsar* of Bulgaria!" Wilhelm snorted with laughter as a comic image flitted into his mind. "You should have seen him at that funeral, clinking his jewels and strutting up and down like an overweight peacock taking a morning stroll!"

He laughed at the memory and the aptness of his simile but, catching sight of Nicholas' indulgent and somewhat impatient smile, he returned to his theme.

"What kind of authority could an elected monarch have, compared to that of a Kaiser, descendant of Frederick the Great, or a Tsar whose lineage can be traced back three hundred years?" He stood up and marched across the room. "The Iberian kings were also there. Manuel of Portugal – where is he now? Skulking in England, desperately trying to regain his throne from the Republicans."

"A terrible business," Nicholas shook his head. "He was fortunate to escape with his life, considering the fate of his father and brother at the hands of anarchists."

"The situation is little better in Spain. The country is in such a constant state of near-revolution that every time King Alfonso hears a motor car backfire, he suspects an anarchist's bomb. Even on his wedding day he narrowly escaped death at the hands of an assassin! How can he possibly play any part on the world stage when he has so many problems to deal with at home?"

Nicholas, obviously disconcerted, bit his lip, "Anarchists are active all over Europe. Russia is not immune to their attacks."

"Oh Nicky," Wilhelm waved dismissively, "I know you have had more than your share of these revolutionary atrocities. In an empire the size of Russia, dissent from some quarters is only to be expected but that does not in the least diminish your authority."

Nicholas silently inhaled the cigarette.

"You know," Wilhelm said, "out of all the other kings at Edward VII's funeral, only one struck me as having the true bearing of a sovereign: King Albert of the Belgians. He's so tall and dignified, he towered over the other mourners, exuding such an air of authority that it seemed a man of such a physique and bearing might have been better suited to ruling a far more powerful kingdom than insignificant Belgium. Italy, perhaps! He is twice the size of little King Victor Emmanuel, but, unfortunately for him, Belgium really is quite irrelevant and, as a constitutional monarch, his personal power is limited."

"Yes," Nicholas murmured distractedly, looking again at his watch.

"So," Wilhelm stepped closer, "apart from you and I, the only other monarch who has the power to shape the future of Europe is Austria's Franz Josef; but let's be honest – at his age, he has neither the desire nor the capacity to face the upheavals of the modern world. Like his empire, he is an anachronism, unable and unwilling to accept the changes that are taking place around him." He moved even closer and looked into Nicholas' eyes, "Do you understand what I am saying?"

Nicholas blinked and shook his head slightly.

"There is no one else, Nicky, only you and I. We alone hold the destiny of Europe in our hands."

The clock chimed nine-forty-five and Nicholas glanced more urgently towards the door.

"Forgive me," Wilhelm said, resting his hand on his shoulder. "You didn't come here to discuss politics and it wasn't my intention to bring all this up now but I am glad to have had the opportunity to speak openly to you. There is so much tension in the air; so much suspicion hovers over our alliances and our foreign interests, and I needed to assure you of my friendship. I don't ever want there to be any animosity between us. You *do* understand that, don't you, Nicky?"

"Of course, I do," Nicholas said sincerely. "Be assured of my friendship and be assured, too, that my greatest desire is for peace."

Wilhelm outstretched his hand and drew him closer. "Bonds of friendship, bonds of kinship and bonds of kingship," he smiled. "We are bound together and I know I can always rely on your support and amity."

Nicholas hugged him warmly and, smiling, turned to the door.

Chapter 6 – The Upper Belvedere Palace, Vienna – May 25th 1913

The evening breeze flowing softly through the open window carried the heady scents of roses into the sitting room and scattered sheaves of papers across the table. Franz Ferdinand gathered them together and, shuffling them into a neat pile, smiled contentedly at the scene of happy domesticity. Two little boys sprawled across the carpet, spinning a globe with wide-eyed fascination, while their elder sister sat entranced by the work of art that her mother was creating. With delicate fingers, Sophie drew a needle in and out of the sampler, embroidering an exquisite flower in threads of blue and gold.

Gazing at her fondly, Franz Ferdinand smiled that his delight in her company had in no way diminished in thirteen years of marriage. On the contrary, the thrill he had felt in the first flourish of love had deepened to such an extent that now his whole being had become synonymous with *Sophie*. The life he drew from her presence or even in contemplating her features was so much a part of him that she was as necessary as the air that he breathed. It was more, he mused, far more than her physical beauty that made her presence so vital. Her strength of character, her courage, her wisdom, her serenity and her unconditional love rendered her indispensable. Quite simply he knew that he could not live without her.

She looked up from her needlework and Franz Ferdinand observed the creases in her forehead and the fine lines around her eyes. There was no denying that humiliation had aged those beloved features but it had added, too, visible depths of compassion.

"Every line on that beautiful face," he thought, *"tells the story of all that she has endured since we met.*

She has stood by me so loyally and lovingly and has brought me more joy than I ever believed possible."

He thought back through many fond memories: their first meeting at the soirée when she was lady-in-waiting to the Duchess of Teschen; the light in her eyes during their earliest conversations; and the unfamiliar thrill in his heart whenever he was in her company. He recalled the happy confusion of realising how deeply he missed her in her absence and the excited anticipation of their next encounter. He smiled to think of their earliest tentative words of devotion, both of them a little afraid and unused to expressions of affection. What a relief it had been when their romance was finally discovered! After months of snatched moments, escaping from prying eyes to share secret kisses and the rising sensations of love, came the exhilaration of announcing openly what had been kept hidden for so long.

It did not matter one jot to him that the wedding had been such a quiet affair. The absence of his family seemed more of a blessing than a snub. Why should he proclaim his vows in front of sneering bigots when the promises he made were between him and Sophie and God? And from that day forward, love had deepened and grown stronger – from the bliss of the honeymoon in Konopischt, through the birth of each of their three children, whose presence here in this idyllic setting was proof of heaven's blessing on this marriage.

His elder son, ten-year-old Maximilian, shuffled onto his knees and, pointing out the borders of Austria-Hungary, told his little brother, "All of this is Great Uncle Franz Josef's empire."

Ernst's nose wrinkled, "Is that *it*? I thought Austria was huge but," he wriggled closer to the globe, "it is tiny compared to the rest of the world."

Franz Ferdinand chuckled to himself and crouched down beside them. "The world is filled with all kinds of exciting places where life is very different from here. There are animals and flowers and monuments and peoples of all different shapes and sizes and colours. In fact, there are so many magnificent sights that sometimes Austria looks quite dull in comparison."

His daughter, little Sophie, jumped down beside him, "Show us all the places you have been, Papa!"

He spun the globe, "Australia. There are animals there the like of which you've never seen."

"Kangaroos!" Maximilian said, causing Ernst to crouch on his haunches and hop across the carpet.

"And koala bears and colourful birds and snakes and venomous spiders and great coral reefs filled with exotic islands with palm trees and fruits." Franz Ferdinand's finger moved to the Far East, "Here in Japan there are ancient Buddhist temples, covered in gold and surrounded by waterfalls. Sometimes young men jump from the top of the temple into the falls; and every afternoon people drink tea in a beautiful ceremony carried out with great precision."

The children's eyes grew wide with fascination, and Franz Ferdinand, relishing their enthusiasm, smiled, "China is surrounded by a great wall, built hundreds of years ago and still there today; and over here in Egypt there are tombs of the Pharaohs that have been there for thousands of years…"

"Pyramids," Sophie said.

Franz Ferdinand nodded, "Such an ancient civilization; so different from…" he spun the globe, "North America, where there is no king or emperor."

"No," Maximilian said, "they have a president as they do in France."

"There *was* a king in France," Sophie said, "but they chopped off his head. Then they had another king and another one but they drove them out of the country."

Maximilian sniffed. "That's nothing. The Serbs butchered their last king and queen and threw their bodies out into the street."

Ernst's eyes opened wide with interest, "Did they?"

Maximilian nodded, "And when Papa's uncle became Emperor of Mexico, they shot him."

"Why?"

"Because," said Maximilian, "they decided that they didn't want him to be Emperor, after all."

Ernst's jaw dropped, "Are people allowed to do that?"

"No one could stop them."

"The Emperor's army should have stopped them."

Maximilian shrugged, "The soldiers didn't want him to be Emperor either."

Little Sophie smiled, "People in Austria would never do that. Everyone here loves Great Uncle Franz Josef and when Papa becomes Emperor they'll love him even more, won't they Mama?"

"I'm sure of it," she replied with a smile but a feeling of unease disturbed Franz Ferdinand's contentment as he turned the globe and his fingers moved over Serbia.

"That's the Balkans," Maximilian said, "where they just fought a war."

Ernst looked at his father, "Why?"

Franz Ferdinand pointed to the globe, "This is Turkey – the Ottoman Empire. The Ottomans or Turks used to be very powerful and, a long time ago, they took over land which these Balkan states – Bulgaria,

Greece and Serbia – believed should have belonged to them. Over the centuries, though, the Ottomans became much weaker so these little states decided to join together and form the Balkan League to reclaim that land."

"And that's what the war was about?"

Franz Ferdinand nodded.

"Did the Balkan League win?"

"Yes they did and all the parties are now meeting in London to draw up a treaty to settle everything."

"So is everyone happy now?"

"Not really," Franz Ferdinand frowned. "They made peace with the Ottomans but then the Balkan states began to squabble among themselves about how they should share out the land. I wouldn't be at all surprised if another war breaks out between Bulgaria and Serbia."

"That's ridiculous!" little Sophie shook her head and stood up. "Why can't they just sit down and talk about it instead of killing each other." She returned to her mother on the sofa, "I don't know why they always want more land anyway. The more land they have, the more problems they have. They really are silly and I am glad it has nothing to do with us."

Maximilian was still staring at the globe and, as his fingers traced the borders of Austria-Hungary, Franz Ferdinand felt suddenly impelled to share his vision of the empire's future.

"Let me show you something," he said, jumping to his feet and hastily searching through his papers for a map. "Sophie is right. The more power kings have, the more problems they have so I've formed a plan to keep everyone happy."

He spread the map across the carpet and smiled proudly at the carefully coloured regions of the empire.

"This is how I envisage Austria-Hungary," he said, crouching between Maximilian and Ernst. "Each of these different colours shows a different ethnic group."

Ernst's nose wrinkled, "Ethnic?"

"People who speak the same language or share the same religion and way of life. Here, we have the Magyars of Hungary; over here the Poles, the Slovenes, the Czechs…Altogether I have counted about twelve to fifteen groups and each one is quite different from the others, with different aspirations and cultures, which makes the role of the Emperor very difficult indeed. He has to keep everyone happy without dividing the empire."

Ernst, losing interest, rolled onto his back, "I'm glad I won't ever be an emperor. It's too complicated."

Franz Ferdinand tousled his hair and smiled.

"I don't think it's complicated," Maximilian said. "I think it's interesting. How can he keep everyone happy if they are all so different from each other?"

"Ah ha!" Franz Ferdinand beamed with delight at the opportunity to explain. "This is my plan. Each of these regions could be given its own council to make laws and organise taxes and so on. The local people would vote for representatives to sit on the council and that way everyone would have a say in the way that their region is governed."

"But then," Maximilian frowned, "each region would be like a separate country and Austria-Hungary wouldn't exist."

"No, no," Franz Ferdinand said excitedly, "because representatives from each of these smaller councils could come here to Vienna, where there would be a much larger council where all the views of all the regions could be discussed fairly and equally. Here they would make the decisions about alliances and trade with other countries and all the policies connected to foreign affairs."

"If they made all the decisions, what would the Emperor do?"

He looked up thoughtfully, "The Emperor is the lynchpin that holds the empire together. According to my plan, he would listen to the views of the different peoples, ensuring that no group became too powerful or too dominant and, if there were disagreements between the different regions, the Emperor would make the final decision about what was to be done. If he were kept fully informed of the opinions of the various councils, he would be in a far better position to make wise and just decisions and the people would feel proud and happy to be part of his empire."

"That's a brilliant plan," Maximilian smiled. "Is the Emperor going to follow it?"

Franz Ferdinand's excitement faded, "I don't think so. When Uncle Franz Josef came to the throne, people thought it was better to build empires by wars than by words. I'm afraid it's very difficult for a man of his age to change his views, particularly when he is surrounded by ministers who cannot see beyond the ends of their noses."

Maximilian leaned closer to the map and studied the various regions, "Is that how the empire came together? Were all these regions won by wars? Hungary, Galicia, Bohemia, Bosnia…"

"Bosnia," Franz Ferdinand groaned, pressing his finger to the map. "Bosnia has officially only been annexed to the empire for five years and it has brought nothing but trouble to the Emperor."

"Why did he annex it?"

"The original motive was honourable enough, I suppose. About fifteen years ago, the Emperor sent in troops to protect the Christians from the Turks who were bent on slaughtering them but, after a decade of occupying the place, he was persuaded to assume it into the empire. The timing was perfect. The Emperor was riding high on the wave of popularity that came with his Diamond Jubilee and his ministers knew that, following their disastrous war with Japan, the Russians wouldn't be in a position to object. It was an ideal opportunity to prove to Germany that we are a powerful ally." He stared more intently at the map, "But it was madness – utter madness. I warned of it at the time but no one listened. We duped the Russians into accepting what we'd done by making promises that we didn't keep and we angered the Serbs by taking land that they believed belongs to them. Now the Russians cannot trust us and the Serbs despise us. It's no wonder they have formed all kinds of patriotic groups who are willing to..." Suddenly aware of Ernst's proximity, he broke off, unwilling to distress him.

"Anyway!" he said, rolling up the map, "That's enough of that for today."

He glanced towards the open window and was about to suggest taking a walk through the gardens to clear his head when the door opened and the attendant announced the arrival of Count Clam-Martinic.

Franz Ferdinand stood up, "Heinrich, this is an unexpected pleasure!"

The Count bowed hastily, "I am so sorry to arrive unannounced and uninvited but..."

"Not at all! You're very welcome and you couldn't have come at a more opportune moment. We were just talking of my travels." He looked down at his children who had gathered in front of their mother, politely awaiting introductions. "You remember my old friend Count Clam-Martinic, who accompanied me on my tour? Perhaps he can remember more details to share with you."

The children looked up expectantly but the Count responded with only the briefest of smiles before turning to their father with an urgent expression. Urgency almost always implied bad news and, from the agitation in his demeanour, it was clear that this was not a social call.

Unwilling to alarm the children, Franz Ferdinand patted Ernst's head, "On second thoughts, it would be a pity to waste so beautiful an evening. Why don't you go outdoors to play in the sunshine?"

Relieved of the duty of making polite conversation, the children smiled brightly and hurried towards the door. Ernst, hopping like a kangaroo, said, "When I grow up, I'm going to travel as Papa did so I can become as wise as he is. I'm going to go to Australia and Egypt and China and..."

The door closed behind them and Franz Ferdinand turned to the Count, who stood sombrely in the middle of the room, his clean-shaven features as pallid as a tombstone.

"You look as if you have seen a ghost, Heinrich. Sit down and let me bring you a drink."

The Count ran his hand over his closely cropped hair, "I thought you should be the first to know so I came as soon as I heard..."

"Heard what?" said Franz Ferdinand, pouring brandy from a decanter and handing it to him.

"It's an extremely sensitive matter." He glanced embarrassedly at Sophie, "If this were to become public..."

Sophie moved to stand up but Franz Ferdinand rested his hand on her shoulder. "My wife and I share everything. Whatever you have to say, you can say in front of both of us."

Clam-Martinic nodded apologetically and, sitting down, took a sip of brandy. "It is unbelievable really..." He put down the glass and pulled on his fingers as he spoke, "You remember some time ago we spoke of our suspicions that there have been serious breaches of security in the Intelligence Corps?"

Franz Ferdinand nodded and sat down beside Sophie, "The ease with which our spies are identified and the speed with which they disappear as soon as they set foot on Russian soil can't be put down to bad luck. Someone must be supplying the Russians with information."

"*Someone,*" the Count whispered. "We now know who that *someone* is."

Franz Ferdinand leaned forwards, "Well?"

"Redl."

The name didn't register and Franz Ferdinand shook his head.

"Alfred Redl – the former Chief of Counter-Intelligence."

Franz Ferdinand reflected for a moment then leaned back, relieved, "Nonsense! I would stake my life on Redl's loyalty. As Head of Counter-Intelligence he developed some of the most innovative practices in the service." Smiling, he turned to Sophie, "They say he was so meticulous that he even sprinkled dust on the chairs where his visitors sat so that he could extract their finger-prints when they left."

Sophie didn't smile. Her eyes were fixed on the Count's pale features.

"That's the irony of it," he said quietly. "Redl was so good at his job that no one had any reason to suspect him. When he moved from counter-intelligence, he was replaced by Ronge – one of his own students, who looked up to and admired him. If the Chief of Counter-Intelligence had no suspicions, why would anyone else doubt him?"

"*Who guards the guards?*" Sophie said quietly.

Franz Ferdinand's smile slowly shrank, "Why suspect him now?"

"A couple of months ago, two packages arrived at the Post Office in Vienna and when no one collected them they were returned to the sender in East Prussia. The German Intelligence became suspicious and sent them on to Ronge, who realised at once they had been sent from an area that is notoriously riddled with Russian spies. When he opened the packages he found they contained around six thousand crowns and the addresses of several undercover agents."

"Six thousand crowns," Sophie's eyes widened. "That's a substantial amount of money."

"Ronge realised it was probably payment for information so he laid a trap. He had duplicate packages made and returned them to the original Post Office here in Vienna, where he installed an alarm so that when someone came to collect them the local police could be summoned to the scene." He paused and sipped the brandy. "Yesterday evening the alarm sounded but by the time the detectives arrived the suspect was disappearing into a taxi. Fortunately, they managed to track down the driver who recalled taking his passenger to the Hotel Klomser. When the officers made a search of the cab they discovered a penknife sheath, which the passenger had dropped, so they took it to the hotel and asked the staff to inquire if any of their guests had lost it. Imagine their shock when they recognised the former Chief of Counter-Intelligence stepping forward to claim it."

Franz Ferdinand's head spun at the revelation. "Did they arrest him on the spot?"

"No. They were so stunned that they contacted their superiors to ask for instructions. Ronge and

Conrad von Hőtzendorf were immediately informed and Hőtzendorf ordered them to arrest him in his hotel room so as not to attract the attention of the other hotel guests."

"Good, good," Franz Ferdinand nodded.

"When they went to his room they found Redl calmly waiting for them. He said he knew why they had come and, offering no defence, he confessed his guilt."

"Redl," Franz Ferdinand gasped, trying to come to terms with the enormity of the implications. "Not just a minion with limited access to information. He knew everything: our defence strategies, our spies, our military capability..."

"And he was passing all that information to the Russians."

"No one suspected anything?" Sophie said.

Clam Martinic shook his head. "Perhaps, if the rest of the Intelligence Corps had been more vigilant, this would have come to light sooner. No one thought to question how he managed to fund such a lavish lifestyle: a mansion in Prague, several houses in Vienna, a collection of expensive cars and…"

"To afford that kind of lifestyle," Sophie said, "he must have been in the pay of foreign agents for quite some time?"

"Possibly a decade or more."

Franz Ferdinand jumped from the chair and moved to the window where he pressed his head against the glass. Outside, his children ran among the roses, cupping their hands around butterflies and skipping over the lawns.

"What sort of man," Sophie said, "could betray his country and endanger the lives of his own people to purchase a few cars and a couple of houses?"

There was silence for a moment then Clam-Martinic cleared his throat pointedly.

Franz Ferdinand turned and raised his eyebrows, "Is there more to this than you have told us, Heinrich?"

"It would appear," he nervously ran his hand over his mouth, "that his original motive wasn't financial gain. The Russians were blackmailing him."

"Blackmail?"

"Redl kept a lover who had very expensive tastes."

"That's common enough," Franz Ferdinand muttered.

"Yes, but in this case," the Count glanced apologetically towards Sophie, "the lover was a young cavalry officer whom he used to pass off as his nephew. It seems that, unbeknown to his colleagues, Redl was homosexual and for years he had been in the habit of paying for the services of boys all over Europe. Maybe some of these boys were Russian spies, or maybe he was seen entering some of the most insalubrious establishments with them. One way or another, the Russians became aware of it and demanded information in return for their silence. It seems to have escalated from there and soon he was receiving large sums of money for increasingly sensitive information."

Franz Ferdinand turned to the window again and hammered the side of his first on the glass, "If the Russians discovered this years ago, why had we no inkling of it?" He recalled the old Emperor sitting at his desk like a relic – the very epitome of this outmoded empire. "Our whole system is ineffectual and out-dated. Would the Germans or the Russians have allowed such a thing to go undetected for so long?"

"It's a great pity…" the Count began.

"A pity?" Franz Ferdinand swung round on his heels, "It's a disaster, Heinrich! Not only has his selfishness cost the lives of several of our agents and endangered the lives of many more, but he has exposed to the rest of the world the sheer incompetence of our Military Intelligence."

"Attempts *are* being made to keep this quiet."

"You know as well as I do that these things have a way of coming out. In no time at all the whole of Europe will be laughing at this shambles."

Clam-Martinic could not dispute it. He sat as still as a statue with his eyes fixed on the floor.

"Well," Franz Ferdinand sniffed, moving to the table to reach for a pen and paper, "we must salvage what we can from this fiasco. Hopefully when he is questioned, he will reveal the extent of his treachery and we can discover exactly what information he has sold to save his precious reputation."

Clam-Martinic looked up suddenly, "Oh no, sir. It's too late for that. Redl is dead."

"What!"

"He killed himself in the early hours of this morning. On Hötzendorf's instructions, the officers handed him a pistol and left him alone in the hotel room to take the most honourable way out."

"Honourable? Suicide is not only a cowardly means of avoiding responsibility; it is a crime against God!"

The Count said something in reply but by now Franz Ferdinand was too incensed to catch his words. A great wave of fury surged through his body from the balls of his feet to the pit of his stomach, gaining momentum as it swelled into his chest and exploded in a roar so loud that Clam-Martinic lurched sideways as though struck by a heavy blow to his temple.

So great was his wrath that for several minutes he could not speak and only when he felt Sophie's hand gently reach for his own, did he eventually manage to gasp, "Suicide or murder…"

The utterance of two coherent words restored Clam-Martinic's balance. He sat upright and, clinging to the brandy glass, said quietly, "I believe that Hőtzendorf thought it was the best way to avoid a scandal. It could be reported that he killed himself in a hotel room for reasons unknown."

Holding fast to Sophie's hand to maintain his self-control, Franz Ferdinand said, "Those who encouraged – or compelled – him to take such an action are as guilty as he is. Sheer incompetence all round! And now he is dead and we shall never know what information he gave to the Russians."

"Actually," Clam-Martinic said, "we *do* know some of it. His home was searched this afternoon and the officers found evidence that he has given Russia all the details of our plans in the event of an invasion of Serbia and…"

Franz Ferdinand, unwilling to hear more for fear he should explode, interrupted urgently, "Heinrich, have a full report sent to me. Contact counter-intelligence and tell them that I want every detail of this case in writing; everything that was found in Redl's homes and a list of his closest contacts. We must be sure that there are no more traitors in our midst. God knows our armies in are in such a poor state already. The last thing they need is any potential enemy to be aware of their plans in advance!"

Clearly relieved at the opportunity of escaping from so volatile an atmosphere, Clam-Martinic stood up, "I'll go at once."

With a slight bow he moved towards the door.

"I take it that the Emperor has been informed?" Franz Ferdinand said.

"Yes, sir. I believe he, too, was greatly disturbed by Redl's suicide. In fact, he was so angry that

Hőtzendorf felt obliged to tender his resignation but the Emperor didn't accept it."

"Oh for pity's sake! Hőtzendorf resigns every other week! I thought I could work well with him but time after time he has behaved so irrationally and impetuously without a thought for the consequences of his actions. This is the last straw. Compelling a man to commit suicide is worse than murder. I wish to God I had never persuaded the Emperor to reinstate him."

Clam-Martinic nodded silently and reached for the door handle. Franz Ferdinand, too engrossed in his own thoughts to pay him any attention was hardly aware of his continued presence in the room until Sophie said, "Heinrich, thank you for coming. It cannot have been easy to be the bearer of such news."

The door closed behind him and Sophie put down her needlework, "Is this really as serious as it sounds?"

Franz Ferdinand opened his arms helplessly, "It proves my point about the extent of the decay at the very heart of the empire. The Emperor is locked into the past, the army is in a mess, and now we cannot even trust our own spies." He closed his eyes, not wanting to see the horrific possibilities. "This couldn't have come at a worse time. With the prospect of another Balkan War looming, the Emperor's cronies will be pushing him more fervently than ever towards an invasion of Serbia and, if the Russians already know of our plans, they will be even more inclined towards military intervention. We would be crushed, utterly crushed and destroyed."

He picked up the globe and, placing it on the table, spun it till his fingers rested on the Balkans.

"I can see it so clearly, Sophie. So much blood will be spilt just so we can hang on to Bosnia and Herzegovina, when everyone knows that our presence there only antagonises the Serbs. It wouldn't be so bad if the Slavs felt that they are valued within the empire but as things stand at the moment they only way they feel they can attract attention to their cause is by forming terrorist groups to commit atrocities. You know they even had a plan to assassinate the Emperor?"

"No?" she gasped.

"Obviously, it came to nothing. I think the would-be assassin lost courage at the last minute but it shows the lengths to which they are willing to go to achieve their ends."

"And the Serbian government supports these terrorists?"

"They deny it but the Emperor's ministers insist that these groups are funded from the highest authorities. If that crazy Hötzendorf had his way, we'd send our armies into Belgrade and crush the Serbs once and for all."

"That seems so extreme..."

"Worse than extreme," he said wearily. "It would be creating a spark that could ignite a conflagration." He moved back to the window, "Can't you feel it in the air when a storm is coming? Even before the clouds gather; even in the midst of a hot afternoon, you sense when it's on the way. Animals feel it more keenly than we do. They gather their young and hurry to find shelter as though they have some kind of intimate communication with the earth and they intuitively know exactly what is going to happen." He turned slowly from the window, "I feel like that now, Sophie. I feel as though I need to gather our children and keep them safe before whatever happens, happens."

She moved to his side and reached for his arm, "But *what*? What will happen?"

"Who knows? You see how everyone is arming so quickly? The Germans and the British, vying with one another for the largest fleet; everyone building bigger and bigger munitions factories and rushing to make alliances so we can all be sure of where we stand when the deluge finally comes…and the worst part about it all is that Austria is way behind the rest of Europe."

"What can you do?"

"I am doing all I can in trying to improve our army and navy but I sometimes feel as though I am simply being swept along in this whole belligerent maelstrom. There is so much anger and tension everywhere." He gazed at her earnestly, "Where has it come from, Sophie? It makes so little sense. All these advances in medicine and industry were meant to improve life for everyone, but instead that learning has been turned to creating more powerful weapons and more means of destruction. Why? Who is behind all of this?"

She shook her head, perplexed.

"The Emperor doesn't want war; the Tsar doesn't want war; I am sure that even the Kaiser doesn't want war and yet here we all are, arming at such a rate as though someone somewhere has planned all of this. Is someone behind it, Sophie? Is someone deliberately inspiring anger and mistrust so that…"

"Oh Franz," she squeezed his arm tightly, "don't you see what you are doing? There is so much anger in your own heart that you see it all around you. You are angry at the court for the way they have treated you; angry at the way they have treated me; angry at the Emperor for failing to listen to you…"

"But he *doesn't* listen to me! He listens to those ministers who are far more obsessed with their own ambition and reputations than with what is best for the empire." He pressed his finger and thumb into the corners of his eyes. "I want to see our children grow up in a country that is peaceful, Sophie. I want you and I to grow old together and to see our grandchildren playing on these lawns and...." His eyes suddenly filled with tears.

"Dear, dear Franz," she said leading him back to the sofa and pressing his head to her chest, "don't entertain these dark thoughts. Listen! Can you hear the children playing?"

He nodded.

"In this moment, think only of their laughter. Put everything else from your mind. None of us can foresee the future but we can enjoy the beauty of this lovely, peaceful evening together."

She ran her hand over his brow to smooth out the creases and, resting his head on her chest, he stared again at the globe.

Chapter 7 – The Alexander Palace, Tsarskoe Selo, Russia – June 1913

Though the sun barely set through the white nights of summer, its brightness did not penetrate the study where Tsar Nicholas sat hunched over his cluttered desk, peering at a series of maps. In the still and stifling air, a cloud of grey cigarette smoke hovered over his head, adding to the darkness of the room. He pulled the lamp closer and ran his finger along the western border of his empire.

"Germany, Austria, Hungary, the Balkans…"

How insignificant those little Balkan states appeared compared to the vastness of Russia. All of them combined could fit into one small Russian province but there was no doubt in Nicholas' mind that, just as a tiny bacillus can lay low or even kill a man, the germ of unrest in that turbulent region could bring about the downfall of empires.

His hand moved over Serbia, Montenegro, Bulgaria and Greece and, reaching for a pencil, he redrew the border of the Ottoman Empire, marking the territories gained by the Balkan League according to the Treaty of London. It was sickening to think that these tiny patches of land had cost so many lives but far more sickening was the thought that it had all been in vain.

From the start, trusting that the union might create stability, he had encouraged and supported the formation of the Balkan League but he had not foreseen that once they had routed the Turks, these states would turn on each other over the division of the spoils.

He leaned back on the green leather chair and looked across the room to the portrait of his father, gazing at him from the opposite wall. 'The Tsar-Peacemaker' they had called him, for steering Russia clear of any foreign war throughout his thirteen year reign.

"Oh Papa," Nicholas sighed, "with all my heart, I wish I could have lived up to your example…"

He thought back to the catastrophe of the Russo-Japanese War, nine years earlier. Defeat by a nation that had appeared inferior had been one of the greatest humiliations of his reign but that dent to Russian pride was nothing compared to the memory of how his brave soldiers had suffered and how many families had been deprived of husbands and sons. At least, he consoled himself, relations with Japan had vastly improved since then, and now, as his eyes returned to the map, he prayed for success in his attempts to broker a lasting peace in the Balkans.

A knock on the door heralded the arrival of Sergei Sazonov, Minister of Foreign Affairs.

Nicholas looked up hopefully, "They received my letters?"

"Yes, sir, and both the King of Serbia and the King of Bulgaria have replied."

"Good news?"

Sazonov shook his head dejectedly, "The Serbs are happy to accept your offer of mediation but the success of the last campaign has gone to the Bulgarians' heads. King Ferdinand refuses to reduce the size of his army and has placed so many conditions on your arbitration that it is rendered meaningless."

"If he doesn't want a peaceful settlement, what *does* he want?"

"If I may?" said Sazonov, leaning over the desk and pointing to the map. "The Bulgarians are demanding that Greece and Serbia hand over to them all of this area so, basically, they will have complete control of Macedonia. In response, the Greeks and Serbs have renewed their alliance and it appears that they are even going to ally themselves with the defeated Turks to combat the Bulgarian threat. There is also a suggestion that Roumania will join the alliance with the Greeks and Serbs."

"This is lunacy," Nicholas shook his head in disbelief. "The Bulgarians will be defeated in no time. What on earth is King Ferdinand thinking?"

Sazonov tugged at his beard, "With all due respect, sir, he seems to be a rather strange and stubborn man with an inflated sense of his own influence. The fact that he chooses to call himself *Tsar* of Bulgaria is, from what I have seen and heard of him, typical of his rather grandiose ideas. He does not accept defeat gracefully and is quick to exact revenge for any perceived slight."

Nicholas, reluctant to undermine a fellow monarch, said nothing but, intrigued by Sazonov's ill-concealed smile, raised his eyebrows questioningly.

"Of course, sir, you are aware of what happened when he travelled to England for the funeral of King Edward VII?"

Nicholas shook his head.

"Apparently, he fell into a dispute with Archduke Franz Ferdinand of Austria about whose railway carriage should take precedence. The Archduke succeeded in having his way and his carriage was placed next to the engine, with King Ferdinand's coupled behind it. King Ferdinand was so incensed by the slight that he refused the Archduke permission to pass through his carriage to reach the dining car so the heir to the Austrian throne was denied any sustenance for the journey."

Nicholas, grateful for the light relief, laughed loudly, prompting a further anecdote from Sazonov.

"On another occasion, while King Ferdinand was staying at Potsdam, Kaiser Wilhelm crept up behind him and slapped him on the bottom."

Nicholas' eyes widened, "Slapped him? Whatever for?"

"I believe the Kaiser saw it as a joke, sir."

"Mm," Nicholas mused, recalling stories of Wilhelm's strange sense of humour and the sadistic pleasure he took in turning his rings inwards to cause pain to his courtiers when shaking their hand. He recalled, too, the even more bizarre tales of the Kaiser ordering members of his cabinet to dance for him, wearing feathers and ballerinas tutus, or to crawl on all fours dressed as poodles.

"King Ferdinand," Sazonov continued, "did not find it in the least amusing. Even though the Kaiser apologised profusely, the King immediately withdrew a lucrative contract he had made with a German armaments factory and took his custom to a French business instead."

Nicholas smiled and shook his head but, as his eyes drifted back to the map, his smile soon faded. "If a man can react so strongly to something so trivial, how will he behave when faced with something more serious? If he insists on taking his country into this war, he is facing almost certain defeat."

Sazonov's moment of humour had passed and his face took on a more sombre aspect, "If the Serbs are victorious – as seems likely – they will feel even more confident about creating their own separate Slav kingdom. Already there are rumours that as soon as they have put down the Bulgarians they intend to invade Albania. Then it's only a matter of time before they try to take Bosnia and Herzegovina from the Austrians."

Nicholas sighed deeply, "The whole situation is so complex; so many conflicting desires and each state believes itself to be justified in its demands." He sat down again and, lighting another cigarette, looked up at the ceiling, weighing his options.

"I will write again to King Ferdinand, impressing on him the seriousness of his actions. He ought to be able to prevail upon his ministers and generals to reach a more peaceful settlement."

Sazonov shuffled back from the desk, "I fear it's too late, sir. King Ferdinand himself is behind much of the aggression. Our intelligence suggests that without consulting his ministers he has already sent an order to his generals to attack both Greece and Serbia. It's widely believed that his aim is to eventually take Constantinople and have himself crowned king there."

"Constantinople!" Nicholas gasped in amazement. "It's a pipe dream!"

"Unless," Sazonov began tentatively, "he has German support."

Nicholas shook his head, "The Kaiser would never encourage such a pointless scheme."

"Wouldn't he, sir?" Sazonov tugged the end of his beard.

Nicholas smiled, "Don't worry, Sergei. The Kaiser might have a strange sense of humour but he is astute enough to realise such a plan would not only destabilise the region further but also create tension between us. Only last month he assured me that his over-riding desire is to maintain peace throughout Europe and he is as keen to remain on good terms with us as we are with him."

When Sazonov appeared unconvinced, Nicholas raised his eyebrows, "Why this suspicion? You have always been in favour of maintaining friendly relations with Germany. I haven't forgotten the vital role you played in helping us to reach an agreement about Persia."

"Yes, sir, and that is why I now have grave doubts about the Kaiser's intentions. According to the latest reports, he has sent one of his generals into Turkey to take charge of sections of the Ottoman army and the garrison at Constantinople. We believe that he intends to control the whole of the Bosphorus."

Nicholas' heart sank, "He would surely have told me of it, if that were the case. He must know that such a move could have serious implications on our trade routes."

Sazonov nodded and watched silently as Nicholas unrolled another map and traced the outline of the Persian Gulf.

"This is all very awkward," he sighed. "Apart from protecting our own trade routes, we mustn't forget that the British are very protective of their interests in Persia."

"I agree, sir," Sazonov nodded vehemently. "That is why I feel we need to be cautious in all future dealings with the Kaiser. We mustn't do anything to jeopardise our alliance with Britain and France."

"I am sure our allies are aware that we will always honour our agreements with them. At the same time, though, we will continue to do everything in our power to remain on good terms with Germany. My priority is to maintain peace not only in Russia but throughout all of Europe."

Sazonov shuffled his papers and appeared to stifle a yawn.

"Yes," Nicholas smiled, "it is late. You had better go and rest now. Come back tomorrow and we will review all these questions again."

With a grateful bow, Sazonov backed towards the door and when he had gone Nicholas stared again at the maps. Like a stone thrown into a lake sending ripples across the surface, the effects of a tiny movement in one part of the world could be felt thousands of miles away; and now, as at no other time in the past, everything seemed to be hanging in so precarious a balance that the slightest fluctuation could throw the whole world into chaos.

His neck ached from the hours of stooping over the desk, and his eyes prickled from poring over plans and documents. He stretched to ease the pain in his shoulders and his eyes alighted on the piles of papers awaiting his signature. The work was never ending. Even if the rest of the world took care of itself, Russian internal politics could consume every hour of every day. He put aside the maps and sifted through the Minister of the Interior's reports of strikes and unrest in the cities.

"*Seven hundred thousand men on strike,*" the figure stuck out from the page like an eye-sore, "*and more are threatening to do the same.*"

So vast a land! So many different cultures, different time zones, different lives – so many millions of people dependent upon his decisions. Such a hotchpotch of cultures and ideals in this empire; so many people with so many demands! So much turmoil here at home, without even taking into account the complexities of international affairs.

He reached for a pen and added a signature to show he had read the document before approving plans from various ministerial departments. For over two hours he worked through the papers until, as the dawn chorus sounded through the window, he could no longer keep his eyes open. He dragged himself from the desk and lay down on the divan at the opposite side of the room where, closing his eyes, he dozed fitfully, his mind too crowded for sleep.

The world was moving so quickly that the face of Russia had changed beyond recognition. It was beneficial, he thought, that his empire was now beginning to keep pace with her neighbours in industry and scientific advancement, but had all this progress come at the expense of the traditions and way of life that had held the country together for so long? The speed of the changes had taken everyone unaware. The liberated serfs swarming into the towns might have come in search of a better life but the cities were ill-prepared to receive them; and the factories that were making Russia a strong competitor on the world stage, were draining the life from her own people.

He prayed for wisdom and the strength to do all that was best for the millions of subjects who counted on him to keep the empire safe. He prayed, too, for peace in the Balkans and in the East until calmness gradually came over him and his mind drifted to the haven of beautiful Livadia – the Crimean estate that seemed like a pleasant dream far removed from this earth and all the pressures of being Tsar.

Chapter 8 – Austrian Military Manoeuvres – September 1913

From the top of a hill, Archduke Franz Ferdinand peered through the disorderly columns of trees at the patterns of fragmented sunlight flickering across the brown earth. The mist of the morning had lifted, revealing a myriad of colours: gnarled roots, like blackened limbs jutting out from the mud; felled trunks covered in purplish moss; dark greens and browns of the undergrowth; and speckles of yellow, dappling the verdant branches. The autumnal scent of burning leaves hung on the air, strengthened by the familiar smell of cordite emanating from the guns in the valley below.

As the clouds of dust whipped up by a cavalry charge dispersed, the blue-clad infantrymen came into view, moving to and fro as in an orderly dance. Around them, artillery officers in their brown jackets stood by their guns, while an occasional flash of red and blue darted across the horizon as a stray horseman returned to his line. From this distance, they appeared so small that they might have been toy soldiers tipped out of a box for a child's amusement and, as Franz Ferdinand narrowed his eyes to view them more clearly, his thoughts returned to the rainy afternoons of his childhood in Graz.

As a boy, he had spent many happy hours examining the colourful uniforms and regimental banners of his painted figures: cuirassiers, dragoons, hussars and foot soldiers; officers on rearing horses, leading heroes to war. Lying face down and pressing his chin to the carpet, he had seen through the eyes of those figures the vibrancy of battle and the glorious spectacle of conquest. Godlike he had planned the fate of his battalions: this man would live; this man would die; one would be decorated with medals and honours;

and one would be shot for dereliction of duty in the midst of the fray. What comfort he had found in that box of bright soldiers! In an unreliable world where, at the age of eight, the death of his mother had brought home to him the uncertainty of life, there was something reassuring about being able to take control of whole armies, moving them forwards with delicate fingers or gathering them together in rough, childish hands. Whether defending the castles of the Danube or fighting on an open plain, his regiments were always victorious and those who were slain died honourably as heroes, struck down in their prime and uttering patriotic speeches with their final breath. The miniature world was safe and beautiful. At the end of the day, the victors and vanquished, the heroes and the cowards, the dead and the living, returned to their satin-lined box, unscathed, for death was only a moment of glory preceding a joyful resurrection.

"If only," he murmured, looking down at the boys in the valley, "real life could be so simple."

For now, as they went through these manoeuvres, the soldiers had no more to fear than those figures he had played with as a child. They were merely toys in the hands of the generals, who moved them thither and yon as in a game. If they stepped out of line the worst they could incur was the wrath of their officers or the temporary loss of privileges, and, like the soldiers of his childhood, at the end of the day they would return safely to their barracks, unharmed and ready to play the same game tomorrow.

"If only they knew..." he sighed. If only they knew that this wasn't a pleasant pastime for the amusement of children. This was the sinister preparation for a seemingly inevitable war.

'Then,' he thought, 'the boxes to which they return at the end of the day will be coffins; death will be *brutal and inglorious, and their mothers and wives will wait in vain for their return.'*

He reached into the saddle-bag of the horse that stood patiently beside him, and pulled out a pair of binoculars. Instantly the tiny figures in the valley grew to manly proportions and the dance, which had seemed so orderly from a distance, turned into a chaotic melee. Infantrymen, out of rank, wandered aimlessly in front of a line of idle guns where artillerymen turned to one another in confusion, as though unsure of their orders and awaiting further instructions. Cavalrymen dismounted and gathered in disorganised groups to chatter and laugh while their horses carelessly champed the grass.

Franz Ferdinand urgently scanned the valley for their Commander-In-Chief and eventually caught sight of Franz Conrad von Hötzendorf, galloping erratically between the lines, waving a sword above his head like a demented Viking intent on terrifying his foes. Though his words were inaudible from the top of the hill, it was clear that he was yelling orders but the only response of those around him was to leap out of his path for fear of being caught in his horse's hooves.

In an instant Franz Ferdinand had mounted his own horse and, pursued by a posse of aides and officers, was charging full speed down the hillside. As though fired by the rider's rising anger, the horse seemed to fly with the wings of Pegasus, leaping tree trunks and boulders, splashing through streams and trampling the kindling to dust. Reaching the valley, Franz Ferdinand pulled at the reins and the horse slowed from a gallop to a canter and down to a steady trot until at last it stood quite still, panting and steaming as sweat dripped from its flanks.

The soldiers, startled by this sudden and dramatic entrance of the heir to the throne, were thrown into confusion. Some jumped to attention and saluted while others set about the tasks to which they had been assigned with greater fervour.

Their Commander-in-Chief, however, was too engrossed in his own ardent oration to notice the Archduke's arrival.

"Come on, lads, put your hearts into it," his voice boomed into the wind. "See yourselves facing those Serbian gypsies! Show them what we're made of!"

For several minutes he continued with an increasingly virulent harangue until at last, catching sight of Franz Ferdinand, he concluded with a theatrical flourish before returning his sword to its scabbard. Tugging at the reins he turned the horse towards the Archduke and, saluting with arrogant confidence, bellowed, "Your Imperial Highness, you see what fire these boys have in their bellies? Every one of them is prepared to lay down his life in the service of the Emperor."

Obviously anticipating a compliment, he paused expectantly but Franz Ferdinand eyed him with contempt. For a few seconds there was silence during which the surrounding aides wriggled clumsily in their saddles until a ripple of disconcertion ran through the lines of foot soldiers, now standing to attention.

Hőtzendorf, unused to being kept waiting even by an archduke, threw back his head impatiently, "This morning, sir, we heard that the Albanians are massing to shake off the yoke of the grasping Serbs. Those gypsies are not satisfied with what they've taken from Bulgaria – they will never be satisfied until they take over the whole of the Balkans. This news has inspired even greater fervour in the ranks. All these boys are eager for their chance to crush the Serb threat once and for all. I trust that you're impressed by what you have seen here today."

"Impressed?" said Franz Ferdinand, raising himself up in the stirrups as the familiar tingling of anger surged through his limbs. "Impressed by this disorganised shambles or by the inappropriateness of your ravings?"

Rather than cowing Hötzendorf, the question triggered a defiant expression, "It is *vital* to fire up the troops to get the best out of them. These…"

"The best? If this is the best they can do, then God help us! All I have seen here is chaos! No control, no order, men wandering aimlessly out of line; no one knowing where he ought to be, and the cavalry so far out of sight as to be beyond the reach of any orders."

Refusing to be subdued, Hötzendorf, too, raised himself in his stirrups like an angry dog poised on its haunches, "Battles are seldom orderly and controlled. Amid the shouts and the shots and the echo of the guns, orders are often inaudible and men need to think for themselves. When their officers' voices cannot be heard, they must drive themselves onward by the power of their passion. Today I have given these men that incentive and a taste of what war is really like."

Franz Ferdinand stared at him, aghast as much at his incompetence as his insolence.

"You have given these men nothing but your own narrow-minded and ill-thought-out opinions. You are not here to fill their heads with your violent politics but to train them into highly skilled soldiers who are capable of defending this Empire. Sword-waving, speeches and cavalry charges! What good are they in the face of howitzers and mortar shells? Anyone would think we were preparing for another Austerlitz or Könnigrätz!"

Hőtzendorf's cheeks turned from ashen to puce and his lips curled into a rabid snarl but Franz Ferdinand, undaunted, continued.

"I can see I was sorely mistaken in persuading His Majesty to reinstate you. I had thought you were a competent general who had the best interests of the army at heart but what I have seen here today shows that you are nothing but a sabre-rattling bigot with no understanding of the nature of modern warfare. You are more likely to lead these men like lambs to the slaughter than to even the faintest hope of victory!"

Through gritted teeth, Hőtzendorf managed to spit, "You are asking for my resignation, sir?"

Franz Ferdinand shook his head derisively, "Ah, once again we see your true spirit! All those fiery words and yet at the first sign of opposition you turn and run."

Leaving Hőtzendorf to seethe, he turned to the officers whose heads were lowered in embarrassment.

"Gentlemen, we have all seen the paintings depicting the glory of battle. As boys, with those images dancing in your heads, you probably played with your toy forts and tin soldiers, dreaming of gallantry and the honour of protecting the beautiful Austro-Hungarian Empire but the days of defending fortresses and face-to-face combat are over. Any future war will not consist of heroic cavalry charges or battles that are settled in an hour or two. Look about you!" He pointed directly towards the line of artillery, "When those guns fire and mortar shells explode, the old military methods will be useless. Have no illusions. There will be no glory, no heroic charges or dramatic sword fights and there will be no room for theatrical displays of individual courage. There will be only bloody mutilation, carnage and horrific destruction. Knowing this, it is the duty of your rulers and ministers to do everything in their power to prevent war by means of negotiation and honourable agreements. If, however, war should become a necessity for the defence of our beloved Austria, then you, as officers will have placed upon your shoulders greater responsibility than any of your forebears ever knew. The lives of your men will depend on your decisions, and in order to gain their confidence you will need to prove yourselves worthy of their respect. This respect does not begin in the midst of the fray; it needs time develop. You must earn that respect now by your example, your commitment to those who serve under you and above all by your competence and ability to unite your forces. The chaos and incompetence I have seen here today is shamefully unworthy of the Imperial Army." His eyes moved along the row of subdued officers, "I hold each of you personally responsible for making the necessary improvements to ensure that your platoons, battalions and regiments work together as cohesive units. In an age where weapons have been developed to destroy hundreds if not thousands of men, it is your duty to ensure your soldiers are well-prepared to defend themselves and each other." He glanced towards Hötzendorf, "There is no place now for theatrics and flourishes. We do not need heroic display. We need a skilled fighting force – nothing more. See to it, gentlemen, that your troops are thoroughly prepared."

His anger abated, he saluted and, without waiting for further excuses from Hötzendorf, dug his heels into the horse's flanks and sped away before his coterie of aides had time to pursue him. As though the words he had spoken had come from beyond him, he was suddenly aware of the horrors that lay ahead if his prophecy came to pass. War would be more grotesque and cruel than any previous battle. He was not so naïve as to believe that all past conflicts had been glorious and painless but now the advances in technology had created weapons that were capable of inflicting unimaginable suffering on such a large scale.

Determined to rid himself of the terrible images, he galloped faster and faster up the hillside until his body settled into the rhythm and his muscles flowed in time with those of the horse. The greater the distance he put between himself and the disorderly manoeuvres, the greater became his sense of freedom. He ducked beneath branches, inhaling the scent of the damp earth, until the trees gave way to a grassy expanse leading towards a ridge where the horse, unprompted, slowed to a steady trot. Franz Ferdinand dismounted and, gathering the reins, led the horse to a shallow pool where, with huffs and snorts, it satisfied its thirst.

Franz Ferdinand stood at the edge of the cliff, shielding his eyes from the glare of the sun and staring across the horizon. A solitary bird soared high across a brilliant blue sky, its wings shining like silver through the thin wisps of clouds where the earth and the firmament merged into one. The air was fresh with the faint spray of the falls that whooshed and trickled onto the green rocks below. The cataract; the mountains; the sky and the glow of September sunlight – it was all so vast and so perfect that every problem on earth seemed insignificant and vanished in the immensity of it all.

It seemed to Franz Ferdinand in that moment, that if he could just see a little further beyond the horizon, he would catch a glimpse of heaven but, even in the midst of his awe, there came a deep feeling of sadness. Summer was fading too quickly and, for some reason that he could not discern, this year its passing felt particularly painful. Each evening for the past week, a peculiar melancholy had disturbed him and he had longed to find some means to slow the hands of the clock to prevent time from slipping through his fingers like sand through an hour glass.

Desperate to drain the last drops of summer to the dregs, he made his way down the jagged rocks and, stepping over fallen stones and gullies, edged along the cliff side until he reached a series of natural steps at the foot of the falls. Tiny caves opened through the eroded rock face and the clear waters trickled in an out of them with a sound so melodic and rapturous that it seemed as though the depths of the earth were playing a mystical concerto.

Sitting down on the pebbles, he pulled off his riding boots and, rolling his trousers to his knees, let the icy water run over his toes. Allured by the autumnal splendour of the sun gleaming through the droplets of the falls and shimmering over the calmer surface below, he waded into the river, displacing the slimy stones on the bed. Knee-deep in the water, he threw back his head and let the spray – so cold and so invigorating – splash over his face and roll down his cheeks like tears. Marbled by the sunlight on the water, shades of purple, ivory and green rippled like a rainbow across the rock face, and Franz Ferdinand gasped with delight. There were no words. There was only wonder flowing blissfully not only through his eyes and limbs but welling up from the very depths of his soul.

"This is....*paradise,*" he murmured and in that instant he was certain that, although he was quite alone, Sophie was somehow beside him, sharing his ecstasy.

He could see her eyes, glowing with joy and, with the same rapturous sense of belonging he had felt when first he gazed into those eyes, he realised that not only their lives but their very souls were inextricably united by the hand of God. He recalled their first meeting when she looked at him with an expression of complete recognition, which he felt, too. For the first time in his life he had understood that until then he had always been alone, finding in his privacy solace from the loneliness that had become so familiar that he had almost forgotten it was there.

"*And now, in this moment, someone,* he had thought, *someone so beautiful, understands and feels it, too.*"

The moment passed but, as she turned from him, he knew that what had happened would remain with him for eternity; that glorious moment when he realized for the first time ever that he was no longer alone.

He stepped back towards the bank and sat down dangling his feet in the fast flowing stream.

"Oh, Father," he prayed, "it is for *this* that Austria must be protected. For this beauty, for this landscape; the flowers, mountains, our heritage…but more than that it is for our families, our way of life and all whom we love." He pressed his hands together, "Dear God, I implore you to avert the catastrophe that seems to be almost upon us." He looked up at the sky, "And grant that whatever happens, Sophie and I will be together always; throughout our lives and through all eternity."

He rubbed the water from his blue feet and pulled on his boots and, as he raised his head to shake the spray from his hair, he caught sight of a figure standing at the top of the falls. Clambering over the stones, he hurried up the slope where an officer stood peering one way then another as though searching for him. Irked that even now duty impinged on these sacred, private moments, Franz Ferdinand coughed and the officer jumped to attention.

"Did you follow me?" he demanded.

"No, sir," said the officer. "I was sent after you with a message from your Chancellery. They said you had come in this direction but I couldn't find you until I saw your horse here so I…"

"What message?" he said grouchily.

"There has been an uprising in Albania, sir. The Albanians are attempting to drive the Serbs from the Luma district."

Franz Ferdinand nodded silently.

"The Serbs have retaliated by committing the most appalling atrocities – bayoneting, burning, looting. They say some villages are littered with corpses and there isn't a single man left alive."

"And this will provide yet another excuse for those warmongers in Vienna to repeat their calls for an invasion."

The officer reached for the reins of Franz Ferdinand's horse and steadied it as he mounted. "Do you have a message for me to take back to your Chancellery, sir?"

"Three words:" he said, "negotiation not war."

The officer saluted and turned away but Franz Ferdinand called after him, "*Not war!* Make sure they understand that."

"Yes, sir."

Dismissed, he disappeared into the trees, and Franz Ferdinand looked up at the heavens, "Half an hour of paradise is all we're allowed before they haul us back to this purgatory on earth."

The ride back was far slower than the ride out, rarely going beyond a steady trot, and with each step homewards, Franz Ferdinand felt increasingly downcast. The moment of freedom had gone and now, with winter drawing closer, the future seemed so bleak and uncertain that he wished he might return to the top of the ridge, to leap into the falls and fade forever into oblivion.

Chapter 9 – Austria - December 1913

Streaks of red flashed across the sky as the fading sun flickered through the blanket of clouds and sank into the horizon like a guttering torch smothered in fog. The day suddenly grew colder almost freezing Franz Ferdinand's finger to the trigger but, despite the stiffness of his joints and the aching in his legs, he refused to yield as long as there was a glimpse of daylight. Even after six hours in the field, the combined scents of wood smoke and gunshot still thrilled his nostrils and the regular flutter, crack and thud above the dog barks and crunching of bracken sounded as melodious to his ears as an overture.

The beaters were beginning to tire and even the dogs had lost much of their early enthusiasm – trotting now, rather than bounding, to recover the prey – but there was still time for one more shot before returning home to the vexing questions that invariably awaited his attention.

Throughout the summer and autumn, events in the Balkans had rapidly unfolded: within two days of turning on their former allies, the Bulgarians, finding themselves attacked on all sides, had been driven into retreat. Their army was routed and all the territories they had won six months earlier were lost. As the defeated troops fled the bloody battlefields, cholera swept through the region and the diseased corpses poisoned the water supplies, killing many more until, by the end of October, the turbulent states had settled into an uneasy peace. To Franz Ferdinand's relief, it had taken no more than a stern warning from Vienna and a whisper from St. Petersburg for the Serbs to withdraw from Albania; and now, in the midst of winter, came a temporary stillness as though, like

Nature herself, anger and resentment lay dormant beneath the frozen earth.

'Perhaps,' he thought, *'men are too busy battling against the cold to think of taking up arms,'* and, though he had little doubt that when spring returned old animosities would revive, for now he was grateful for a respite from the endless talk of war.

He raised his gun towards the darkening sky but, rather than firing, he loosed his finger on the trigger, confounded by the unexpected bleakness of his thoughts. Several times during his recent visits to Vienna, a deeply disturbing sensation had oppressed him and now, as he stared into the black December evening, vivid images of the Emperor's ministers danced before his eyes. Not for the first time, it occurred to him that the stony glares, to which he had long been accustomed, had intensified, as though the familiar antagonism of the courtiers had developed into outright hatred. Formerly, he might have dismissed their silent antipathy and he would even have understood the anger in Hötzendorf's eyes, but now came a feeling that his enemies were uniting against him and perhaps even laying a trap for his demise.

He blinked away the thoughts and nodded to the beaters, now barely more than silhouettes in the semi-darkness. Moments later the fluttering of wings set his reflexes on edge. He raised the gun and, pointing the barrel the perfect distance ahead of the flight, pulled on the trigger. Seconds later came the familiar thud as the bird dropped lifeless to the ground.

Applause and calls of 'well done, sir!' echoed over the field and Franz Ferdinand, turning to his companions, smiled, "Shall we give the birds a break and call it a day?"

Stamping their feet to shake away the cold, the attendants gathered the guns and dragged the bags across the field.

"A good day's shoot, eh, Jaroslav?" he said to his brother-in-law, but, as his eyes moved towards the bags, a sense of anti-climax dragged at his heart. A mass of bloody feathers and beaks was visible through the neck of the sack, and the beady eye of a pheasant's corpse stared directly at him. He reached into his pocket for a hip flask and took a gulp to combat the cold and the feeling of weariness that suddenly came over him. Dozens of dead birds in one day might have displayed his unerring skill as a marksman but the excessive slaughter of specially plumped creatures, bred primarily for amusement, suddenly filled him with revulsion.

As they strode back towards the house, Jaroslav inhaled contentedly, "There's nothing quite like the thrill of the shoot, is there?"

Like the recoil of a rifle, Franz Ferdinand's mind propelled him backwards through the years until the corpses of the hundreds of thousands of beasts he had slain seemed to lie in his memory like a great animal necropolis.

He turned to his friend, Clam-Martinic, "Do you remember the hunt in Australia, Heinrich?"

Whether or not Clam-Martinic answered, Franz Ferdinand did not know. His thoughts were too absorbed in recollections of the grand tour that took him from the Suez Canal to the farthest reaches of the British Empire.

"Can't remember the exact number of kangaroos we bagged altogether, but on the first day alone I shot five as well as about twenty wild turkeys and a few emus."

"Is that right?" Jaroslav said with admiration.

"Just over eleven years ago," Franz Ferdinand nodded, trying to shake away the gloomy thoughts.

"Some of the finest taxidermists in the world live in Australia," Clam-Martinic said, "so we brought back a collection of wonderful specimens."

"Interesting, isn't it," Jaroslav said, "how the hunter must adapt to his prey? Did you even hear about the way they hunt tigers in Nepal?"

Franz Ferdinand shook his head.

"The Maharajah, apparently, is a first-rate shot and he travels with an entourage of around fourteen thousand people and over two thousand elephants."

The twilight had faded and now only the lanterns illuminated the path back to the house. Franz Ferdinand peered through the darkness, imagining the scene.

"When the Maharajah decides to go hunting, the beaters start to flush out the tiger days before his party arrives. Once the tiger has been tracked, it is surrounded by a huge circle of elephants – sometimes a couple of hundred of them. They gradually narrow the circle until there's no escape for the tiger and the hunters can move in for the shoot."

"Imagine," Franz Ferdinand murmured, "the poor tiger completely unaware that he is being tracked and the net is slowly closing in on him."

Jaroslav stopped and stared at him, "A great hunter like you, Franz? I never thought I'd hear you express such concern for the prey."

"Neither did I but now…"

Jaroslav waited, anticipating an explanation, but when none was forthcoming he prompted, "But now, what?"

Franz Ferdinand looked around to make sure the beaters were out of earshot.

"I sometimes feel like that tiger."

"You?" Clam-Martinic frowned, laughed and shook his head in one movement.

"There are times," he whispered, "when I feel as though I am being watched and hunted just like that Nepalese tiger. One day, perhaps, I will be walking or driving along, unsuspecting, and will suddenly find myself surrounded and trapped by those who wish to kill me."

"Nonsense!" Jaroslav slapped his back. "Who would want to kill you?"

"I have enemies; I am sure of it."

"Well, I dare say that you're not the most popular man in Vienna but that's a far cry from someone wanting to kill you."

Franz Ferdinand pulled the hip flask from his pocket and took another swig before nodding to signify that they should walk on. For a short while they continued in silence but, as they gained ground on the rest of the party, he stopped.

"I want to tell you something. A couple of years ago I had a mausoleum prepared for myself and Sophie in the chapel at Artstetten."

"Yes," Jaroslav sighed as though he didn't wish to discuss it. "You mentioned it at the time."

"If the ministers have their way they won't let us be buried together. They'll put me in the family sepulchre with the rest of the Habsburgs but because of their damned snobbery they won't allow Sophie to be interred there with me."

"Franz," Jaroslav said with mounting impatience. "I know all of this."

"But if anything should happen to me, you *will* take good care of Sophie and the children, won't you? Promise me that, Jaroslav, and you, too, Heinrich. And promise me that when the time comes, you'll see that Sophie lies beside me."

Clam Martinic frowned, nodding in agreement, but Jaroslav, determinedly jovial smiled, "You've made your wishes clear so often that there is really no need to mention this again. Of course I would see they were all taken care of but why bring this up now?"

He shrugged, "Who knows? Maybe it's because it's virtually the end of the year and each time an old year passes I feel such a sense of my own mortality."

"Dear God!" Jaroslav laughed. "Look on the bright side. One year over but a new one beginning; 1914 could be the best year ever! You never know, it might even be the year when we have a new Emperor – hail Your Imperial and Apostolic Majesty, Emperor Franz Ferdinand!"

He shook his head and, forcing a smile, walked on but the darkness hung on his heart like a shroud and the night, which had descended so swiftly, felt as cold as a tomb.

December dragged slowly by and, in an effort to convince himself that his growing sense of unease was irrational, Franz Ferdinand sought distraction in the pursuits that had always brought him solace. Through the dark days of winter, he pored over horticultural books and articles, seeking out new breeds of roses to plant in the spring; he labelled and categorised his collections of foreign and ancient artefacts, examined his hunting trophies, and made plans for the renovation and redecoration of his various estates. In the evenings he found comfort in the cosy family gatherings, discussing music with Sophie or telling tales to the children and joining them in their games.

Christmas passed with the typically cheerful family celebrations but the New Year brought the usual commands to attend dinners and dances, as was expected of the heir to the throne. The stateliness of the ballrooms and the perfectly ordered steps of Strauss waltzes might, Franz Ferdinand thought, appear civilized to outsiders but to him they were nothing but a pleasure-seeking frenzy designed to combat ennui. The longer he watched the dancers swirling across the floor, the greater became his disgust at the shallowness of their lives. One social season was no different from the next: the same faces, the same families, the same intrigues and machinations; false smiles and fake laughter and a repetition of the conversations that had gone on year after year for as long as he could remember. This, too, he thought as he watched the old Emperor enjoying the attention of sycophantic devotees, was part of the Habsburg tradition that had come to symbolise all that was alien to him. Had Sophie been beside him, he knew he might have felt differently but, unable to bear the thought of placing her in a situation that invited humiliation, he had come alone. Even so, it irked him intensely to listen to hours of idle chatter while his neighbours bombarded his ears with tedious details of their families but if he dared to mention his own wife and children he was met with nothing but silence or disapproving sighs.

Year after year he had endured the same tortuous tedium; glancing frequently at his watch, scarcely able to believe that only minutes had passed since he last checked the time, but this year something greater than boredom gnawed at him. As officers and princesses danced before his eyes, their faces gradually faded until, rather than seeing the glittering spectacle of a shimmering Viennese ballroom, he felt himself to be viewing a grotesque *danse macabre*.

"The charnel house of Fontanelle…" he thought aloud as a story he had heard in Italy many years before, drifted through his mind. Some centuries ago, he was told, the graveyards of Naples were so overcrowded that by night many skeletons were removed and secretly buried in shallow graves outside the city walls. They remained forgotten until floods swept the region, washing the relics into the streets. The horrified citizens gathered the bones and placed them in a cave which soon became the charnel house of every vagrant, pauper and cholera victim who died in the city. There they lay for decades until a kindly priest, pitying their indignity, had them disinterred, listed and cleaned to give the poor souls a dignity in death, which they had never known in life. Now, apparently, quite a cult had grown around the bones, and pilgrims came from all over Italy to honour them and ask for their blessing.

Even during the telling, the story had a strangely charming effect, and now, as the ballroom appeared like a shadowy mirage before him, he had the eerie sensation that the whole of Austria were about to become that charnel house. He stared across the room and the shapes of the dancers took on new forms – white silk gowns blackened before his eyes, smiles contorted to grimaces, and faces turned into skulls like those that once floated through the streets of Naples. He found himself wondering how it must feel to be forgotten in some cave, no grave for grieving relatives to bring flowers, no tomb or sarcophagus as a monument to a life once lived. In spite of the heat of the crowded ballroom, he shivered at the thought of how dreadful it would be to lie cold and forgotten and unknown.

He stepped back into the shadows and the music's steady rhythm flowed with hypnotic momentum lulling him into a melancholic and introspective trance. Echoes of the officers' voices behind him were strangely reassuring – life was still going on to distract from the fear that suddenly overcame him. At the other side of the room, the elderly

Emperor shuffled, pausing to make conversation in a low voice, inaudible above the higher-pitched laughter of the princesses chattering and flirting in corners. The dresses of the dancers billowed like waves, as they twirled in the arms of their inamorati and, in spite of his natural antipathy towards them, Franz Ferdinand half-wished he were young enough to share their excitement.

For a moment, he was back in childhood, enjoying the affection of the loving stepmother who had supported him in all his endeavours and graciously encouraged his love for Sophie. He remembered the winter evenings, sitting by the fire in Graz, listening to poets reading aloud; and the vigorous excursions through the Alps, swimming in rivers, making camp fires and tramping home by the light of a lantern.

The laughter of the princesses grew louder and Franz Ferdinand turned in their direction as chandeliers cast gleams of candlelight on their limbs, giving the impression that they were gradually disintegrating before his eyes. Their voices dimmed, like the dying notes of a half-caught song, and the foggy memories of his distant past enfolded him like a shroud. He was vaguely aware of an image of his mother, like a photograph in the back of his mind, but the edges of the image were blurred and yellowed, timeworn, perhaps, by the decades since her passing. No sooner had he turned his attention to the memory than it faded to be replaced by the recollection of seeing her cold and white as alabaster in her coffin. Recoiling from the thought, his eyes darted towards the princesses, longing for their laughter to dispel his dark thoughts but, though they continued to enact their joyful dance, it seemed that some unseen hand had muted their voices for, though their lips moved and their teeth showed, only silence issued from their mouths.

In one glance Franz Ferdinand's eyes shifted from the princesses to the old Emperor, to the hazy pictures in his memory and in that instant, in that glorious and terrifying moment, the dead and the living, the old and the young were all one. And he, too, was one with them, uncertain whether he were really present or simply a ghost looking on. If the other guests should look in his direction, he doubted that they would see him; he doubted that he was even there at all. He might have been a seer from another era, viewing this future that had yet to arrive.

"Dead, sleeping…" he murmured.

Slowly, he curled in on himself like a daisy at sunset. He drew his arms into his sides and, bending his knees like folding petals, crouched against the wall until his eyes beheld nothing but the endless sea of swirling dancers. Like a great tide, the ceiling, the chandeliers, the music rolled over him and he knew that somewhere beneath the shiny floor, beneath foundations and stone, discarded shells of souls lay buried in the earth. There was nothing fearful about that; nothing more fearful than the brittle casing of mussels and winkles strewn on the sand by departing waves. But where had they gone – all those souls that once animated the flesh and the bone; all those heart beats pounding with sorrow and laughter – where were they now? In some vast expanse of whiteness beyond the sky? In the arms of a gentle Mother-God who nursed them forever in a tender embrace?

The great swirls of intricate patterns cast by the shadows of dancers on the shimmering floor and on the gilded walls and ornate frescoes above his head, drew him in and, in that moment, he had no idea who he was, nor how old he might be, nor how young. Perhaps he had lived since time began or perhaps he had yet to be born; and as the mysteries floated around him like the feathery wisps of a dandelion clock, he knew he would be happy to stay there forever, in that moment of unknowing, in that shrouded and hallowed silence that held him with greater warmth than the wife who was absent or the mother who had died when he was so young and whom he suddenly missed so deeply.

Chapter 10

"Uncle Franz?" Karl said, standing directly in front of him though Franz Ferdinand seemed unaware of his presence. "Uncle Franz, are you alright?"

At last he stirred and, as his eyes regained their focus, he blinked several times like a child startled from sleep.

"I'm sorry," Karl stepped backwards. "You seemed so distant. I thought you might be unwell?"

"No, no," he shook his head quickly, "I'm fine." He pulled a handkerchief from his pocket and dabbed at his forehead. "It's unbearably warm in here, isn't it?"

"Yes, it *is* very warm." Karl looked across the room to where the Emperor sat watching the dancers, "Uncle Franz Josef mentioned earlier that he was having difficulty breathing in such an oppressive atmosphere."

"This place is always oppressive. Every time I come here I feel as though I am suffocating."

"Would a little fresh air help?"

Like a schoolboy unexpectedly released from a tedious lesson, Franz Ferdinand turned eagerly towards the door and as they stepped from the chatter of the ballroom to the cooler corridors his mood lightened. Brightly and with genuine interest, he asked after Karl's family and his eyes shone with childlike delight when Karl made similar inquires about Sophie and the children. The greater the distance they put between themselves and the rest of the guests, the more briskly he walked and the more freely he smiled until suddenly, passing an ante-room, he stopped abruptly.

Karl followed his eyes through the open door to where a small group of men stood in a conspiratorial huddle. Franz Ferdinand's smile inverted to an expression of disgust at the sight of the court's First Chamberlain, Albert Montenuovo.

"Look at him," he whispered, taking Karl's sleeve and drawing him into the shadows. "His Majesty's guard dog! Have you ever been able to enter the Emperor's study without that loathsome Montenuovo sniffing around? I swear no one can so much as piss in this palace without him being aware of it."

Karl winked mischievously, "It's to be hoped it's a royal piss. They say he spends hours studying family trees to check the suitability of the Emperor's guests."

Franz Ferdinand stiffened, "Pompous upstart! It's not as if he has any great credentials – the son of Napoleon's widow and an officer in her guard! You should have seen how he gloated when he came to read the proclamation debarring Sophie and our children, from the succession."

Karl, embarrassed by his bitterness, twitched his lips sympathetically and began to walk on but Franz Ferdinand pulled him back.

"Wait, I want to see who is with him..."

Like a pair of spies in the shadows, they peeped into the room to see Krobatin, the Minister of War, and the military commander, Conrad von Hötzendorf, talking in animated whispers. Also present were the Prime Minister, Sturgkh, and the Foreign Minister, Berchtold.

"Who is that?" Franz Ferdinand said, pointing to a man whom Karl instantly recognised.

"Berchtold's adjutant – Alexander von Hoyos."

"Hoyos," Franz Ferdinand stepped out of the shadows and walked on towards a staircase, "why does that name sound so familiar?"

"He's the son of Josef von Hoyos, a friend of the late Crown Prince."

"Ah, yes," Franz Ferdinand pressed his palm against the cool marble of the banister. "Hoyos was the man who discovered Rudolf's body, wasn't he?"

"I believe so." Karl shivered unexpectedly as though a ghost had suddenly drifted past and, judging by the gravure of Franz Ferdinand's expression, it seemed that he felt it, too.

In silence they continued down the stairs to the entrance where footmen pulled open the doors and a blast of cold air rushed into the hallway sending a chill like the touch of icy fingers across Karl's cheeks. Seemingly oblivious of the cold, Franz Ferdinand strode out into the courtyard where coachmen sat shivering and warming their hands on the lamps. Guiding Karl from their hearing, Franz Ferdinand pulled a cigarette case from his pocket and under the pretext of shielding the flame of his match from the wind turned to the wall.

"Tell me," he said confidentially, "what did you make of Rudolf?"

"Me?" Karl shrugged. "I was less than two years old when he died. To be honest, I barely remember him."

"Mm, I suppose not," Franz Ferdinand puffed at the cigarette and glanced furtively across the courtyard. "All the same, I am sure you have heard the rumours about his death."

He waited as if he were expecting a reply but Karl, unwilling to voice an opinion, stamped his feet against the cold and looked up at the stars dotting the icy sky.

"From the very beginning there were rumours," Franz Ferdinand continued as though thinking aloud, "but at the time I paid them no attention. When a young prince dies in bizarre circumstances – a suicide pact with his mistress in such a romantic setting as the Mayerling hunting lodge – it's bound to give rise to speculation, isn't it? That's what I thought it was: idle speculation."

Karl glanced at him and his uncle seemed to take that as encouragement to go on.

"You see," he flicked a flake of tobacco from his lip, "I had watched Rudolf's decline from an enthusiastic and well-read young man, to a depressive and unpredictable morphine addict, riddled with gonorrhoea and obsessed with dark thoughts."

Karl silently cupped his hands together and blew into them, wishing he had remained in the ballroom.

"Throughout the last six months of his life, there was such an air of morbidity about him that a tragedy seemed inevitable." Franz Ferdinand frowned. "He was preoccupied with death. He always had been since his childhood when he saw a man in the palace grounds dying in agony after deliberately taking caustic soda…"

Karl grimaced.

"…but towards the end, that dark obsession became stronger. The fact is, knowing him as I did, I wasn't surprised to hear of his death and so I paid no attention to the rumours."

Karl, beginning to feel drawn into the story, remembered the contradictory accounts he had heard. "It seems," he said quietly, "there is such mystery about the details of what happened to him. Perhaps that is why so many rumours still circulate."

Franz Ferdinand, suddenly more animated, nodded quickly, "Yes! That's what I thought, too, and I put the mystery down to the Emperor's shame and his determination to keep the matter as secret as possible. You know that he views the monarchy as sacred and so it was vital for him to keep the scandalous details from the public. Besides, he would have seen it as his paternal duty to salvage what he could of Rudolf's reputation."

"Surely there was more at stake for the Emperor than simply protecting his reputation." Karl said. "There was the matter of his son's eternal salvation."

Franz Ferdinand raised his eyebrows and Karl struggled to find the right words. "I am sure that the Emperor wanted Rudolf to find in death the peace that eluded him in life but, considering that suicide is a mortal sin and brings with it the penalty of being denied the right to be buried on hallowed ground, wasn't it odd that Rudolf was given a full requiem and Catholic burial?"

"The Emperor held several clandestine meetings with various bishops and they reached an agreement with the Vatican. Naturally," Franz Ferdinand smiled cynically, "they would want to keep *that* quiet."

Karl frowned, finding it hard to believe that his beloved Church, normally so dogmatic in its adherence to tradition, could bend its teaching so easily to accommodate the Emperor's request.

"The ironic thing is," Franz Ferdinand said, with the same cynical smile, "Rudolf had rejected the Church. He considered it too repressive and its bishops too political. That was another source of dissention between him and his father."

Karl shook his head sadly.

"You're shocked?" Franz Ferdinand said and, lowering his voice to little more than a whisper, added, "You would be even more shocked if you knew what I am thinking."

Karl looked directly into his eyes, certain that he *did* know exactly what his uncle was thinking.

"I, too, have heard rumours," he began but at that moment Franz Ferdinand stepped suddenly away from the wall and, drawing himself to full height, stood openly in the middle of the courtyard with his eyes fixed on the entrance.

Karl turned to see Berchtold, Hoyos and Hötzendorf walking swiftly from the palace towards their separate carriages. Franz Ferdinand threw down his cigarette and strutted forwards as though planning a confrontation but all three men bowed their heads against the biting wind and seemed not to notice him. To the clopping of hooves and the rolling of wheels, their carriages disappeared towards the gates and Franz Ferdinand stood for some minutes staring after them into the night before turning back to Karl and uttering a single word, "Redl."

Karl frowned, not understanding.

"Redl," he repeated. "You heard what happened to him?"

Karl nodded. Even if he hadn't been told the details of the case, the story of the spy's double-dealing, detection and subsequent suicide had been leaked by hotel staff and reported in newspapers for all the world to read.

"Do you see where I am leading?"

Karl shook his head uncertainly and Franz Ferdinand, rubbing his hands together, nodded towards the entrance, "Let's go back indoors; it's warmer there and there is less chance of being overheard."

On a table inside the entrance, a buffet was laid out to provide the guests with sustenance for their journey home. Franz Ferdinand helped himself to a dish of soup and invited Karl to do the same before leading him into a small side-room where, closing the door, he sat down at a table and placed a napkin over his lap.

Karl sat opposite him and took several spoons of soup before his uncle spoke again.

"You're a good man, Karl, high-principled, devout and honest."

He looked down, embarrassed by the compliment.

"Tell me, then, what is your opinion? Which is the graver sin: suicide or murder?"

Taken aback by the question, he paused before replying, "They are equally grave since they both destroy the life that God has given and God alone has the right to take."

Franz Ferdinand slurped his soup, clearly dissatisfied by the reply.

"They are equally grave, too, because they both offend against the commandment: *Thou shalt not kill.*"

Franz Ferdinand laughed and dabbed the corners of his mouth with the napkin, "Oh, we are so good at adapting the commandments to suit our own purposes, aren't we? We bandy them about with such self-righteousness: *thou shalt not kill*...unless, of course, thou art killing our enemy or executing a criminal or following a general's orders." He shook his head, still smiling to himself and took another spoonful of soup. "Forgive me, Karl, I'm not mocking. It's just that the older I grow, the more often I find myself faced with moral questions the answers to which seemed so simple when I was young." He pushed the soup dish away and leaned back in the chair. "In any case, I think we agree that suicide and murder are equally grave offences?"

Karl nodded, "Though, more often than not, those who take their own lives do so when they are not of sound mind and they cannot be held responsible for their actions."

"Ah ha!" Franz Ferdinand lunged across the table, "In which case, if a person of unsound mind were encouraged or even permitted to commit suicide, wouldn't you say that the person or people who gave that encouragement were guilty of murder?"

"Yes," Karl said without hesitation, "I would."

"And that, Karl, is precisely what happened to Alfred Redl. Even though he pulled the trigger, those who placed the gun in his hand and made it clear what was expected of him, were the real culprits. Therefore, it was not suicide but murder."

Karl put down his spoon and whispered, "Are you saying that that is what happened to Rudolf."

"No, no," he leaned back again. "I don't think that at all but if our agents have no qualms about causing a man like Redl to commit suicide, they would probably be equally willing to commit outright murder."

Karl ran his finger along the edge of the table, wondering if this was an appropriate moment to voice his own suspicions.

"Everyone knew how unpredictable Rudolf had become," Franz Ferdinand continued. "We had all seen his decline and so we readily accepted the story that he had killed himself. Now though, nearly twenty-five years later, the more I think of it, the less sense it makes. His addictions and his unhappiness were the result of his inability to effect the changes he wanted to make. His relationship with the Emperor was so fraught because he had so many progressive ideas that he longed to implement but his father treated him as though he were still a child. In sheer frustration, Rudolf sought relief with his mistresses and his medications. Think about it, Karl. If those ideas hadn't mattered so much to him, he could have settled comfortably into a life of opulent decadence, as so many of our uncles and cousins have done. It was *because* those ideas mattered so much to him that he could not bear to see them dismissed and ignored."

Karl nodded trying to predict where he was leading.

"If these things were so important to him, would he then abandon them by resigning himself to despair and taking his own life?"

"Perhaps, if he thought he could never be in a position to change anything…"

"But that wasn't the case. He knew he would be Emperor one day and when that day came he would be able to do all the good he had planned. No matter how long he had to wait, that thought alone would have kept him from complete despair."

Karl could no longer restrain his opinion, "That is exactly what Zita and I think. We have often discussed it and we cannot accept that a young man of so much promise would willingly take his own life. Then, there are all the discrepancies in the story. How many bullets were fired? Some say as many as six; and I have heard it said that there were defence marks on Rudolf's hands as though he had been in a struggle."

"So you think he was murdered?"

He inhaled sharply, "Rudolf was known to dislike our alliance with Germany, wasn't he?"

Franz Ferdinand nodded.

"Zita's brothers believe that he was approached by the French government in the hope that he would stage a coup against his father and seize the throne. The French believed that he would then sever relations with Germany in favour of an alliance with France. Rudolf refused to participate and was murdered to ensure that the plot never came to light."

Franz Ferdinand, unimpressed, shook his head, "Why would the French murder the one man in Austria from whom they had most to gain? No," he stood up, "that is one of the least likely explanations I have ever heard."

Slightly deflated, Karl lowered his head, "What do you think happened?"

He opened his arms in a gesture of honesty, "I truly don't know, Karl, but if he *was* murdered, I suspect his killers were closer to home."

Karl pushed back his chair and crossed the room to stand beside him.

"Rudolf was not popular with many of his father's ministers. They saw his liberalism as a threat and they realised that once he became Emperor, their own positions would be untenable."

"You are suggesting he was killed by our own people?"

Franz Ferdinand shrugged and stood for some minutes staring into space, lost in his own unfathomable thoughts, which Karl felt powerless to interrupt.

Eventually, he turned and said, "In the past, I believed that kings and emperors made all the decisions for their people. Now, though, I see it very differently. For the most part, monarchs are merely the actors who take centre-stage. Their lines are scripted for them and their movements are stage-managed by faceless people whom the audience never sees. Even in an autocracy like Austria-Hungary, so much goes on behind the scenes where ministers and politicians plot and intrigue among themselves. They see their monarchs as little more than puppets. They make plans that suit their personal ambitions and increase their own sense of power, and they manipulate their emperors into accepting and implementing those plans at whatever cost to their countries. Then comes the cruellest part of all: when the drama turns into tragedy, these people withdraw into the shadows leaving the emperor to shoulder all the blame."

Karl frowned, "I cannot believe that an emperor anointed by God could be so easily influenced."

"Most emperors who take their coronation oath seriously have the good of their people at heart but even the most astute of them cannot see with his own eyes all that is happening across his empire. These shady people know that; and so, with carefully woven words, they persuade him that unless he follows this course or that course, the country will suffer. They conceal things that they don't want him to know and they scare him into accepting their ideas."

"*Scare* him!" Karl laughed in disbelief.

"Yes," Franz Ferdinand nodded emphatically. "The ability to inspire fear is the politician's most powerful weapon. Men react totally irrationally when they are afraid. Even in Biblical times, wasn't it fear of losing their authority that prompted the Sanhedrin to hand Christ over for crucifixion? And wasn't it the fear of repercussions from Rome that prevented Pontius Pilate from setting him free? Imagine being able to harness that fear and twist it to your own ends. That is a tactic that politicians have mastered. Create an enemy, create something or someone to fear, and then persuade the people that you alone can protect them from the impending disaster. If the people believe you – and skilled politicians ensure that they do – they will do whatever you ask of them: they will fight your wars, pay your taxes, and allow their own freedom to be curtailed, all the time believing that you are acting for their highest good."

Karl ran his hand across his brow.

"These politicians employ the same tactics when dealing with their emperors. They say, 'unless you implement harsh laws, more people will suffer' or, 'unless we take up arms against this country or that country, we will be invaded,' and all the time, unbeknown to their king, they are striking deals among themselves or with their foreign counterparts."

"But *why*?" Karl blinked, "Why would they do such a thing?"

"Money, power…"

"And for *that,* they would not only betray the trust of an emperor but also endanger the welfare and lives of their fellow countrymen?"

Franz Ferdinand smiled at him gently and spoke in the tone of a patient schoolmaster to an innocent pupil, "The more noble the emperor, the easier it is for the unscrupulous to take advantage of him. Good men, who act from the highest motives, believe that those around them are equally noble. I hate to disillusion you, Karl, but the truth is that there are many ambitious and self-seeking men in positions of authority. Who would have believed that someone like Redl, on whom so much of our country's security depended, would sell us out to protect his pathetic reputation and to fund his lavish lifestyle?"

"That was a particularly unpleasant case."

"Believe me, Redl is not the only one who would be willing to sacrifice all that we hold dear to further a greedy ambition. Every day secret agreements are reached between politicians, arms manufacturers, bankers, spies and newspaper proprietors. There are always people who place their personal gain before the good of the country."

Karl returned to the table and, sitting down, rested his head in his hands. The evening had begun so brightly in the glamour of the ballroom, yet now, alone with his uncle, he felt suddenly drained and exhausted.

Franz Ferdinand came to stand behind him and rested an avuncular hand on his shoulder, "I am so sorry, Karl," he said softly. "I didn't intend to distress you but men in our position *must* see what is going on or there is no hope for our country or our people."

A line from the Gospel ran through Karl's mind, *'I am sending you out like lambs among wolves; be as wily as serpents and as gentle as doves.'*

Franz Ferdinand smiled at him kindly, "One day, you will be emperor. Be prepared." He patted him on the shoulder and stepped backwards, "It sometimes feels to me as though a great struggle is taking place – a struggle the like of which we have never known before. The world is changing so rapidly and people are no longer content to be ruled by kings whom they never see, or emperors in distant cities. The better educated they are, the more they realise that they have the ability and the right to make their own decisions and to have a say in the laws which govern them."

Karl turned around sharply, "Are you saying we would be better off as a republic?"

Franz Ferdinand's eyes widened in shock, "No, absolutely not! A monarch is the unifying force within his country, and when kings are ousted there is invariably a vacuum which power-seekers leap eagerly to fill. Look at what happened in France after the revolution. Has there ever been such a blood-bath in the whole of history?"

Karl smiled with relief.

"I *do* believe, though, that we must keep abreast of the times. There is a need for greater freedom so that the many cultures within the empire feel that they are valued and their voices are heard."

Karl, suddenly inspired, said, "Yes, yes – I agree! With all my heart I respect and admire the Emperor. He is such a strong link in a chain has kept the dynasty alive for hundreds of years but I think, too, that there is a way to adapt to our present age without discarding our valuable traditions."

Whether or not he deliberately intended to dampen Karl's enthusiasm, Franz Ferdinand's brow furrowed and his voice was more solemn, "I firmly believe that there are forces at work – not only here in Austria but right across Europe – who would willingly dispense with monarchs so that they might seize power for themselves. There are many who preach freedom from what they call the oppression of tyrants, but their real motive is envy and a desire for power. What frightens me, Karl, is the thought that these people would willingly manipulate us into a situation where war becomes inevitable. To all intents and purposes, it will be seen as an imperial war between kings but in fact they will use kings and princes as scapegoats. The whole tragedy will have been engineered by unseen characters who will use the ensuing chaos to set up their puppets in our place."

Karl was certain that, had he not known Franz Ferdinand better, he would have thought such a notion was nothing more than the brooding imaginings of a paranoid mind. The idea of an orchestrated plot to create such a horrendous scenario seemed more likely to have come from a dark fantasist than from a rational and well-educated archduke but there was something so certain and yet so ominous in Franz Ferdinand's eyes that Karl, though unwilling, felt obliged to believe him.

"What can be done?" he said helplessly.

"We must choose our advisors carefully and, as far as possible, take nothing on trust without seeing and studying the facts for ourselves. This is where I fear Uncle Franz Josef fails. He is too easily swayed by the opinions of his ministers, most of whom are as blinkered as he is. With no foresight or awareness of the consequences, they would willingly lead us into an invasion of Serbia and..."

His face flushed, and Karl, fearing he was about to erupt into one of his legendary rages, hastily interrupted, "And Rudolf? How is he connected to this?"

The question instantly quelled Franz Ferdinand's anger and his florid face turned ashen. He took several seconds before replying and, when he did, his voice was low and grave. "I don't know whether or not he was murdered – it *could* just as easily have been suicide – but there is no doubt that certain ministers had a motive for such a crime. Rudolf made no secret of his dislike of many of his father's advisors, and they saw him as a threat to their own positions. Now, Karl," he opened his palms and looked up at the ceiling, "I find myself in the same situation as Rudolf. I have made no secret of my opinion of those warmongers and sycophants who surround the Emperor and, though I don't give a damn for their opinions, I am not oblivious to the hatred they feel towards me."

Shocked and embarrassed, Karl stepped forwards to protest but Franz Ferdinand halted him with an ironic smile.

"No, don't attempt to spare my feelings. It's the truth. They hate me and the feeling is mutual. I have made many enemies here in Vienna: not only do members of our own family shun me, but Montenuovo despises me, Berchtold and the others can barely tolerate me and I have even succeeded in alienating that hot-head Conrad von Hötzendorf. Good God!" he laughed loudly, "How dreadful it must be for them to think that, out of all the possible Habsburgs, I am heir to the throne!"

Uncertain how to respond, Karl smiled awkwardly.

"Oh, how they must dread the day when I become Emperor! I'll bet every time the Emperor sneezes or looks slightly under the weather, they are thrown into panic, wondering how much longer they can continue in their cosy little niches!"

Deeply discomfited, Karl shook his head but Franz Ferdinand refused his reassurance.

"Wouldn't it be so much easier, if I were out of the way? After all, they have nothing to gain from me. They don't expect me to father an heir to continue the dynasty; they know I will not support their mad invasion plans; and they undoubtedly know that I have already drawn up lists of trustworthy ministers to replace the lot of them. To them, the reign of Emperor Franz Ferdinand would be a disaster. Life would be so much better for them without me."

Karl stared at him and whispered, "What are you saying, Uncle?"

He stepped closer, "We have seen that Redl was easily disposed of; and we have our suspicions about what might have happened to Rudolf. Now, *if* it were possible to remove the Crown Prince who was popular and loved by the people, wouldn't it be convenient to remove an unpopular archduke whom few outside his immediate family would mourn?"

"No!" Karl stared aghast. "I refuse to believe that."

Franz Ferdinand looked at him silently for a moment, then his face melted into a smile, "Ah, dear Karl, you are such a good man, you cannot conceive of evil in others. Well," he patted his back and led him towards the door, "if I'm wrong, I trust you will put all this down to my own dark nature." He opened the door and inhaled deeply, "But if something untoward should happen to me, perhaps you will remember this conversation and it will serve as a reminder to keep your eyes open and be wary of whom you trust."

Karl nodded sadly and with slow, heavy steps walked silently back towards the ballroom.

Chapter 11 – Potsdam, Germany – February 1914

Crown Princess Marie of Roumania swept into the Grotto Hall of the Potsdam Palace as though she were making an entrance onto an ancient Greek stage. The glistening of shells and semi-precious stones embedded in the walls enhanced but did not detract from her sense of her own radiance, for a place of such beauty was a fitting backdrop to the role she had chosen to play.

Stepping over the intricacy of colour that swirled across the marble floor, she looked up and sighed with delight at the paintings on the ceiling.

"*The Three Graces* - Joy, charm and beauty!" she whispered, aware that she embodied them all and, as her eyes moved over *Venus and Amor,* she saw too, her own reflection in the image of the Goddess of Love.

"Venus, lover and mother," she thought aloud and, with more satisfaction than pride, realised how well she played those two roles in her own life and in the lives of her people.

Even after bearing six children – the youngest only the previous month – her figure had lost none of its youthful allure and, although she was now approaching forty, age had augmented rather than diminished her charm. Loved and viewed with adulation by the crowds, she had perfected her portrayal of the mystique of royalty and performed her role with such finesse that she even believed her own myth.

As a young girl, naïve and romantic, her head had been filled with passionate tales of the Age of Chivalry, and it seemed now that she had come to completely embody the princesses of her childhood dreams. Like the alabaster statues of goddesses, situated in alcoves around the Hall, every pose was captured to perfection, emanating poise and grace; and, like the waters rippling from the indoor fountain, every step, every turn and every movement flowed with unique charm.

Bathing her eyes in the opulent surroundings, it was clear to Marie that such gifts as heaven had bestowed upon her must be used for the good of all. She could not – and had no desire to – deny the pleasure of entering a room and seeing all heads turn in her direction, or the way that men's eyes widened whenever they looked her way; but the beauty with which she had been endowed was not solely for her own amusement, it was a powerful means of bringing joy into the world.

It's a great honour, she thought, *to be able to raise men's spirits simply by one's presence, or to have a charisma that causes a wounded soldier to forget his pain. A dowdy princess serves no purpose whatsoever, but one who radiates light is like a lantern shining in the darkness of her people's lives.*

For a moment she considered how different life might have been had she been born in a lowlier station but such a life, she quickly decided, could never have brought her fulfilment. With every cell of her being, from the tips of her ring-bedecked fingers right down to her toes, she knew herself to be a woman of destiny, born to shine as a Queen.

She looked again at the ceiling and, as she smiled at the prospect of all she would achieve when her husband eventually succeeded his uncle to the throne, it occurred to her that had she not been so young and naïve, she might have made a better match. Hadn't she turned down a proposal from the future King of Britain? And wouldn't her many talents have been better employed in a more powerful nation than that which her grandmother, Queen Victoria, had described as 'semi-barbaric Roumania'? And yet, she had grown to love that country and its people, whose mystical temperament resonated so harmoniously with her own.

In spite of the disappointments of the earliest years in Bucharest, her marriage, too, she thought, was not without its compensations. It was true that at only sixteen years old she had been all but forced into accepting the diffident Nando's proposal and, before she knew it, had found herself married to a virtual stranger in a foreign land. It was equally true that, following the horror of her wedding-night, those early years had opened her eyes to a reality which contrasted sharply with her youthful, romantic dreams. In a stifling court with an unfaithful husband, she could easily have followed many other princesses into suffocating oblivion, but – she smiled at the thought – with her instinctive sense of self-preservation she had not only refused to be crushed but had recreated herself and her role in the world. Rather than bewailing her fate, she complimented Nando's mistresses, and rejoiced that his indifference allowed her the freedom to spend time with the dashing Prince Barbo Stirbey. What other husband, she wondered, would have willingly employed and befriended his wife's paramour? And what other prince would complacently accept the child of their affair as his own? All in all, she thought, the arrangement with Nando worked extremely well. In public their played their role to perfection, while behind closed doors with mutual and friendly acceptance, they enjoyed their separate lives.

A booming voice echoed across the hall, "Ah, there you are, Missy! I was looking for you." She turned gracefully to see Kaiser Wilhelm striding towards her, "Nando is not with you?"

"No, he went for a short walk with our son before dinner so I seized the opportunity of admiring the treasures of your palace."

He smiled and proudly ran his hand over the jewel-encrusted wall, "It *is* a beautiful room, isn't it? We Germans do these things so well. You would never find such exquisite artwork in any of the English palaces."

"That's true," she laughed lightly, amused by his pride. "There is only one other place in the world which compares to this."

"Oh?"

"The Amber Study of the Catherine Palace in Russia."

He grinned triumphantly, "Which proves my point!"

She raised her eyebrows and he took delight in explaining, "You didn't know that the Amber Study was a gift to Tsar Peter from King Frederick Wilhelm of Prussia?"

She shook her head.

"The Tsar was here in Potsdam when he saw and admired the amber panels. Frederick Wilhelm gave them to him as a gift and in return the Tsar gave him a couple of hundred Russian soldiers to serve in his army. So you see, one of Russia's finest treasures originated here in Germany."

Marie smiled and he gesticulated towards the door, "Allow me to show you more of our splendours."

As they walked towards the corridor, his eyes moved over the walls with as much pride as if he had built the palace with his own hands.

"Speaking of German treasures," he said, "while you are here, would you do me the honour of taking part in a ceremony for the opening of our new library."

"A library?" she turned to him with genuine interest.

"It is a monument to culture and learning. People tend to view us as a great military empire but we are far more than that. German scholars and writers have always been at the forefront of debate in so many fields. Some of the greatest literature in the world flowed from German pens and we want to instil that great heritage into our children. The library will be our gift to posterity." He paused for a moment and ran a finger across his moustache, "Unfortunately, my wife is unable to return for the opening but your presence would greatly enhance the ceremony and I would very much like to hear what you think of the architecture and style."

Flattered by his tone, Marie stopped in her tracks, barely able to disguise her surprise. Until now he was one of the few men who had seemed immune to her charms. In his company she had always felt insignificant – a mere younger cousin whom he still viewed as a child – yet suddenly, his manner had changed and he addressed her as though she had miraculously blossomed into a person in her own right and one whose opinion he valued.

"I would be honoured," she said.

"That's settled then," he smiled, "and I am sure my people will be delighted to see this as a mark of friendship between Germany and Roumania."

Marie smiled, too, but beneath her contentment came the inkling of suspicion that his flattery was more political than personal, and her distrust heightened when he said, "There has been so much upheaval in the Balkans of late that I am sure King Carol recognises the importance of having strong allies to support Roumanian interests."

Deliberately refusing to be drawn, Marie said, "Thank goodness the Balkan conflict is over. The Bulgarians were quite intoxicated by the gains in the earlier war and seemed to view themselves as invincible."

"It worked out well for you, though, didn't it? By the time your Roumanian troops arrived, all the fighting was over and they marched in and took what they wanted."

Marie concealed a wince, "It was not quite like that. We might have missed the worst of the fighting but the aftermath was equally terrible. The suffering was so immense that, had I not seen it with my own eyes, I would never have believed it."

"Yes," the Kaiser smiled, "I heard that you ignored King Carol's warnings and made personal visits to the Bulgarian side of the Danube."

"I had no choice. Our soldiers were suffering terribly because the cholera outbreak had created such panic that the doctors fled, leaving them to die untended. They needed me. They needed someone to take charge and create order and, as their Crown Princess, it was my duty to do that."

Warmth shone from his eyes, "You were very courageous to go into the camps in the middle of an epidemic."

"What else could I do? The medical staff listened to me and, because of my position, I was able to raise funds and draw people's attention to what was happening. I can honestly tell you, Willy, that were it not for my intervention, many more men would have died."

"Then I am sure that you won their hearts."

She nodded, unable to deny it.

"And I am also sure that, since your people adore you, you hold great sway in the King's court."

She laughed dismissively and he stopped and turned to her again, "Missy, it would be most beneficial for King Carol to adhere to our treaty and strengthen Roumania's alliance with us."

"Treaty?" she raised her eyebrows in feigned ignorance.

"Come now," Wilhelm laughed, "it's an open secret that your King has made certain agreements uniting Roumania with us and Austria-Hungary."

"If such a treaty exists, it's small wonder it remains a secret. The Roumanians in Transylvania feel great antipathy towards the Hungarians and with good reason. The way that Emperor Franz Josef encouraged the Magyars to oppress them politically and religiously has not been forgotten."

Wilhelm nodded, "The Austrian Emperor has made many mistakes but he cannot live forever and we must look to the future not the past. You have probably heard that he is suffering from a serious bout of bronchitis."

"Apparently it is an annual occurrence for him."

"This time his condition is far worse than usual. It wouldn't surprise me in the least if it were to develop into something more serious that would finish him off."

Marie frowned at his heartlessness but he seemed oblivious of her disapproval.

"In any case, it is only a matter of time before Franz Ferdinand succeeds him and I am sure you are aware that the Archduke has a great personal attachment to Roumania."

"As I understand it, Franz Ferdinand despises the Magyars. He has never managed to master their language and he views the whole of Hungary with suspicion."

The Kaiser laughed, "All the more reason for him to take Roumania's side in any dispute. He has not forgotten that King Carol and Queen Elizabeth showed such respect to his wife and, for that reason alone, he will do everything in his power to settle any disagreements between your people and his."

Marie smiled and walked on but it was several seconds before he followed and reached her side.

"I do hope you will think over what I have said about strengthening the ties between Roumania and Germany. Perhaps you might even speak of it with the King?"

He waited in anticipation but when she did not respond he said nonchalantly, "I shall be visiting Franz Ferdinand in a few months. It's an informal visit so there will be plenty of time for me to speak with him of your concern for your people in Transylvania. Perhaps in return you might ensure that King Carol..."

"Willy," she said theatrically, "I am becoming suspicious of your motives in inviting us here. I was under the impression that it was purely an act of hospitality on your part but now I wonder..."

His great, booming laughter echoed too loudly along the corridor and he placed his hand on his heart in a gesture of sincerity, "I assure you my motives were entirely personal. I always relish the opportunity of meeting with my cousins so when I heard you were passing through Berlin I seized the chance of enjoying the pleasure of your scintillating company."

Although he had not allayed her suspicions, she allowed herself to succumb to his flattery.

"Well," she teased, "as a mere woman, I have no say in politics so if there were anything you wished to discuss on that score, it would be far better to approach my husband. After all, Nando is the heir to the throne, not I."

He chuckled, "I *never* underestimate the power of a beautiful woman, particularly when she is married to a man who is – how shall I put it? – of a diffident nature."

She threw him one of her most enchanting smiles before shaking her head and walking on. They had reached the Marble Gallery and, stepping inside, Marie beamed with pleasure at the way the light, reflected from the windows by mirrors, flooded the room and illuminated the glistening gilt ceiling.

Clearly enjoying her obvious awe, Wilhelm smiled, "Since we must avoid politics shall we confine our conversation to family and friends?"

She nodded, "I must say I am somewhat surprised to hear that you've accepted Franz Ferdinand's invitation."

"Why?" His boots clicked across the red jasper and marble floor, "Do you think it is beneath me to be the guest of an Archduke who married a lady-in-waiting?"

"Oh, good heavens, no! I think their story is rather touching."

"You women are such romantics! Grandmama was exactly the same. She could be as intransigent as you like in some respects but the moment she heard a love story she happily threw caution to the wind! Do you remember how she encouraged Cousin Eddy's passion for that French princess, regardless of the political repercussions? And how she provided a home for the King of Hanover's daughter when he refused to allow her to marry a commoner? Great Queen that she was, like all women she was still a soft-hearted romantic."

Marie cringed inwardly at his patronising tone but, without dropping her smile, she replied, "Romance aside, I share Grandmama's aversion to the snobbery that is prevalent in so many other courts. Didn't you always think that, in spite of the popular perception of the court of Queen Victoria, she was one of the most open-minded and tender-hearted monarchs in the whole of Europe? It was *she* who made Britain great and set the standard for the rest of the world."

It amused her to see him bristle at the mention of Britain's greatness but he quickly disguised his irritation with a smile and change of subject.

"So, if it is not his wife's status, what surprises you about my acceptance of Franz Ferdinand's invitation?"

Her eyes travelled over the shining chandeliers, "I have only seen him on one or two occasions so I am not in a position to judge but from all accounts he is a rather difficult character, not at all accommodating in his conversation and rather brusque in his manner."

"I am very fond of him. I appreciate his straightforward way of speaking and his reluctance to engage in small talk. He is trustworthy; and, to be frank," he strutted across the gallery, "he is far more perspicacious than the old Emperor; so when he invited me to Konopischt to view his roses, I…"

"His roses?" she interrupted with a bemused smile.

"Yes," Wilhelm nodded. "I know it sounds rather odd that a clumsy-looking man of such a masculine temperament should indulge in so feminine a pursuit but apparently Franz Ferdinand is an avid rose breeder. After Uncle Bertie's funeral I found him wandering in the gardens at Windsor Castle, examining the petals and bushes. He told me he has often travelled incognito to different countries simply to seek out new strains and different methods of cultivation."

Marie, pleasantly surprised by the revelation, said, "I know that he is a renowned as hunter but I had no idea that he is an equally keen gardener. There is obviously far more to him than meets the eye."

"Yes, I think there is. I always thought he looked aloof and humourless but when I saw him enthralled by something as simple as a flower, he seemed as approachable as a child."

Marie smiled and Wilhelm moved closer.

"He is also a man of progressive ideas. Austria-Hungary under Franz Ferdinand will be a very different place from Austria-Hungary under Franz Josef. You see, Missy, he understands that the world in the twentieth century is very different from how it was in Grandmama's day. He recognises the need for changes and he has the drive to implement them. He will make Austria stronger and then we, as the Central Powers, will hold sway over the whole of the continent. We see ourselves not as conquerors but rather as the custodians of peace. As the daughter of the Duke of Coburg, I am sure you can see the benefits to Roumania of an alliance with us."

She spun around, "My father was Duke of Edinburgh before he was Duke of Coburg."

"Ah," he raised his eyebrow, "so you consider yourself more English than German?"

"Naturally! I am English by birth and German only by accident, and now, I suppose, I consider myself Roumanian, too." She mused for a moment before continuing, "It's the same for everyone in our family, isn't it? We are all a mixture of so many nationalities."

This time, he could not disguise his irritation, "I am German, thoroughly German."

"Though your mother was English?"

"When I was a small boy," he laughed but his laughter sounded forced and insincere, "I had a nose bleed and I told my mother that it was only my English blood that poured out. What was left was entirely German."

"If only it were all so simple," she sighed wistfully. "You see, I am the product of so many different cultures. My upbringing was truly cosmopolitan, and I can never forget that, although on my father's side, I am the granddaughter of a British Queen, on my mother's side I am also the granddaughter of a Russian Tsar."

"Indeed," said Wilhelm thoughtfully. He moved to a chair by the window and, after running his hand across the red leather seat as though inspecting it for dust, he sat down. "And now you intend to strengthen that Russian connection by having your son marry the Tsar's daughter?"

She stared at him askance.

"Why else would you come here to take him away from his military duties in Berlin, and drag him off to Russia unless you intended to encourage a Russian match?"

"No, no," she said quickly, "we are only putting out feelers, as it were. The young people haven't even met yet and absolutely nothing has been decided."

"I see," he said dubiously.

"In fact I have serious doubts that anything will come of this."

His eyes widened, "Really?"

"There are so many considerations to take into account."

"Not least the health of Nicky's daughters?"

She stepped closer and looked down at him uncertain what he was implying.

"Another open secret," he said. "Even though it is never mentioned, we both know that Nicky's family has been cursed by the bleeding disease that afflicts so many members of our extended family."

Marie leaned back against the wall, "So it's true that the Tsarevich has haemophilia?"

"Apparently so, although they try to keep it a secret."

"How tragic," she said sincerely.

"It *is* tragic and all the more tragic that there is no means of predicting where it will strike. It makes things very awkward. Usually, any royal house would be delighted to arrange a match with a daughter of the Tsar, but what family would dare to risk introducing such a terrible illness into their dynasty?"

His words confirmed Marie's unvoiced fears.

"Tragic," he said again, shaking his head as he stood up, "and they are all such lovely girls, too; so open-hearted, innocent and so devoted to one another."

He was silent for a few minutes and the arrogance in his expression sank into a doleful, almost child-like sadness. When he eventually spoke, his voice was far softer than formerly.

"I am so fond of Nicky and his family; it would be a terrible, terrible thing if we were ever to find ourselves in conflict with one another."

For the first time, it occurred to Marie to question his motive in pressing her for a Roumanian alliance. After all, she reluctantly admitted to herself, although Roumania might provide a convenient buffer between Russia and Serbia, the country was of no major significance on the world stage and the balance of power would hardly be affected whether King Carol favoured the Central Powers or the Entente.

She looked closely at Wilhelm's face, from which the mask of arrogance had slipped, and his vulnerable expression aroused tender, maternal feelings in her. He looked so like a lost little boy abandoned in his nursery and desperate for the company of a friend that it seemed to Marie that his desire for Roumanian support was based more on his personal longing for acceptance than political expediency. When he looked up at her again, the fiery pride in his eyes had vanished, replaced by helpless desperation.

"War," he said quietly, "would be truly horrific. Our family would be utterly devastated. We would be fighting not only cousin against cousin but brother against brother, sister against sister, parents against their own children."

She nodded.

"You have to understand, Missy, that that is why I am doing everything in my power to ensure we have peace. You *do* understand that, don't you?"

She opened her arms noncommittally.

"You must realise that as long as Germany is respected and allowed to prosper, I offer the hand of friendship to all nations. Sometimes I fear that if anything disastrous should happen, I will be seen as the aggressor but it will not be my doing. I want only to protect the wellbeing of my people and to maintain the balance of power so that we can live in peace."

Not doubting his sincerity, she smiled at him warmly but she couldn't help but doubt that so impetuous and erratic a man, who had difficulty maintaining balance in his own thoughts and behaviour, would ever be able to maintain the balance of power across Europe.

Chapter 12 – The Schönbrunn Palace, Vienna – February 1914

A dry, hacking cough interspersed with bronchial wheezing echoed along the corridor as Franz Ferdinand approached the Emperor's study and, though mildly ashamed of so malevolent a notion, he could not suppress the hope that each gasp might be the last. A brief silence from the other side of the door caused him to pause and hold his breath in anticipation. If his uncle were to slip away now, everything would fall into place. Reforms to create greater co-operation between the provinces of the empire could be implemented; alliances with neighbouring states could be strengthened; and competent and trustworthy men would replace those warmongers in power. If the Emperor would slip away now there was even a chance of rebuilding the stability of Europe.

The coughing began again and Franz Ferdinand's spirits sank at the thought that his uncle seemed destined to live forever. He walked on, consoling himself with the hope that this illness might at least render him more amenable, when suddenly the door flew open and the too-familiar figure of Prince Montenuovo emerged from the study.

Franz Ferdinand's shoulders stiffened as Montenuovo, standing as unwelcome and obtrusive as a boulder in the entrance, stared defiantly into his eyes. For a minute or more, they snarled at one another like two angry dogs waiting to pounce, until the Prince, subdued by the Archduke's superior status, was obliged to yield with the most begrudging of bows.

"Your Imperial Highness," he muttered as courtesy demanded but, as he raised his square head with a supercilious sneer, Franz Ferdinand's loathing intensified.

"Your Imperial Highness will be pleased to see that His Majesty is much improved today," he said with obvious sarcasm. "We are all greatly relieved that the doctors have predicted a full recovery."

The implication was obvious and when Franz Ferdinand didn't reply, Montenuovo, deliberately baiting him, went further, "His Majesty is so loved and so devoted to the empire that we dread to think what will happen when he is gone."

Resisting the impulse to strike him for his insolence, Franz Ferdinand lurched forwards, compelling him to step aside and let him pass, but no sooner had he crossed the threshold, than Montenuovo's rude, imperious voice echoed across the study, "His Imperial and Royal Highness, Archduke Franz Ferdinand of Austria-Este."

The Emperor was not in his usual position at his desk but sitting in an arm chair, a rug thrown across his knees and another pulled over his shoulders. Pale and gaunt, his face had so skeletal an aspect that he might have just emerged from a grave and when he looked up his eyes were so narrow that he seemed barely capable of raising their lids.

Disarmed by his fragility, Franz Ferdinand's antipathy lessened and, bowing, he asked with genuine concern, "Are you feeling a little better today?"

Another lengthy bout of coughing prevented an immediate reply and Franz Ferdinand's concern turned first to revulsion and then to alarm. Much as he eagerly anticipated the Emperor's death, he had no desire to be present when that event occurred. He strode to a side table and poured a glass of water but, as he extended it towards him, his uncle waved it away and, with a gargling inhalation, shook his head.

"It isn't as bad as it sounds," he eventually managed to say and, regaining his breath, dabbed his watery eyes with a handkerchief. "The doctors tell me I am over the worst."

"I'm pleased to hear it."

With a guttural snort the Emperor smiled, "Are you really?"

Franz Ferdinand could only nod in response, which seemed to amuse the Emperor.

"I'm sorry to disappoint you, Franz, but I have a good few years left in me yet."

Prince Montenuovo, hovering like a guard dog by the door, gushed sycophantically, "The whole empire is praying for your recovery, sir!"

To Franz Ferdinand's satisfaction, the Emperor paid him no attention but gesticulated towards a chair, "Sit down, Franz. It makes my neck ache looking up at you. Sit down so we can talk."

He obeyed and sat bolt upright in such a superior position of health and strength that he felt emboldened to speak with an air of authority. For a moment he considered demanding Montenuovo's dismissal but on reflection concluded that so pompous a man would find greater humiliation in being ignored.

Shifting his chair into a position from which he could keep Montenuovo in sight, he reached into his pocket and withdrew two envelopes.

"I have received two very interesting letters. The first is Kaiser Wilhelm's response to my invitation to spend a weekend with us at Konopischt this summer. Sophie and I are delighted that he has accepted."

There was something so exquisitely pleasurable in seeing Montenuovo squirm at this news that Franz Ferdinand pressed further.

"The Kaiser has always shown the greatest respect to my wife. He often mentions how impressed he is by her wisdom and intelligence."

The Emperor stifled a cough, "It will of course be an unofficial visit?"

Franz Ferdinand nodded, "He will be accompanied by Admiral von Tirpitz who is keen to see our rose garden."

"Rose garden?"

"Apparently, Tirpitz is also an avid rose-breeder.

"Strange sort of interest for a sailor."

"Not really." Franz Ferdinand smiled. "Cultivating a rose garden requires the same skills of organisation, planning and imagination as maintaining a navy. I suppose, too, that gardening provides him with some relief from the pressures of his office."

"And I suppose that you will seize the chance of learning all you can about how we might improve our own fleet."

As though the Emperor had not spoken, Franz Ferdinand continued, "Once the Kaiser and his party have left, I propose to open my gardens to the public for the day. The roses are at their best in June and I should like to give the local people the opportunity of experiencing their beauty."

The Emperor's face crumpled in confusion.

"This gesture might also help to create a stronger sense of connection with your subjects. When walls and gates and guards stand between us, it's unsurprising that we often appear aloof and unapproachable and the people feel cut off from us. By inviting them into my gardens I hope to show that, in spite of our different roles, we too are as human as they are."

Suspecting that the next bout of coughing sprang from the Emperor's disapproval, Franz Ferdinand chose to ignore it and, opening the second envelope, withdrew a letter, which he perused with satisfaction as he waited for the coughing to subside.

"General Potiorek wrote to me..."

"Potiorek?"

"The Governor of Bosnia and Herzegovina."

The Emperor shook his head, "I thought I appointed that other fellow...what's his name? Bil...Bil.." he frowned deeply, ploughing through his memory until Montenuovo sprang to his assistance.

"Bilinski, sir."

"Bilinski." Franz Josef nodded, "I thought I appointed him as Governor."

To Franz Ferdinand's annoyance, Montenuovo again intervened, "Leon Bilinski is the *Civil* Governor, sir. Potiorek is the Military Governor. I understand that there is great deal of friction between them since Bilinski favours a tolerant approach to governing the region whereas Potiorek prefers to take a firmer, more aggressive stance."

"That doesn't bode well in such a capricious place. If our own governors can't see eye-to-eye what hope is there for the Slavs and Bosnians?"

Montenuovo agreed and was about to say more but Franz Ferdinand, increasingly irked by his unbidden interference, shook the letter.

"Potiorek has invited me to inspect the summer manoeuvres in Bosnia. I should like your permission to accept the invitation."

The Emperor peered at him through tired, red eyes, "Considering the strength of anti-Austrian feeling in the region, that wouldn't be wise. It might be better to postpone the visit until things settle down."

"Will things *ever* settle down if we remain out of sight?" Franz Ferdinand stood up to add height to his argument, "How can the Bosnians feel part of the empire if the empire is never personified for them in an official visit?"

Franz Josef looked up, "So already you see yourself as the face of the empire? I am not dead yet, Franz."

Unable to think of an appropriate response, Franz Ferdinand changed tack, "As Inspector-General of the Army, it is my duty to inspect the troops wherever they are stationed. To decline such an invitation would be seen as cowardice."

"Not cowardice, but prudence," the Emperor said. "Your presence could so easily inflame an already volatile situation."

"Or," Franz Ferdinand said earnestly, "it could calm the situation and help bring the different factions together."

"No, Franz. It is too great a risk."

The Emperor closed his eyes, signifying an end to the discussion, and Franz Ferdinand, deflated once more by his intransigence but reluctant to press him while his health remained fragile, sighed resignedly. He moved towards the chair and was about to sit down again when Montenuovo interrupted for a third time.

"Forgive my intrusion, sir, but may I express an opinion?"

The Emperor, without opening his eyes, nodded carelessly.

"General Potiorek is renowned for his strict security measures. In fact he is so meticulous in these matters that he is viewed as quite tyrannical. He would never have issued such an invitation without being certain that he can guarantee the Archduke's safety."

Franz Ferdinand, astounded by this unexpected show of support, stared at him, and the Emperor opened his eyes and blinked several times.

"What's more, since His Imperial Highness would be attending manoeuvres and inspecting the troops, the visit would draw attention to our strong military presence, which would make the Serbs think twice about making further claims on the region."

"The Serbs," the Emperor grimaced as though the word tasted unpleasant. "I was half inclined to agree with Hötzendorf that we should have declared war on them for their invasion of Albania."

Franz Ferdinand shook his head, "Hötzendorf has become so aggressive that he won't be satisfied until we have invaded just about every country in Europe! Had we gone in heavy-handedly, we would have been seen as the aggressors and, no doubt, Serbia's allies would have rushed to her aid."

The Emperor nodded to himself and Franz Ferdinand returned to his chair, "Didn't that situation prove that diplomacy is the best way of dealing with the Serbs? At the Tsar's request, they withdrew peacefully from Albania without one Austrian bullet being fired or one Austrian life being lost."

"Diplomacy," the Emperor murmured. "Yes, you are right, Franz. Diplomacy is always the better course."

"Which is why this visit to Bosnia could be so beneficial."

The Emperor looked at him and Franz Ferdinand, sensing a glimmer of hope, eagerly explained, "Potiorek suggests that I spend two or three days inspecting the troops and attending the military manoeuvres before paying an official visit to Sarajevo to meet with the civil dignitaries in the city. We are hoping to speak with local leaders and representatives of different ethnic groups to find common ground and ways in which we can create a greater sense of cooperation and unity of purpose."

The Emperor frowned ponderously, "Put like that, I can see the benefits of such a plan but it will take a good deal of organisation. When were you hoping to go?"

"Towards the end of June; a couple of weeks after the Kaiser's visit."

"Is four months sufficient time to make all the necessary arrangements?"

Franz Ferdinand looked down sheepishly, "The invitation actually came some time ago but I didn't want to trouble you with it while you were unwell."

The Emperor raised his eyebrows, "So, just as my ministers come here pretending to seek my advice when in reality they want nothing but my signature to approve their plans, you have made your arrangements and organised everything but only now see fit to seek my approval?"

Franz Ferdinand shook his head adamantly, "I would do nothing without your permission. Potiorek's arrangements are only suggestions; nothing has been finalised."

The Emperor leaned back and closed his eyes so tightly that Franz Ferdinand feared he had fallen asleep but at length he stirred and looked towards Montenuovo.

"Since you have responsibility for the Imperial bodyguard here in Vienna, you will ensure that Potiorek has organised appropriate protection for His Imperial Highness."

"Of course, sir."

Franz Ferdinand's eyes widened with hope, "Does this mean I have your permission to go?"

The Emperor nodded wearily, "But you *must* be careful, Franz. If anything should happen to you, the consequences would be catastrophic not only for your family but for the whole empire."

Franz Ferdinand was so delighted that he reached for the Emperor's gnarled hand and, pressing it warmly, said with uncharacteristic affection, "Uncle, nothing will happen to me; I will probably be safer in the streets of Sarajevo than I am here in Vienna. If I thought there was the slightest danger, do you think I would be willing to place Sophie at risk?"

"Sophie?"

At last came the moment for which he had been waiting and he made no attempt to restrain his elation as he fixed his eyes on Montenuovo. "Did I not mention that the invitation was for both of us? Potiorek is arranging for Sophie to meet with several groups of local women – Muslims and Christians – and he says that the Bosnian people are very eager to see her. In fact," he laughed, "according to Potiorek, needlewomen are already busy stitching banners of her image to display in their windows as we drive past."

While the Emperor was suddenly caught in a further fit of coughing, Montenuovo did not so much as blink; and Franz Ferdinand, eager to leave at the height of his triumph, saluted, "Thank you, sir. I can see that this meeting has tired you so with your permission I will leave, wishing you a full recovery."

He backed towards the door and, smiling brightly, hurried to the waiting car.

Chapter 13 – Konopischt Castle, Bohemia – June 12th 1914

The cone-topped turrets jutting out above the trees, and the shy smiles of Franz Ferdinand's children gave Kaiser Wilhelm the pleasant impression that he had stepped into the magical world of a fairy-tale in which he was the dashing hero. On either side of the broad walkways, clusters of bright flowers exuded a heady fragrance while the low hum of bees and the trickling of fountains played an enchanted melody through this Bohemian idyll. Such a profound sense of peace pervaded the gardens that Wilhelm was quite content to forget all affairs of state and he knew he would be happy to spend the rest of the weekend listening to Franz Ferdinand and Tirpitz discussing their roses, or chatting with Sophie and her children about their cheerful games. It pleased him immensely to hear the little ones laugh at his jokes and to see the genuine delight in their mother's eyes whenever he addressed her directly. It required so little effort to treat her with the courtesy that the Austrian court had denied her and it was clear that every compliment he paid to Sophie increased Franz Ferdinand's gratitude and cemented their deepening friendship.

Not that the compliments were insincere; on the contrary, the pleasure he took in Sophie's conversation surpassed his expectations. Her intelligence was far superior to that of many princesses he had known, and her respectful response to his attention left him with the happy certainty that she appreciated and deeply admired his wisdom and humour.

He gesticulated across the gardens to where the children were darting to and fro among the trees, "You are fortunate to have such a beautiful family."

She gazed fondly in their direction, "Yes, we *are* truly blessed;" and, smiling, she turned towards him, "and you, too, have been blessed with such fine sons and a beautiful daughter."

"And grandchildren;" he beamed, "five of them already! Who knows where the time goes? It seems only yesterday that my boys were no bigger than Maximilian and Ernst but suddenly they are all grown men. I can hardly believe that my eldest son, Wilhelm, is already thirty-two years old. At that age I had been Emperor for three years."

"They grow so quickly," she nodded wistfully. "That is why Franz and I want to spend every possible moment with them."

Wilhelm smiled, envious of the love that flowed so obviously between them. "The older they grow the further they drift from us and, where once they were eager to seek our guidance and follow our advice, they turn to rebel against us. Well," he shrugged, recalling his contempt for his parents' liberal ideas, "that's the nature of youth, I suppose."

"'*The young people of today,*" she said, "*have bad manners, contempt for authority, they show disrespect to their elders; they no longer rise when elders enter the room. They contradict their parents and chatter before company...and are tyrants over their teachers...'*"

He looked at her questioningly.

"Socrates," she smiled. "Strange to think that he wrote these words all those centuries ago and people still say the same thing of young people today."

He laughed, impressed not only by her knowledge but also by the carefree way in which she spoke with him. Neither overawed in his presence nor eager to ingratiate herself, there was a naturalness in her manner which contrasted sharply with the rehearsed poses and practised prattle of many of the hostesses who entertained him on foreign tours. So refreshed was he by the ease with which their conversation flowed that he had a sudden, overwhelming urge to reward her and show his appreciation.

"Maximilian, how old is he now?"

"Eleven."

"A fine young man! What a dreadful shame that he is denied the right to succeed his father."

She moved her parasol from one hand to the other and played awkwardly with the handle as though discomfited by the statement.

"Naturally, I don't mean to meddle in your affairs or your country's internal politics but, now that I have met your children, their situation seems terribly unjust and I wish that I could do something to rectify it."

Too loyal and too discrete to reply directly, she responded with a subtle smile but the sadness in her eyes wrought in him an even greater desire to demonstrate the strength of his friendship.

"Tell me," he said, "is there any truth in the rumour that, although Maximilian is barred from the Austrian throne, there is still a chance that he could inherit the crown of Hungary?"

She glanced at him with such a startled expression that Wilhelm was taken by surprise. Perhaps the idea had never occurred to her or no one had ever before pointed out such a possibility. He smiled, eager to be the bearer of such interesting information.

"As in my country, where I am both German Emperor and Prussian Kaiser, your dual monarchy means that Emperor Franz Josef is both Austrian Kaiser and King of Hungary, is he not?"

"Yes."

"I understand that the strict rules governing the Austrian succession do not apply in Hungary. Therefore, although the law might prevent Maximilian from becoming Emperor, it is possible that he could succeed his father as King of Hungary."

She stopped and stood quite still for a moment, then shook her head and said very quietly, "Franz and I have discussed this but we don't want to create any disharmony within the empire."

"No, of course not," he shook his head quickly, suddenly aware of the dangerous implications of his suggestion and regretting having mentioned it. Austria-Hungary was already a weak enough ally without creating further divisions in the fragmented empire.

"Besides," she said, looking towards Maximilian, "the pressures of kingship are so great that we are grateful that our children will be spared that responsibility."

He nodded but, angry with himself for his ill-thought-out suggestion and dissatisfied that he had failed to impress her, his mind ran rapidly through other possibilities.

"All the same, I am also sure that you want your children's gifts to be used to the full."

"Naturally."

"I can see great potential in Maximilian. He's an intelligent boy and, as the Archduke's son, he is familiar with the demands of politics and power."

She acknowledged the compliment and the light in her eyes encouraged him to continue, "Once there were only two ways of gaining a crown: conquest or inheritance. Now, of course, things are different. Greece, Bulgaria, Albania, Roumania and Norway – all of these countries offered their thrones to foreign princes." He mentally scoured Europe for an available kingdom but Sophie seemed far less ambitious.

"Several of those foreign princes were unceremonious ousted when they failed to meet the expectations of their people."

"That's true," he nodded. "A throne – particularly a Balkan throne – can be a most precarious place to sit. Somewhere a little safer might be more suitable for Maximilian; somewhere under our protection..." An idea dawned on him and he slapped his hand against his thigh, delighted by this flash of inspiration. "Alsace-Lorraine!"

She blinked and he nodded rapidly.

"Yes, yes...Since we took the region from the French forty years ago, it has been as much a thorn in our side as Bosnia-Herzegovina is to Austria but in recent years the place has become more settled."

"Really?" she said apprehensively, leaving him in little doubt that she was well aware of continued unrest in the region.

"Occasionally," he shrugged, playing down the extent of the Alsatians' resentment, "there is some friction between our officers and the older people who still view us as invaders but I have often thought it would be to everyone's advantage if we were to appoint a non-German governor for the region. An Austrian would arouse far less antipathy than a German and, since the French have so little respect for hereditary titles that they make a habit of killing or deposing their kings, they would be far more amenable to a governor who had been rejected by an imperial family. All in all, Maximilian would be the perfect man for the job!"

"Man?" Sophie's eyes widened. "Maximilian is only eleven years old."

"Oh yes, I realise that he is just a child at the moment but, as we were saying, they grow so quickly and it's important to think ahead. In a few more years he will be old enough to take his place in the world and he deserves a position of prestige. Alsace would suit him perfectly. I will think of an appropriately dignified title for him and, obviously, as the region is part of my empire, he would remain under my protection so you need have no worries for his safety."

Elated by his own brilliance, Wilhelm smiled, basking in the certainty that his thoughtfulness and wisdom had impressed her. Eager to maintain and deepen her admiration, he was about to consider similar positions for her other children when suddenly Admiral von Tirpitz, who had been walking ahead of them, stopped and, with a gasp of delight, stooped to scrutinise a rose. He bent so low that his long beard, almost touching the ground, appeared to have sprouted from the soil like a great bushy shrub and when, with child-like curiosity, he launched into a series of questions about horticultural techniques, his mouth was so close to the rose that he might have been addressing it directly.

Sophie, raising her parasol to create a shade from the sweltering sun, stepped closer and commenced a description of her husband's methods of rose-breeding. Though it seemed unlikely that this was a deliberate ploy to escape from his company, Wilhelm, disgruntled at being deprived of her attention, turned instead to her husband.

Franz Ferdinand, who, until now, had been strolling some distance behind them, seemingly more interested in his gardens than his guest, made a few trite comments about the landscape and layout of Konopischt before guiding Wilhelm into a greenhouse out of earshot of the rest of the party.

The humid air, drenched in the intoxicating scents of summer, bathed his face with a fine mist that trickled from his brow like sweat as Franz Ferdinand pointed out the diverse species and the different types of soil required for various shrubs. Oblivious of the sauna-like heat, he continued his monologue at some length until Wilhelm pulled a handkerchief from his pocket and pointedly mopped his brow.

"Forgive me," Franz Ferdinand said. "I am so passionate about the gardens that I sometimes forget how dull my conversation sounds to other people."

"No," Wilhelm said, tweaking his moustache to ensure that the humidity had not softened the wax and caused it to droop, "it isn't in the least dull. When someone is fascinated by a subject, his passion is infectious. Although botany has never been a great interest of mine, I always enjoy listening to an expert."

Franz Ferdinand's taut face softened, "I'm hardly an expert. I just find gardening therapeutic. I suppose everyone must have something to take his mind off the pressures of the day. The British king, I believe, collects stamps; my uncle, the Emperor, loves taking long walks; and…."

"Now that the Emperor has recovered from his illness, he is remarkably fit for a man of his age, is he not?"

Franz Ferdinand nodded grouchily, "I sometimes think he will live to be a hundred."

The phrase recalled to Wilhelm an amusing story he had heard and he burst into such a fit of uncontrollable laughter that his host stared at him in bafflement as though fearing he had lost his mind.

"I'm sorry, Franz," he eventually managed to gasp. "What you said reminded me of something. I don't know if there is any truth in it."

Franz Ferdinand's brow creased into a perplexed frown.

"The parrot?" Wilhelm prompted.

"Ah," said the Archduke, slumping onto a bench, "so the story reached Potsdam?"

Still laughing, Wilhelm nodded, "We only heard the gist of it. What exactly happened?"

Shaking his head, Franz Ferdinand smiled, "We were in Vienna when one of our parrots – a beautiful creature! – escaped from the Belvedere. We thought we had lost him forever but he had flown into some public gardens where he was found and taken to the local police station. Unfortunately, he was a very gifted bird with great powers of imitation and he soon began repeating all kinds of things that I had said in private to Sophie."

Wilhelm, bent double with laughter, clutched his sides and, croaking like a parrot, said, "He'll live to be a hundred, Sophie! He'll live to be a hundred!"

"That was bad enough," Franz Ferdinand sighed with a smile, "but there were other comments about various members of the family and the court, and the damned bird was so gifted that the police actually recognised my voice!"

Wilhelm's laughter thundered so loudly that it seemed to shake the glass of the greenhouse, "They brought him back to you?"

He nodded, "Since then I have taken great care not to speak my mind in the presence of a parrot."

Tears welled in Wilhelm's eyes and it was some time before he was sufficiently composed to be able to draw the conversation to more serious matters.

"You really dislike the Emperor and his court so intensely?"

"I would be a hypocrite to deny it, and the feeling is mutual. People speak so highly of the importance of the family but it seems to me that family members assume they have the right to treat their relatives in ways that would never be tolerated among other groups of people. Manipulation, control, mockery, ill-manners…if we treated our friends as we treat our family, we should soon find ourselves completely isolated." He paused for a moment and then, as though a dam had burst within him, a tirade of such ferocity poured forth from his mouth that Wilhelm was stunned. Every hidden grievance, every slight he and Sophie had endured, and all the frustration he had kept hidden for years erupted in a volcanic stream of ire; and when he had completed the lengthy litany of wrongs he had suffered, he continued with a bitter criticism of his uncle's political policies and military strategies.

"...to yield, as he did, to the Hungarians' demand for a dual monarchy, was a disgrace! And now, his pig-headed obstinacy over Bosnia-Herzegovina has created such animosity with the Serbs that it is only a matter of time before something triggers another wretched war in the Balkans."

The heat of his rage so filled the already stifling greenhouse that Wilhelm, desperate for air, pushed open the door and, leaning against the jamb, breathed deeply. Though he had no desire to involve himself in the internal disputes of the Habsburgs, he stared pensively across the gardens, weighing up all possible responses. The Emperor might be in perfect health now but the recent bout of bronchitis demonstrated the fragility of his hold on life. Sixty-six years on the throne must have taken their toll, and his personal tragedies had surely left their scars.

Franz Ferdinand, on the other hand, was young and robust and, even if the rumours of his seizures were true, it was only a matter of time before he took on the mantle of Emperor. Besides, Wilhelm mused, a man who had reigned for so many decades was far less malleable than one who had yet to wear a crown, and, much as Franz Josef was keen to maintain a strong alliance with Germany, he was not as appreciative of the Kaiser's personal friendship as Franz Ferdinand was.

Wilhelm glanced back into the greenhouse where the Archduke, his anger exhausted, ran his hand across his damp brow and shook his head as though waking from a trance. Though he could not discern exactly what it was, there was something about this man that appealed to Wilhelm: perhaps it was the potency of his unyielding opinions and his determination to abide by his decisions regardless of what anyone thought – such strength of mind was certainly an admirable quality – or perhaps his attraction lay in the fact the he appreciated and valued Wilhelm's judgement more than any other prince in the whole of Europe. Whatever the cause, Wilhelm suddenly felt a great empathy with him for, though he had suffered none of the snubs and slurs that Franz Ferdinand had endured, he had often felt that seething rage which the Archduke had so powerfully expressed. He ran his right hand over his withered left arm, recalling the pains and traumas of childhood, and he recognised the deep sense of frustration in Franz Ferdinand's eyes.

"Well," the Archduke eventually sighed apologetically, "as you can see, my temper is as hot as the sun. Sophie chides me for it and urges me to keep it in check but…"

Wilhelm stepped back into the greenhouse and sat down beside him. "I agree with you, Franz. Our greatest trials often come from within our own families. Unlike our friends, we did not choose these people and yet we are expected to live harmoniously with them although we have absolutely nothing in common except happening to have been born of the same parents or grandparents."

Franz Ferdinand, obviously embarrassed by his outburst, sighed deeply and said nothing.

"Sometimes," Wilhelm said more earnestly, "it is right to vent our anger and it doesn't surprise me in the least that you feel so affronted by the way you have been treated. The heir to the Habsburg throne deserves the utmost respect, as does his wife. The way that people have treated Sophie is inexcusable."

"Thank you," Franz Ferdinand murmured, and Wilhelm, eager to cultivate the deepening sense of empathy, patted his shoulder.

"You might be aware that one of my sons is in a similar situation to yours."

Franz Ferdinand shook his head.

"Oskar – my fifth son – is to marry my wife's former lady-in-waiting."

The statement sparked Franz Ferdinand's interest and he looked up through wide eyes.

"Of course, it is viewed as a *mésalliance* and there has been a good deal of opposition within the court." Wilhelm ran a finger over his lips, concealing the fact that he had been the chief opponent until prevailed upon by his wife to consent to the match. "Consequently, I have not been able to raise the girl to the rank of Princess of Prussia but she will be treated with the respect she deserves as a daughter-in-law of the Kaiser. My wife is very fond of her so, of course, she will always be welcome in our home."

Franz Ferdinand's lips flickered into the briefest of smiles.

"Did you know," Wilhelm said, "that at the time of your wedding, I wrote a letter to the Emperor, asking him to accept Sophie as a member of the family?"

"So, too, did Tsar Nicholas of Russia but my uncle paid no attention. Even when the Pope himself wrote, the stubborn old man refused to yield. But that is only part of it. The personal insults we suffer on account of his intransigence are nothing compared to his failure to understand the way in which his empire is fragmenting."

Wilhelm leaned closer and said quietly, "Don't worry, Franz. Your time will come. Many years ago, when my parents were set on a course that would have led Germany into becoming some kind of liberal reflection of England, with no standing at all on the world's stage, I suffered exactly as you are suffering now. My opinions were dismissed as of no value and no one was prepared to listen to my advice. Do you know what I did?"

Franz Ferdinand shook his head and Wilhelm stood up.

"I found a photograph of myself and I wrote across the bottom of it, *I bide my time.* You see, Franz, that is all it was – biding time, knowing that eventually my plans would be realised and I would be in a position to make Germany the great nation she is today."

"You succeeded."

"Yes," he nodded adopting the stance he had taken on the photograph, "and one of the chief reasons for my success was that I refused to be dominated by old men who had been around for so long that they believed themselves to be indestructible. At the beginning of a reign it is vital that a new Emperor stamps his authority on his ministers or he will find himself repeating the mistakes of his predecessors. When I came to the throne Chancellor Bismarck had been dominating the court for decades and he believed that, because I was young, he could manipulate me into agreeing to all his policies. I don't deny that he had been a good servant to the country – it was largely thanks to him that the unification was so successful – but by the time I became Emperor, his ideas were out-dated. He would have prevented German expansion and, worse, he would have had me begin my reign by sending troops against my own people! He didn't understand, you see, that times had changed. He didn't appreciate the social problems caused by rapid industrialisation and he didn't realise that unless we took an expansionist approach to foreign policy, we would be left behind while all the other European powers grew in strength."

Franz Ferdinand looked up at him attentively.

"Your uncle is not entirely to blame for the problems of Austria-Hungary. He is an old man and, like Bismarck, he comes from another era and the challenges we face today are beyond his comprehension. One might say Franz Josef represents the past, and Franz Ferdinand, the future. Your time will come, Franz, and when it does you must be fully prepared to implement whatever changes are necessary for the good of Austria and her allies."

Franz Ferdinand cleared his throat and, glancing towards the door as though fearful of eavesdroppers, whispered, "I *am* prepared. I already have a list of ministers who will be appointed to different departments and I have drawn up a map of the way in which the separate states of the Empire will be given greater autonomy. Even my portrait has been painted in readiness for my accession."

"Good, good," Wilhelm said, delighting in his superiority, "and alongside these domestic changes, I am sure you have put a great deal of thought into foreign policy and strengthening your alliances?"

"Yes, yes indeed," he nodded. "You know how deeply committed I am to our alliance with Germany."

"We reciprocate that commitment and promise that you will find no firmer ally."

"That is very reassuring," Franz Ferdinand's eyes narrowed, "particularly considering the present state of affairs in the Balkans. I am sure you're aware that the Emperor's narrow-minded ministers are constantly urging him to authorise an invasion to prevent the Serbs from becoming more powerful."

Wilhelm frowned, "Are there sufficient grounds to warrant an invasion?"

Franz Ferdinand laughed ironically, "Oh I am sure that sooner or later they will find an excuse and if they cannot find one, they will create one."

Wilhelm, not understanding, frowned more deeply, but Franz Ferdinand, offering no explanation, changed tack.

"It is ludicrous that so much blood could be shed, and has already been shed, for the sake of these little Balkan states. Is it right that Serbia – a land of a few plum trees and a pack of unruly scoundrels – should hold such sway over the great nations of Russia, Germany and Austria, and influence our alliances and foreign policy?"

Wilhelm, unable to follow his train of thought, shook his head and sat down again.

"Instead of wasting so much effort squabbling with these petty states, it would be more beneficial for everyone if we were to find a means of improving relations with our neighbours. Over the years we have been very wary of the Russians and they have viewed us with deep suspicion. This is a most unsatisfactory state of affairs for neighbours who share a border. I believe that the best way to ease the tension in the Balkans and prevent further conflict is for all the Great Powers to work together. As things stand, the Balkan states can play us off, one against another; the Serbs have Russian support; the Bulgarians have German support and so on; but if we were able to develop more harmonious relations with one another, the threat from these little states would diminish or disappear altogether."

"You are suggesting greater co-operation with Russia?"

"Yes," he said firmly. "That is exactly what I am suggesting, if the Tsar would be amenable."

Wilhelm thought for a moment then smiled, "I am sure the Tsar would be delighted to hear what you have just said. Nicky and I are old friends – his wife is my cousin, don't forget – and I can state unequivocally that he would be more than willing to do whatever he can to create greater harmony in Europe. He has enough problems of his own without worrying about foreign affairs: half his country is on strike, from all accounts, and he is totally unprepared for war. Besides, he is a pious man with no appetite for conflict."

Franz Ferdinand's features softened into a smile.

"Trust me," Wilhelm said. "I know Nicky very well and I am sure that his greatest desire is to live peaceably with his neighbours. However, I also think it would be beneficial for us to cultivate friendship and alliances in the Balkans to counter-balance the growing Slav influence."

"I agree. I believe that the only way to resolve the tension between ourselves and the Serbs is by dialogue but, as things stand at the moment, thanks to the bellicose ranting of the Emperor's ministers they are deeply suspicious of us and fear that we intend to destroy them."

"Fear," Wilhelm murmured. "Fear is the most dangerous emotion of all. What was it that Shakespeare said? '*In time we hate that which we oft do fear...*'"

Franz Ferdinand nodded distractedly. "If we were to develop closer relations with the Serbs' Balkan allies, we would be able to alleviate that fear and build trust which would eventually enable us to reach agreements that would satisfy everyone."

Wilhelm jumped to his feet and gesticulated towards the gardens. Franz Ferdinand followed him outside where he picked up a stick and drew a map in the soil.

"Here we have Serbia; to the south, Greece."

"And the Greeks are part of the Balkan alliance with the Serbs."

Wilhelm smiled, "Since my sister is Queen of Greece, I am confident that the Greeks would be happy to ally themselves with us. Now then," he prodded around in the soil, "to the west we have Bulgaria – still reeling from the recent defeat and desperate for our support – and Roumania. If we can entice the Roumanians with flattery and a few concessions, we shall soon have them eating out of our hands." He looked up thoughtfully, "The only difficulty is that there is such antipathy between them and the Hungarian Magyars that they are unlikely to want to enter into an alliance with the Emperor of Austria-Hungary."

Franz Ferdinand stiffened as though about to embark on another angry explosion but this time he managed to restrain himself, "The Hungarians are a lawless rabble and if I were in the Emperor's position, I would do everything in my power to bring them to heel. I have great sympathy with the Roumanians and a great personal attachment to King Carol."

"Excellent!" Wilhelm beamed. "And, as we are looking to the future, I trust you have an equally high opinion of the Crown Prince and my cousin, the Crown Princess?"

"They are most accommodating and charming."

"Charming," Wilhelm laughed. "The Crown Princess would be delighted to hear you say that. She thrives on flattery and, since she holds more sway than her diffident husband, if we win Marie over to our way of thinking, we can safely assume that the rest of Roumania will follow."

Voices sounded across the lawns and, seeing Sophie and Tirpitz approaching, Wilhelm trampled over the soil to erase the map. He slapped Franz Ferdinand on the back, "We have made our positions clear, I think."

Franz Ferdinand nodded, "It has been a very rewarding conversation."

"Yes it has." He looked up at the bright sunshine and inhaled contentedly, "Between us Franz, we will show the world that the Central Powers have risen to their true place at last. No longer dominated by the old order, with you and I at the helm, Germany and Austria-Hungary shall steer this generation safely into a Golden Age. Future generations will look back at us with gratitude and say; *these were the kings who brought peace and prosperity to their countries and to the whole of Europe!'*" He stood for a moment imagining statues of himself rising alongside those of his illustrious forebear, Frederick the Great.

"I am glad we have had this opportunity to talk frankly and uninhibited by ministers and politicians."

"So am I," Franz Ferdinand said sincerely. "Now I am even more confident that our visit to Bosnia will prove beneficial."

"Ah yes," he said, strolling slowly towards the rest of the party, "the trip was reported in our German newspapers a couple of months ago."

"Really?" Franz Ferdinand raised his eyebrows, "I wouldn't have thought it was significant enough to merit a report."

"Your government must have thought it was."

"Our government?"

Wilhelm shrugged carelessly, "I presume that the government gave the story to our press."

Franz Ferdinand stopped with a strange, quite fearful expression but Wilhelm, content that the conversation had reached a happy conclusion, pretended not to have noticed.

"When do you go?"

"The week after next," he said quietly.

"Jolly good! I shall be thinking of you when I am in Kiel reviewing my fleet." He looked up again at the brilliant blue sky, "Summer is the very best time of year for reviewing the troops, isn't it!"

He strode off towards Sophie and Tirpitz but suddenly turned back, "Just one thing to remember…"

Franz Ferdinand looked at him earnestly.

"Be careful not to repeat any of our conversation in the presence of your talking parrot!"

He strutted along the walkway and his laugher boomed like thunder across the gardens.

Chapter 14 – June 1914

Black clouds like funeral palls draped the green cupolas and shrouded the urns and statues along the roof as the motor car moved slowly down the broad esplanade from the Belvedere Palace. Though he had never been particularly fond of the place, Franz Ferdinand felt suddenly compelled to turn and look back at the palace as one might take a last fleeting glance when leaving a dearest friend. As his eyes moved over the baroque façade, however, it was not grief that caused his heart to beat a little more quickly, but relief and the sense of freedom that always accompanied his departure from Vienna. For all its romantic beauty and architectural splendour, the city had come to epitomise frustration, suffocation and despair. On so dark a day as this, even the brilliant Belvedere looked dull and dreary; and the wide variety of shrubs and flowers, normally so colourful and bright, drooped towards the earth as though tired of straining for the sun.

He turned back and smiled at Sophie and, as the ominous storm clouds swathed and swaddled the towers and trees, the sense of liberation was greater than ever. For the past month he had felt more optimistic and content than at any other time in his life. Event after event had reassured him that the sense of foreboding, which had occasionally unnerved him while preparing for this visit to Sarajevo, was nothing more than a sign of imminent change. It was almost impossible to believe that, after all these years of frustration, his words were finally being heard and that at last Sophie was receiving the honour and respect she deserved.

He recalled with pleasure their recent trip to the races where the colourful crowds swayed along the edge of the racetrack like a tangle of flowers in an English cottage garden. Sunlight, pouring over parasols and panoplies, had brought such delight to his heart that his laughter had run as freely as the horses haring towards the finishing line. It was not merely the rare escape from the pressures of work that brought this rush of exhilaration; it was rather the tumultuous cheering as Sophie stepped into the Imperial Stand. Oh, that Montenuovo had been there to hear it! And that the entire Imperial Family could have seen the way in which the crowds hailed her as though she were their future queen! Never again would any of them dare to snub this woman so loved by the people. Never again would they dare to view her with disdain.

He smiled with deep satisfaction and silently uttered a prayer of thanksgiving. As if it were not enough that his own people accepted Sophie, the Kaiser's visit had added to his joy. Wilhelm had treated her with the deference he would have shown to an empress, and he had treated Franz Ferdinand as though he had already inherited the throne.

His thoughts turned to the last few days spent with the children in his castle at Chlumetz. The bliss of their laughter as they played their happy games and their bright eyes shining with excitement as he told them tales of distant lands brought such ineffable gratitude to his heart that the only words he could find for his prayer were those from the psalm, *"Truly, my cup runneth over..."*

As the motor car moved through the ornate gates of the Belvedere, the first raindrops fell on Prinz Eugen Strasse. Suddenly a wild wind whipped through the branches, scattering the leaves that swirled like dancers spinning together in the air and falling softly to the ground. A clap of thunder boomed like a drum, then the clouds burst and the rain pounded the pavements and streamed down the windows with such melodic power that it seemed as though the Viennese sky had somehow absorbed the music of the ballrooms and concert halls and was echoing it back to the earth. The more powerful the storm, the greater became Franz Ferdinand's sense of liberation and, as streaks of fork lightning flashed through the darkness, his heart beat against his ribs like a young bird flapping against a bony cage on the point of finding freedom.

Such unfamiliar elation caused him to laugh and, tapping his hands on his knees, he began to hum and then sing Strauss's joyful and invigorating *Radetzky March*.

Sophie stared at him in astonishment but he sang all the louder and soon, infected by the same exultation, she sang, too, her soft soprano voice blending harmoniously with his deep bass tones. The streets of Vienna, which had for so long seemed like a prison to him, were suddenly awash with the glory of the storm, and at each thunder clap he raised his arm to conduct the divine orchestration while Sophie swayed and all but stamped her feet on the floor of the motor car.

When the joyful duet concluded with a final crescendo, they laughed together as cheerfully as children enraptured by an enchanted tale.

"Oh Lord," he gasped breathlessly, "I am going to miss you so much, Sophie!"

She squeezed his hand, "It's only a couple of days till we meet again in Bad Ilidze."

"Even a couple of minutes apart from you feels like an eternity!"

She frowned with sham severity, "It's your own fault. If you hadn't stubbornly refused to travel through

Hungary, you could have come with me instead of taking such a circuitous route."

"If I pass through Budapest the Hungarian ministers will expect me to go out and meet them."

"Would that be such a bad thing?"

"They dislike me – why aggravate them by my presence?"

"Because one day you will be their King."

He looked up thoughtfully, "When that day comes, the ministers will have all the more reason to dislike me."

She frowned at him, "Why?"

"I have been thinking that when I succeed as Emperor, I will refuse to be crowned King of Hungary until the government passes the reforms that are so badly needed. I will start by demanding that they grant universal suffrage so that the people are given the chance to elect their own ministers and government officials."

She gazed at him adoringly, "My love, when you are finally in a position to do all the good you have planned, the Hungarians and all the rest of your subjects will love you and recognise you as the noblest and most devoted Emperor that Austria-Hungary has ever known."

The tenderness in her eyes inflamed him with a powerful desire to take her in his arms and kiss her but, in so public a place, all he could do was reach for her hand and dispel his passion by bursting into an even more rousing rendition of the *Radezky March*.

By the time they reached the station, his spirits had reached such a peak that even the moment of separation from Sophie could not dampen his joy. With the eyes of so many attendants fixed upon them, he politely took her hand and, gently brushing her finger to his lips, said, "I wish you a comfortable journey and I shall be counting the hours until we meet again."

She responded with a smile and he turned towards the platform where his own train waited to take him to Trieste, whence he could make the next stage of the journey by sea.

"Good heavens!" he said, looking around the anxious faces of the station officials, "Whatever is the matter with everyone today? Has a little fall of rain made you all so miserable?"

A sheepish attendant stepped forwards and nervously explained that the storm had caused a failure of the lighting in the Imperial train. Franz Ferdinand brushed aside the apology with a shrug and peered into the sepulchral gloom of the candlelit carriage.

"Good grief," he laughed, boarding the train and settling himself by the window, "it's so dark, it's like entering a tomb. Not to worry. As soon as we leave Vienna, I am sure there will be nothing but blue skies and sunshine."

Few of the many journeys in his life had been more invigorating for Franz Ferdinand than the voyage along the Dalmatian Coast from Trieste to Bosnia. Standing on the deck of the *Viribus Unitis,* inhaling the fresh Adriatic air, his thoughts returned to the travels of his youth, and a series of half-forgotten memories flowed through his mind in a clear rejuvenating stream. Recalling peoples and places and the dreams that had inspired him all those years ago, he felt young again. He breathed more easily, walked more freely and smiled more readily than he had smiled in years; but it was not nostalgia that inspired him to contemplate each scene from the past with the studious attention of a critic observing a work of art; it was rather his desire to glean from each experience ideas for improving the lives of the Austro-Hungarian people. Revitalised by the power of the ocean, he felt stronger and more certain than ever that all his plans were on the point of coming to fruition. His accession seemed imminent and, just as the mighty dreadnaught ploughed effortlessly through the waves, he saw himself fearlessly cutting through centuries of outworn traditions to establish peace, freedom and progress throughout the empire.

Even the arrival of the morning newspapers – normally so disheartening – added to his optimism. Alongside the reports of his progress towards Sarajevo, were images of the German Emperor, dressed in the uniform of a British Admiral, touring a British dreadnaught that had sailed to Kiel for the regatta. It was clear from Wilhelm's smile that he welcomed this visit from the Royal Navy and, like Franz Ferdinand, his greatest desire was for mutual respect and friendship between the nations of Europe.

The photograph of the dreadnaught reminded Franz Ferdinand, too, that this voyage on the *Viribus Unitis* provided him with an ideal opportunity to examine the strength and capacity of this recent addition to the Austrian fleet. Four mighty turrets mounted with triple guns overshadowed further rows of armaments, while submerged torpedo tubes jutted out from the bow and the broadsides. Recalling the disgust he had felt when attending naval manoeuvres some years earlier, Franz Ferdinand listened intently to the officers' descriptions of the calibres of the guns and extent of their range, and it filled him with immense satisfaction to know that the implementation of his recommendations had led to so many improvements that even Kaiser Wilhelm couldn't fail to be impressed by so powerful a vessel.

The contrast between the dreadnaught and the yacht, to which he transferred on the Dalmatian coast, was reflected clearly in the changing vista. From the deck of the gunship he had stared into the unfathomable depths of the sea, awed by its vastness and power. Now, as the statelier *Dalmat* moved steadily along the Neretva River, he gazed across the softer scenery of sleepy towns, church spires, hills and ancient towers. So calm a landscape soothed the remnants of anxiety that had clouded his plans for this visit and, by the time the red roofs of Metkovic came into view, he felt more alert and invigorated than he had felt in months.

The final stage of the journey by train was made all the brighter by the knowledge that Sophie would already have arrived at the spa town of Bad Ilidze, not far from Sarajevo, and as soon as he had inspected the military manoeuvres he could hurry to her waiting arms. Such was his mood that even the presence of Conrad von Hötzendorf could not dampen his spirits. On the contrary, it was gratifying to see how efficiently the troops performed their tasks when Hötzendorf, who had come only as an observer, was relegated to the side lines. So impressed was Franz Ferdinand by the organisation of the manoeuvres and the proficiency of the Military |Governor, Potiorek, that, despite his dislike of social gatherings, he actually relished the opportunity of entertaining the officers and local officials at a banquet in his hotel that evening.

Roses from the South and *Artist's Life* sounded softly from the strings of the Sarajevo Garrison Orchestra as Franz Ferdinand, sated by the feast, stepped out into the gardens of the Hotel Bosnia. The amber beams of the setting sun sparkled through the bubbles that rose like jewels in his champagne flute, and the scent of newly-mown lawns drifted on the balmy air. So tranquil was the scene and so mellow his mood that it was impossible to believe that this region could ever have been so hotly disputed or have caused so many problems for the Emperor. Officers mingled in cheerful groups, chattering and laughing without a care, and even Hőtzendorf's craggy features seemed to have softened a little this evening. Like a vision of an angel, Sophie floated from one group to another with effortless confidence and it amused Franz Ferdinand to think that he, who had been prepared since childhood to sparkle on such occasions, stood like a silent spectator looking on, while Sophie competently set the guests at ease.

Gradually she made her way towards him and he hoped that his smile conveyed the depths of love and appreciation that words could not express.

"Franz," she said quietly, nodding towards a thin man arrayed in a pride of military medals, "who is that?"

"I'm so sorry," he said, feeling suddenly gauche, "I should have introduced you earlier. He is Oskar Potiorek, the Military Governor who invited us here. Come, I would like him to meet you."

He took her arm and led her across the garden to where Potiorek stood talking with Hőtzendorf but, as they approached, Hőtzendorf made a slight bow and, with an inaudible excuse, withdrew.

After responding respectfully to Sophie's greeting, Potiorek assured her, "Everything is in order for your visit to Sarajevo tomorrow, Your Highness. Perhaps it has been mentioned that a group of Moslem ladies would be greatly honoured if you would be willing to speak with them at the City Hall?"

"Yes," Sophie smiled, "we have seen the itinerary and I am very much looking forward to meeting them."

Potiorek made a slight bow and turned to Franz Ferdinand, "Count von Harrach has placed his motor car at your disposal for tomorrow, sir. With your permission, he will act as your personal bodyguard and he and I will travel with you in the motorcade."

Franz Ferdinand nodded.

"There will be six vehicles in all. Curcic, the Mayor of Sarajevo, and Gerde, the Police Commissioner, will take the first; we will take the second. My Chief of Staff, Merrizi and Count Boos-Waldeck will accompany Baron Morsey, Baron Rumiskirch and the rest of your suite in the remaining cars."

"Excellent," Franz Ferdinand smiled. "I know we can reply on you to ensure that everything passes without incident."

Potiorek glanced across the gardens towards Hötzendorf, "It is four years since Bosnia was honoured by a visit from a member of the Imperial Family, so I am sure that tomorrow will be remembered for a long time to come."

A sudden breeze swept through the garden, rustling the leaves and rippling the white linen table cloths until the champagne glasses clinked and tinkled like mystical bells. Franz Ferdinand shivered and let out an involuntary moan.

"Franz?" Sophie looked at him earnestly, "What is it?"

"Nothing," he cringed exaggeratedly, "someone just stepped on my grave, that's all!" To distract from his embarrassment he laughed loudly and, looking around the garden, changed the subject.

"Where is Dilinski?"

Potiorek awkwardly dug his foot into the lawn, "He isn't here, sir. We thought it would be inappropriate to invite him."

Franz Ferdinand raised his eyebrows, "What is inappropriate about inviting the Civil Governor of the region?"

"This is a military event and you came here to inspect the manoeuvres, so there seemed little point in his attending. In fact," he frowned, "we didn't even see the necessity of officially informing him of your visit."

"That's a pity," Franz Ferdinand said. "It would have given us the opportunity of seeing Bosnia-Herzegovina from a different perspective." He glanced at Sophie and, unwilling to create any discord on so pleasant an evening, let the matter drop. "Never mind; there will be other opportunities as I am sure we will return here before too long."

"Indeed, sir." Potiorek nodded and, with a slight raise of his hand, Franz Ferdinand signalled that he was dismissed.

When he had gone, Franz Ferdinand took Sophie's arm and together they strolled through the garden, enjoying the scents and sounds of the season and making polite comments to their guests until darkness descended and the party began to disperse.

Finally alone beneath the stars, Franz Ferdinand drew Sophie closer.

"Fourteen years ago tomorrow…" he whispered, tenderly gazing into her eyes.

"The happiest and most blessed fourteen years of my life."

"And mine," he sighed contentedly and looked up at the blue-black sky. "Look, even the stars have come out to celebrate our anniversary! The whole of heaven is rejoicing with us."

"You know," she laughed lightly, "I didn't sleep a wink the night before our wedding."

"Neither did I. I spent the whole night thanking God for bringing you to me, and praying that I would make you happy."

"God answered your prayers," she smiled.

"Yes," he said softly, "he did." He nodded towards the hotel, "Did you see that they have set up a little chapel especially for our visit?"

"Yes. I visited it earlier. It was very kind of them to go to such trouble."

"Let's go there now," he said, "just you and I. Let's go and make our vows again."

The light danced in her eyes, "Again?"

He nodded, "There's something strange in the air tonight. It feels as though..." he shook his head, trying to find the words. "It feels as though everything is just beginning for us. Tomorrow when we drive through Sarajevo, the people will see you as you really are. You don't have to hide away any longer, giving precedence to all those inane archduchesses or letting them treat you so disparagingly. It's *your* time, Sophie. Your time and my time...and now that the whole world is opening before us. Let's go and renew our vows before God and pray that the next fourteen years will be even more beautiful than the last."

She smiled and hand-in-hand, they walked through the moonlight towards the little chapel.

Chapter 15 – Sarajevo – June 28th 1914

The sudden juddering of the wheels after the steady click-clack of the past few miles caused Franz Ferdinand to look up from his papers and put down his pen. Great clouds of steam swirled outside the windows – a sure sign that the train would soon be approaching the station. He was about to summon his aide when, through a mirror on the opposite side of the saloon carriage, he caught sight of Sophie's reflection.

Perhaps it was the sunlight accentuating the loveliness of her complexion, or perhaps it was the prospect of their first public drive together that made her appear more beautiful than ever today. For fourteen years he had prayed for the moment when she would sit beside him to receive the recognition of the crowds and now, at last, on the joyful anniversary of their wedding, that day had come. He turned to the window and, seeing the sun's rays burst through the clouds and gleam across the bunting and hanging baskets lining the platform, he offered a silent prayer of thanksgiving.

Today, more than ever, it was clear that his star was in the ascendant and all he had dreamed and planned was coming into being. The severity of the Emperor's recent illness had demonstrated his weakness, and already influential people were looking to his successor.

Sophie looked up and smiled, "You look so happy today."

"Of course, I am happy! I have the honour of presenting my beautiful wife to the people. Have you any idea how proud that makes me?"

She laughed coyly and he moved closer, reaching for her hand. "As I said last night, this really is *our* time, Sophie. Not only are the people eager to accept and honour you, but at last I also have the opportunity to implement some of my own ideas instead of being bound by the out-dated views from Vienna."

"Franz," she said cautiously, "you must not openly contradict the Emperor."

"I won't do that. With a hint here and a nod there, I can make my intentions clear without any reference to his jaded policies. Look at what we've already achieved: the improvements to the army and navy; a firm friendship with the Kaiser, and today I'll be able to suggest that it's only a matter of time before the Bosnian Slavs are given a measure of autonomy. That will quell any lingering unrest and completely undermine the Serbs' demands for a separate Slav Kingdom."

"You really think so?"

"I am sure of it. The Emperor doesn't understand that times have changed. His policies come from the last century and his advisors think that he can hold the Empire together by brute force. That might have worked once but nowadays people are better informed. They have a voice and they want that voice to be heard. The best way – the *only* way – forward is through conciliation. Once the people realise that it is in their interest to remain a part of Austria-Hungary, they won't need to…"

The compartment door opened and Franz Ferdinand broke off mid-sentence as two members of his suite, Morsey and Rumerskirch, appeared.

Rumerskirch held out the Archduke's green-plumed helmet, "We're arriving, sir. This is Sarajevo."

The train drew alongside a platform crowded with waiting dignitaries, many of whom Franz Ferdinand recognised from the previous evening.

"General Potiorek looks so gaunt," Sophie said.

Morsey followed her eyes, "It isn't surprising considering the strain he is under – constantly a target for the Black Hand."

"Black Hand?"

"A Serbian terrorist group made up of lawyers, journalists, military officers and all kinds of riff-raff. According to our intelligence their numbers are growing rapidly. There must be over two thousand of them now."

"And they're all here in Bosnia?"

"Oh no, most of them are in Serbia." Franz Ferdinand stood up and straightened his jacket before taking his helmet from Rumerskirch. "They come here from time to time with various hare-brained plans."

"Not long ago," Morsey said, "one of them tried to kill Potiorek with a poisoned dagger."

"Good grief! No wonder he looks to tense."

Franz Ferdinand, desperate to avoid causing her any anxiety, scowled pointedly at Morsey, who hurriedly tried to make up for his tactlessness, "Of course that attack was unsuccessful. Potiorek's security arrangements are second to none. Besides, with such a strong military presence in Bosnia, this is probably the safest place in the empire."

Franz Ferdinand brushed a speck of dust from his sleeve, "I sometimes wonder whether the reports of the Black Hand's activities are exaggerated. Is there any evidence of actual atrocities that they have committed?"

Morsey mused for a moment, "Their leader, Dimitrijevic, who goes by codename of Apis, was involved in the assassination of the late King and Queen of Serbia."

Franz Ferdinand grunted, "That was an entirely internal Serbian affair and has nothing to do with us. What's more, it was over ten years ago. What has this

Apis done since then apart from spouting hot air?" He threw back his shoulders and smiled at Sophie, "Come, let's not keep the crowds waiting."

As they stepped onto the platform, the assembled dignitaries bowed in unison and, to Franz Ferdinand's delight, Potiorek gesticulated to a child who curtseyed and handed Sophie a bouquet of roses. The blush of their fragile petals matched the radiance of their recipient's complexion, and their fragrance filled the station and hung on the warm, damp air.

"If you would come this way, sir," Potiorek said, guiding the party towards a waiting motorcade but, as an officer held open the door of the second phaeton, Franz Ferdinand paused.

"Is the cover really necessary?"

"It was raining earlier, sir, so we thought..."

"And now," he looked up at the sky, "the sun has come out to greet us. Have the cover pulled back so the people can see us."

As the attendants hurried to obey him, Franz Ferdinand smiled at Sophie, "I want everyone to see you today. Soon your face will be better known than those of all the archduchesses in Vienna!"

The moment the vehicles left the station, a great roar erupted from the crowds, who raised flags and threw flowers across the road. Arms waved, necks craned to catch sight of the visitors, and the ripple of rapturous applause flowed like a river welling into an ocean. The warmth of the reception took Franz Ferdinand by surprise and he smiled in delighted amazement that the people of such a hostile region were showing greater respect and affection to him and to Sophie than they had ever received in Vienna.

"I am glad you chose not to deploy the troops," he said to Potiorek. "So often on these visits they stand like a solid wall between us and the people."

"It didn't seem necessary, sir." Potiorek gesticulated into the crowd, "The people are delighted by your visit so there was no need to bring in the army when a scattering of policemen is enough to maintain order."

"I didn't expect to see so many people," Sophie beamed, as the crowds responded to her smile with even greater fervour.

"It is a national holiday," Potiorek explained, "the start of a week of celebrations, so the people were free to come out and greet you."

"A holiday?"

"St. Vitus' Day."

"St. Vitus' Day?" Franz Ferdinand raised his hand to acknowledge the cheers. "The anniversary of the Battle of Kosovo?"

Potiorek glanced around vaguely, "Yes, I believe so."

Franz Ferdinand frowned; he had been so swept up in the thoughts of this visit coinciding with his wedding anniversary that he had quite overlooked the date's significance to the Serbs.

"In which case," he said quietly, "I trust that our visit won't be seen as a provocation."

Potiorek, with a puzzled expression, shook his head.

"Five hundred years ago the Christian Serbs were defeated by the Turks at Kosovo," Franz Ferdinand explained, "but to this day they continue to hail those heroes as symbols of Serbian independence. There's even an old legend that on St. Vitus' Day the rivers still run red with the blood of the Christian heroes."

"I had forgotten that you're a historian, sir," Potiorek smiled. "I hope that will make this afternoon's visit to the museum even more enjoyable for you."

The driver steered towards a military barracks where a guard of honour stood awaiting inspection. Franz Ferdinand alighted from the vehicle and, reaching for Sophie's hand, pointedly drew her to his side. No longer would she walk some paces behind him or remain out of sight. Now she would take her rightful place as his partner and equal. Through the clattering of sabres, the soldiers stood to attention and the boom of the gun-salute echoed over the walls and resounded through the streets like a fanfare trumpeting Sophie's emergence into the public gaze.

When the inspection was complete, they returned to the vehicle and, as the motorcade continued on its way, Potiorek outlined the plans for the rest of the day. Franz Ferdinand replied with positive comments, his eyes moving over the banners embroidered with his image, when suddenly a crack sounded across the street.

"Brilliant," Harrach huffed. "That's the tyre blown. Now we'll have to…"

Before he could finish, the phaeton suddenly lurched forwards at the same moment as Franz Ferdinand saw something fly through the air towards Sophie. He raised his hand to protect her and the missile struck his arm, landed in the folded roof and bounced off onto the road behind them.

A deafening explosion split the air, followed by a moment of silence, then gasps and cries replaced the cheering of the crowd. The phaeton screeched to a halt, hurling the passengers against the seats. As though propelled by a catapult, Harrach leaped out and ran back along the route they had taken. Franz Ferdinand, turning to watch him, saw behind them on the road a thick cloud of dust and the shattered bodywork of a limousine around which a mass of people stood crowding and screaming.

Sophie, her face white with horror, gasped, "Drive on quickly!"

Seconds later, Harrach returned and, breathlessly jumping back onto the running board, ordered the chauffeur to accelerate. Without a moment's hesitation, he revved the engine and sped through the streets so quickly that his passengers were obliged to cling to the seat to maintain their balance.

No one spoke again until the motor car screeched to a halt at the City Hall, where rows of officers lined the steps, clearly surprised by the speed of the guests' arrival. The driver turned anxiously as though fearing for the safety of his passengers and only when he saw that all four of them were uninjured did he let out a deep sigh.

"I am so sorry, Your Imperial Highness."

"Sorry?" Franz Ferdinand raised his eyebrows.

"I saw something flying through the air towards us. That's why I stopped. Then I heard the explosion and…"

"My good man," Franz Ferdinand patted his shoulder, "I think you have just saved our lives. What's your name?"

"Loyka, sir. Leopold Loyka."

"Well, Loyka, we are in your debt."

Other vehicles from the motorcade began to arrive and, as Franz Ferdinand and Sophie stepped from the phaeton, the Archduke, observing the whiteness of the faces around him, strode towards Baron Morsey, "Who was in the motor car behind ours?"

Trembling, the Baron almost choked as he answered, "Count Boos-Waldeck and Eric von Merrizzi. We don't know what has happened to them."

"If you will come inside, sir," Potiorek said urgently, "I will find out."

By now, news of the events had reached the attending crowds and their cheers as Sophie and Franz Ferdinand appeared on the steps resounded with even greater fervour.

"Are you alright?" Franz Ferdinand whispered to Sophie, while Harrach darted around them like a protective puppy.

"I felt a sting in my neck. I thought it was a wasp or some other insect but it must have been part of the explosion."

Only then did the extent of the danger dawn on Franz Ferdinand and the horrific realisation that Sophie could have been hurt or even killed, caused a torrent of rage to well up inside him. He stamped up the steps towards the Mayor, who immediately launched into a fulsome speech, expressing the city's thanks to His Imperial Highness for his visit.

Unable to restrain his anger, Franz Ferdinand approached him menacingly, "Thanks? Your thanks! A strange kind of gratitude when we come here in peace only to have bombs hurled at us! It is an utter disgrace and..."

"Franz," a gentle whisper immediately dispelled his anger and he turned to see the softness in Sophie's brown eyes.

"Go on then," he nodded grouchily to the Mayor, "get on with your speech."

The City Hall was buzzing with officials and officers, scurrying backwards and forwards as though their busyness might somehow allay the tension that filled the air. The planned reception continued as arranged but the joyful enthusiasm that had greeted them at the station had sunk into a far more sombre atmosphere. Repeatedly turning to Sophie to restrain his temper, Franz Ferdinand suggested that the rest of the day's engagements be cancelled until he had received a full account of exactly what had happened and the extent of the injuries suffered by the members of his suite.

"Franz," Sophie said softly, "the Moslem ladies are waiting to meet me. I should not like to disappoint them."

"Very well," he agreed and, as the attendants led her towards a staircase, he strode into a large reception room and sat down at a table, waiting for Potiorek to return from his investigations.

"I suppose," Morsey said, coming to rest beside him, "we knew that this visit would be dangerous. The Emperor had doubts about the wisdom of your coming here."

Franz Ferdinand clenched his hand into a fist and slammed it down on the table, "We cannot allow ourselves to be intimidated. The huge crowd that turned out to greet us is proof that there are many people here who are loyal and devoted to the Crown. My only regret is that other people have been hurt on my account..."

The door burst open and Potiorek marched into the room accompanied by Harrach and the Police Commissioner, Gerde.

"Well?" Franz Ferdinand demanded, twisting in his chair. "Boos-Waldeck and Merrizzi?"

"Their injuries are not as severe as we first feared, sir," Potiorek said. "Merrizzi has suffered a wound to his head but the doctors are satisfied that he is going to be alright."

"Thank God for that," Franz Ferdinand sighed with relief. "Was anyone else hurt?"

"Several bystanders were hit by debris from the explosion but, as far as we know, there is nothing too serious. It was a grenade. The culprit has been arrested."

"No doubt he is a Serb?" Morsey said.

Gerde stepped forwards, "Obviously we haven't yet had time to question him properly but we have ascertained that his name is Cabrinovic. He was born here in Sarajevo but has spent much of his time in Belgrade."

"Without a doubt he's a member of the Black Hand," Potiorek growled. "His suicide attempt is typical of those cowardly renegades."

"Suicide?" Franz Ferdinand said.

Gerde nodded, "As soon as the grenade exploded, he jumped over the bridge and threw himself into the river, intending to drown himself. Fortunately, the water there is only a few inches deep and, with the help of the public, two of my officers managed to drag him out, whereupon he immediately swallowed a capsule which he claimed contained cyanide."

"That proves it," Potiorek said. "It's common for the leaders of the Black Hand to supply their minions with poisons so that if they are captured, they don't break down under interrogation."

Franz Ferdinand frowned pensively, recalling the fate of Alfred Redl, "The Black Hand are not the only ones to promote suicide. It seems to be the answer to everything nowadays."

"Well," Potiorek shrugged. "Cabrinovic was no more successful in killing himself than he was in his attack. The cyanide didn't have the desired effect. He is alive and, apart from vomiting all over the place, he is…"

"…well enough to be questioned?" said Franz Ferdinand.

Gerde nodded, "My officers are interrogating him as we speak. I promise you, sir, we will get to the bottom of this. We will find out exactly who was behind this attack and see that they are brought to justice."

"It's obvious who was behind it," Potiorek said impatiently. "The Serbs are behind every atrocity we suffer. The country is riddled with fanatical nationalists and the sooner they are crushed the better."

Franz Ferdinand, frowning, sat down again and the others hovered around him like ghosts, their white faces and dark eyes inspiring in him a powerful sense of foreboding.

"It seems to me," he murmured, "that crushing a nation seldom achieves the desired effect. It only gives rise to resentment which, in the long run, leads to more uprisings and violence."

"What's the alternative?" Potiorek said. "If a place is the breeding ground of criminals and assassins, there is no option but to bring it to heel."

Franz Ferdinand pressed his hands together as in prayer, "When we arrived here, the reception we received was warm and welcoming, wasn't it?"

Potiorek agreed.

"And you say that the crowd turned on this Cabrinovic and helped the police to apprehend him?"

"That's right, sir," Gerde said.

"So you see," Franz Ferdinand opened his hands like conjurer, "we have already won the support of the majority of the people. The outrage that they feel at this attack might even increase their support for us and, when more concessions are granted to the different regions, there will be no place at all for assassins and radicals. We will achieve far more through cooperation than we can ever achieve by military might and it's important to remember that we cannot blame an entire nation for the madness of one or two hotheads."

"Ah," said Morsey, nodding like a wise old sage, "that explains it."

Franz Ferdinand turned to him quizzically.

"Thirty-odd years ago, the Russian Emperor had freed the serfs and was on the point of granting a constitution which would have reduced his own power in favour of his government and the people. One would think that this would have satisfied the anarchists, who were constantly airing their grievances and plotting all kinds of atrocities in the name of freedom, but it had the opposite effect. Rather than placating the insurgents, it inflamed them because they were afraid that, if people were content with the Tsar's concessions, they would no longer listen to the revolutionaries who wanted to completely overthrow the autocracy."

"So they blew the Tsar to pieces before he could implement the changes," Franz Ferdinand said.

"Yes, sir," said Morsey gravely, "and I hate to be pessimistic but, since your views on granting greater autonomy to this region are quite well-known, the Black Hand must fear you even more than they fear a tyrant."

His eyes met Franz Ferdinand's and were filled with such doom that the Archduke physically trembled. He gripped the edge of the table, determinedly retaining his composure.

"The Serbs are not the only ones who fear my reforms," he mumbled and the faces of the Emperor's ministers drifted through his mind. "The greater the show of public support for Sophie and me, the more they fear me; and the more they fear me, the more they despise me." An even more disconcerting notion began to dawn on him, "And then, of course, there are people for whom the disintegration of Austria-Hungary would be beneficial. They do not want me to implement changes that would create more stability. They want chaos because wherever there is chaos there is the opportunity of seizing power for themselves." He turned urgently to Gerde, "Keep a very close watch on Cabrinovic. *Nothing* must be allowed to happen to him, you understand?"

Gerde nodded.

"Whoever he is, I doubt that he was acting on his own initiative but before we jump to any conclusions about who was behind this, we need to know all the facts. Find out everything you can about his contacts, his background and exactly who provided him with the explosives and cyanide."

Potiorek sniffed, "The interrogation will, of course, be thorough but it's clear that this is the work of Serbian nationalists. Who else but those crazy fanatics would dare to carry out such an attack?"

When Franz Ferdinand didn't answer, Harrach turned to Potiorek, "Under the circumstances, it would be advisable to cancel the rest of the day's engagements so that His Imperial Highness can leave the region as quickly as possible."

"Nonsense!" Potiorek said. "The culprit has been arrested. The danger is passed."

Harrach stared at him, "There could well be others waiting to complete what Cabrinovic began."

"Oh really!" Potiorek snorted. "Do you think Sarajevo is filled with assassins?"

"Who knows? And it isn't a risk we should be prepared to take."

Potiorek sighed deeply and pressed his hand to his brow, "The decision is yours, Your Imperial Highness. Do you wish to continue as planned or should we cancel the rest of the events?"

Franz Ferdinand pushed back his chair and paced back and forth again, weighing the options.

"If something untoward should happen to me here, it could have very serious consequences. Any attempt on my life will be seen as an attack on Austria herself, and regardless of what they think of me, the Emperor and his ministers could not let that go unpunished. My death would provide them with the perfect excuse..." he broke off, imagining Hőtzendorf and the ministers gloating over his coffin.

"The perfect excuse for what, sir?" Morsey frowned.

"The perfect excuse to invade Serbia."

Potiorek's face twisted through a series of emotions, "But, surely..."

"No," Franz Ferdinand interrupted decisively. "Taking everything into account, we would be foolish to remain here. My wife and I will leave as soon as possible but first I have a duty to visit those who were injured. Make the necessary arrangements for me to go to the hospital."

"Yes, of course, sir."

Morsey said, "With all due respect, sir, since their injuries are not serious, wouldn't it be better to leave at once?"

"No," Franz Ferdinand replied. "I will not place myself in a position that could give those warmongers in Vienna the excuse they are looking for, but neither will I neglect my duty to those who were injured on my account. Morsey, find my wife and tell her of this change of plan. Ask her to wait here until I return from the hospital. The rest of you, go and sort out the motor cars and drivers."

Like a small platoon they marched in step towards the door and were about to leave when Franz Ferdinand called to Potiorek,

"Oskar, the driver we had this morning – Leopold Loyka, wasn't it?"

"Yes, sir?"

"His quick reactions saved our lives. Have him drive me to the hospital."

"Very good, sir."

"And see to it that he doesn't take the most obvious route. I am sure there will be no further incidents but, in case there are other would-be assassins waiting to pounce, we don't want to be too predictable."

"We can avoid the main thoroughfares and turn off from the Appel Quay towards Franz Josef Strasse and..."

"Whatever you think is best," Franz Ferdinand waved his hand dismissively.

When they had gone, he sat down and, resting his elbows on the table, joined his hands in prayer. Images formed like photographs on the darkness of his eyelids: the laughing faces of his beautiful children as they ran on the lawns at Artstetten; Sophie, beside him on the balcony, holding the rose he had placed in her hand. In his mind he wandered through the familiar rooms, past the trophies gathered during his travels; along corridors and into sitting rooms where he watched his children practising the piano; his daughter with her pretty ribbons and his sons in their brilliant white sailor suits; down, down he went into the ornate chapel where he saw himself kneeling to thank God for the wisest decision he had ever made: to marry Sophie, who had brought him more joy than he had ever believed possible. With his eyes still closed, he saw himself rise from his knees and move towards the chapel door when he noticed the space he had created four years previously to house his and Sophie's tombs. He opened his eyes and stared at the opposite wall, aware of the dampness of a fearful sweat around his collar...Was he really so close to occupying that space in the Artstetten chapel?

He shook his head and stood up, reassuring himself that such thoughts were only a reaction to the shock of the morning's events but, as he heard the sound of approaching footsteps, a deep unease caused him to pray silently, *"Dear God, take care of my family when I am gone.."*

Sophie stood between Potiorek and Morsey in the doorway and as Franz Ferdinand moved towards her she said quietly, "Fourteen years ago, you sacrificed the support of your family and the goodwill of the Emperor and his court to marry me. You risked everything so as not to abandon me. I have no intention of abandoning you now."

Franz Ferdinand frowned towards Morsey, who shook his head helplessly.

"The Baron told me you wished me to wait here while you visit the hospital."

"It's a precaution, that's all. There's no need to…"

She silenced him with a smile, "Wherever you appear in public today, my place is at your side."

The resolution in her tone and the certainty in her eyes said that, even if he had wanted to, it would have been impossible to dissuade her.

"Very well," he turned to Potiorek, "let's go."

By the time they reached the entrance, the officials and representatives of different Churches, who had been hovering in doorways all morning, had regrouped and formed an unlikely guard of honour down the steps. Franz Ferdinand rested his hand on Sophie's as she clung to her folded parasol and walked with a confident smile towards the waiting phaeton.

"I'll ride on the running board beside you, sir," Harrach announced. "That way I can shield you from any attack."

Franz Ferdinand raised an eyebrow, "I trust that won't be necessary."

When the guests were seated, Potiorek took his place with his back to the engine and signalled to Loyka to pull away. In the wake of the morning's events, the crowd had dwindled but still a rapturous ovation greeted their departure.

"Sophie," Franz Ferdinand whispered ruefully, acknowledging the cheers from the roadside, "I wanted everything to be perfect for you today. I am *so* sorry that it has turned out so badly."

"No," she smiled, "it hasn't. In spite of what happened, we can be grateful that no one was seriously hurt; and what I will remember of today is the warmth of the reception we received. I can't wait to tell the children about it."

He smiled at her fondly and inhaled the scents of the River Miljacka, flowing peacefully through the town. As the phaeton continued along the Appel Quai, his eyes moved beyond Harrach, standing on the running board beside him, to the sunlight glistening like a handful of diamonds scattered on the surface of the water.

It was all so peaceful and so calm that the chaos of the morning seemed to be fading to a distant memory when suddenly Potiorek turned abruptly and shouted to the driver, "Stop! Stop! You're going the wrong way!"

The vehicle slowed down, "This is the route I was given, sir."

Potiorek glanced sheepishly at Franz Ferdinand before replying, "There was a change of plan. You should have been told. Go back towards Franz Josef Strasse."

Without a word, Loyka began to reverse when the sound of two cracks split the air. A thud struck Franz Ferdinand's neck but the pain was so sharp that for a moment he was barely aware of it until he felt the sticky warmth of blood in his mouth. Sophie's ashen face appeared in front of him, her eyes filled with terror, "For heaven's sake, what's happening…"

He could not reply. She sank lower and lower, her head sliding over his chest as she slumped to the floor. A deep red stain spread over the whiteness of her dress and, in his horror, he wanted to hold her, to reach and help her but he could not move.

"Sophie, my little Sophie, don't die…live…you must live for our children…"

He could not say more. He was vaguely aware that the vehicle was now racing through the town, and Harrach had climbed in beside him,

"Are you in a great deal of pain, sir?"

Sophie….Sophie….the children….He could think of nothing else. There was no pain, there was only confusion. It must be a dream, a nightmare…it could not be real.

"It's nothing…It's nothing at all…"

There *was* nothing more: only light, only peace; and Sophie beside him forever.

Chapter 16 – Vienna – 29th June 1914

Every bone in his body ached as Emperor Franz Josef sat as still as a corpse, staring at, but not reading, the mountain of telegrams and reports spread across his desk. In the past twelve hours, hurrying back from his country residence to Vienna, he had helter-skeltered through so many emotions that now he felt as if he had been dragged by wolves across a rugged mountain range. The initial shock had soon surged into anger, which in turn gave way to guilt at the realisation that, were it not for the political repercussions, his nephew's death might be more of a relief than a tragedy. Perhaps, since no earthly power had been able to prevent his wilful flouting of the dynastic laws, God had seen fit to intervene to restore the rightful order. Such thoughts led briefly to resignation – after all, it seemed the lot of the Habsburgs to suffer such violent deaths – but now resignation had sunk into sorrow. Having lived through the murder of his brother and wife and the suicidal madness of his son, he would have thought that one more outrage would barely move him, but somehow the bullet that had killed Franz Ferdinand had also struck his own heart.

Weary and exhausted, he hardly knew what to feel but it seemed that the faces of the four men standing at the opposite side of the desk reflected the conflicting emotions that swirled in a maelstrom through his head.

His eyes moved over each man in turn, alighting first on the face of his Foreign Minister, Count Leopold von Berchtold. The deep frown lines in his forehead and the creases in his lower lids accentuated the earnest intensity of his eyes, giving him the appearance of a lion, calmly alert and ready to pounce on its prey. His expression suggested that he was coolly and carefully calculating the most effective reprisal and required only a word to fire him into swift and decisive action. In his face Franz Josef saw the reflection of his own instinctive reaction to the news: this was not merely an attack on a single archduke; it was an act of defiance aimed at the whole House of Habsburg.

Standing erect beside Berchtold, the military Chief of Staff, Franz Conrad von Hötzendorf, pushed out his chin as though trying to suppress an angry outburst. The thickness of his white moustache could not conceal the snarl of his lips as he strained like an angry bulldog tethered to a leash. Though relatively small in stature, such was the fire in his eyes that Franz Josef was certain that his appetite for battle was so great that he did not really care whom he fought, as long as he was fighting someone to avenge this affront to Austrian pride. The Emperor empathised with his anger and, were it not for his age and experience, he thought he too might be willing to lash out at any perceived enemy who had dared to attack his empire.

In contrast to the belligerent expressions of Berchtold and Hötzendorf, the Chamberlain, Prince Montenuovo, struggled to conceal a smile. Undoubtedly he was aware of Franz Ferdinand's plans to remove him from office at the first opportunity and now he was silently gloating in his enemy's demise. Beneath that smug expression, however, the Emperor detected something more sinister as though he was not only gratified by the Archduke's death but would have willingly congratulated the man who carried out such an atrocity. In spite of his disgust at such a thought, Franz Josef was painfully aware that, deep within his soul, he shared Montenuovo's relief that Franz

Ferdinand, with his unorthodox ideas and morganatic wife, would no longer be such a thorn in his side.

Finally, the Emperor's eyes alighted upon his great-nephew, who was now his heir. Perhaps, at only twenty-seven years old, Archduke Karl retained the sensitivity of youth, or perhaps it was a mark of his noble spirit that, of all the men in the room, he alone demonstrated genuine shock and grief at what had occurred. Although his eyes were fixed on the carpet with a self-abasement which contrasted so sharply with the outspokenness of his late uncle, it was clear from the flush of his cheeks that he had been weeping, and, were his own eyes not so weary, Franz Josef thought he too might have wept not only for Franz Ferdinand but also for all the other terrible tragedies of his reign.

With aching joints, he picked up one of the reports and waved it across the desk, "Well, gentlemen, I suppose you want the details."

None of them replied but Karl looked up from the carpet.

"The assassin – a nineteen-year-old Bosnian Serb named Gavrilo Princip – was seized by the police only seconds after he fired the fatal shots. He attempted to kill himself with the same gun but when the angry crowd wrestled it from him he swallowed a cyanide capsule, which had no effect other than causing him to vomit. So, having failed in his suicide attempts, he is now in custody."

"Only nineteen years old," Karl sighed.

"Obviously," Berchtold replied officiously, "he wasn't acting on his own initiative."

The Emperor shook his head, "It would appear that Cabrinovic, who carried out the earlier attack, and Princip were part of a group who had come to Sarajevo specifically to carry out this murder. General Potiorek and Police Commissioner Gerde are in the process of rounding up several others who were known to be involved."

"In that case," Hőtzendorf snarled, "they should round up the whole of the Serbian government!"

Karl glanced at him, "From what I have read, the Serbs are as horrified as anyone by what has happened. Their government has denounced the Black Hand and declared a state of mourning."

"Words, mere words..." Hőtzendorf grunted. "Our legation in Belgrade has no doubt at all that the Serbs are behind this."

Unwilling to enter into a political dispute, Franz Josef returned to his original report. "The most unfortunate part of it all," he said, "is that when the first attack failed and Franz Ferdinand safely reached the City Hall, Princip had given up hope of carrying out his plan and had decided to return home. He went into a shop and, purely by chance, as he emerged onto the street the Archduke's motor car reversed alongside him."

Karl's eyes widened, *"Reversed* alongside him?"

"There had been a last minute change of plan, apparently, but the driver hadn't been told. It seems he missed a turning and was told to go back, which he did at exactly the same moment as Princip stepped out of the shop. Since he didn't have time to detonate a grenade, the killer pulled out a pistol and fired point blank."

A deeply troubled frown creased Karl's brow, "It seems almost incredible that he should reverse right into the path of the assassin."

Franz Josef nodded, "Had they kept going, Princip would have been too late."

"That wouldn't have made any difference," Hötzendorf boomed. "If this Serb hadn't got him, another one would have."

Karl ran his hand over his brow, "That the motor car should stop *there,* right in front of him…so close that he could see their faces…"

The others looked at him questioningly.

"No matter what hatred possessed him to do such a thing, and no matter how many grievances he believed he had against Austria and poor Uncle Franz, how could he possibly have been so cold-hearted as to murder an innocent woman?"

Montenuovo glared at him, prompting Karl to continue, "If the killer were so close, he must have aimed directly at Sophie, too. Why would he do that? She had no political role; she wasn't even accepted as part of the family…"

"A lady-in-waiting had no right to ride beside him in public anyway," Montenuovo shrugged callously.

Karl winced but Franz Josef, unwilling to either defend or contradict him, shook the report, "Potiorek thinks that Sophie saw the gunman and deliberately placed herself in front of her husband in order to shield him. The other eye-witnesses are not so sure since it all happened so quickly. In any case," he looked again at the paper, "they were not even aware that she was injured at first. When she slipped to the floor of the motor car they thought that she had fainted in shock. It was only later that they realised she had died within seconds of the shooting."

Karl gulped as though swallowing tears, "Their poor, poor children! They meant everything to Uncle Franz and now…"

"And now," Hötzendorf interrupted rudely, "we must exact the severest punishment." He turned to the

Emperor, "How many times have I said that the only way to prevent this kind of violence is an outright invasion of Serbia?"

Berchtold smiled, "Over twenty times in the past six months, I believe."

"And if my advice had been heeded, this could have been avoided. This is nothing less than a declaration of war and now we must retaliate with the utmost severity. One word from you, Your Majesty, and we can mobilise the troops without delay. Seventeen days, that's all it will take to prepare the mobilisation, and another seventeen days to complete it. The Serbs will be crushed in no time."

Karl, in a quiet voice, said, "We cannot punish an entire country for the crimes of one or two men."

Hötzendorf turned and addressed him as though he were a junior officer, "It isn't just one or two. They are *all* behind this. Crush the lot of them, I say. Show no mercy. What mercy did they show the Archduke?"

Karl's innocent eyes were wide with shock and he looked earnestly at the Emperor, "Uncle Franz wasn't killed in Serbia. He was killed in *our* territories and we have no evidence that the Serbian government had any involvement in it."

Hötzendorf was about to reply but Berchtold said calmly, "I understand there has been a strong backlash in Sarajevo. The Bosnians are so appalled by this outrage that they are exacting revenge on all the Serbs in the region. Shops looted, schools destroyed, houses set ablaze…The ferocity of their anger shows the depths of their disgust and they expect us to impose the severest punishment on the perpetrators. There has never been a more opportune moment for us to take decisive action against Serbia. Not only do we have a legitimate reason and public support for an invasion, but we also have a chance to show the world that Austria-Hungary will not tolerate such atrocities."

Hötzendorf strongly agreed, "The Serbs are so lawless and uncivilised that they are incapable of ruling themselves. Look at what they did to their last king and queen – literally butchered and hacked to pieces! Look, too at the crimes they committed in Albania. The only way to bring them to order is a complete occupation of their territories."

Franz Josef's head ached and he suddenly felt very old. Throughout his long reign, his devotion to the empire had been unwavering but now he had neither the stomach for a fight nor the desire to extend his borders. What good would it do to acquire more acres of land and more diverse peoples when there was so much discord and disintegration in the areas he already ruled? Of course, he told himself, he had a duty to his successors and to posterity but, as he glanced towards Karl, he couldn't help thinking that it would be cruel and futile to leave so young and innocent a boy a legacy of even more hostile regions to govern.

On the other hand, Franz Ferdinand's assassination could not go unpunished.

"The way that things are balanced," he eventually said, "it would be unwise to risk incurring the wrath of the other powers for the sake of obscure little Serbia."

Berchtold stepped closer, "All of Europe is shocked by this murder. Britain, Russia and Germany – all have declared a state of mourning. Not only do they understand the legitimacy of our cause, but they *expect* us to exact punishment. No other country would tolerate such a blow to their national pride and if we fail to act now Austria will be viewed with scorn as weak and spineless."

"Be that as it may, unless we have evidence that the Serbian government was behind this plot, we have no legitimate reason to take any action against them. We must give the Serbs an opportunity to show that they neither planned nor condoned this crime."

Hötzendorf huffed impatiently but Franz Josef raised his hand to silence him, "Before we go any further, a thorough investigation must be carried out to discover whether or not their government gave any assistance to these assassins."

Berchtold nodded, "With your permission, sir, I will appoint someone at once to carry out this investigation, and may I suggest that in the meantime, we draw up a series of demands to present to the Serbian government."

"What kind of demands?"

"That they should co-operate fully with our investigations and openly withdraw any support for these nationalist groups."

"Very well."

"And if these demands are not met?" Hötzendorf growled. "Or if this investigation shows that the government was behind this?"

"Then," the Emperor said quietly, "I suppose that at some point war will be inevitable."

Berchtold smiled indulgently, "I will call the council together at once and we will prepare the demands."

Hötzendorf sniffed, "You had better not take too long about it. The time is ripe for action and we don't want to let this opportunity slip through our hands."

"On the contrary," Berchtold smiled, "it could serve our purposes to let the Serbs sweat for a while. While they're wondering what we are going to do, you will have time to muster the troops."

Karl's frown deepened, "You are saying that war is a foregone conclusion?"

"Oh no, sir. If they meet all our demands, everything will be settled diplomatically but, while we wait," he turned to Franz Josef, "it would be advisable to liaise with Berlin to ensure we have German support for whatever action might be necessary."

Franz Josef nodded, "The Kaiser has, of course, been informed of the details and has expressed his deepest sorrow and outrage. As soon as he received our telegram, he cancelled the rest of the events at the Kiel regatta and returned to Berlin so that he could offer us any assistance we need. I think he genuinely cared for the Archduke."

Berchtold raised his eyebrows, "In which case, he will be anxious to have the guilty parties brought to justice."

Franz Josef agreed and signalled that his visitors were dismissed but, as Berchtold and Hötzendorf moved towards the door, Karl lingered by the desk, "Forgive me, Uncle, but isn't there another matter that we need to discuss?"

"Mm?"

"The arrangements for Uncle Franz and Sophie."

"Today they lie in state in Sarajevo and tomorrow their bodies will be brought back to Vienna."

"And when they arrive?"

Montenuovo, who had been on the point of leaving, turned back, "You can leave all that to me, sir. I will make all the necessary preparations."

"I would like to be informed of the arrangements," Karl said. "If there is any part I can play in their funerals, I would be honoured to do so."

Montenuovo smiled sardonically and, after
bowing to the Emperor, strutted from the room. When
he had gone, Karl looked into Franz Josef's eyes.

"Uncle," he said softly, "I am so sorry for what
has happened. After all the tragedies of your reign, this
latest murder must be causing you so much anguish.
Please, be assured that I will do everything in my power
to support you in any way I can."

His voice was so tender and sincere that it
touched Franz Josef deeply. In spite of his aching
bones, he pushed back his chair, moved around the desk
and hugged him warmly.

"God bless you, Karl," he murmured.

Chapter 17 – Vienna – July 2nd 1914

Like a lone sentry in a far-flung outpost of a crumbling empire, Karl stood to attention as the train chugged into the station. Turning neither to the left nor the right, he looked across the platform, half-hoping that even at this late hour other members of the family might appear. He had followed the reports of the coffins' sojourn from Sarajevo to Trieste; he had read of the bare-headed crowds silently lining the route and the officers standing as a guard of honour at each station. Even as the dreadnaught, *Viribus Unitis*, bore their bodies across the Adriatic, Franz Ferdinand and Sophie had been given the dignity of a flotilla; but here in the darkness of Vienna, the capital of the empire to which he was heir, no such honour attended the Archduke's return.

In this time of personal grief and international mourning, Karl could barely fathom the depths of Montenuovo's petty-mindedness. Not only had he succeeded in preventing foreign royalties from attending the funeral but he had even managed to keep the Habsburgs at bay.

"All this," Karl thought, *"for the crime of marrying the woman he loved,"* and, lowering his eyes, he uttered a silent prayer, thanking God that Franz Ferdinand and Sophie could now rest together forever.

When the coffins had been brought from the train, he returned to his motor car and signalled to the driver to follow the hearse on its mournful way. No crowds lined the route, no bowed heads or lowered flags – only the darkness of the sleeping city welcomed Franz Ferdinand home. It wasn't, Karl observed, that the Viennese shared Montenuovo's callousness or the

Habsburgs' resentment but rather that no one had been told that the train would arrive so late in the night. Had Montenuovo had his way, the whole ceremony would have been conducted in private like some shameful family secret. At least, Karl thought, the Emperor had ignored the chamberlain's protestations that a lady-in-waiting had no place in the Royal Chapel, and had insisted that both bodies should lie in state for a few hours before the funeral the following day.

Slowly, slowly the cortege moved through the silent streets and Karl's thoughts drifted back to the moment when he first received news of the murder. Taking a late lunch with Zita in the summer house of his villa at Wartholz, his mind had been far from the events unfolding on the streets of Sarajevo. In the warmth of the June afternoon, amid the scents of roses and the bird song in the trees, the peace of the long summer days seemed set to last forever. The first indication that anything was amiss was the servants' inexplicable delay in serving the next course of the meal. Instead of bringing more plates to the table, they eventually arrived with a telegram from Franz Ferdinand's adjutant, Rumerskirch. Though mildly surprised that Rumerskirch should have any reason to contact him, Karl, relaxing in the beauty of the gardens, was totally unprepared for the news that the telegram contained. When his eyes alighted on those dreadful words, the starkness of the message had struck him so forcefully that for a moment he felt as though he too had been hit by the bullet that killed Uncle Franz.

"How dramatically things can change in so short a time," he murmured as the cortege continued on its weary way. Only four days ago he was enjoying the idyll of a bright summer afternoon yet now that serenity was shattered, Uncle Franz was gone, his children were orphaned, and Karl himself was thrust from relative obscurity to the role of heir apparent.

"Now," he thought, "more than ever, Uncle Franz Josef will need my support..." and his thoughts moved on to the gathering in the Emperor's study three days earlier. He saw again Hötzendorf's aggressive expression and the intransigence in Berchtold's eyes, and it occurred to him that, no matter how the Serbs responded to their demands, these men – and many others besides – were intent on using this murder as an excuse for an invasion. How ironic it was that these people, who had viewed Uncle Franz with antipathy, were now filled with such self-righteous indignation that they would willingly use his death as justification for a war!

The sombre procession eventually came to a halt at the Hofburg Palace and, as the pallbearers carried the coffins towards the chapel, Karl lingered in the courtyard and looked up at the stars. It seemed so short a time since he and Uncle Franz had escaped from the ball and stood on this same spot, their breath mingling and hanging in clouds on the icy air. Now, in spite of the warmth of the summer night, a chill ran down his spine and, as clearly as if the Archduke were still there beside him, Karl heard again the words he had spoken:

"...if it were possible to remove the Crown Prince who was popular and loved by the people, wouldn't it be convenient to remove an unpopular archduke whom few outside his immediate family would mourn?"

An alarming image of the murder caused Karl's muscles to stiffen as a series of vague suspicions, which had been swirling like flies through his head, merged together into one coherent idea – an idea too repugnant to contemplate.

In the four days since the murder, as more details had come to light, numerous questions had haunted him: why was the visit arranged for a national holiday – a day of such sensitive significance to the Serbs? Why was the route lined so sparsely with policemen and no military protection whatsoever; and why, following the first attack, was Uncle Franz driven in an open car towards the hospital? Why was the driver not informed of the change of route? And wasn't it convenient that he was told to reverse straight into the path of the killer?

Karl pressed his head to the cold stone wall of the Hofburg, which, from the few remains of the original medieval building to the magnificent baroque grandeur of the eighteenth century, read like a history book of Habsburg rule.

"In the past, I believed that kings and emperors made all the decisions for their people." Uncle Franz had said, *"Now, though, I see it very differently...Even in an autocracy like Austria-Hungary, so much goes on behind the scenes where ministers and politicians plot and intrigue among themselves. They see their monarchs as little more than puppets..."*

Could it be that when these people realised that they could never use Uncle Franz as their puppet, they had found a way to remove him, just as Rudolf had been removed?

He shook his head and tried to reassure himself that such notions were the result of grief and confusion but Franz Ferdinand's words rang even more loudly through his ears:

"Wouldn't it be so much easier, if I were out of the way?...To them, the reign of Emperor Franz Ferdinand would be a disaster. Life would be so much better for them without me."

Approaching footsteps brought temporary relief from his torment and he looked up to see Montenuovo mincing from the entrance with such a spring in his step he might have been dancing.

"Everything is in place, sir, if you would care to come inside."

Karl followed him into the dimly lit Gothic chapel where the air was heavy with incense, beeswax and candles. Reverently he moved towards the catafalque where his uncle's ornate coffin rested, surrounded by the symbols of his estate: his military sword and badges of office, his helmet and Imperial Orders. Karl closed his eyes and, kneeling, murmured the prayers for the dead:

"*Subvenite, Sancti Dei, occurrite Angeli Domini.*

Suscipientes animam ejus. Offerentes eam in conspectu,

Altissimi."•

He blessed himself and stood up, preparing to repeat the same prayer for Sophie when, to his horror, he realised the depths of Montenuovo's malice. Almost two feet lower than her husband's coffin, Sophie's was barely visible and, despite the fact that she had been raised to the rank of Highness, the only decorations were her fan and gloves – the symbols of a lady-in-waiting.

Karl's eyes met Montenuovo's, "You would humiliate her even now?"

The prince blinked in response.

"The lowliest peasant in Austria," Karl whispered, "is accorded dignity in death and people

---

• "Come to his assistance, ye saints of God; come forth to meet him, ye angels of the Lord, receiving his soul. Offering it in the sight of the Most High…"

honour his last wishes. Doesn't it occur to you to think of what the Archduke would have wanted?"

"Yes, sir," Montenuovo replied brightly. "His Imperial Highness requested that he and his wife be interred side by side in his castle at Artstetten. We are allowing him that."

"*Allowing* him?" Karl stared, outraged by his arrogance, but before he could say more his eyes alighted on the tabernacle lamp and he could not permit himself to vent his anger in the house of God. He looked again at Sophie's coffin and said calmly, "How will the children feel when they see how their mother is treated? Haven't they suffered enough already?"

"Don't concern yourself with that, sir. The children won't see this. Their mother's family is taking care of them and they won't be attending the funeral. All the places here are reserved for those of royal blood or specific positions in the government, and, of course, foreign ambassadors."

Karl shook his head sadly and looked down at Sophie's face, so white and calm in her coffin.

"I will see that your children are well cared for," he promised and, dropping to his knees, closed his eyes and repeated the prayer.

The following afternoon as Montenuovo unceremoniously hurried the congregation from the chapel, Karl stood before the altar, scarcely able to believe the speed with which the Cardinal Archbishop of Vienna had raced through the funeral rite. Until now, every requiem that he had attended – including that of his father, whose life had been less than exemplary – had been lengthy and reverent ceremonies but for Uncle Franz and Sophie, Cardinal Piffl had barely set foot on the sanctuary steps before he was sprinkling the catafalques with holy water and muttering inaudibly the final words of the rite:

"*In Paradisum deducant te Angeli, in tuo adventu suscipiant te martyres et perducant te in Civitatem Sanctam Jerusalem...*"

Taking one last glance at the coffins, Karl genuflected before the tabernacle and fervently repeated the prayer: "*May the angels lead thee into Paradise; at thy coming may the martyrs receive thee and lead thee to the Holy City, Jerusalem...*"

Less than half an hour after the service had begun, he stepped from the chapel and heard Montenuovo firmly bolt the door behind him. It was customary on such occasions for the congregation to gather for a banquet but, since no foreign princes or monarchs had been permitted to attend, and the ambassadors who had been sent in their place were eager to return to their embassies, the day fizzled away as though nothing out of the ordinary had happened.

The Emperor appeared too tired and weary for company and so, having offered a few sympathetic words, Karl excused himself and walked pensively through the many courtyards of the Hofburg. With every step the only memorable lines from the service sounded through his ears:

"*Dies irae, dies illa, solvet saeclum in favilla...*"

"Day of wrath, that dreadful day, the whole world shall lie in ashes..." he whispered, when suddenly the sound of raised voices echoed from the Medieval Gate where three men stood talking loudly.

Striding in their direction, Karl immediately recognised them as the Czech Princes Kinsky, Schwarzenberg and Lobkowitz, who had knelt reverently in the chapel and seemed genuinely saddened by the deaths. Seeing him approach they turned in unison and, though their greeting was polite, there was an obvious hostility etched into their faces.

"Gentlemen, it is a sad day…" Karl began in a conciliatory tone but rather than placating them his words provoked anger.

Prince Kinsky was the first to speak, "A sad day and a thoroughly shameful one!"

"Shameful?" Karl said, uncertain of his meaning.

"Had I not seen this for myself, I would never have believed it."

"Montenuovo," Prince Lobkowitz said, "should be publicly humiliated and dismissed at once for such an affront. How dare so vile and insignificant a creature dishonour the Archduke and his wife in this way!"

Though his own feelings were slightly less vehement, Karl immediately warmed to these men who shared his disgust at the treatment of Sophie and Franz Ferdinand.

"It *is* a great insult to my uncle's memory…" he began but Prince Kinsky interrupted,

"If I were in the Emperor's position I would have Montenuovo flogged for this."

Lobkowitz agreed, "As if it were not enough that they treated Her Highness so atrociously in her lifetime, they now go out of their way to abuse her in death."

"And as for that excuse for a requiem…" Kinsky said so angrily that he could barely blurt out his words and looked to Schwarzenberg to speak for him.

"Who told the Cardinal to rush through the service and why were there so few mourners? We know that many foreign royalties wished to attend but they were not allowed to do so. King Carol of Roumania was actually turned back at the border!"

Appalled by this information, Karl shook his head, "I had no idea."

Kinsky, regaining his composure, said, "Even our own people were turned away. Crowds had gathered to file past the coffins. Many had patiently waited in line since dawn, and others had made the effort to travel from different parts of the empire but almost four hours before the service began Montenuovo had the doors locked and refused them entry."

"It would be understandable," Schwarzenberg said, "if the public were to be given another opportunity of paying their respects but we have just been told that there will be no formal procession to the station. The bodies are to be shipped away in the night like a pair of executed criminals."

"At least," Kinsky said bitterly, "when they reach Artstetten they will be given the honour they deserve. I thank God that the Archduke had the foresight to make provision for himself and Her Highness in Bohemia where they have always been shown the respect and affection that was so sorely denied them in Vienna."

Karl stared down at the ground and said quietly, "I know it is small consolation but I agree with everything you have said. I was very fond of my uncle and I know that all of this has been conducted in a shameful manner. The Emperor, however, is not to blame. He…"

"The Emperor *allowed* this to happen," Kinsky said. "It is common knowledge that he intensely disliked Archduke Franz Ferdinand and I dare say that he is more than relieved by this turn of events."

"No!" Karl protested loyally. "It's true that they disagreed about many things but the Emperor is truly horrified and saddened by what has happened."

Kinsky shook his head scornfully and opened his mouth to say more but Schwarzenberg urgently intervened as though fearful of what his companion had been about to say.

"You must understand, Your Imperial Highness, that the Archduke was the only member of your family who truly understood and respected the Bohemian people. As in so many other parts of this empire, there is a feeling among the Czechs that we are issued with orders from Vienna by people who have no understanding of our culture and our way of life. Archduke Franz Ferdinand was different and, of course, his wife was one of our own people. The Choteks might be sneered at here, but in Bohemia they are a highly respected family."

Lobkowitz nodded, "Unlike the ministers or even the Emperor – to whom, I assure you, we remain devoted – the Archduke listened to us. We even hoped that when he eventually succeeded to the throne he might restore the Kingdom of Bohemia as an autonomous region within the empire in much the same way as the Kingdom of Bavaria is both autonomous and part of the German Empire."

Karl nodded thoughtfully and wondered whether it would be imprudent to suggest that, like Uncle Franz, he recognised the need for greater freedom and self-government in the various provinces.

Schwarzenberg, seeming to read his thoughts, said, "Of course, this is not an appropriate time to discuss your future plans but, as you are now heir, perhaps you will consider what we have said and honour the Archduke's memory by implementing some of his ideas."

"Uncle Franz had many plans for reform. He was well-travelled and well-read and, though as yet I lack his wisdom and experience, I hope that one day I will be able to combine our great traditions with some of his more progressive ideas."

"Then I suggest," said Kinsky, "that you keep your views to yourself until you are in a position to execute them."

Karl, disturbed by his ominous tone, ran his foot over the cobbles, inadvertently kicking a stone that flew across the courtyard and ricocheted on the opposite wall.

Schwarzenberg moved closer, "The details of exactly what happened in Sarajevo remain unclear. Perhaps you could elucidate?"

Karl opened his hands helplessly, "The killer, Gavrilo Princip, was a nineteen-year-old Bosnian who believed that by assassinating Uncle Franz he would further the cause of a South Slav Kingdom. Princip wasn't working alone. There were several would-be assassins in the street that day..."

"We have read all of this in the newspapers but it makes so little sense," Kinsky said impatiently. "Doesn't it strike you as odd that a group that is allegedly comprised of Serbian officers, ministers and lawyers should choose a set of incompetent kids to carry out such an attack?"

"I suppose," Karl said, "young men like Princip are malleable. It is easy to train them into believing their actions are justified, and their leaders view them as dispensable."

Kinsky's eyes narrowed, "Imagine if we were planning the assassination of someone as important as the heir to an empire. Whom would we choose to carry it out – a tubercular boy who, from all accounts, hadn't even held a gun until a few months ago, or a skilled marksman with experience of weapons?"

Karl shook his head, "What are you suggesting?"

"Is there any proof that this boy was acting on behalf of the Black Hand?"

"The Emperor has ordered a thorough investigation so we must wait for its findings."

Kinsky threw back his head, "The investigators will find whatever they are told to find, which undoubtedly means they will implicate the Serbian government in the murders."

Karl glanced warily across the courtyard.

"You are aware, I suppose," Shwarzenberg said, lowering his voice to a whisper, "that the Serbian Prime Minister, Pasic, warned our ambassador in Belgrade that a plot was afoot and the Archduke's life would be in danger if he travelled to Sarajevo?"

Karl, increasingly unnerved, shook his head.

"Pasic had received word that these assassins were planning to disrupt the visit and he gave orders that they were to be arrested at the border."

"*And,*" Lobkowitz said, "three days before the Archduke left Vienna, the Serbian envoy gave Bilinski, the Civil Governor of Bosnia-Herzegovina, the same warning but in every case these warning were ignored."

"*Why?*" Karl frowned.

"Why indeed?" Kinsky looked up at the sky. "One thing is certain, there are several men within our own empire and even more international intriguers who had far more to gain from His Imperial Highness' death than the Serbs had. When did the Archduke receive his invitation to Sarajevo?"

Karl shrugged, "I don't know. A few months ago, I would imagine."

"Around the time of the Emperor's illness, perhaps?"

"Perhaps."

"The thought that the Emperor might die must have triggered a great deal of fear in certain circles.

Everyone knew that the Archduke had already prepared lists of the ministers whom he would remove from office; and everyone knew, too, that he had no intention of supporting an invasion of Serbia."

"There is no proof," Schwarzenberg said, "that these boys were linked to the Black Hand. Even if they were duped into believing that they were acting on behalf of that group, who is to say that that was actually the case?"

Karl's stomach churned, "You are saying that his murder was planned by ..."

"No," Schwarzenberg interrupted, "we are accusing no one. We are merely making observations."

Lobkowitz nodded, "Who knows what goes on in the shady world of spies and agent provocateurs?"

"You must admit," Kinsky said, looking directly at Karl, "that the timing and manner of His Imperial Highness's death couldn't have worked out better for many of those ministers in Vienna if they had planned the whole thing themselves. Now, they can remain secure in their positions of power; and this very public killing has provided them with the perfect excuse they were seeking to invade Serbia."

Again Karl remembered Franz Ferdinand's words on the evening of the ball: *"...What frightens me, Karl, is the thought that these people would willingly manipulate us into a situation where war becomes inevitable. To all intents and purposes, it will be seen as an imperial war fought by kings but in fact the whole tragedy will have been engineered by ministers and generals who will then use the ensuing chaos to set themselves up in our place."*

"And," Kinsky said, "they must be rejoicing that they are not only rid of the Archduke, but also his wife whom they all treated so appallingly."

"Isn't it strange," Schwarzenberg nodded, "that Princip was as close to Her Highness as I am to you, yet he claims that he killed her by accident?"

Karl stared at the ground, weighed down by so many conflicting thoughts and emotions that for several minutes he could not speak and when he eventually did so, his voice trembled, "What do you want me to do?"

"Nothing," Kinsky said. "There is nothing to be done. The investigation will produce its report, and history will record these events accordingly but, with all due respect, Your Imperial Highness, be aware that very few world events are ever quite as simple as they are presented for posterity."

"Indeed," said Lobkowitz. "Documents disappear, investigations run into insurmountable obstacles, and the truth is lost in the fairy tales that are told to keep the public happy. It is so often the case that beneath these stories, there are layers upon layers of artifice, and even when we have a glimpse of the truth and the immediate culprits are unmasked, there are many more who lurk in the shadows and whose guilt is never uncovered."

Karl nodded sadly. Just as the news of the murder had shattered the beauty of a summer afternoon, so, too, had Uncle Franz death wrecked the idyll of the age of innocence.

"Whether or not we will ever know the truth of what happened in Sarajevo, there *is* something we can do now to honour Uncle Franz and Sophie."

The three princes looked at him with interest.

"There are still crowds outside who would like to pay their respects as the bodies are taken to the station."

"Police cordons have been set up to keep the people away."

"The police will give way to the new heir apparent. Gentlemen, perhaps you will join me in leading the crowds in procession so that we can at least mark the Archduke's departure from Vienna in a manner that's honourable and fitting."

Chapter 18 – Potsdam, Germany – July 5th 1914

Papers floated to the floor like snowflakes as Kaiser Wilhelm flung a fistful of telegrams across the study. He flounced back and forth, irked by the failure of his Chancellor, Bethmann-Hollweg, to share his rage with sufficient vehemence.

"It is *not* within the remit of an ambassador to interfere in the decisions of foreign governments! The role of our ambassador in Vienna is to make representation on my behalf and to keep me informed of developments. Isn't that so?"

"Yes, Your Imperial Majesty."

"Well then," he snatched one of the telegrams and shook it violently, "by what authority is Tcshirschky attempting to dissuade the Austrians from taking immediate and forceful action against these murderous Serbs?"

Bethmann pressed his hands together, "As I understand it, sir, the ambassador *is* urging the Austrians to take action but to avoid acting too hastily or impulsively without considering the consequences."

"It is not Tcshirschky's business!" Wilhelm yelled so loudly that the Chancellor flinched. "It is imperative that the Austrians *do* act swiftly and decisively. They have been far too patient for far too long and unless they act now the Serbs will go from strength to strength and no one will be able to contain them."

"With all due respect, sir, the Austrians' caution is understandable. When a man has been affronted it is only natural that he should react in the heat of the moment but this can lead him into situations he might later regret. The same is surely true of nations."

Wilhelm, astonished by his calmness, stared at him aghast before strutting across the room and tugging sharply at his beard. "*That,* Theo, is an affront and, in this case you would do well not to react hastily since I am your Kaiser and Emperor."

Berchtold, without blinking, ran his hand over his chin with a confused and somewhat indulgent expression which greatly annoyed Wilhelm.

"There is an enormous difference between an affront and an outrage and we are not talking of an affront! We are talking about the cold-blooded murder of the heir to the Austrian throne! And, as for the heat of the moment, let me remind you that it is now over a week since this atrocity took place and still there has been no visible response from Austria."

The Chancellor looked down subserviently, "I believe, sir, that this is partly due to divisions within the Austro-Hungarian Empire. In Vienna they are crying out for military action but Tisza, the Hungarian Prime Minister, is urging restraint, not least because he fears that an invasion of Serbia will be met with strong resistance from Russia and her allies."

"Excuses, excuses! The Tsar has far too much to concern him at home. Half his country is on strike, for heaven's sake! He wouldn't be willing to risk all-out war for the sake of those Serbian Philistines."

Bethmann nodded but appeared unconvinced.

"Trust me," Wilhelm said more calmly, "I *know* the Tsar. The last thing he wants is to become involved in what is essentially a private matter between Austria-Hungary and Serbia."

"And yet *we* are involved."

The hint of dissention in Bethmann's voice re-ignited Wilhelm's anger. He slammed his fist against the desk, "It is vital to our interests that Austria appears strong. If the rest of Europe believes we've allied ourselves to a weakling, it undermines our own prestige and endangers the security of the German Empire. Don't you understand, Theo? Ever since the days of my uncle, King Edward VII, the British have been weaving plots and forming alliances with our neighbours to encircle us and leave us isolated? That is why our alliance with Austria is so vital and why we must show the world that any attack against our allies is seen as an attack against us and will be sternly dealt with. It is the only way to maintain peace and the balance of power."

Bethmann frowned, "It would be a disaster if Britain were to become involved in this."

As quickly as Wilhelm's temper had ignited, it cooled again. "No, no, no," he said, revelling in his own ready grasp of affairs, "This has nothing to do with Britain. My brother is on holiday in England and he has confirmed that King George is appalled by the murder of the Archduke. Britain has no intention of meddling in what goes on in the Balkans."

Balkans - as soon as he spoke the word, a shiver of anxiety ran down his spine and he recalled the warning of the wise old Chancellor Bismarck, whose views had dominated his childhood and youth: '*If there is ever another war in Europe, it will come out of some damned silly thing in the Balkans...*'

For a second, doubting his own understanding, he wished Bismarck were still alive and present to offer advice and reassurance.

"Of course," he said, "I am not advocating an immediate invasion or anything of the sort. I am sure there are other ways to teach Serbia a lesson but something has to be done and it has to be done quickly."

To his relief, the door opened and an officer announced, "His Excellency, Ambassador Szogyeny-Marich and Count von Hoyos of the Austrian Foreign Ministry."

Wilhelm turned to Bethmann, "Now we can find out exactly what is happening and make our position clear."

A moment later, the aged Austrian ambassador entered the study accompanied by a dapper man with a narrow moustache and curiously gloomy eyes. The latter marched determinedly towards Wilhelm and, after the usual salutations, handed him a letter.

"His Imperial and Apostolic Majesty, Emperor Franz Josef asked me to give this to you in person," he said with a bow.

"The death of his nephew must have come as a terrible shock to the Emperor," Wilhelm said, reaching for a letter-opener. "How is he?"

"Saddened and disgusted, sir."

"As indeed we all are. Archduke Franz Ferdinand and his wife were close personal friends of mine. I trust that the Emperor intends to deal with their murderers with the maximum severity."

Hoyos nodded, "Many Serbs have been rounded up in Sarajevo and six of the suspected seven conspirators have been arrested already."

"Then I hope you will make an example of them to show the world that we do not tolerate the murder of kings and princes."

"Unfortunately, sir, most of them are too young to incur the death penalty."

"If they are old enough to commit murder, they are old enough to take the consequences." Wilhelm pulled the letter from the envelope, "Obviously, they were acting on orders from some higher authority."

"Oh yes, sir. There's no doubt that political and military figures in Belgrade put them up to it. How else did they obtain their weapons and the cyanide capsules they were carrying in case of arrest? That is why it is imperative that we strike a blow at the Serbs, isolating them from their allies and denying them any opportunity of carrying out further attacks. The sooner we act the better."

After a cursory glance, Wilhelm held up the letter, "It seems that Emperor Franz Josef is not convinced that military action is the ideal solution."

Hoyos, taken aback, looked to Szogyeny, who hesitated before replying, "I believe, sir, that the Emperor is very much in favour of firm action but he wishes to be sure of your support."

"Of course, he has my support," Wilhelm said, wounded that he should doubt it. "I do not make alliances only to break them in a time of crisis."

"No, sir. I'm not suggesting that…"

As the older man stuttered to find an excuse, Hoyos interrupted, "The truth is, sir, we wish to know where we stand if Russia decides to intervene."

Wilhelm, laughing, turned to Bethmann, "What *is* this obsession with Russian intervention? Russia, like the rest of the world, is disgusted by this crime. Didn't the Tsar order an extended period of mourning for the Archduke?"

"Yes, sir – twelve or fourteen days, I believe."

"Well then, that proves where Russian sympathies lie."

Hoyos pressed a finger to the corner of his droopy eye, "The problem is that we are receiving conflicting reports. Tsar Nicholas has condemned the murders but at the same time Hartwig is vociferously assuring the Serbs that Russia will protect them in the event of reprisals from Vienna."

"Hartwig?" Wilhelm's nose wrinkled at the unfamiliar name.

"Nicholas Hartwig, the Russian ambassador to Serbia. He is an ardent Pan-Slavist whose makes no secret of his pro-Serbian sympathies or his mistrust of Austria. Some years ago he ingratiated himself with the royal family in Belgrade by facilitating a marriage between the Tsar's cousin and the Serbian king's daughter."

Wilhelm nodded, vaguely recalling the event.

"Since then, Hartwig has developed one of the most complex networks of spies in the region and is so popular among the Slavs that they jokingly call him the King of the Balkans."

Wilhelm dismissed the epithet with a wave of his hand, "A large fish in a small pond, nothing more."

"Quite so, sir, but his assurances of Russian support are increasing the Serbs' confidence and making them less compliant. The Serbs need to fear us again or our borders will never be safe and our provinces will always be open to attack. Unfortunately, while Hartwig convinces them that Russia is their protector, they think they have nothing to fear from us no matter what crimes they commit."

"We can soon put a stop to his antics," Wilhelm smiled. "Once it is known that Austria has the full support of the German Emperor there will be no more mention of Russian involvement. Trust me, gentlemen, the Tsar is not prepared for war and so this *Hartwig's* promises are all bluster."

Hoyos beamed with satisfaction spurring Wilhelm to reiterate his support.

"Bethmann, have a telegram sent at once to Vienna. Inform His Imperial Majesty that Germany will support any action he deems necessary. Let him know, too, that we expect Austria to find a suitable means of avenging this heinous crime with the utmost urgency."

Bethmann blinked in shock but before he could speak, Hoyos said, "We are drawing up a series of demands that we intend to present to Serbia."

"I see," Wilhelm nodded, not seeing at all.

"Emperor Franz Josef and certain Hungarian politicians felt it was necessary to give the Serbs the opportunity of showing remorse for their actions."

"Remorse? What good is that if they are free to repeat their crimes and continue to cause unrest?"

"Our demands will be...shall we say, *extreme.*"

"How extreme?" Wilhelm frowned.

"Extreme enough to ensure that they will never again be in a position to carry out such atrocities."

"Excellent. The world must realise that no civilized country will stand idly by while Serbia remains a breeding ground for assassins."

Bethmann hummed to himself before asking, "Forgive me, but is there any definite evidence that the Serbs were responsible for the Archduke's murder?"

"Oh yes, there is plenty of evidence," Hoyos said without being drawn into specifics.

"In which case, could you give us details of that evidence, or even an idea of the demands that you intend impose on them?"

Hoyos' lips twitched, "The precise wording hasn't yet been decided but I can assure you that the demands will be harsh and unambiguous, leaving the Serbs in no doubt at all as to our intentions."

Bethmann smiled insincerely, "Perhaps I am being a little slow here, but what exactly *are* your intentions?"

Wilhelm, irritated by his questions, shook his head as though the Chancellor were an imbecile, "I would have thought that was obvious! The Serbs must make reparation for these murders."

Hoyos nodded, "But we must go further. The Archduke's assassination is not an isolated incident. It is merely the most prominent example of the Serbs' determination to take complete control of the Balkans. If their ambition is allowed to continue unchecked, there will be further outrages and it is only a matter of time before they become too powerful to contain. Already, Your Imperial Majesty, we are in a vulnerable position with Russia to the east and Britain and France to the west. If we allow the Serbs to continue to gain strength we could find ourselves susceptible to attack from the south as well."

"Encirclement," Wilhelm murmured.

"Yes indeed, sir."

"That cannot be allowed to happen," Wilhelm sat down and, taking a cigarette from a case, tapped it against his desk. "It would be in everyone's best interest to draw up your demands and deliver them as soon as possible, while the memory of the Archduke's murder is still fresh in people's minds."

Szogyeny, who until now had said very little, moved closer to the desk, "Actually, sir, since the French President is visiting Russia this month we thought it better to wait until he has returned home so that this matter doesn't arise in the discussions between the President and the Tsar."

Wilhelm nodded. "This is a private matter between Austria and Serbia. There is no reason for anyone else to discuss it."

"Of course, you are right, sir," Szogyeny said, "but, at the same time, we feel it would be beneficial to garner as much support as possible from the other Balkan states and so it might prove useful to approach

King Ferdinand of Bulgaria with a view to forming an alliance."

"With Bulgaria?" Wilhelm laughed at his mental image of the portly king. "What would be the point in that? The country is still reeling from the effects of the last Balkan War, but," he shrugged and, pushing back his chair, stood up, "you must do as you see fit. Now, gentlemen, I would appreciate it if you would inform Vienna at once that I will support any action you choose to take and then, perhaps you might care to join me for lunch."

They muttered their thanks and he strutted towards the door, "And make sure you also convey my sincerest condolences to the Emperor on the death of his nephew."

"Of course, sir."

As they bowed in unison, a vivid memory of his visit to Konopischt floated into Wilhelm's mind.

The recollection of the children's laughter, Sophie's smiles and Franz Ferdinand's gentle attention to his roses, almost brought tears to his eyes and suddenly the political and international implications seemed as nothing compared to the unexpected and quite overwhelming grief he felt at the thought of the tragedy that had befallen so loving a family.

When he spoke, his voice no longer came out in the decisive tone of a powerful emperor, but rather in that of a wounded child, deprived of a dearest friend, "I would have liked to have attended the funeral. I was very fond of Franz Ferdinand and Sophie and it would have meant a lot to me to have been able to honour their memory."

Szogyeny looked down at his feet and Hoyos bit his lip awkwardly.

"From what I have been told, the service was hardly befitting of the heir to the throne. Is it true that, had it not been for the intervention of Archduke Karl and several Czech princes, there would have been no public procession at all?"

Hoyos made several incomprehensible sounds as he struggled for an excuse, "Considering the circumstances of the Archduke's death, we were anxious not to endanger any more lives. For that reason it was deemed wisest to keep the public as far away as possible and to advise all foreign royalties to stay away."

"That was not the reason I was given," Wilhelm frowned. "I was told that in view of the Emperor's poor health, it was to be a quiet ceremony. Had I known it was a matter of my personal safety, I would have been prepared to take that risk for my friend. You see, Count, Germany stands by her friends at any cost."

Hoyos squirmed before replying, "I am sure that such sentiments from the All-Highest Kaiser will bring great comfort to Emperor Franz Josef in his dreadful loss."

Wilhelm dismissed the visitors and, when they had gone, he stood for some seconds shaking away the memories of Konopischt before turning to Bethmann.

"There now. That was easily arranged. If our ambassador in Vienna had expressed my orders instead of his own opinions, all this would have been sorted out days ago."

Bethmann smiled, "And now that it is sorted out, sir, you can enjoy your cruise."

Wilhelm pulled out a chair and sat down again at his desk, "Under the circumstances, it might be better to cancel that trip in case of any further developments."

"Oh no, sir, no," Bethmann said with gusto, "there's really no need to do that. Jagow is leaving today for his honeymoon so, if the Foreign Minister is entitled to take a break, surely the Emperor is, too?

After all the upheavals of recent weeks, you, sir, more than anyone deserve a holiday."

Wilhelm eyed him with suspicion, "If I didn't know better, Theo, I would think you were trying to get me out of the way."

Bethmann's excessive denials increased rather than alleviated his suspicions.

"No," he decided. "I shall stay here until this blows over. The cruise can be postponed until the Serbs have sent their response."

"But, sir," Bethmann said, "if you cancel your holiday now it could create the impression that we are anticipating a conflict, whereas, if you continue as planned, the rest of Europe will see that everything has been settled decisively and satisfactorily."

"Hmm," Wilhelm mused, tempted by the thought of the freedom of the ocean and the blue skies over Norway. "Everything *has* been settled satisfactorily, hasn't it?"

"Yes, of course, sir. You have honoured your agreement with Austria; Emperor Franz Josef will be grateful for your support; and by your wisdom and perspicacity you have averted what could have been a serious international crisis. Now you can enjoy your holiday, knowing that you have left everything in good order."

He leaned back in his chair and lit the cigarette. "Can I be sure that no one will do anything rash during my absence?"

"There is nothing more to be done. The Serbs will comply with the demands and by the time you return from Norway everything will have been settled."

"Very well," he exhaled the smoke slowly. "Even emperors deserve a holiday and if I cannot trust my ministers to keep everything in order while I'm away, whom can I trust?"

Bethmann smiled serenely, "Quite so, sir."

Wilhelm leaned further back in his chair and resting his feet on his desk imagined inhaling the fresh air of the fjords and the feel of the cool sea breezes blowing over his face.

Chapter 19 – Vienna – July 9th 1914

With a swing of his cane and a swagger in his step, Count Leopold von Berchtold strolled towards the Reichsratsgebäude, home of the Imperial Council. The waters of the Pallas Athena Fountain glistened like stars in the sunlight and, as Berchtold looked up at the imposing statue of the Goddess of Wisdom, he rejoiced in his good fortune at having been born in Vienna. Seat of splendour and pageantry; home of the Spanish Riding School and the world-renowned Hofkapelle; centre of mathematics, physics, and the new science of psychology – was there a city in the whole of Europe more cultured and beautiful than Vienna? It was of no small significance, he thought, that this was also the birthplace of Strauss and Schubert. Music seeped through the streets, from the booming bells of St. Stephen's Cathedral to the swish of the rivers and the trickling of fountains. On days like this even the most serious politician felt inclined to dance.

It might have appeared in recent years that Austria was steadily sliding into decline and these brilliant buildings, no less than the Schönbrunn and Hofburg, were merely 'whited sepulchres concealing dead men's bones and corruption' and yet this morning it seemed to Berchtold that Franz Ferdinand's death had signified a halt to that decline and had breathed new life into the empire. Now, free of the prospect of being ruled by that hot-tempered pessimist with his unsuitable wife and unsociable manner, there was an opportunity for men of ability to shape a glorious future for Austria-Hungary.

Better yet, since the aged Emperor was long past his prime and the new heir was but an inexperienced boy, there had never been so ideal a time to wrestle power from the grasp of the Habsburgs and hand it over to their ministers. Of course, there must always be Emperors – like the ornate palaces and ancient cathedrals, they were a necessary part of the pomp and spectacle of Vienna – and these Emperors, like the majority of their subjects, must continue to believe that their word was law, since autocracy was integral to the empire. In truth, though, in this modern age, the birth-right to power was an anachronism and it fell to men of learning and ambition to take control of affairs.

Tipping his hat to a passing group of ladies, Berchtold smiled. Not only had he had the good fortune to be born Viennese, but his life had been blessed in so many other ways, too. The great wealth of his family had enabled him to benefit from an excellent education, which had undoubtedly provided opportunities for his entry into the political sphere, but it was thanks to his own innate talents and charm that he had risen so quickly to the heights of his career. At first his appointment as Imperial Foreign Minister had filled him with dread as his inexperience and relative youth had caused him to doubt his ability to deal with so many complex issues. In the midst of the Balkan Wars he had even been accused of indecision and vacillation and, looking back now, he had to accept that the charge was probably justified. Since then, though, he had become more secure in his post and his confidence had reached such heights that he knew that in this present crisis there would be no doubt or hesitation. He would act resolutely. His mind was made up: Conrad von Hötzendorf would have his Serbian war.

On cue, his eyes alighted on the striking features of the Commander-in-Chief, standing in front of the fountain with Major General Alexander von Krobatin, the Imperial Minister for War. Berchtold quickened his pace and, swinging his cane towards the statue of Athena, smiled brightly, "Behold, the Goddess of Wisdom presiding over our proceedings on this this glorious morning!"

Hőtzendorf glanced at the statue, "It's significant that she wears armour and carries a spear."

"Indeed she does," Berchtold nodded, "and, if you look at her right hand, you will observe that she also carries Nike – the Goddess of Victory."

Krobatin, with even greater urgency than Hőtzendorf, turned towards the entrance of the Reichsratsgebäude, "So how are we to proceed?"

"All in good time," Berchtold smiled, leisurely dipping his hand into the trickling waters of the fountain. "We don't want to create the impression that anything is amiss. In fact, gentlemen," he nodded pointedly to the array of medals decorating Hőtzendorf's uniform, "I was thinking that it might be a good idea if you were both to take your summer vacations."

Hőtzendorf and Krobatin stared at one another in confusion.

"The Emperor is away at Bad Ischl; the Kaiser has embarked on a North Sea cruise; and I dare say that as soon as the French President leaves Russia, the Tsar will retire to one of his summer estates. Why don't you follow their example and take a holiday? The Tyrol is beautiful at this time of year and the mountain air would do you a world of good."

Hőtzendorf's face creased into a fiery frown and he was about to speak when Berchtold moved closer and said quietly, "Don't you understand? In order to ensure that our plans are carried out smoothly, it's vital that we give the impression that nothing out of the ordinary is happening. If military leaders are seen constantly milling around the Reichsratsgebäude, people will begin to suspect that something is brewing, whereas, if you are out of the way, they will assume that we are simply preparing a set of reasonable demands with which we expect the Serbs to comply so that the whole business can be painlessly resolved."

"Demands or compromises?" Hőtzendorf said.

Berchtold smiled, "Don't worry. You will have your war. The demands I have in mind are so extreme that the Serbs will find it impossible to accept them; and once they have rejected them, the rest of Europe will see that we are fully justified in carrying out an immediate invasion."

"And in the meantime..."

"In the meantime, we lull them into a false sense of security while, from a distance, you set to work preparing your regiments for the attack."

Hőtzendorf turned to Krobatin, "It would be helpful to provide the troops with maps of Belgrade and the surrounding regions."

Krobatin nodded, "And we need to formulate the precise strategy."

Berchtold laughed, "Hőtzendorf has spent years preparing such strategies. I am sure he has everything already in place."

Hőtzendorf, unsmiling, said, "I have warned the Emperor so many times that one day war with Serbia would be inevitable."

"And now you can revel in the knowledge that you were right and that day is almost upon us."

Hőtzendorf nodded but Krobatin was less convinced, "That day will never come if we cannot persuade the Emperor to authorise an invasion. The Hungarians are still urging caution and their Prime Minister never stops bleating about the dangers of such an attack."

"Tisza can easily be dealt with," Berchtold said, shaking the water from his hands. "His greatest fear isn't war itself, but rather that if we assimilate Serbia into the empire, the Slavs will outnumber the Austrians and Magyars put together. Once that fear is alleviated, it shouldn't be difficult to bring him around to our way of thinking."

"And how do you propose to do that?" Krobatin said.

"I will promise him that we will not take so much as an inch of Serbian soil for ourselves. We will go in, teach them a lesson, disarm them and withdraw."

Hőtzendorf stared at him in horror, "That's *it*? We withdraw and give them the opportunity to rebuild, rearm and continue to flourish?"

"Calm down," Berchtold laughed. "You've already seen the plans we have for the division of Serbia but there is no need to mention that to Tisza."

Now it was Hőtzendorf's turn to laugh, "If I fell so easily for your promise, I am sure that Tisza will be equally easily fooled."

"Yes," Krobatin said, "but will the Emperor? They say that Tisza writes to him almost daily urging him to show clemency towards the Serbs."

Berchtold, leaning back against the fountain, looked up at the sky and let the sun caress his face, "His Majesty never reads those letters. In fact, he never receives them."

"What?"

"The poor old Emperor is still in mourning for his nephew. It would be cruel to add to his troubles by presenting him with opposing opinions. As an act of kindness and for his own protection, I have put measures in place to ensure that Tisza's letters are intercepted."

Hötzendorf laughed loudly, "You're a sly old fox, Poldi!"

Berchtold smiled and, pushing himself away from the fountain, waved his cane towards Reichsratsgebäude, indicating that they should walk on.

"The only other problem I can foresee," Hötzendorf said, "is how we are going to overcome the Emperor's fears about Russian intervention. I heard directly from Giesl at our embassy in Belgrade that this Russian fellow, Hartwig, is wandering around assuring all and sundry that the Tsar won't stand by if we take up arms against Serbia."

"Hartwig is a loose-cannon, from all accounts," Krobatin said. "He's renowned for making decisions without authority from St. Petersburg."

"All the same, if word of his promises reaches the Emperor, it will increase his reluctance to authorise an invasion."

"Hartwig," Berchtold repeated the name several times. "Don't worry, I am sure we have nothing to fear from him. Besides," he tapped his breast pocket, "I have with me a telegram from Berlin."

His companions stopped and stared at him expectantly.

"Hoyos and Szogyeny report that the Kaiser has not only promised us his full support but he would be disgusted if we fail to seize this opportunity of crushing Serbia once and for all."

Krobatin almost leapt with delight, "This is exactly what we needed. And the Kaiser has as good as said that he expects us to start the invasion?"

"To be honest," Berchtold said, stepping from the warmth of the sunshine into the cool, pillared atrium, "I suspect that Hoyos has exaggerated the response but the Kaiser is a proud man and once he has given his word, or is believed to have given his word, he will not be prepared to lose face by backing down."

Hötzendorf puffed out his chest and walked more quickly, "Once the Emperor hears of this, he will have no option but to give his assent to our plans." His heavy tread thudded on the marble floor and his voice echoed on the walls so clearly that Berchtold, fearful of eavesdroppers, nodded pointedly towards the groups of ministers and officials hovering in the hall.

"Now we must prepare our demands," he said theatrically, "and since we are sure that they will be complied with, you can both take this chance of escaping from the heat of the city to the fresher air of the mountains."

Hötzendorf leaned towards him and whispered, "You *will* keep us informed?"

"Naturally, and when the Serbs reject our demands, you and I can approach the Emperor together. Now go and enjoy your holiday, knowing that when you come back everything will be in place for your war."

Karl knelt in the chapel of Schloss Wartholz, silently recalling the words of the reading:

"...*and Aaron shall lay his hands upon the head of the live goat, and confess all the faults of the sons of Israel and all their transgressions and all their sins...and the goat shall bear all their sins...*"

The priest gave the final blessing, and sunlight shone through the stained-glass windows and poured over the altar and aisle, bathing Karl in a so bright a glow that it seemed as though heaven itself were illuminating his darkest suspicions.

"*The scapegoat,*" he thought, "*one innocent creature blamed for the sins of a nation,*" and with more desperation than fervour he rose to join in the final prayers, invoking the intercession of the Blessed Virgin and the saints.

"Holy Michael, defend us on the day of battle; be our safeguard against the wickedness and snares of the devil..."

Even the familiarity of the lines increased rather than soothed his anxiety. He recalled being taught as a child that, following a disturbing revelation, Pope Leo XIII had written these prayers to be said at the end of every Low Mass. The Pope, he was told, was descending the steps of the sanctuary after Mass when he fell into so deep a trance that the surrounding cardinals feared he was dead. When eventually he revived, he recounted his troubling vision: a conversation between Jesus and Satan, in which Satan claimed that if he were given one hundred years free rein, he could destroy the Holy Catholic Church and bring the world under his command. The Pope then heard Jesus say, "So be it..." and immediately witnessed an image of terrifying proportions as though the whole of hell had been let loose over the earth.

Karl inhaled sharply in horror at the thought of what such a scene might entail: deceit and intrigue; plotting and murder; death and the destruction of war on a scale that could hardly be imagined...

He stared ardently at the crucifix.

"Most Sacred Heart of Jesus, have mercy on us. Most Sacred Heart of Jesus, have mercy on us. Most Sacred Heart of Jesus, have mercy on us."

He thought of Franz Ferdinand's orphaned children; the Emperor and all the peoples of Austria-Hungary, and he entrusted them all to the care of the Sacred Heart, the Blessed Virgin and St. Michael.

When the priest had left the altar, Karl looked down at his young son Otto, sitting between him and Zita, who held their new little daughter in her arms.

Otto smiled cherubically but when Zita looked up at him, he knew that she, too, was oppressed by vexing questions. He stepped out from the bench and, after genuflecting before the tabernacle, led his little family out into the morning sunshine.

Otto ran ahead, skipping cheerfully through the flowers, pursued by his nannies, while Zita handed over the baby, six-month-old Adelheid, to a nursemaid.

"What's bothering you?" Karl said as they strolled towards the summer house. "You looked so troubled after Mass."

"Did I?" she shook her head and was about to deny it but he knew her too well for deception.

"Whatever it is, you know can tell me."

"It will probably sound ridiculous," she shrugged embarrassedly.

He shook his head, "Tell me anyway."

"Do you think it's possible that there are hidden forces intent on destroying the Church?"

At first the notion seemed so implausible that his immediate response was to remind her of Christ's promise that the gates of hell could not prevail against his Church, but the intensity of her expression and the memory of the Pope's vision was so unnerving that he said quietly, "What makes you think that?"

"I don't know exactly. I just feel that there is something going on, on a far wider scale that we can imagine. It seems to me that Uncle Franz's murder is more significant than any of us has realised yet."

"I know; I feel that, too," he whispered and reached for her hand.

"If someone were intent on destroying the authority of the Church, wouldn't they begin by attempting to destroy the Christian monarchies in Europe?"

"Cut off the head so the body withers?"

She nodded, "Do you remember how often Uncle Franz spoke of ideas and dreams being far more powerful than military might?"

"He said that if someone wished to gain control of a nation, they would first have to understand the ideals and aspirations of the people." Karl smiled sadly, "I think Uncle Franz *did* understand those aspirations. He wanted people to have greater freedom and a greater say in how they were governed and…"

"…and now he is dead. Isn't it strange, Karl, that the one man who might have succeeded in uniting the different cultures and bringing stability to the empire, should be killed in such questionable circumstances? This might be a wild and ridiculous notion but I can't help thinking that there are people who would prefer to see the disintegration of Austria-Hungary and all the Christian nations of Europe."

"In order to seize power for themselves?"

"Yes, and in order to do that, they must first create chaos and disorder, driving people into such desperation that they reject their kings, their religion and the established order and become like sheep without a shepherd, helplessly searching for any new idea that appears to offer stability and freedom."

They walked in silence for a while until Karl said, "You think Uncle Franz's murder was part of such a plan?"

"Yes. I do."

"But who would do such a thing? And who would be *able* to implement such a plan?"

"Some people believe that there are several secret groups and societies who have been behind many of the most appalling and tragic events of the past hundred years. Freemasons, occult societies…" She suddenly stopped and turned to him, "Do you remember shortly before our wedding I was granted an audience with the Pope?"

"Yes, you told me how supportive he was and that he said he was very happy about our marriage."

She bit her lip, "But I didn't tell you *all* that he said. He spoke of you as though you were already the heir and when I reminded him that you were only second-in-line to the throne as Uncle Franz was the heir, His Holiness' response was very strange."

"Strange, in what way?"

"He turned from me and said very seriously that Franz Ferdinand would never be Emperor. How did he know that?"

Karl shook his head uncertainly, "He is a saintly man, and many saints have prophetic powers."

"Perhaps so; or perhaps he was already aware that plans had been made to kill him."

So many thoughts pounded through Karl's brain that he could no longer bear it, "Oh Zita! I am so full of suspicions and uncertainties and I can't even begin to make sense of any of them. Are we caught up in some wider intrigue or is it just that the shock of the murders has led us to create problems where there are none?"

"*Something* is definitely going on, Karl," she said certainly. "I don't know what it is, but I feel it and it disturbs me."

Karl kicked at a clump of grass, "How can we possibly see the bigger picture when we don't even know what is going on under our noses? I should have stayed longer in Vienna to find out exactly what is happening and what the ministers are planning. I keep telling myself that everything is going to be settled peacefully and, since a fortnight has passed since Uncle Franz' murder, if there were going to be reprisals, they would have begun by now; but when I think about Hötzendorf and Krobatin and the rest of the war party, I can't believe they are going to let this opportunity for war pass them by."

When Zita didn't reply, he sought to counter his own argument, "Then again, if Uncle Franz Josef were concerned that something is about to happen, he wouldn't have told me to come back here and continue the holiday."

"Unless he wants to keep you free of all intrigue so no blame can ever be attached to you."

He frowned at her.

"On the other hand, does the Emperor himself have any idea what is happening? How can he, when he is out of the way at Bad Ischl?"

They had reached the summer house where the servants had placed a jug of coffee and the morning newspapers.

"Well," Karl said, sitting down at the table and flicking through the pages, "according to this, nothing important seems to be going on. Berchtold has sent some official named Wiesner to Belgrade to report on the findings of the inquest; the boys who committed the crime are still being questioned; oh and look," he turned to her brightly, suddenly cheered by the news, "Hötzendorf is preparing to leave for the Tyrol."

Zita leaned over her shoulder, "He's taking a holiday?"

"Doesn't that prove that there are no plans for an invasion? After all these years of calling for Serbia to be crushed, Hötzendorf wouldn't be running off to Innichen if something dramatic were about to happen."

Zita poured the coffee and he continued to turn the pages, feeling greater relief by the moment until a small article caught his eye.

"Oh no," he said and his spirits sank to the depths. "Hartwig, the Russian ambassador to Serbia has suddenly dropped dead: '...*while visiting our ambassador, Baron Giesl, at the Austrian Legation, to convey his condolences on the murder of His Imperial Highness Archduke Franz Ferdinand, the Russian ambassador to Belgrade, Count Nicholas Hartwig suffered a heart attack and died instantly... "'*

Zita shook her head, "It's very unfortunate, and even more unfortunate that it happened at our embassy."

"Unfortunate," Karl said, "or remarkably convenient?"

Chapter 20 – Bad Ischl – 21st July 1914

From the balcony of the Kaiservilla, Emperor Franz Josef stared across the green meadows towards the distant mountains. For over sixty years the familiarity of the view had brought comfort and inspiration to his heart. In times of doubt, the solidity of the changeless landscape had reassured him that all was well; and in times of sorrow, the Alpine breezes had soothed his grief as lovingly as a mother might caress a wounded child. In his younger years he had often scaled those distant peaks, and the permanence of the mountains confirmed his faith in the stability of his empire.

Always, this place had brought healing and restoration to his soul, and yet today its beauty hung like a great weight around his heart. Perhaps it was simply the realisation that he was no longer the lithe young man who had climbed to the heights with such ease, but rather, like the ancient trees with their gnarled routes and twisted limbs, he had grown old; or perhaps it was the sense that the certainties that had sustained him for over eighty years were being swept away like dust on a summer breeze.

Not since the Reformation had Europe known such a tumult of conflicting ideas, threatening to throw all that was safe and secure into chaos. In those far off days when the Church was being torn apart by schism, the Holy Roman Empire had stood firm against the sweeping tide of change, but now the successor of that empire, Austria herself, was at the very heart of the storm.

Perhaps Franz Ferdinand had been right, he thought, when he warned that dreams were more powerful than weapons, and that ideas could never be conquered by war. Every day new philosophies emerged to undermine everything that had held society together and even to challenge the belief in God's anointed kings. Widespread education had made men discontented with their lot and now that they had eaten the fruit of the Tree of Knowledge, Eden must be destroyed. Study had made men cynical and new scientific and theological research challenged not only the social order but even the eternal truths of his beloved Roman Catholic Church.

"Have I lived too long?" he sighed, gazing wearily towards the mountains as the debonair figure of Count Leopold von Berchtold appeared, striding across the courtyard. "There was a time when everything was clear and everyone knew where he stood, but now nothing remains of that certainty."

First, Darwin had questioned the veracity of the scriptural accounts of Creation; then David Strauss had gone so far as to deny the divinity of Christ. In mathematics and physics, too, men like Cantor and Boltzmann had thrown the accepted truths into disarray; while art, which had once raised Man's spirits towards the Divine, had sunk into appealing to his basest instincts. Then there was this dreadful fellow, Freud, infecting men's minds with his bleak and bestial view of humanity, disregarding the teachings of ages that Man was made in the image and likeness of God.

As Franz Josef turned from the balcony, the door opened and Berchtold stood before him, smiling as though he had come bearing wonderful news. After a preliminary greeting and polite inquiry as to whether the Emperor was enjoying his holiday, he moved to the centre of the room, impatient to proceed with the business that had brought him here to Bad Ischl.

"Did Your Majesty have an opportunity to examine the document that I sent yesterday?"

Franz Josef silently sat down and spread a series of papers across a table.

Berchtold, officiously erect, said, "I think you will find, sir, that our demands are comprehensive and unambiguous. With your permission, Ambassador Giesl will present them to the Serbian government the day after tomorrow."

Franz Josef peered at a list of questions he had written earlier in the day.

"Before we continue," he said without looking at Berchtold, "do we have a report yet from Wiesner's investigation?"

There was a noticeable hesitation before Berchtold replied, "We know that the Serbs were behind the assassination."

Franz Josef looked up at him, "Do we have proof?"

"Evidence is gradually coming to light. We have ascertained that Princip and his fellow conspirators were given pistol training by a Bosnian named Ciganovic who, together with Major Tankovic also supplied them with weapons."

"Ciganovic and Tankosic?" Franz Josef's eyes moved to the end of the document, "I see here that you demand their arrest but who are these men and what is their connection to the government? They are just names to me, nothing more."

"Milan Ciganovic works as a railway official but we are certain that that is merely a cover for his subversive activities. He is a close associate of Colonel Dmitriejevic and Major Tankosic – both prominent officers in the Serbian army and founder members of the Black Hand."

"One or two rogue officers do not prove the involvement of an entire country and yet here," he pointed to the opening paragraphs, "you are as good as demanding that the Serbs admit their guilt."

Berchtold feigned laughter, "The weapons were traced back to a Serbian military depot. We are certain that Tankosic was not the only officer involved in this conspiracy but we have reason to believe that it was he who informed Prime Minister Pasic of their intention to assassinate the Archduke."

Franz Josef raised his eyebrows, "And Pasic passed that information to our embassy but it was ignored."

"The fact is, sir," Berchtold said, "Archduke Franz Ferdinand's murder cannot be treated as a single event. It was the culmination of many years of aggression directed towards us. Even if we cannot prove a direct link to the Serbian government, it's clear that they have at least condoned anti-Austrian propaganda and allowed these seditious groups to go unchecked."

Franz Josef nodded silently and, with greater urgency, Berchtold leaned over the document.

"For the first time, the whole of Europe can see the extent of the Serbs' aggressive intentions towards us. In the past our complaints have gone unheeded by our neighbours but this assassination has shown that Serbia is a training ground for assassins who will stop at nothing to achieve their aims. There has never been a more opportune moment for us to wipe out this threat while we still have universal sympathy."

Such was the light in his eyes and the eagerness in his tone that Franz Josef peered at him sceptically, "Anyone would think that you were rejoicing in my nephew's murder."

Stunned by the accusation, Berchtold shook his head vehemently, "No, sir, no. I am horrified and disgusted by what has happened, which is why I am so desperate to prevent further atrocities. As long as the Serbs continue to permit the circulation of anti-Austrian propaganda and allow subversive activities to go unpunished, we will remain a target for every anarchical group in Belgrade. If we do not act now, how many other members of your family will fall victim to assassins?"

Franz Josef, trusting his sincerity, nodded.

"This is why," Berchtold continued, "we are insisting that the Serbs outlaw subversive propaganda and arrest anyone found in possession of such material. It is vital, too, that we ensure that they do everything possible to prevent weapons from being smuggled over the border into Bosnia, and that they order the immediate arrest of those officials who have allowed that to happen in the past. Under the circumstances, sir, everyone can see that these are reasonable demands."

"Very reasonable," Franz Josef agreed, and Berchtold's confidence seemed to increase.

"In which case, sir, do we have your authorisation to deliver the document?"

The Emperor frowned deeply. Berchtold's arguments were convincing and yet there was something disconcerting in the urgency of his manner. Behind the mask of reason, it seemed something sinister was afoot as though, between the lines of the justifiable demands, a secret agenda was concealed. He read again through the document, searching for possible points of contention.

"*This*," he eventually said, pressing his index finger to a particular line.

"Yes sir?"

"Can we really expect the Serbs to allow our investigators to participate in the prosecutions on Serbian soil?"

Berchtold's eyes widened, "I see no problem in that. If they are as innocent as they claim and have nothing to hide, I am sure that they will welcome our help in bringing the perpetrators to justice."

Franz Josef read through the entire document once more before agreeing, "Very well, you have my permission to send this." He pushed back his chair and stood up, "Let's hope it has the desired effect. If the Serbs agree to end these attacks, at least some good might come out of my nephew's murder."

"Yes, sir," Berchtold gathered the papers. "The Archduke will not have died in vain."

"Let me know the moment we receive their reply."

"Of course, sir," Berchtold bowed and hurried to the door, unable to contain his eagerness to send the authorisation to Vienna.

Chapter 21 – Peterhof, Russia – July 24th 1914

For the seventh time Nicholas picked up the document convinced that he must have made a mistake but, no matter how many times he read it, the message was shockingly clear. This was not a set of reasonable demands but an ultimatum couched in such self-righteous terms that its contents made him cringe. Over and over the Austrians wrote of their benevolence and patience, claiming in a tone of injured innocence that they had only wanted peace. Nicholas shook his head. If that were true why had they annexed Bosnia-Herzegovina in the first place? And why were they behaving now like a bully holding a weaker child by the throat?

He reached for the telegram recently arrived from Prince Alexander of Serbia, urgently requesting his help. Its conciliatory tone, contrasting so sharply with the Austrian demands, gave at least a glimmer of hope that a compromise might be reached. Nicholas pulled a cigarette from the case and was about to light it when he saw that the one he had lit only five minutes earlier, still glowed in the ashtray amid a mountain of butts. In the stillness of the afternoon, clouds of smoke hung, unmoving, above his desk, prickling his eyes and creating such a sense of suffocation that he suddenly needed air.

Dropping the papers onto his desk, he pushed open the door and strode towards Rastrelli's Ceremonial Staircase with its magnificent frescoes of Aurora and Genius. Passing golden statues and ornate banisters glistening in the July sunlight, he came to the first floor balcony where his young son, Alexei, stood, leaning on the balustrade, staring out towards the ocean.

Nicholas stopped to gaze at him and so many emotions flooded through him that he thought he might weep. Never had a child brought such joy and such sorrow to his parents: this angelic creature, the joy of his family and the hope of the dynasty, had often been so close to death that it seemed a miracle that he had survived his nine years. At times his agonising condition was so unbearable that Nicholas had even thought that death might be a blessing for him, yet the prospect of losing him was more than he could bear and on days like this, when he was well, his vivacity flooded the whole palace with light and love.

"Serbs, too, have sons whom they love," Nicholas thought, "as do Austrians, Germans and Russians…" and the possibility of so many families being torn apart by war rendered him still more determined to find a way to ensure peace.

He stepped forwards, and Alexei, hearing his footsteps, turned and smiled with delight, "Papa! I didn't know you were there."

The radiance of his features was so refreshing after the oppressive heat of the study that Nicholas spontaneously crouched with outstretched arms to embrace him.

"They said you were busy and not to be disturbed," Alexei said, hugging him warmly.

"I am waiting for the Foreign Minister to return. He should be here any minute."

Alexei leaned back to view his face, "You look worried again. Is Sazonov bringing bad news?"

Nicholas shook his head, "He's been meeting with the Council of Ministers and he's going to bring me their report, that's all. So!" he looked up brightly, "I have a few minutes to spend with my favourite son!"

"Your *only* son!" Alexei laughed and led him back to the balustrade where they stood together gazing out to the horizon.

A canal, six hundred metres in length, stretched towards the misty Baltic harbour, and from either side of the waterway came the whooshing and gushing of fountains. Narrowing his eyes, Nicholas could just about make out the figure of Samson prising open a lion's jaws from which a great surge of water spouted forth.

"You see there," he said, "that statue was erected in honour of our ancestor, Peter the Great."

Alexei nodded, "I know, Monsieur Gilliard told me. He said that Tsar Peter built this place to outshine the French king's palace at Versailles to show the world the might and beauty of Russia." He peered into the distance, "You can't see it from here, but there's a grotto by the harbour surrounded by golden heroes and gods that stand as symbols of the Tsar's power. Monsieur Gillard says that, like the ancient Roman emperors, the Tsars of Russia have been hailed almost as gods for centuries."

Nicholas tousled his hair, "That's right, they have but we are not gods, Alexei. We are men just the same as the poorest peasant in Siberia or the lowliest factory worker in Moscow. The difference is that the poorest peasant can dream of a different life and in time might see his dream fulfilled. We, on the other hand, are denied such dreams. We have wealth and we have servants and we have all this splendour but from the moment we are born our lives are mapped out for us and there is nothing we can do to change that."

Alexei stared at him in amazement, "Don't you *want* to be Tsar?"

Nicholas was thoughtful then leaned over to whisper, "If I had a choice, I'd leave all this behind and buy a little dacha somewhere in the country. I would work the land, chop wood and plant wheat, and your Mama would read and sew and maybe teach in a little school, which you and your sisters would attend. We would be an ordinary happy little family untroubled by all these important questions and responsibilities."

"But you are the Tsar of All the Russias! People obey yours orders and kiss your shadow when you pass and…"

"You would think that standing here amid all this magnificence, the Tsar of the All the Russias would feel like the most powerful man on earth but the truth is, Alexei, when I see this opulence and think back to my ancestors, I don't feel like a mighty Tsar at all. I feel like a very small man on whose shoulders a heavy burden has been placed."

Alexei's face fell in disappointment.

"You see, there is a difference between Nicholas the man and Nicholas the Tsar. I am just a man like any other man but a Tsar is so much more than a man – he is a symbol for his people; a symbol of the splendour and sanctity of Russia. It isn't for me to question why God called me to this role. It's my duty, that's all – my duty to obey God's will and adhere to the oath that I made at my coronation."

"And one day," Alexei said, quietly, "I will have to take the same oath and all that responsibility, too."

"Don't worry," Nicholas smiled, "you will be well prepared – better prepared than I was." He thought back to his accession, "We believed that my Papa would live for a very long time and so I wasn't fully trained in all the things that a Tsar needs to know…" He caught sight of Alexei's pale face and shook his head quickly, "For you it will be different. Mama and I will make sure that we teach you well so that when your time comes, it will all be so much easier."

Alexei slipped his hand into Nicholas', "I hope I will be as great a Tsar as you are…as great as Peter the Great!"

Nicholas laughed gently, "What do you think, Alexei? What makes a great Tsar? Is it one who conquers his enemies and expands his empire at any cost? Or is it one who leads his people in peace and maintains order and stability?"

Alexei ran his fingers over the balustrade, "I suppose that to be a great Tsar you first have to be a good man and love your people."

"'*Out of the mouths of babes*…'" Nicholas smiled. "Pray for me, Alexei. Pray that I will be a good man and…"

A cough distracted them and Nicholas turned to see an attendant, hovering at the entrance to the balcony.

"Your Imperial Majesty, the Minister of Foreign Affairs has arrived."

Nicholas nodded and, kissing Alexei's head, whispered, "Pray that I will be a good man and a wise man, too, so I can do the very best for our people."

He hurried back to the study where Sazonov stood in the doorway, a stack of papers tucked under his arm, and his face lined with consternation.

"Sergei," Nicholas said, snatching the Austrian demands from the desk, "I take it you've had time to discuss this?"

Sazonov sighed, "It's impossible, isn't it, sir? There is no way that these terms can be met. This is as good as a declaration of war."

Nicholas beckoned him closer and signalled that he should close the door. "Let's not be too hasty. I am sure that there is something we can do to reach a compromise."

Sazonov blinked despondently and Nicholas picked up a telegram, "Prince Alexander of Serbia has asked for our help."

"The Council of Ministers anticipated such a request, sir, and has made various suggestions for your approval."

Nicholas nodded distractedly as he re-read the telegram, "The Prince reiterates that he and his countrymen whole-heartedly condemn the murder of Archduke Franz Ferdinand and they are eager to ensure that the perpetrators are brought to justice. That being the case, they will be equally willing to take action to suppress anti-Austrian propaganda and to outlaw the group that carried out the attack."

"Yes, sir," Sazonov said, "but the Austrians want so much more than that. They insist that Austro-Hungarian agents be allowed to operate within Serbia to enforce justice. That would violate the Serbs' constitution and would be as good as handing over their sovereignty to Austria. What's more, if the Serbs agree to this, the Austrians will feel free to meddle in Serbian affairs whenever they choose."

Nicholas nodded, "But there are many points here that the Serbs *are* willing to accept."

"Count Berchtold has made it clear that unless they comply with *all* the demands it will be taken as a refusal and the Austrians will consider themselves entitled to launch an invasion."

Nicholas stared at the document, inhaling deeply as he tried to decide upon the best course of action. "It's unreasonable to expect a response within forty-eight hours. Since this arrived yesterday evening there is only one full day left to negotiate or come to any kind of agreement."

"It's obvious, isn't it?" Sazonov shook his head pessimistically. "In giving the Serbs only forty-eight hours to respond, the Austrians knew there wouldn't be time to reach a reasonable compromise. Even the manner in which this was delivered shows their true intentions."

Nicholas raised his eyebrows.

"Prime Minister Pasic wasn't in Belgrade and his subordinate refused to accept it in his absence so the Austrian ambassador dropped it onto his desk and walked out. Apparently Berchtold has instructed him to vacate the embassy and return to Vienna as soon as he receives a reply. That proves that no matter what response the Serbs give, the Austrians don't want or expect the demands to be met. They want war."

"No," Nicholas said. "There is no justification whatsoever for an invasion. Even their own investigator – what was his name?"

"Wiesner."

"Yes, Wiesner; even he reported that there was no evidence to implicate the Serbian government in the murder."

"It makes no difference, sir. They are determined to destroy Serbia and no amount of argument is going to stop them. Since the Kaiser has pledged his support they see themselves as invincible."

Nicholas tried to remain hopeful, "Sergei we can't let this happen. We must explore every possible avenue of negotiation before this escalates out of control. Is Pasic back in Belgrade yet?"

"Yes, sir. He returned early this morning."

"Contact him at once. Urge him to proceed with extreme caution. He mustn't do anything that could be seen as a provocation to Austria."

Sazonov's lips twitched, "He has already ensured that these demands are made public and has distributed the details to all European governments so that everyone can see the impossible position in which Austria is placing him."

"Has there been any response?"

"The British Foreign Minister said he has never seen such harsh demands and even a senior German minister is reputed to have said that he considered the demands too extreme."

"Good, good," Nicholas smiled, becoming more optimistic. "If the Austrians are aware of these responses, they will be less inclined to go in heavy-handedly. We must try to arrange some form of international conference as soon as possible."

"I fear we would be wasting our time, sir. I don't believe the Austrians have any desire to attend a conference or to accept any form of negotiation."

Undaunted, Nicholas said, "If they are shown that there is a possibility of achieving their aims without bloodshed, how can they refuse?"

Sazonov nervously ran his finger around the perimeter of his notes, "The question is: what exactly *are* their aims?"

"Isn't it obvious? Whether or not the Serb government had any involvement in the Archduke's murder, it cannot be denied that they have permitted the distribution of subversive literature and made only the weakest of attempts to suppress the groups who are violently hostile to Austria. To some extent, we must agree that the Austrians are justified in demanding an end to such activities in order to prevent further outrages."

When Sazonov appeared unconvinced, Nicholas re-read the list of Austrian demands.

"You see," he said, "it could be argued that even these extreme measures – insisting that Austrian agents be allowed to operate in Serbia – are justified to the extent that the Austrians feel they cannot trust the Serbs to adhere to any promises they might make. If, however," he looked up and smiled, "we were able to negotiate an agreement to ensure that these subversive activities cease, the Austrians might be satisfied."

Sazonov remained sceptical, "I doubt it, sir. In fact," he hesitated, "I don't think this has anything to do with the Archduke's murder. That is merely a convenient excuse. Their true intentions are far more sinister."

Nicholas, intrigued, sat down, "Go on..."

"I believe that their aim is to annex and divide the Serbian territories, which would significantly reduce our influence in the Balkans."

"No," Nicholas said, shuffling through the disorderly piles of papers on his desk, "I received a telegram from Prince Koudachev in Vienna this morning. He had just come from a meeting with Berchtold who assured him that the Austrians have no territorial aims."

Sazonov nodded, "I spoke with the German ambassador, Count Pourtalès, yesterday evening and he told me that Berchtold had given him the same assurance. He stressed that it was not in the interest of Austria-Hungary to assimilate more Slavic peoples in the empire and that their sole aim was to prevent further attacks."

"Well then?" Nicholas said.

"I am not convinced that Berchtold is telling the truth and when I pressed Pourtalès as to whether Germany would come to the support of her ally even if it turned out that the Austrians had a quite different agenda, he refused to give me a direct answer."

Nicholas gave up the search for the telegram and threw his hands into the air, "The only way we can find out exactly what they want is through direct discussion. We *must* arrange an international conference."

Sazonov pointlessly glanced at his watch, "With less than thirty hours till their ultimatum expires, how can we possible arrange such a meeting?"

"We must buy more time," Nicholas said firmly. "Send an urgent message to Berchtold, requesting an extension."

"And if he refuses?"

"Warn him that if Austrian troops cross the border into Serbia, we will view it as an unprovoked attack and come at once to the assistance of our allies. When he hears that, he won't refuse."

Sazonov stepped backwards and said very quietly, "Does this mean you intend to mobilise the army?"

Nicholas hesitated as memories of the disastrous Japanese campaign ran like a news reel through his mind.

"We cannot make a threat without showing we are prepared to carry it out," Sazonov prompted.

"I trust it won't be necessary to carry it out. If the Austrians see sense and agree to negotiate, everything can be worked out peacefully."

"I'm sorry, sir," Sazonov looked down at the carpet. "Unless we at least make a show of mobilisation, we will not be taken seriously. After all, it isn't that long ago that we objected to the annexation of Bosnia-Herzegovina but the Austrians marched in anyway and we did nothing."

Nicholas leaned back and lit a cigarette, "Did you discuss this with the Council of Ministers?"

Sazonov nodded and flicked through his notes, "Realising the seriousness of the situation, they have considered various possibilities. It could be seen as a provocation to Germany if you were to order a general mobilisation of the entire army but a partial mobilisation might be effective."

"Partial?"

"Yes, sir – mustering only those troops who would be needed to defend Serbia and to protect our border with Austria. The Council have asked that, if necessary, you will authorise the mobilisation of the troops in the districts of Moscow, Kiev, Odessa and Kazan; and also have the Baltic and Black Sea fleets held in readiness."

"Yes, I will do that *if* it becomes necessary," Nicholas said, with great emphasis on the 'if'.

"The Council also suggested that General Sukhomlinov at the War Ministry should start amassing and organising supplies."

"Only as a precaution."

"Of course, sir. And," he paused and looked again at his notes, "there was one more suggestion from the Minister of Finance."

"Yes?"

"Bark requests your permission to begin withdrawing our investments and assets in Germany and Austria-Hungary."

Nicholas sighed, exhaling the smoke from his cigarette, "Do they really believe that this is going to deteriorate into a full European war?"

"They feel we should be prepared for any eventuality."

"Very well, let them make these preparations but in the meantime we do everything in our power to contain the situation and prevent it from accelerating out of control." He stubbed the cigarette into the ashtray and stood up, "First, we must negotiate an extension of the time-limit for the Serbs' response. Once the Austrians have agreed to that, we will try to persuade them to negotiate by giving them an opportunity to express their grievances and their intentions without resorting to military intervention. Get in touch with the British Foreign Minister to see if he is willing to co-operate. Grey is well respected and the British have no specific interests in the Balkans, so he might be the man to lead it."

"You don't think that Austria would object to that, sir, since Britain is our ally?"

"If they prefer, we could refer the whole matter to the International Tribunal at The Hague – a disinterested party should satisfy everyone."

Sazonov nodded but he was far from convinced, "Supposing that, in spite of all our efforts, the Austrians refuse all attempts at conciliation?"

"Then they leave us with no choice. We are duty-bound to protect Serbia."

No sooner had he said it than Nicholas' heart sank into his stomach at the thought of the inevitable consequences.

"Willy…" he thought aloud.

"I beg your pardon, sir?"

"I must write to the Kaiser. He has great influence over the Austrians and he has no more desire for war than we have."

"He is away, sir, touring the fjords, I believe."

"At such a critical time?"

Sazonov cynically raised his eyebrows, "It's unlikely that the Austrians would have acted without his agreement, which suggests that these demands were prepared before he left Berlin."

"Then why wait until now to send them?"

"The timing speaks for itself. They waited until President Poincaré had left, in order to prevent you from discussing this with him."

Nicholas bristled at the notion of such manipulation but there was no time to waste on resentment.

"Find out when the Kaiser is due to return to Berlin. I need to contact him to make our position clear. He has assured me on numerous occasions that he has no enmity towards us and his greatest desire is for peace. In the meantime, I will write to Prince Alexander and urge him to accept as many of the Austrian demands as possible. Go now, Sergei, get in touch with Berchtold and the Austrian ambassador tell them we need more time."

With a low bow, Sazonov backed away and, as he disappeared through the door, Nicholas raised his eyes to the ceiling and whispered a prayer for peace.

Chapter 22 – Bad Ischl, Austria – July 28th 1914

Conrad von Hőtzendorf's heavy tread echoed on the yellow walls as he marched towards the Kaiservilla with the gait of a general leading his troops to war. Berchtold, striding to keep pace, clenched his fists at his side, silently rehearsing the speech he had prepared for the Emperor. So far everything had fallen perfectly into place; the most difficult part was over and all that was required now was Franz Josef's signature authorising the invasion.

As they neared the door, the smell of cooked herbs drifted through a downstairs window and mingled with the scent of freshly-cut grass. The fragrance was so enchanting that Berchtold walked more slowly and was suddenly struck by the incongruousness of the setting and the business that was about to take place. In the evening sunlight, birds, perching on the lowest branches of the trees, chirruped in blissful innocence, and wild Alpine flowers dotted the green meadows leading away to the mountains.

"What's the matter?" Hőtzendorf growled like a spluttering engine.

"I want to be sure of what we are going to say."

"We'll tell him the truth. The Serbs haven't met our demands and he must sign an immediate order for mobilisation."

"Yes," Berchtold said quietly, glancing at the open windows, "we must tell him the truth but not the whole truth."

Hőtzendorf puffed like a steam train, "Of course we won't mention that there is no evidence of the Serbian government's involvement in the Archduke's murder or that the spineless Serbs wrote such a snivelling reply. It shows what pathetic cowards they are to yield so easily, offering to do virtually everything we asked!"

"They did so, on the advice of the Tsar. If the Emperor were to hear that he asked for more time…"

"This has nothing to do with the Tsar! It's not his business. All the Emperor needs to know is that the demands weren't met so unless we invade immediately our word will count for nothing and those Serbian renegades will continue to wreak havoc. Come on," he waved towards the entrance as though he were waving a sabre, "let's get this over with quickly."

Berchtold didn't move. "You do realise," he said, "that the Emperor's greatest fear is a European war. If the Tsar adheres to his promise to protect Serbia, this could lead to…."

"Forget the Tsar! Concentrate instead on presenting the Emperor with the basic facts. The sooner he signs the order, the sooner we can get the invasion underway before the Tsar or anyone else has time to intervene. By this time next month, we'll have Serbia completely under our control."

"Next *month*? It will take that long?" Berchtold frowned.

"It will take another two or three weeks before the army is fully equipped and organised, but by then we'll have shelled Belgrade to the ground and the rest of the country will fall in no time."

Emperor Franz Josef stood at the window, peering across the green meadows as the two figures drew closer to the entrance. In such a perfect setting on so peaceful an evening, it was painful to think that so many battles had bloodied and sullied the history of this most beautiful country. It seemed so short a time since his soldiers were marching to combat the Prussians, and the vivid images of that ignominious defeat still haunted his memory. Ironic, he thought, that now those same Prussians were Austria's staunchest ally.

"What's it all for?" he sighed as he watched Berchtold and Hötzendorf step through the door. "So many lives lost, so much bloodshed and suffering and what does any of it achieve? A moment of glory, a little more land – the same story told again and again through the centuries and, rather than improving anything, we spiral further into destruction."

He turned from the window and shuffled to a table to await his visitors. Like the sound of an approaching army, their footsteps pounded the corridor and even before they had entered the room he knew what they were going to say. So many times he had seen in their eyes an insatiable appetite for war, and for so long he had tried to hold them back as they strained like wolves on a leash, but now his arms were tired and his heart was so weary that he doubted he had the strength to curb their ferocity any longer.

Suddenly they were standing before him, their brows rigid with determination. Berchtold talked at some length but Franz Josef was too distracted by the fiery urgency in Hötzendorf's eyes to pay any attention to his words.

"...so you see, Your Majesty," he eventually came to the point, "we have done everything possible to give the Serbs an opportunity for peace but, since they have rejected our proposals, there is no other option open to us. We must take immediate military action." He placed a document on the table, "With your signature, sir, we can mobilise at once and in three days we will be prepared to issue the declaration of war."

Franz Josef's eyes moved over the words on the page. His mind ran back through the countless documents he had signed since the beginning of his reign and he recoiled from the thought that one stroke of his pen could send so many men to their deaths.

"When exactly did we receive the response from Belgrade?" he eventually said, causing Berchtold and Hötzendorf to exchange wary glances.

"Five-to-six this evening, I believe," Berchtold said.

"Just five minutes before the expiry of the forty-eight hours?"

"They came up with the most bizarre excuse for leaving it so late. Apparently they couldn't find a typist with sufficient linguistic skills to translate their response into French!"

In such circumstances, his laughter sounded inappropriate and the Emperor, deliberately solemn, said, "Were they hoping we would give them more time?"

Again the two men exchanged glances before Berchtold replied, "We did receive such a request from both Britain and Russia but, as we pointed out, it is a month since the Archduke's murder and we cannot wait any longer. Besides, our demands were reasonable and comprehensive so there was nothing that required a great deal of discussion."

Franz Josef looked at his watch, "So the Serbs sent their response at five minutes to six and now it is only ten minutes past seven. In little more than an hour you have had time to draw up this mobilisation order and declaration of war, and bring it here?"

Berchtold smiled uneasily and Franz Josef fixed him in a penetrative stare, "Or was this already prepared since you intended to persuade me to authorise an invasion, no matter how the Serbs responded?"

When Berchtold stuttered to reply, Hötzendorf came to his aid, "It was necessary to be prepared, particularly when we received reports that the Serbs had begun to mobilise even before giving us their response."

Shocked by this revelation, the Emperor looked again at Berchtold, "Is that right?"

"Yes, sir. Around three o'clock this afternoon they began calling up their reserves. In fact, they are already shelling our borders."

"If we don't act immediately," Hőtzendorf said, "Austrian lives will be needlessly lost."

The Emperor looked down at the document.

"Some of our regiments have already moved towards the border and…" Hőtzendorf began but he stopped mid-sentence when the Emperor looked up at him.

"I wasn't informed."

Berchtold quickly intervened, "It was a precautionary measure. Naturally, your loyal subjects are very angry about the murder of the Archduke, and the strength of anti-Serb feeling occasionally spilled into violence. The troops were sent to the border solely to keep the peace and prevent any backlash from the Serbs."

'All this for Bosnia-Herzegovina,' Franz Josef thought. 'Is it really worth so much bloodshed to cling on to regions, which have no desire to be part of my empire?'

He pushed the document away. "Gentlemen, sixty-six years ago when I came to the throne, Austria was in a state of turmoil. There were so many insurgents and anarchists trying to destroy the great traditions of our country that we were in danger of civil war."

Hőtzendorf impatiently cleared his throat but Franz Josef paid him no attention.

"At the time I believed that in order to preserve the empire it was necessary to take severe and uncompromising action against those who sought to create chaos and to disrupt our way of life."

Hőtzendorf's hand edged towards the document, "Absolutely true, sir: swift and decisive action."

"Consequently, I signed the death warrants for many men and I believed that in so doing I was serving God and my country. Now, though," his brow furrowed, "I am so much closer to standing before the throne of God and I often wonder how I shall face him with so many deaths on my hands. How shall I answer when he asks how I responded to his commandment, *thou shalt not kill?*"

Hőtzendorf moved to reply but Berchtold, with a sycophantic smile, spoke first, "In recent years, sir, you have pardoned far more political criminals than have been executed. The people love you for it and appreciate your mercy and kindness. God will do the same."

Franz Josef balked that this man should dare to speak for God but, clearly unaware of his own arrogance, Berchtold continued, "Unfortunately, here on earth, nothing is ever quite so straightforward. There are times when it is necessary to kill in order to prevent further killing."

Hőtzendorf could no longer contain his impatience. "With all due respect, this isn't the time for an ethical or theological debate. We need action. As soon as Your Majesty signs the mobilisation order, we can return to Vienna and put everything into place so that on Monday morning we can commence our bombardment of Belgrade."

"Bombardment?" the Emperor said. The word sounded horrific, creating images of injured civilians: women and children, who had no political influence and had played no part in Franz Ferdinand's murder.

Hötzendorf, oblivious of these concerns, said, "I estimate that it will take about three weeks for all our forces to be fully up to scratch so in the meantime we will begin by shelling. If we…"

Berchtold, clearly sensing the Emperor's unease, restrained him with a glance and said, "Unless we control the Serbs, their attacks will continue and many more Austrians, whom God placed under your protection, will lose their lives. The whole world understands that we are not the aggressors here. We are defending our people."

Still Franz Josef hesitated, and Berchtold adopted a lighter tone, "We will probably find that there is little resistance to the invasion, in which case there will be very few casualties and very little bloodshed. Many Serbs are appalled by what happened to the Archduke and, since they understand the legitimacy of our cause, they will see no reason to oppose our march on Belgrade."

Franz Josef looked at him cynically, "Do you really expect me to believe that?"

"One thing is certain," Hötzendorf said. "The sooner we take action, the less prepared they will be. If we strike now, before they have time to muster their army or rally their allies, our losses will be minimal."

"Their allies?" The word increased Franz Josef's unease.

"There is nothing to worry about," Berchtold said, glaring at Hötzendorf. "We have been assured that the rest of Europe will sit back with folded hands while we take whatever course is necessary."

"You are certain of that?"

"Yes, sir," he smiled confidently, then his expression suddenly because more serious. "There is just one concern: the German Emperor stressed that if we fail to act, we are in danger of losing his support. He does not wish to be seen as carrying a weak ally."

Franz Josef stared at the document. Perhaps he had been over-cautious. There was no denying that something must be done and, if every peaceful avenue had been explored without success, the only way to uphold Austrian dignity and protect his people was to send his troops into Belgrade.

"You can assure me," he said, picking up the pen, "that there will be no reaction from Russia?"

"Russia?" Berchtold's eyes widened. "The Tsar was appalled by the Archduke's murder. He knows only too well from the assassination of his own grandfather that the only way to deal with these criminals is to take firm action."

Franz Josef nodded and frowned.

"I have been in constant contact with the Russian ambassador and with your ambassador to St. Petersburg," Berchtold persisted. "They understand that we have been driven to take a firm stand and they know that we have the full support of Germany. The Tsar is too preoccupied with dealing with the strikes in his own country to be bothered by something as trivial as this and he has said many times that his army is not prepared for war. The last thing he wants is to involve himself in a local dispute between us and Serbia."

"Think of the annexation of Bosnia-Herzegovina," Hötzendorf said. "The Tsar did not intervene then. He will not intervene now."

"Very well," Franz Josef said reluctantly, "go ahead. Do whatever is necessary."

He picked up a pen and, signing his name, authorised the declaration of war.

The sun's rays shimmered on the calm surface of the fjord as Kaiser Wilhelm stood on the grassy bank gazing at the mountains of Balholm, rising up from the earth like wise old giants – their ancient features chiselled by the vicissitudes of nature, and the snow along their ridges like white strands of uncut hair.

He looked down into the fjord, and his reflection, monstrously distorted by the ripples, stared back at him in a grotesque caricature. His proud moustache seemed to have grown to enormous proportions and his eyes, magnified by the sunlight on the surface of the water, took on a wild voracious appearance. How different was this from the image he had taken such pains to cultivate! The great, heroic scholar-soldier of his dreams was contorted now into a gargoyle-like creature, hideous and depraved. Was *this* how history would remember him, if this petty Austrian dispute should lead to a European war? Would posterity forget his successes in peacetime and present him instead as the aggressor, responsible for these damned demands and the subsequent slaughter?

He plunged a stick into the water, violently swishing away the reflection and, as he turned again to the mountains, sorrow and disappointment tugged at his heart.

'Posterity,' he thought ruefully, *'will see me as neither the hero nor the aggressor. I will be forgotten; overlooked and cast aside.'*

A great wave of self-pity washed over him. No matter what efforts he made, no matter how brilliant his mind, noble his plans or altruistic his intentions, he remained that same little boy desperately trying to impress a mother who failed to appreciate him.

Deep-rooted frustration tightened like a belt around his stomach and he wanted to scream aloud and hear his voice echo through the mountains, shattering the peaks and causing avalanches to boom through the valleys: "Why don't you see me? Why don't you hear me? I am the Kaiser, the successor of Frederick the Great!"

The uniforms, the parades, the cheering crowds and military displays – none of these, or even the combined memories of them all, had been able to exorcise that demon of self-doubt from his soul.

Laughter echoed from the deck of his yacht, *Hohenzollern,* moored in the bay, and for one dreadful moment came the terrible thought that he was the cause of the joke. Yes, they pandered to him, those officers and, like the ministers in Berlin, they nodded with their 'yes, sirs,' and 'no, sirs'; they flattered and cajoled with exaggerated respect and responded to his orders with alacrity but did they really think him so unintelligent that he could not see through their masks? They were no different from his mother – in their eyes he was still a helpless and deformed child whom they wanted to hide away. Did they honestly believe he was too blind to know why they had encouraged him to take this vacation? Weren't they making decisions in his absence, which were really his to take, leaving him – their Emperor and Kaiser! – to discover what was happening from the Norwegian newspapers?

The list of demands had been delivered; every other ruler in Europe was poring over its contents and making decisions that would affect the future of the world, while he was here, pushed aside, discarded and ignored.

Self-pity and frustration took their usual course and surged into anger. He stamped fiercely on the ground. Now they would listen to him. This time everyone would hear. *He* ruled and he was the one to whom they must pay attention. At the top of his voice he yelled, "Make ready. I must return at once to Berlin!"

And with the fire of anger and determination in his belly, he prepared for his next dramatic entrance onto the world stage.

Chapter 23 – Potsdam, Germany – July 29th 1914

Gripped by a rage so powerful that his body felt too small to contain it, Wilhelm stormed along the corridors of Potsdam spilling a trail of recriminations.

"This is what happens in my absence," he roared at the ministers striding to keep pace. "On all sides there is nothing but deceit and incompetence! Three days during which all of Europe was scrutinising the Serbs' response and making preparations for war, yet the German Emperor was left to forage for news from foreign papers!"

He turned, expecting a reply, but so great was his fury that no one seemed capable of responding.

"And now I hear that the Austrians are bombarding Belgrade, and the Tsar is preparing to mobilise his army. How did all this happen? And why wasn't I warned of it? Didn't it occur to any of you imbeciles to inform me of something as drastic as an imminent declaration of war?"

The Chancellor, Bethmann-Hollweg, said quietly, "We couldn't inform you, sir. We knew nothing about it."

He turned sharply, "What?"

"I fear we have been duped by Vienna."

"Duped?" the word revolted him.

"We thought that the Austrians would be content when we saw the Serbs' response to their demands but now it's clear that from the start they wanted nothing less than war. Once they had received assurances of your support, they began preparations for their attack without even bothering to tell us."

Too incensed to reply, Wilhelm stared menacingly at the Chancellor until he shrank like a beaten dog.

"I understand, sir, that the only course open to me is to offer my resignation."

"Resignation!" Wilhelm exploded. "Oh no, you have cooked this broth and now you will stay and eat it."

He marched on and, barging through the door of his study, seized a handful of telegrams, barking a line from each one before hurling it to the floor,

"'*I beg you in the name of our old friendship'... 'I trust in your wisdom and friendship...'* You see? Even the Tsar of Russia expects me to sort out this mess that was not of my making!"

Bethmann stepped forwards tentatively, "According to our ambassador in St. Petersburg, the Tsar is eager to avoid war at all costs."

"Of course the Tsar doesn't want war; I don't want war; and I very much doubt that Franz Josef wants war, so how has it come to this?"

Hoping for a helpful response, he looked to the men who had followed him into the study but Bethmann stared feebly down at his feet; the Foreign Minister, Jagow, gazed vacantly into space; and Admiral Tirpitz silently tugged at his beard. Only, Moltke, the Army Chief of Staff, and Falkensteyn, the Minister of War, showed any sign of animation. Moltke, with the bold expression of a veteran campaigner, scrutinised the globe on Wilhelm's desk as though he were mentally measuring borders and terrain, while Falkensteyn stood with his hands behind his back like a general inspecting his troops.

"Well?" Wilhelm demanded. "Is anyone going to furnish me with the details of how this fiasco came about?"

Bethmann scrambled through a folder of papers, "At eleven o'clock yesterday morning, the Austrians sent a telegram to the Serb Prime Minister, Pasic, issuing a declaration of war." He paused and looked up, "I suppose they had to issue the declaration by telegram rather than sending an envoy since their staff withdrew from the Austrian embassy in Belgrade as soon as they received the reply to their demands."

"For pity's sake," Wilhelm yelled, "I don't give a damn *how* the declaration was delivered; what concerns me is *why* it was delivered before we knew anything about it! Only yesterday, when I was finally able to see the Serbs' response, I was under the impression that most of the demands had been met and it was time to start peace negotiations." He glared at Bethmann, "Didn't I order you to start a peace process?"

Bethmann nodded.

"Then how has it come to this?"

"I don't know, sir. We are all shocked by this turn of events. It was so unexpected that when the Serbs received the telegram they thought it was a hoax until the Austrians began firing shells across the Danube. Overnight the military action intensified as Austrian gunboats bombarded Belgrade from the River Sava."

"In response," Moltke said, his eyes still fixed on the globe, "the Serbs blew up one of the main bridges to prevent ground troops from entering the city."

"And while that was going on," Wilhelm kicked at the scattered telegrams, "I was in communication with the Tsar who assured me that his intentions were peaceful yet first thing this morning I hear he has authorised preparations for a general mobilisation! Why didn't he warn me of his intentions? And why is he involving himself in this anyway?"

Bethmann raised his eyebrows, "Apparently public opinion in Russia is running so high that the Tsar has been under a great deal of pressure both from the people and from his ministers."

"Public opinion!" the words exploded like a grenade. "He is an autocrat; he cannot allow himself to be swayed by public opinion!" His eyes alighted on a line from a telegram, "'*An ignoble war...*' he calls this. There is nothing ignoble in taking harsh measures against those who perpetrated the murder of the heir to the throne and if Nicky thinks otherwise he is putting every crowned head in Europe at risk. He must understand that. He *must!* Good grief! His own grandfather was blown to bits by insurgents and I don't imagine he considered his father's swift response to that atrocity ignoble!"

"According to Ambassador Pourtalès, the Tsar understands the Austrians' desire for justice but he cannot condone the invasion of Serbia, particularly when there is no evidence that the Serbian government was behind the assassination. He hopes that by sending his troops to the Austrian border, he can buy time to arrange some form of mediation. He has suggested presenting the case to the International Tribunal at The Hague."

"Yes, yes, yes..." Wilhelm waved his hand impatiently, "I know all this. He said as much in his telegrams and I assured him that I supported that idea but how can we negotiate if he goes ahead with this mobilisation? If he would hold back and let us deal with this, it would soon be settled and peace would be restored but if he continues with this aggressive stance, he will be responsible for setting the whole of Europe alight!"

"The trouble is," Jagow said despondently, "the rest of Europe doesn't see it that way. The Austrian attack has changed everything. All the sympathy that was felt for Austria following the Archduke's murder has shifted now to the Serbs."

"*Poor little Serbia*," Wilhelm grimaced, "and if we come to the aid of our allies, we will be seen as the aggressors!" Like a host of taunting demons, distorted images of his own reflection danced before his eyes. "The Austrians should never have acted without our consent. I will not be blamed for this!"

Moltke's pimpled face appeared in front of him, "There is no reason for anyone to view Germany as the aggressor. If this should escalate into a wider conflict, Russia will be to blame." He rested his hand on the globe and pressed his finger to the vast sprawling mass of the Russian Empire. "By the terms of our alliance we have a duty to defend Austria-Hungary in the face of a Russian attack so, if the Tsar proceeds with mobilisation, the only question is how quickly we, too, can ready our troops."

Bethmann stared at him in alarm, "The consequences would be disastrous. As His Majesty said, we would be seen as the aggressors while the Tsar is desperately trying to find a peaceful solution."

Wilhelm gasped indignantly, "*I* am trying to find a peaceful solution! The Tsar has asked me to mediate and that is precisely what I intend to do."

Moltke looked up, "But, as you said, sir, how can you mediate while the Russian army is poised to attack? It would appear that the Tsar has left Your Majesty with no choice but to issue an ultimatum."

Wilhelm, jolted from anger to fear, gulped audibly, "Ultimatum?"

"The Tsar must abandon his mobilisation plans or we will come to Austria's aid...unless, of course, Your Majesty is considering reneging on your promise to our allies...."

Wilhelm's heart beat so quickly it sounded through his chest like the echo of a million soldiers marching to war, "I never renege on my promises but let's remember that there is still time for this catastrophe to be averted. We agreed to support Austria if ever she were to come under direct attack from Russia, and as yet that is not the case."

He sat down at his desk, trying to steady himself and hoping that, if his ministers noticed how violently his hand was trembling, they suspected the cause was rage rather than fear. A thousand memories rushed through his head: the family gatherings, the jokes and the laughter; Nicholas' gentle violet-blue eyes shining as he watched his pretty daughters running in the sunshine; the gifts exchanged between cousins; and the merry wedding parties reuniting so many members of this huge extended family.

"Nicky must be persuaded," he murmured. "He *must* be persuaded to stand down before he plunges us all into an abyss from which there is no escape."

"Yes, sir," Moltke said, "everything is now in the Tsar's hands. If he wants peace, he need only abandon his mobilisation plans."

"And if he doesn't?" Bethmann asked.

"Then it will be mutual butchery between all the civilised nations of Europe."

Wilhelm, wincing at such a prospect, leapt from his chair and strutted around the room in an attempt to dispel his rising agitation.

"This is all sabre-rattling on the part of the Tsar. Nicky would never betray me like this. I will write to him again. I will call his bluff. I will warn him that if his mobilisation goes ahead, I will order a full mobilisation, too. That will solve everything. He is a peaceful man with no desire for war, and he knows that the strength of the German Imperial army is far superior to that of his own. I will tell him…"

He was suddenly aware of the perplexed and curious expressions of his ministers as their eyes followed him around the room as though he were losing his mind.

"There *is* still hope," Bethmann said in a tone which Wilhelm considered patronising. "If the Austrians make their intentions plain, there is a possibility that Russia can be appeased." He nodded pointlessly at the globe, "The Russians' greatest fear is that the Austrians will annex Serbia in much the same way as they annexed Bosnia-Herzegovina, thereby reducing Russian influence in the Balkans and upsetting the balance of power in the region."

Wilhelm, sensing a glimmer of hope, nodded with interest.

"If the Austrians could be persuaded to give an assurance that they will make no territorial claims in Serbia and will go no further than occupying Belgrade for a limited period, the Russians will probably be satisfied."

It seemed too simplistic to be possible but so desperate was Wilhelm to find a solution that he threw back his head and barked determinedly, "Let's waste no more time. Bethmann contact our ambassador in Vienna and have him impress on the Austrians the importance of clearly defining their aims. Then find the Austrian ambassador in St. Petersburg…what's his name?"

"Count Szapary, sir."

"Tell him to swallow his pride and plead with the Tsar to stay out of this."

Bethmann nodded and, as he began to back towards the door, Moltke stepped forwards to study the globe more intently.

"What of our other allies or potential allies?" he said. "Have they given any indication of where they stand in this?"

Jagow shook his head, "The Turks have sent a confidential missive offering to form an alliance with us if we should come into conflict with Russia but there is no support whatsoever from our closer allies. The Italians have made it clear that they have nothing to gain from supporting Austria, and the Bulgarians have declared their neutrality. The Roumanians remain non-committal."

Moltke groaned but Wilhelm shrugged carelessly, "Forget them. I never trusted the Italians or their dwarf of a king; and as for that oaf who rules Bulgaria…They were never reliable allies and the fewer nations involved in this, the better."

Moltke's eyes narrowed, "We can't overlook the likelihood that Russia's allies will come rushing in at the first opportunity. How are the French and British responding to this?"

"It seems certain," Jagow said, "that the French will stand by Russia. We believe they have already given an assurance that they are prepared for action. The British have refused to give any indication of their intentions but they seem to be on the point of declaring neutrality."

Admiral Tirpitz, who until now had been listening to the proceedings with the expression of a wise old owl, suddenly stirred.

"Then why did they fail to disperse their fleet after their summer manoeuvres at Spithead? And why were their ships spotted racing towards Scapa Flo overnight?"

Wilhelm's anxieties increased.

"I don't think we need to read anything into that," Jagow said. "They prevaricated when the French asked if they would pledge support in the case of a conflict and they have no interest in Serbia or the rest of the Balkans."

"Whatever happens," Wilhelm said desperately, "Britain must remain neutral. Summon their ambassador and make whatever deals are necessary to ensure that they stay out of this."

"*Whatever* deals?" Tirpitz said solemnly. "The British want to rule the waves. If they think we will give them whatever they want, they will insist that we reduce our naval capacity."

Wilhelm frantically threw his arm in the air, "Use your initiative! Offer them something that will keep them happy without undermining our strength and dignity."

Jagow nodded tentatively and the tension that filled the room was so great that Wilhelm could no longer stand it.

"Go now," he said, "all of you. Do everything you can to avert this disaster before it's too late."

In the balmy evening sunlight, the steady thud of the ball on the tennis court at Peterhof had a therapeutically mesmeric effect, calming the painful rigidity that had gripped the Tsar's muscles all day. The more strenuous the game, the greater the relief and, as one ominous thought after another arose, he hammered the ball more fiercely until sweat poured from his brow and his white naval shirt clung like a wet sail to his shoulders.

Willy was a bore and an exhibitionist but he would never start a war. The frantic tone of his telegrams showed more agitation than aggression and, in spite of his bluster and impulsiveness, he was not so rash as to embark on this path with no thought for the disastrous consequences.

The ball flew over the net and as it twanged against his racquet, Nicholas caught sight of his Foreign Minister, Sazonov, marching quickly towards him. The seriousness of his expression and the urgency in his step wrought in Nicholas a flurry of emotion, which he channelled into the final rally, powering the ball with such speed that it bounced back and forth across the court, sending his sailor-opponent leaping in all directions until he collapsed to his knees in defeat and gasped, "Your game, sir. You win again."

Nicholas strode across the court to shake his hand, "If only everything could be settled by something as agreeable as a tennis march."

"Do you wish to play again, sir?"

He glanced at Sazonov, rushing towards the baseline, "What I would *like* and what I must do seldom coincide. Now I am afraid I must engage in a far more serious game…"

Leaning the racquet against the net, he picked up a towel and, wiping the sweat from his face, turned to the Foreign Minister who, breathless with anger and exertion, omitted the usual courtesies.

"The Austrians are shelling Belgrade!"

As though struck by a poleaxe, Nicholas stood, stunned and immobile.

"They've left us with no choice, sir. We cannot delay the mobilisation any longer."

Nicholas, determinedly maintaining his calm, nodded toward the steps leading to the palace, "We mustn't rush into anything until we know all the details."

Sazonov, striding up the steps beside him, gasped, "The details are quite plain, sir. A couple of hours ago the Austrian ambassador came to me, pleading that we should remain neutral. I believe that the German Kaiser asked him to do that. I informed him that we had no desire for war but we could not stand by if Serbia were attacked."

Nicholas nodded.

"He assured me that the Austrians, too, want peace and their sole intention is to eradicate subversive propaganda and activities. I was half-inclined to believe him but..." he paused to regain his breath, "as we were talking, the telephone rang and I was told of this unprovoked bombardment."

Nicholas frowned, "How did Szapary respond?"

"He seemed stunned at first but then began to rant about how this is no concern of Russia's. To be honest, sir, our meeting concluded with a great deal of anger both sides."

Without a word, Nicholas continued to the top of the steps.

"We promised we would protect the Serbs," Sazonov said, "and now Belgrade is being destroyed. Sir, you have no option but to order an immediate general mobilisation against Austria and her allies."

Nicholas looked up at the sky, recalling Wilhelm's assurances of friendship, "You mentioned that the Kaiser had asked the Austrian ambassador to come?"

"Yes, sir, I believe so."

"Then perhaps the Germans were not expecting the bombardment, either. If there are divisions between the Central Powers, we could limit ourselves to a partial mobilisation aimed solely at Austria without provoking Germany."

Sazonov shook his head, "When Szapary had left, I contacted the German ambassador, Pourtalès. He insisted that if there are any troop movements on our part, Germany will immediately mobilise, too. The Germans are prepared to stand by Austria no matter what happens."

They had reached the palace where Nicholas stopped and, leaning against the cool walls, grasped at one last hope.

"I am still awaiting a reply to my last telegram to the Kaiser. I asked him to act as mediator in the hope that he could restrain Austria…"

Sazonov opened his mouth to speak but Nicholas, unwilling to hear his objections, continued, "I believe that he is sincere in his wish to avert a European war. In fact, Sergei, he seems quite desperate to maintain peace."

Sazonov lips curled cynically, "Perhaps, so, sir, but his ministers do not give that impression and, while we wait for him to find a peaceful solution, Serbian civilians are being killed."

Nicholas half closed his eyes, praying for insight and wisdom.

"Very well," he eventually said, "I will authorise the general mobilisation with immediate effect but make it clear to everyone that this is solely a defensive measure. As long as there is a possibility that the Kaiser can restrain the Austrians, we will not cross over the border; and as soon as the bombardment of Belgrade ceases, I will rescind this mandate."

Chapter 24 – July 29th–30th 1914

The clock in the study ticked as irritatingly as a bluebottle buzzing round the room. Eight-forty-five, nine o'clock, nine-fifteen, nine-thirty…the pendulum, swinging hypnotically to and fro, had probably always clicked this loudly but Nicholas had not noticed it before. Perhaps the room had never been so quiet; or perhaps his nerves had never been so on edge, causing every sound to grate on his ears and increase the tension in his muscles.

Resting his elbows on the desk, he pressed his head into his hands and closed his eyes. The disparity between who he was and the role he was called to play was more apparent and painful than ever. Nothing would have pleased him more than an obscure life, quietly raising his family and living in harmony with God and his neighbours. He opened his eyes and glanced around the study which, like the private apartments in all of his palaces, bore witness to his desire for simplicity. From the outside, these glorious edifices dominated the landscape, creating an impression of splendour and opulence, but here behind the façade and beyond the gilded state chambers, the family rooms were inexpensively furnished with items from *Maples* in London; the walls, far from being bedecked with priceless art works, were covered with ordinary family photographs and sacred icons.

Few people, Nicholas thought, ever penetrated that façade of splendour; and still fewer people saw beyond his role as the Tsar.

"What was it that Rousseau said?" he mumbled to himself. "'*Man is born free but is everywhere in chains…*'" and it seemed that, from the moment of his accession, a Tsar was fettered by stronger bonds than those which bound the most dangerous or abject of prisoners.

For the past twenty years, everything in his life had been subjugated to his role as 'Little Father' of his people, and at times the responsibility for the wellbeing of his millions of subjects had seemed far too great a weight for one man to bear. Muscovites, Estonians, Georgians, Armenians, Siberians, Poles – the number of people relying on his decisions was as endless as the overwhelming series of titles heaped upon him at his coronation: Tsar of all the Russias, Tsar of Novgorod and Astrakhan, Sovereign of Armenia, Lord of Tchernigov and Turkestan…The list went on and on like a litany, and, like the supplicants who poured out their litanies in desperate prayers, so too did his people look to him now to keep them safe; to protect the borders of the empire and to adhere to treaties and agreements made with foreign allies.

The immensity of such responsibility was crushing. By one stroke of the pen he could pardon a condemned prisoner or authorise the movement of armies to send thousands of men to their death. Far from filling him with pride, this godlike role ran so contrary to his natural inclinations that it confounded him utterly to think that out of all the men in Russia God should have chosen him to be Tsar.

He thought back through the three hundred years of the Romanov dynasty and the mysterious legend of his predecessor, Tsar Alexander I. In 1825, after reigning for almost a quarter of a century and defeating Napoleon's army, Alexander was said to have died of typhus at the age of forty-seven. In spite of the public funeral and interment in the family vault, rumours persisted even to this day that the ceremony was merely a show, when in fact he had abandoned the throne to live out the rest of his long life as a monk named Feodor Kuzmitch in the wilds of Siberia.

"Feodor Kuzmitch..." Nicholas smiled sadly. In the midst of so much personal pressure and international tension, what could be more appealing than to slip away into anonymous seclusion?

"And yet...and yet..." he sighed, fixing his eyes intensely on an icon, "I will not shirk my responsibility or forget my coronation oath."

The sound of hurried footsteps approaching the door jolted him from his reverie and he jumped from his chair as Fredericks, the Minister of the Imperial Court, appeared in the entrance.

"Your Imperial Majesty," he bowed, almost falling over his feet in his eagerness to hand over a telegram, "this has just arrived from the German Emperor."

Oh please God...Nicholas prayed silently as he snatched it from his hand but, as he read the message, his heart sank.

"It's no good," he said, shaking his head. "We cannot go ahead with this."

Fredericks' eyes widened.

"Willy is right. If we continue with our military preparations, a European war will be inevitable. I cannot do that, Fredericks. I cannot subject my people – and all the peoples of Europe – to this. Get me Sazonov on the telephone. I need to call off the general mobilisation before this goes any further."

Fredericks nodded quickly, "And do you wish to send a response to the German Emperor?"

Nicholas bit his lip, "It's so difficult communicating by telegram; everything can be misconstrued. If only I could meet him in person, we could..." he broke off, shaking his head. "Obviously there isn't time to arrange that but I can send a personal envoy to explain our position more clearly. Yes, call Sazonov," he nodded urgently towards the telephone, before snatching a pencil from the desk and hastily scribbling a note, "and have this sent immediately to the Kaiser. He needs to know that I have cancelled the general mobilisation and am sending someone to him right away."

By the time his note was written, Fredericks was holding out the telephone and Sazonov's apprehensive voice sounded through the receiver.

"But, sir," he protested in response to Nicholas' command, "we cannot keep issuing orders then rescinding them. Tension in the ranks is already running high and this indecision is unsettling and damaging to the morale of the army."

Uncharacteristically irked by this implied criticism, Nicholas answered sharply, "It is better for morale to be damaged than to send men needlessly to their death! I have made my decision and will not be pressured into provoking Germany when the Kaiser is doing his utmost to maintain peace!"

A brief silence followed and it was clear that Sazonov was startled by this outburst. When he spoke again his voice was far more subservient, "Of course, sir, you know the Kaiser's intentions far better than I do…"

"Yes," Nicholas interrupted, "I do. I know that he has sent his ambassadors to urge restraint on the Austrians."

"Perhaps so, sir, but our ambassador in Berlin informs me that Count Berchtold has refused to place any limit on the Austrians' military activities or to give any indication of their war aims. Meanwhile, the shelling continues and, though the Austrians have not yet been able to cross the river into Belgrade, the Serbs are coming under the most brutal, unprovoked attack."

Nicholas' certainty waned and he pressed his hand to his eyes, desperately seeking a solution.

A shuffling of papers sounded through the phone-line, then Sazonov said, "I have before me a copy of a manifesto just released by Prince Alexander of Serbia, which makes clear the extent of Austrian aggression. He is urging his people to defend their homes and their families. Sir, can we stand idly by when innocent civilians are being massacred?"

Such an appeal was impossible to refuse, and Nicholas said very quietly, "Go ahead with a partial mobilisation against Austria with effect from..." he glanced at the clock, "midnight."

Sazonov sighed with satisfaction before continuing more tentatively, "In such a volatile situation, sir, would it not be better to continue with the general mobilisation against Germany, too? We do not know how the Kaiser will respond and it would be as well to be prepared if he orders his troops to come to Austria's assistance."

"No," Nicholas said decisively. "We will defend the Serbs but we will go no further."

"Of course, you realise, sir, that if the unthinkable were to happen and we should come under attack from Germany, it could take several weeks for all your armies to be gathered from the different parts of the empire, whereas the Kaiser's army could be readied in a matter of days."

"No," Nicholas said again. "The Kaiser will not send his army against us. Don't forget that he remained supportive to us when the rest of Europe opposed our war with Japan; and if he had any desire to attack us, he would have done so when we were virtually defenceless during the uprisings in 1905. He remained a true friend then and he will remain a true friend now."

"I sincerely hope so," Sazonov said with such incredulity that Nicholas felt obliged to bring the conversation to an end.

"Fredericks is sending a telegram to inform the Kaiser that I have cancelled the general mobilisation and I intend to send a personal envoy to Berlin tonight to impress upon him that we have no dispute with Germany. For all his faults, the Kaiser is a personal friend of mine and a man of honour. He will understand our position and use his influence to restore peace. I will let you know as soon as I receive his response and I expect you to inform me immediately of any new developments. It doesn't matter how late it is, I shan't be sleeping until this whole mess is resolved."

Nicholas replaced the receiver and glanced again at the clock. It was going to be a long and wakeful night and he could only hope that these sleepless hours would lead to a peaceful conclusion.

As the sun rose over Potsdam, Wilhelm rode through the Sansoucci Park, throwing back his head to let the fine morning mist wash the drowsiness from his eyes. He could scarcely remember when he had last slept, and even when, in the early hours, he lay down to doze for a while, his thoughts buzzed and battled so frantically that rest had been impossible. Throughout the whole of the night, as telegrams passed back and forth between countries, Bethmann had returned again and again with an increasingly taut expression to deliver more alarming news. By dawn it was obvious that the Austrians were not only refusing to limit their military ambitions to a temporary occupation of Belgrade, but they were actively organising a general mobilisation against Russia. Despite all Bethmann's attempts at persuasion and restraint, Berchtold appeared to be incapable of understanding that he was dragging his country and her allies into a terrible war.

Wilhelm dug his heels into the horse's flank and galloped more quickly across the park in an attempt to flee the fearful thoughts that assailed him. If his efforts at mediation failed, the many successes of his reign – the progress in industry and the arts; the improvements in education and workers' benefits; the splendour of the Imperial Navy and the advancement of Germany's standing in the world – would be forgotten in the butchery of battle. The faster he rode, the more desperately he longed to hurtle on, beyond the park, beyond Berlin, and beyond the premonitions of slaughter that danced before his tired eyes.

His sole consolation was the knowledge that, if this war should come about, no army in the world was better trained, equipped and disciplined than his own. There was no doubt at all that his loyal battalions would soon prove victorious whomsoever their enemies might be and for one brief second the prospect of riding triumphantly at the head of a conquering army brought a rush of exhilaration through his limbs.

The momentary thrill quickly faded into horror as the dome of the Temple of Friendship came into view. Slowing his horse to a steady trot, he realised, perhaps for the first time in his life, how deeply he valued the friendship and affection of his extended family. One of the greatest pleasures of his reign had been his ability to entertain and impress his many cousins who came as guests to Potsdam. It pleased him to welcome them into his home, to amuse, and lavish gifts upon them; to offer advice and to see the fond admiration in their eyes. Above all, he wanted….no, *needed*…the feeling of belonging and being loved. His armies might conquer Europe; his navy might become the envy of the world, but what good would that do if none of his cousins and lifelong friends could appreciate or share in his victories? What joy could there be for a mighty Germany Emperor if he had made enemies of his own family?

He gently pulled at the reins and, dismounting, sat down on the steps of the Temple of Friendship to relive the many happy meetings with his cousins. He recalled Queen Victoria's Golden Jubilee procession through London; and the day twenty years before, when, thanks to his intervention, his cousin, Alix of Hesse, had finally accepted the proposal of the young Tsarevich Nicholas of Russia. There had never been a more joyful reunion than that day when so many of his relatives gathered in Coburg for the wedding of Alix' brother. Queen Victoria, was there, too – the great matriarch, clucking over her grandchildren like a great mother hen fussing over her brood of chicks. In those days, there was no antagonism or mistrust. There was only the certainty that Grandmama's dream of a peaceful Europe united by family ties had become a reality.

Surely, he thought, these bonds of kinship were strong enough to prevail against this rising madness. No one in this family of kings and emperors wanted war. He leaned back against a pillar and looked up at the dome.

"If *we* do not want war, who does? Who has anything to gain from it?"

An unnerving idea began to dawn on him. Queen Victoria's descendants were not the only family populating the courts of Europe. While kings and queens paraded on a public stage, other shadier characters connived behind the scenes to fulfil their own ambition. As intricate as the web of his royal relations, was the hidden network of a few other families, who had gradually infiltrated governments and made unseen alliances in their quest for wealth and power. Through their own dynastic marriages these families of bankers and businessmen had, within a few generations, worked their way through the courts of Europe and beyond, manipulating monarchs and markets to suit their own ends.

He recalled the coterie of financiers and industrialists who surrounded King Edward VII, and the part they played in controlling international banks. Had their influence on Uncle Bertie not helped to draw Britain away from her natural affinity with Germany, to form an alliance with republican France?

Wilhelm's jaw clenched at the shocking realisation that, far from holding the reins of power, he and his fellow monarchs were being played off against each other like toy soldiers in someone else's game.

Wars were expensive; the cost of maintaining and equipping an army was immense, and, while arms manufacturers and industrialists grew fat on their profits, the prosperity of nations was squandered in pointless slaughter. Bankrupted by battle, to whom could kings turn for assistance but to these same international bankers who had profited from virtually every war of the past hundred years?

He gripped the edge of the step. There was far more at stake here than simply the amassing of a personal fortune at the expense of a nation – if this war came about, the control of Europe could so easily fall into unscrupulous hands. As opposing armies exhausted themselves in battle, and kings were turned into beggars, pleading for a loan, these men could decide which side to fund and which to abandon, effectively controlling the outcome of the war. In truth, though, there would be no victors, for whoever won would remain indebted to these bankers, paying off the exorbitant interest for years, even decades to come.

Hints and insinuations to which he had paid little attention before, suddenly took on a new importance. Only three years ago, the British Prime Minister, Asquith, had commented on the way in which the German press was being controlled by one or two families, who could feed the masses with whatever information they chose. Was this not equally true of other nations? Were the peoples of Europe being roused into frenzy for a war which would ultimately destroy the established order, taking away each nation's autonomy and handing complete control of industry, wealth and government to these few for whom so many lives would be lost?

Invigorated by the realisation that he had seen through their plans, Wilhelm hastily remounted the horse and rode with even greater alacrity back to the New Palace, where an ashen-faced Bethmann stood at the entrance awaiting his return. Even before Wilhelm dismounted, the Chancellor thrust out another handful of reports.

"I'm sorry, Your Imperial Majesty. The news isn't good. In spite of all my efforts, the Austrians refuse to negotiate or compromise and war seems inevitable."

"Nonsense!" Wilhelm leapt eagerly from the saddle. "I will not allow Germany to be dragged into this. As long as my fellow-emperors and I continue to work together, I am certain we can reach an amicable solution." He strutted towards the entrance, "Is there any news from my brother in England?"

"Yes, sir." Bethmann, hurrying after him, fumbled through his papers, "Prince Henry explained to King George your proposals for negotiation and he has forwarded the King's response."

Wilhelm snatched the telegram from his hand, "My brother is – alas! – a child as far as politics goes, but he does have the ability to make himself agreeable to people so I dare say he was the best man to deal with the English." He looked over the telegram and nodded with satisfaction, "Excellent! You see, my dear Theo, your pessimism is premature. King George is eager to work with us to show that Germany and Britain are united in their desire for peace."

"And yet, last night when I spoke with the British ambassador and asked him to give an assurance that Britain will stay out of this, he treated my suggestions with disdain."

Refusing to listen, Wilhelm read on, "King George agrees that this can be settled through negotiation if the Austrians agree to go no further than Belgrade."

"But that's the problem, sir," Bethmann whined. "I have spent all night trying to gain that assurance but Berchtold ignores my requests for a compromise. Now the Austrians have even gone so far as to call up their reserves to mobilise against Russia."

Refusing to be dismayed, Wilhelm shook his head, "I shall write at once to Emperor Franz Josef. He cannot allow himself to be dictated to by ministers who may well have their own agenda that has nothing to do with the welfare of their people."

Bethmann shook his head, not understanding but Wilhelm had no desire to explain. He walked on, still reading the letter from his brother.

"King George is grateful for my mediation and eager that I should continue to put pressure on Austria. In the meantime, his government is urging the French and Russians to suspend any military preparations so that we can negotiate peacefully."

Bethmann sighed loudly and ominously.

"What?" Wilhelm demanded.

"It's too late. We have just received news that preparations for the Tsar's partial mobilisation against Austria is already underway."

Wilhelm stopped abruptly, "No. No. That *cannot* be so. Last night he agreed to cancel the mobilisation. He would not lie to me."

Bethmann raised his eyebrows apologetically and held out a further telegram, "It seems, sir, that the Tsar *did* cancel the mobilisation but, after consulting with his ministers and hearing of the Austrians' bombardment of Belgrade, he changed his mind. His troops are already preparing to move to the Austrian border."

Wilhelm, choking with anger and fear, seized the telegram. "What's he playing at!" He threw back his head in disgust, "First he asks me to mediate then goes behind my back to prepare for war! How can he claim that this is a defensive measure when Russia isn't even being attacked?"

He snatched the rest of the papers from Bethmann's hands and scattered them across the entrance hall. "Why should I bother? I have done all I can and this is how they respond! Very well, then, I shall mobilise, too. They want war so let them have it but God help them! My army is the most powerful fighting force in Europe and when it is roused to full strength they will all rue the day they paid no attention to my warnings!"

Brushing Bethmann aside, he stamped up the stairs to his private apartments where, slamming the door behind him, he threw himself onto his bed and buried his face in the pillow.

Chapter 25 – July 30th 1914

All morning so many heavy footsteps had come and gone from his door that Nicholas was sure that they must have worn a deep gully in the corridor as visible as the frown lines their conflicting reports had wrought in his brow. First came the bespectacled Prime Minister, Goremykin, frantically running his fingers through his excessive moustache and looking ten times older than his seventy-four years. It was vital, he said almost on his knees in supplication, that war be avoided at all costs. Then came the countless attendants and messengers bringing further telegrams and reports from across the continent and the different regions of the Russian Empire. Now, as the Council of Ministers gathered at the other side of the desk, Sazonov, in a panic, warned that Germany was preparing for war and the Kaiser had abandoned his attempts at mediation.

Various other ministers with equally grave faces nodded and agreed. One after another they stepped forwards with their gloomy assessments and ominous predictions:

"The Central Powers never had any intention of accepting a peaceful solution. From the moment the Austrians received the Kaiser's support, they began preparing for war."

"A half-hearted mobilisation against Austria will serve no purpose whatsoever if we find ourselves under attack from Germany."

"There is no other course now but a general mobilisation."

They leaned over maps and pointed out borders, predicting from which direction the most ferocious attack would come, and their voices clashed in a cacophony of chaos until Nicholas, no longer able to bear it, pushed back his chair and called, "No!"

Stunned by his outburst and frowning in confusion, they stared at him.

"Our sole aim is to protect Serbia and I have given the Kaiser my word that I will *not* mobilise against Germany."

They glanced warily at each other and for several minutes there was silence until Nicholas said quietly, "We have no quarrel with Germany and I still believe that the Kaiser will use his influence to restrain the Austrians."

Again there was silence until Sazonov inhaled sharply, "Your Imperial Majesty, the Kaiser has made plain that, whatever happens, he intends to honour his alliance."

His words clearly echoed the sentiments of the rest of the council and, like a group of unruly children vying for attention, they rushed to his support.

"The moment we intervene to prevent the Austrian advance, we will find ourselves under attack from Germany."

"How do we know that the Kaiser's mediation isn't really a distraction to give the Germans time to rally their troops and take us unprepared?"

"The longer we delay, the greater the risk."

"They are laughing at us! They think we are bluffing and will back down at the first show of opposition."

"If we don't show our strength now, we will not only sacrifice our influence in the Balkans but also lose all credibility as a major power, leaving the Central Powers free to do whatever they like. The Kaiser has been longing for an opportunity to display German military might and…"

Their words washed over him as Nicholas turned to the window to look out at the gathering clouds shrouding the mid-morning sun. Though he did not doubt the sincerity of their warnings, he realised that not one of these ministers knew Willy personally as he did. Yes, he loved his military pageants and martial displays but there was no aggression in that. He was as proud to prance about on the deck of a British dreadnaught in his British Admiral's uniform as he was to pose with his own Prussia cavalry in the helmet of the Death's Head Hussars. He might be impulsive and unpredictable but he was loyal to those whom he loved. When his close friend, Eulenburg, became embroiled in a scandal that might well have threatened Willy's own reputation, he had not abandoned him or allowed the rumours to damage their friendship. More importantly, Nicholas thought, throughout the most turbulent years of his reign, Willy's support had been unwavering. His personal affection for his cousins was evidenced by his many gifts for Nicholas' children and the warm wishes with which he always concluded his letters.

This was the Kaiser whom Nicholas knew, so why should he doubt his sincerity now when he had firmly reiterated his desire to maintain peace? Besides, Germany was flourishing, the economy was booming and industry prospered – would he really be willing to sacrifice that for a war that nobody wanted?

Still the ministers babbled through their alarming lists of reasons to doubt him but Nicholas had heard enough. He stepped past them to the door and, gripping the handle, said, "Gentlemen, I have made my decision. We continue as planned with the *partial* mobilisation."

"But surely…" someone began.

Nicholas raised his hand, "I trust the Kaiser and will not turn my army against him."

"And if he turns his army on us?"

The insubordination and lack of deference in the question greatly annoyed Nicholas and he retorted irritably, "I have given my orders and expect them to be obeyed. This meeting is concluded."

He threw open the door and, leaving the ministers to their mutterings, strode swiftly out to the gardens. He walked on and on, faster and faster, beyond the fountains and canals, over meadows and flower beds through the humid heat of the early afternoon, until at last he came to a beach leading to the wide expanse of the Baltic. Trickling waves hissed over stones, grinding them together, crunching them against broken shells and the severed claws of dead crabs. Driftwood, covered in slimy seaweed lay across the pebbles – timbers from ancient wrecks, perhaps, and branches that had fallen from trees on eroding cliff tops. He leaned against a boulder, running his fingers over the clinging limpets, and stared towards the horizon.

The sea's steady rhythm flowed soothingly and the timelessness of the scene was as calming as a lullaby. But for the outline of modern ships in the harbour, it could have been any era, any age. Any moment a fleet of Viking longboats might rise up on the horizon, for the sea still carried the echoes of the clanging of their shields and spears. Perhaps the fleet of his ancestor, Peter the Great, might float into view – *Poltava, Saint Catherine, Shlisselburg, Narva* and *Ingermanlanda* – returning from their victory over the Swedes or clinking with the jingling of gold and weighted by the cloths brought in from the Low Countries. It would not have surprised him to see the bow of a sinking man-o-war, blown off course and drifting towards the rocks, as the voices of its seamen reverberated on the cliff in desperate pleas for help.

He shook himself from the daydream and strode across the sand to let the sea spray bathe the sweat from his face. The droplets were so refreshing and invigorating, and the water so clear and alluring that he hastily pulled off his clothes and let them fall like a mountain of snow onto the sand. Running, he plunged naked into the sea and, as the waves rose to meet him, he raised his arms and let himself fall forwards, allowing the tide to carry him further from the shore. The chill of the icy Baltic on his skin, the salty taste of the waves on his tongue, he swam in sheer exhilaration as free as a salmon returning to its home, until all tension and fear and all thoughts of war vanished into the ocean.

When his fit of self-pity was exhausted, Wilhelm rolled from his bed to the wash-stand where he gazed at himself in the mirror.

"You are the Kaiser, the All-Highest Emperor of this great nation. Will you allow yourself to be dominated by lesser men? Wake up! There is no time for defeatism."

He splashed water over his face and smoothed his moustache before saluting to the image, "Now, let's sort out this mess!"

He marched towards the council room from which raised voices echoed. The Foreign Minister, Jagow, sitting alone in one corner, stood up as Wilhelm entered but Moltke and Bethmann were too engrossed in a heated argument to be aware of his arrival.

"Don't you realise," Bethmann shrieked, "that is the exact opposite of what His Majesty wants? It runs contrary to all his orders and…"

Moltke interrupted with such force that Wilhelm half-expected him to seize the Chancellor by the throat, "What do you expect? Am I supposed to sit back and do nothing while the Russians march in and take East Prussia?"

"His Majesty specifically stated that…"

"His Majesty is blinded by family loyalty! He might have faith in his little Russian cousin but I am not so easy to fool and I will not…" Suddenly noticing Wilhelm he broke off, wide eyed in horror.

"You will not what?" Wilhelm said.

Moltke opened his mouth to reply but seemed incapable of speech.

"Well?" Wilhelm stepped closer, "You had enough to say a moment ago, but who is the fool now?"

Moltke shook his head and rapidly ran his hand over his mouth, "Forgive me, sir, I didn't mean…"

Wilhelm stared him in the eye, purposely prolonging his discomfort.

"I am sorry, sir, but I had to do something."

"About what?"

Moltke looked at Bethmann who shook his head in disgust, "I have spent the past twenty-four hours trying to persuade the Austrians to show restraint and all the while General Moltke has been telling his counterpart in Vienna that the Austrians must order a full mobilisation against Russia!"

"Is this true?" Wilhelm demanded.

Moltke nodded, "The Russian mobilisation is more extensive than we first believed. At least four divisions are already on the move and yet I heard directly from Conrad von Hötzendorf that the Austrians troops are concentrating solely on Serbia, which leaves East Prussia wide open to a Russian attack."

"So you took it upon yourself to offer advice without my authority?"

"With all due respect, sir, the situation is changing so rapidly that there was no time to seek your permission and, as Commander-in-Chief of your army, it is my duty to do everything in my power to ensure the safety of Germany."

Wilhelm, incensed by his arrogance, was about to respond in a ferocious tirade when a newspaper lying on the table caught his eye. The startling headline immediately diverted his anger into horror and, forgetting Moltke, he snatched the paper, "What's this?" He held it out to Bethmann, "'...*His Imperial Majesty has ordered a general mobilisation and extensive war preparations are already underway....*'"

Bethmann shrugged, "Editors print whatever they choose in order to sell more newspapers."

"But this is untrue," Wilhelm said, aghast at his lack of concern. "It's a complete fabrication and a dangerous and incendiary fabrication at that! These papers are read all over the world and if stories like this are believed, the damage could be irreparable. Are they trying to provoke war?"

Asquith's warning about the power of the press, and the thoughts that had occurred to him earlier that morning in the Temple of Friendship returned to him with alarming clarity. This was exactly the way that monarchs were manipulated into unwanted wars.

"This has to be stopped now. Call the newspaper offices. Tell them to cease printing immediately!"

As Bethmann hurried to the telephone, Moltke, clearly relieved to have escaped the Kaiser's wrath, said, "Even though this report is false, it echoes the prevailing sentiment. All the other nations of Europe are preparing for war. Our people expect us to do the same or we could find ourselves in a very precarious position."

Wilhelm, still deeply disconcerted by the suspicion that he was being manipulated by unseen forces, murmured, "They *are* trying to provoke a war."

"The Russians, sir?" Molkte said.

Wilhelm shook his head but Moltke, not understanding, continued, "If war is inevitable, the sooner we are begin to implement our plans the better. There is no doubt that our troops are better prepared than any other force in Europe so if we act quickly this whole conflict can be brought to a swift conclusion, leaving us in a more powerful position than ever before."

"The longer war continues, the greater the profits for those schemers behind the scenes," Wilhelm said.

Moltke looked at him curiously but was too engrossed in his plans to attempt to understand, "As long as we counteract any attempt at encirclement, we can achieve a satisfactory victory."

"*Encirclement,*" Wilhelm said quietly, "this has always been the greatest threat to us."

"Yes, sir," said Moltke, "the worst things that could happen for us would be for us to be attacked on two fronts – Russia to the east, France to the west, which is why it is fortunate that we had the foresight to prepare for such an eventuality." Suddenly animated, he leapt towards the table and unrolled a map. "We know that throughout this crisis the Russians and French have been in constant communication but we do not know for certain whether or not the French will come to Russian support in the event of a war."

Jagow moved to his side, "In order to discover the French intentions we intend to ask them to give an assurance of neutrality."

"Neutrality?" Wilhelm laughed ironically. "The French despise us. In the unlikely event that they agree to remain neutral, we could never trust them to honour that agreement."

"Ah," Moltke smiled, pressing his finger to the map, "we have thought of that. As a guarantee of their neutrality, we will ask them to hand over to us the garrison forts at Verdun and Toul until the conflict is over."

"They will never agree to that! They will join forces with Russia and we will be attacked on both sides."

Moltke's eyes gleamed with excitement, "If you recall, sir, ten years ago when the French began making overtures to Russia, Schlieffen, prepared for just such an eventuality."

"Schlieffen?" Wilhelm muttered.

"My predecessor as Chief of Staff."

Wilhelm nodded and Moltke pointed to the map, "May I?" He spread his huge palm across Russia, "The various divisions of the Russian army are scattered all over the empire. It will take at least six weeks for the Tsar to organise his troops and bring them to our eastern borders. That leaves us plenty of time to concentrate on disabling the French and forcing them to surrender before they can come to his aid. We estimate that within forty days our troops could take Paris. By the time Russia is fully prepared, the Tsar will be isolated and the strength and discipline of our army will soon overcome any resistance. In no time at all we will find both France and Russia suing for peace and willing to comply with whatever demands we choose to make."

Wilhelm raised his eyebrows, "We take lunch in Paris and tea in St. Petersburg?"

Moltke smiled indulgently, which irked Wilhelm, causing him to adopt a more serious tone. He ran his finger over the French border, "How do we propose to bypass all these heavily armed forts?"

"Schlieffen's original idea was to avoid that border by sweeping through Holland, Luxemburg and

Belgium but, as I see it, there is no need to involve Holland. We simply move directly through Belgium. The flat terrain will facilitate a speedy advance."

Bethmann, having concluded his telephone call, moved to the table, "The Belgians have declared their neutrality in the case of any European conflict."

"Exactly," Moltke smiled, "so they will offer no resistance. We will send a request to King Albert asking him to allow us to pass through his country."

"As soon as the French become aware of our plans they will come out to meet us and the whole of Belgium will be turned into a battlefield! How could King Albert possibly agree to that?"

Moltke smugly raised his eyes to the ceiling, "He will be powerless to object. Our Second Army alone has over three hundred thousand men – if we send about thirty-four divisions to his border, the King will have to let us pass."

"Unless," Wilhelm said, "he appeals to Britain for help. The British agreed to protect Belgian neutrality…"

Instantly his mind ran back to his boyhood holidays in England – the toy fort at Osborne and the childish battles in which he was always the victor. His heart rose and sank in one moment. Life was so different in those days; wounds were not real and scars always faded by teatime.

"We have nothing to fear from the British," Moltke said. "They have too many problems with the socialists and the Irish to want to involve themselves in mainland Europe."

Bethmann shook his head, "When our ambassador asked the British Foreign Secretary about his country's intentions, Grey wouldn't commit himself but insisted that he couldn't guarantee neutrality."

"Common cur!" Wilhelm suddenly snapped, half-absorbed by his childhood memories. "There was a time when Britain was a good friend to Germany but since the days of my buffoon of an uncle, King Edward VII, the British have gone out of their way to treat us as rivals and hinder our progress. Very well! If they involve themselves in this, we shall strike them where it hurts the most; we will take their greatest possession – the 'jewel in their crown'. Jagow, have agents sent into India to stir up a Moslem revolt. That will give those deceitful traitors something else to think about and if we are to bleed to death in this war, the English will at least lose India!"

As though he had not spoken, Jagow turned to Moltke, "Thirty-four divisions entering Belgium, you say?"

Moltke nodded.

"If the greater part of our army is involved in that move, won't that leave us unprotected to the east?"

"As I said," Moltke smiled, "the Russian army won't be ready for weeks. The Austrians can hold off the Tsar's few divisions until we complete our conquest of France." He turned to Wilhelm, "This is why I was urging the Austrians to order a complete mobilisation. I know that Your Majesty has done everything in his power to maintain peace but you have been deceived, sir. Now it is time to show that the German Emperor will not be dictated to by foreign powers. By carrying out this plan, we can quickly take complete control of this situation and you, Your Majesty, will go down in history as the greatest ruler since Frederick the Great."

Jolted from anger and nostalgia, Wilhelm stared at him pensively, trying to reconcile his conflicting emotions.

"You see, sir," Moltke said more forcefully, "until now we have never had an opportunity of witnessing a unified Germany defending herself against her enemies. Success in this venture will not only ensure that we are no longer at risk of being encircled by foreign powers, but will also serve to create a sense of national pride. However," he lowered his voice, "if we fail to act we will appear weak and unreliable and a force to be dismissed in the eyes of the world."

Weak? The word revolted Wilhelm. He eyes moved over the map, comparing the size of Nicholas' vast empire to his own, and remembering the wise old Chancellor, Bismarck, whose advice on foreign affairs had always proved so sound.

"Austria and Russia," he said, recalling Bismarck's insistence that good relations with both were vital for German stability.

Again, he wished that Bismarck were still here to advise him, Surely he, who had so easily embarrassed and quashed the liberal views of Wilhelm's own parents and played so great a role in unifying Germany, would know the best course of action to take now. He viewed the faces of the ministers standing before him – for all the strength of their opinions and all the guile in their eyes, not one of them inspired the confidence that had exuded from that 'Iron Chancellor.' It was instantly clear to Wilhelm that he must now show that decisive leadership for which he had been born.

Weakness…whatever happened, he could not appear weak. He threw back his shoulders and tucking his hands into his belt said, "Since the rest of the world has taken up arms it is time for us to show that Germany, too, means business."

Moltke smiled hopefully, "You will authorise a general mobilisation?"

"No, sir, please!" Bethmann suddenly intervened with as much terror in his eyes as a condemned man facing his executioner.

Wilhelm, shaken by his desperation, stared at him.

"Please hold back just a little longer. Neither the British nor the French have mobilised; the Tsar has only authorised a partial mobilisation which is not directed against us; and, in spite of General Moltke's interference, even the Austrians have only a partial mobilisation against Serbia. If we were to mobilise now, we could well be making the situation so much worse. Surely, sir, you are not willing to sacrifice the blood of so many of your loyal soldiers, and your own reputation as a peaceful Emperor, while there is even the remotest chance of peace."

Hurled once more into confusion, Wilhelm shook his head.

"General Moltke would have you presented as a conquering hero, but will that really be the case? It would be a dreadful misrepresentation of your reign and all you have done for your people if you were to go down in history as nothing but another Prussian warlord."

Wilhelm winced but Bethmann went further, "You see, sir, your people love you because you have maintained peace throughout the entire twenty-six years of your reign. What other monarch can claim such an accolade? The British have fought the Boers; the Russians have fought the Japanese; the Austrians have lived in constant disharmony with the Serbs; but since Unification, Germany has shown herself to be a peace-loving place. We are a modern nation – a nation of the future not the past. We don't squander our success on fruitless campaigns, and so the country has prospered. Can we cast all that aside for the sake of this squabble between the decaying Austro-Hungarian Empire and unruly Serbs?"

Wilhelm stared down at the carpet, trying to imagine how he might be seen by posterity. Bethmann was right – this *was* a different era than that of his hero, Frederick the Great. Even Frederick, he thought, had gained greatness not through his many successful military campaigns but through the prosperity, education and culture he brought to his country.

"For the sake of my people," he eventually said, "I will stay my hand a little longer. I will give the Tsar one more chance to back down, and you, Bethmann, will do everything you can to impress upon Austria the necessity of accepting immediate mediation."

Moltke groaned loudly but Wilhelm, unwilling to hear an opposing argument for fear of being persuaded to change his mind, turned and walked from the room.

"As unpredictable as the weather," he heard Moltke whisper behind him. "One minute he hates the British, the next he wants to form an alliance with them. One minute he calls the Tsar a weakling and a traitor, the next he…"

Pressing his hand to his ear to block out Moltke's voice, Wilhelm hurried away along the corridor.

Chapter 26 – July 30th 1914 –
Schloss Wartholz, Lower Austria

Karl lay in the long grass looking up at the myriad of shades of blue and silver streaking the summer sky. A cloud floated by like a prehistoric monster lost in a fathomless expanse of ocean, followed by faces and figures from mythical tales; giants with shields, and fire-breathing dragons, the Habsburg eagle, and heavy grey whales.

In spite of the beauty of the season and the peacefulness of the gardens, he felt deeply troubled. He had hoped that by spending this time alone with Zita he might regain the tranquillity that had deserted him of late, but now, as the afternoon faded into evening, the sense of impending tragedy intensified. For the past week he had told himself that the alarming headlines were nothing more than the journalists' need to create a crisis in order to sell papers; after all, he had thought, if anything significant were happening, he, as heir, would be among the first to be told. No official information had come from Vienna, and the sole communication from the Emperor – a brief note announcing the declaration of war on Serbia – implied that this was a minor conflict which would be settled in a matter of days.

That alone had been disconcerting. It seemed remarkable that, while the conspirators awaiting trial maintained that they had acted entirely of their own volition and refused to implicate any specific group in their crime, the Emperor had, without tangible proof, accepted his ministers' insistence that the Serbian government was to blame, and authorised the declaration of war. If the decision had been taken in the days immediately following Uncle Franz' death, it might have been put down to a reflex reaction to such an appalling crime but the month's delay between the murder and this offensive cast the situation in an entirely different light. In that time, it had become apparent that not only was there no evidence of the Serbian government's involvement but also that the Prime Minister, Pasic, had been strenuously seeking to outlaw and disperse the Black Hand. Moreover, the young hot-heads who carried out the crime, had stated quite clearly that they had no particular allegiance to Serbia, as their intention was to create an entirely new and independent state of Yugoslavia.

Even more perplexing was the Emperor's explanation that the bombardment of Belgrade began in response to Serb shelling. The Emperor stated unequivocally that he only authorised the offensive when Berchtold informed him that Austrians were under attack; yet, clearly that wasn't the case. The Serbs' were desperate to avoid war, and every report confirmed that the Austrian attack was unprovoked. Why had Berchtold deliberately deceived the Emperor?

Karl stared intently into the sky as he thought of a disturbing letter which Zita had received that morning from her cousin, Queen Elizabeth of the Belgians. According to the Queen, her husband, King Albert, fearing an imminent invasion, had ordered the strengthening of the fortifications at Liège and was preparing similar defensive measures at various sites along the German border. If the peace-loving King of neutral Belgium felt sufficiently alarmed to take action, surely the more belligerent nations must be readying themselves for war on a far wider scale.

He turned to look at Zita, sitting on the grass beside him and peering intently at the bark of a tree. Feeling his eyes upon her, she blinked and said quietly,

"Nature can be very frightening, can't it? It all appears so calm and beautiful on the surface but look a little closer and there are layers upon layers of murders and massacres going on all around us."

She pointed to a fly, flapping frantically in a hopeless attempt to escape from a spider's web.

"It is the same everywhere:" she said, looking up at the tree top, "birds killing worms and flies; bigger birds killing smaller birds…and no matter how civilised the gardens appear or how carefully they are tended and tamed, the same daily violence continues; daily horrors, daily massacres…"

"Or daily wonders," Karl said, rolling onto his stomach and resting his chin on his hands. "Eggs hatching, seeds growing, buds, blossom, new life…"

She smiled and leaned back against the tree, "Yes, of course you're right. I am just being pessimistic."

He rolled over again onto his back and closed his eyes against the glare of the sun. But for the buzzing of the fly and the rustle of birds in the branches, there was silence for a while but he sensed, even through closed eyes, that Zita was laboriously considering some troublesome question.

"Karl," she eventually said, "I read that last month Cardinal Pacelli, on behalf of the Pope, presided over the signing of a Serbian Concordat with the Vatican. Do you know anything about it?"

"Yes," he sat up and nodded enthusiastically. "It's a means of ensuring freedom of worship for Roman Catholics in Serbia. Considering that we began our occupation of Bosnia-Herzegovina to protect religious freedom, it was perhaps the Holy Father's means of ensuring the same freedom throughout the rest of the Balkans, without the need for further invasions or annexations."

"Was the Emperor informed of it in advance?"

"I don't think so. There was no reason why he should have been since it was an agreement between the Vatican and the Serbs."

"And yet, until now, hasn't there been an unspoken arrangement whereby the Vatican has relied upon the Emperor to protect the interests of Catholics in the region?"

Karl nodded, "Which is precisely why it is such an inspired move. There is enough animosity between us and the Serbs without bringing religious differences into it. I think perhaps the Holy Father saw it as a means of easing the tension between us."

Zita, with a deeply troubled frown, shuffled closer, "Doesn't it seem significant that this Concordat was signed only four days before the murder of Uncle Franz and Sophie?"

To Karl is seemed no more than a coincidence. "What do you mean?" he said.

"The timing seems odd and, putting that together with the Pope's prophecy about Uncle Franz never becoming Emperor, I can't help wondering..." the sentence trailed off and she stared into space, frowning in contemplation.

Karl lay down again but her words played and replayed in his head and wove their way through his own suspicions creating a tangle of confusion and doubt.

Everything was falling into place exactly as Franz Ferdinand had predicted, yet the likelihood of one chance event or even a whole series of chance events precipitating a war seemed impossible. As the days had passed, the connection between the murder of Uncle Franz and the heated discussions taking place between ambassadors and ministers had become so tenuous that his death seemed to be nothing but a spark to ignite a well-orchestrated and pre-planned explosion. Once again Karl recalled the shady figures whom Franz Ferdinand had described as controlling monarchs and the destiny of nations. It wounded him deeply to think that his uncle's death had been used – or even planned – to provoke a conflict that could lead to the downfall of empires and the undermining of religion in Europe. What was even more painful and abhorrent was a terrible question gnawing at his brain: could it be that these shady figures lurked even in the hallowed halls of the Vatican and they, too, knew in advance of the plan to kill Franz Ferdinand?

Disgusted that he could even think such a thing, he sat up, convinced that this was but a ruse of Satan, who as St. Sebastian had warned, *"strains every nerve to secure the souls which belong to Christ."*

"It's all so confusing," he said to Zita. "Will you come with me to the chapel?"

As they walked back to the villa, he reached into his pocket and, pulling out his rosary, prayed silently for protection and guidance. By the time he had finished one decade, the rush of fear had passed and he was about to begin the second *Pater Noster* when an attendant charged towards him, urging him to hurry as the Emperor was waiting to speak with him on the telephone.

Breathless with running, he lifted the receiver and before he had finished gasping a greeting, he heard a frail voice on the crackling line.

"My dear boy, the situation has taken a very dangerous turn. It's better that I do not give you too many details now as I cannot be certain of the security of the telephone line…"

Karl looked up as Zita walked silently into the room.

"I will send a telegram in a day or two with more information but in the meantime I need you to prepare for a tour of Hungary to rally support. In the coming days we are going to need the whole of the empire behind us. Do you understand?"

"War?" Karl whispered.

He hesitated, "I fear it will be on a far wider scale than I had envisaged."

Karl's heart sank, "Whatever I can do to help, uncle, you know you have my full support and I place myself at your service."

Zita stepped closer and rested her head on his shoulder.

"Then pray for me Karl; I need your prayers now more than ever since even the Pope has…"

"The Pope?" Karl said.

"He has denied me a blessing. Our ambassador informed him that we have declared war on Serbia, and he asked for a blessing for me but the Holy Father replied that he would sooner curse me for what I have done."

Karl stared at Zita in horror.

"I cannot understand it," the Emperor continued. "Only a couple of day ago, the same ambassador reported that Pope Pius had spoken of the importance of maintaining and strengthening Austria-Hungary as the Church's stronghold in Europe. He clearly expressed his belief that the Serbian threat must be firmly dealt with to avoid the disintegration of the Empire. Yet now…"

His voice was weary and sad but Karl could find no words of comfort to offer him beyond the reassurance, "Zita and I will go at once to Hungary as you asked and then I must return to my regiment."

"No, no. Leave it for a couple of days. Wait for a telegram. Miracles happen from time to time and there is still the slightest chance that the worst might be avoided."

"Then we will pray for that more fervently than ever."

"God bless you, Karl."

A click and the line buzzed, but Karl waited some seconds before replacing the receiver.

"You don't need to explain," Zita said. "It's obvious what he wanted to tell you."

Stunned, Karl could only say, "This is a disaster – a terrible disaster. The Pope has refused to bless him. What is going on, Zita?"

He flopped into a chair and she sat down on the floor at his feet.

"This must be heart-breaking for the Emperor," he said, staring at a crucifix on the opposite wall. "He has such devotion to the Holy See – in fact ten years ago he was responsible for the election of Pope Pius."

Zita looked up, "Really?"

"The Conclave was about to elect Cardinal Rampolla but for some reason Uncle Franz Josef intervened and used his power of veto to prevent his becoming pope."

"Why?"

"There were many rumours about Rampolla's connection to Freemasonry – all of which I am sure were unfounded – and other stories about how he favoured the Serbs and the Slavs over Austria. Perhaps Uncle Franz Josef's greatest objection, though, was that Rampolla was known to have strong opinions about modernising the Church."

"Whereas Pope Pius has done everything possible to strengthen tradition."

Karl nodded, "The poor Emperor must be in complete despair about his response to the war with Serbia."

"And, for the Pope to take such a stand, he, too must be in despair about what is happening."

Karl slid from the chair and sat down on the floor beside her, "It's all become so murky, hasn't it? The politics of the Church and the politics of nations...forgive me, but all of this seems so very far removed from the Gospels and all that Christ taught."

"I know," she soothed, "but we must hold to our faith now more than ever. Let's pray, Karl."

He pulled the beads from his pocket again and together they whispered the rosary.

Like a condemned man anticipating the arrival of his executioner, Nicholas stood in the doorway of his study torn between the hope of a last minute reprieve and weary resignation to his fate. Sazonov's voice had sounded so ominous that Nicholas, unwilling to hear his news via a telephone line, had cut him short and requested that he come in person to the palace, but now, as he waited for him to appear, the delay only prolonged his torment.

Alongside the terrible prospect of war itself, came the torture of uncertainty as to how such a conflict would progress. If everything could be concluded in a matter of weeks or months, there was every chance that Russia would come through it unscathed. With a standing army of almost six million men and as many again in reserve, the sheer weight of numbers would be sufficient to overcome any immediate assault by the Central Powers. If, however, the enemy were able to withstand the first onslaught, the Russian Empire was ill-equipped to maintain a sustained engagement. The railways were not prepared to convey endless lines of men and supplies to the front; the armament factories could not cope with too vast a demand; and the arrival of foreign imports would be severely impeded if the

Baltic ports should come under attack. His thoughts returned again to the Japanese War – a war that his ministers and generals were certain they would win. Then, as now, the Russian troops outnumbered those of the enemy but by the time they had completed the long trek through Manchuria, the men were in no fit state to fight; half their guns and horses had been lost en route, and the 'short victorious war' that his ministers had predicted, ended in a slow ignominious defeat.

The thought of inflicting more suffering on his soldiers was painful enough but when added to the realisation of what war would mean to the civilians at home, the scenario was even more unbearable. On a personal level, too, there were so many considerations to take into account: wouldn't it break his wife's heart to see her native Germany under attack from her adopted homeland? And how would he tell the children that their cousins in Hesse and Prussia were now their foes?

Sazonov's footsteps sounded along the corridor – slow and unsteady as though he, too, were trying to postpone the inevitable.

"Your Majesty," he said solemnly, "all our reports suggest that the Kaiser is preparing for war. It isn't possible to delay the general mobilisation any longer."

"You are certain of this?" Nicholas' voice came out in a whisper.

"Even the German newspapers have published details of the extent of their preparations. If the reports were not true, the Kaiser would not have allowed them to go print."

Nicholas stepped backwards into the study, "Do you realise what you are asking of me, Sergei? Do you understand the suffering that will come from this?"

Sazonov exhaled loudly, "Yes, sir, I do and I know that you have tried so hard to prevent this but the Central Powers are intent on destroying our influence in the Balkans and are arbitrarily slaughtering our allies in Serbia. What more can we do?"

Nicholas felt the blood rush from his face. His heart thudded and an agonizing wrench churned in his stomach. "I know that you're right," he eventually managed to say. "Go ahead with the general mobilisation and may God help us."

Chapter 27 – Potsdam – July 31st 1914

Wilhelm stood at the window trying to muffle the voices of his ministers and silence the clamour inside his head. For over half a century he had dreamed of a glorious military victory that would elevate him to the status of King Frederick the Great but, even in his most vivid imaginings, he had never considered the fate of the vanquished or envisaged that such a triumph could cost him the friendship – or even the lives – of those he held dear. In his dreams, he had seen himself admired and revered by his fellow monarchs, and his empire as the model to which every nation aspired. He had imagined that Germany's military might would be the envy of all the peoples of Europe; and her scientific and cultural advances would earn veneration and respect throughout the world.

Now, though, stark reality had invaded his dreams. His fellow monarchs – cousins and friends – had deceived and betrayed him; they smiled at him while plotting the demise of his empire, and they spoke of friendship while laughing behind his back. In that moment it seemed that the whole of his life had been nothing but a series of fantasies and now, in his fifty-sixth year, he was suddenly confronted by the truth. Once he had laughed at the madness of King Ludwig of Bavaria, dressing up as the mythical knight, Lohengrin, and playing in his fairy-tale castles in boats drawn by artificial swans on artificial lakes; yet now, as he stood in the midst of his ministers' raised voices, he realised that, no less than Ludwig, he too had lived in a dream.

He had never commanded an army in the field or even witnessed a battle, yet his wardrobes were filled with military uniforms like costumes for his fantasies or play clothes for a childish game. Only six weeks earlier, as he strolled through the gardens of Konopischt, he had seen himself as a fairy-tale hero who could magically settle all international crises by a wave of his hand. With Franz Ferdinand, he had planned to create stronger ties with Russia; he had foreseen that between them they could bring stability to the Balkans and, without compromising German prestige, would bring peace to the world. Now, Franz Ferdinand lay cold in his tomb; chaos reigned in the Balkans; Russia was readying herself for battle; and Germany was being dragged into someone else's war.

He turned and looked at his ministers' desperate faces and his lips curled in self-loathing. How could he have been so foolish as to think his ideas would be heeded? And how could he have been so naïve as to trust his so-called friends? From Britain, George was sending messages of support while his naval warships raced through the Channel; and from Russia, Nicholas sent messages of peace while his army prepared to attack.

'How could I have been so mistaken about Nicky?' he thought, 'It never crossed my mind that the malleable and affectionate boy would stand so firm against my warnings and advice. Why is he doing this? Who has deceived him into seeing me as the enemy?'

"...no doubt whatsoever," Moltke was telling Bethmann. "My officers in East Prussia have seen it with their own eyes. The Tsar has sealed the border and mobilisation notices have been posted in all the cities, towns and outlying villages."

Bethmann's face was as white as a sepulchre. Only hours earlier, he had been eagerly announcing that at last the Austrians might be willing to compromise and accept a peace plan proposed by the British Foreign Secretary. Now he stood mute and motionless, holding between his fingers a telegram from Ambassador Pourtalès in St. Petersburg, confirming the Russians' general mobilisation.

The normally taciturn Foreign Minister, Jagow, looked up at the ceiling as though seeking divine inspiration, "All the major powers are anticipating war. The markets and banks are in turmoil – the London Stock Exchange closed earlier today, giving no indication of when it will re-open. Interest rates have taken a sharp increase. Here, as in Austria, food prices are soaring and people are pledging all kinds of securities in order to gain advances from the banks...."

'Ah yes,' Wilhelm thought, 'the banks. Like rats scurrying from a sinking ship, these bankers have a nose for detecting an imminent disaster long before kings and emperors are aware of the danger. What is it? Some kind of instinct? Or have they deliberately created the disaster?'

"Everyone," Jagow continued, "is preparing for war."

"Everyone," Moltke said, "except the German army." He turned to Wilhelm, "How much longer can we wait, Your Majesty? If we don't act now, the Russians will be pouring into East Prussia unimpeded. The Italians refuse to honour their agreements with us; the Austrians are too busy concentrating on Serbia to protect our borders; and the Roumanians and Bulgarians are prevaricating. Soon we will find ourselves quite alone against the combined armies of Russia and France; and who can say how long it will be before the British seize a chance to strike? For the sake of the Fatherland, we must ready ourselves. I beg you, sir, issue a state of martial law and authorise an immediate general mobilisation."

"No," Bethmann pleaded. "Wait just a little longer. Britain hasn't made any definite commitment and, if the Austrians accept these new peace proposals, the Tsar will surely cancel his mobilisation."

Moltke threw his arms in the air, "We have waited long enough! The Austrians have had weeks to come to an agreement but they have resisted all attempts at mediation and Emperor Franz Josef has ordered a general mobilisation. Why should the Tsar trust them now? And why should we trust the Tsar? Yesterday he told His Majesty that he would not raise his army against us yet only hours later – without even the usual courtesy of informing us of his intention – he, too, ordered this general mobilisation. Sir," he turned again to Wilhelm, "there is only one way of preventing a Russian attack. We must send an ultimatum warning the Tsar that unless his army stands down, we consider ourselves at war."

'Now,' thought Wilhelm, *'they have backed me into a corner and played me for a fool. Nicky and I are mere pawns in their hands but, God damn it, if I must play their game, I will play it to win and when this is over they will come to realise that the All-Highest Kaiser has seen through their schemes and will never again allow himself to be so callously manipulated.'*

He drew himself to full height, "Germany will not be toyed with any longer. It is time to show that we mean business."

Bethmann shrank visibly but Moltke's eyes glowed with satisfaction, "The ultimatum is to be sent?"

Wilhelm nodded, "If, within twelve hours of receiving it, we have not received assurances that the Tsar has withdrawn his troops from the Austrian border, we are at war."

"And the French?" Moltke said.

"Tell them they have eighteen hours to declare their neutrality or we will unleash on them the mighty army of the Fatherland!"

Bethmann's head hung so low that he might have been weeping, "Even if that means invading neutral Belgium?"

"The Belgians have a choice," Moltke said coldly. "If King Albert allows us safe passage, our troops will behave impeccably and cause him no harm."

"You know as well as I do that he cannot do that."

"Then we will take Liège and watch the rest of Belgium crumble."

"No," Wilhelm said. "My Imperial Army is not a pack of marauding invaders. We are not in dispute with King Albert and it contravenes all laws of decency and chivalry to invade a neutral country."

"Your Majesty," Moltke said with a hint of exasperation, "we did not create this war but if we must fight, we must ensure that we suffer as few casualties as possible and achieve a swift victory."

"Not at the expense of innocent civilians," Wilhelm said, his confidence rapidly ebbing away. "We have no authority to invade Belgium."

"As soon as the first shot is fired, we will find ourselves attacked on two flanks: France to the west, Russia to the east. Our only hope of success is to crush the French as quickly as possible so that we can turn our attention to Russia."

Annoyed by his patronising tone, Wilhelm said, "Do you think I don't know this?"

Moltke, unflinching, met his eyes, "Then may I ask how would Your Majesty suggest we defeat the French without passing through Belgium?"

"By the same route as the French will launch their attack; the route my grandfather's army took in the Franco-Prussian war."

"Via Alsace?" Moltke smirked and, turning to the table, boldly unrolled a map, "And when we reach the border, how do you propose we bypass these heavily-armed forts?"

Wilhelm stared helplessly at the map.

"Verdun, Moulainville, Douaumont and the rest...they have all been significantly strengthened since the Franco-Prussian War. I suppose," he grinned with obvious sarcasm, "like the armies of old, we could lay siege to them and, after months of waiting around, we might eventually starve them out only to find that while our attention was fixed on the French, the Russians have sneaked in through the back door!"

Angered as much by his own inability to find a solution as by Moltke's insolence, Wilhelm snatched the map and flung it across the table, "You are getting ahead of yourself, General. The French might yet declare their neutrality and, when the Tsar receives our ultimatum, he is sure to back down. Why are we wasting time discussing hypothetical battles when there is still a chance that war can be avoided?"

He turned to Jagow and Bethmann, "Prepare the ultimatum and have it sent to Pourtalès in St. Petersburg with orders that he deliver it at once. When you have done that, contact our ambassador in Paris and have him demand that the French declare their neutrality or face an imminent invasion."

Moltke waited as though he, too, expected to be given an order but when Wilhelm, ignored him and moved to walk out, he said defiantly, "Does this mean, Your Majesty, that Germany is now under martial law?"

Wilhelm turned and glanced at him.

"It would be a wise decision, sir. We need to close the borders and ensure that your troops are in place for any eventuality, howsoever we choose to proceed."

Wilhelm nodded, "Begin preparations but hold off the mobilisation until we see how the Tsar responds to the ultimatum."

The fragrance of incense and the chanting of priests brought their familiar reassurance as Nicholas stood in the chapel of Peterhof, his eyes closed and his hands clasped tightly in prayer. For the first time in weeks, his thoughts were more settled and his muscles less tense as a deep serenity pervaded his soul with the sense that a power far greater than his own held everything safely in its hand. Here, in this atmosphere of sanctity and calm, he could, for a little while at least, let go of the frenzied and conflicting messages with which his ministers had been bombarding him, and listen instead to the whisper of God to whom everything was clear.

Empires, he thought, rise and fall; tsars come and go; and all that remains is a name in a history book or a portrait in a gallery, but God is timeless, changeless and infinite. With his eyes still closed he joined in the chanted *Te Deum* and the powerful prayer of praise soothed his spirits. The vice-like stiffness in his shoulders eased and, with every line, his limbs relaxed.

"*...The glorious company of the Apostles praise thee. The righteous fellowship of the prophets praise thee. The noble army of martyrs praise thee. The holy Church throughout all the world doth praise thee...*"

Even his eyes, which had been so weary from reading countless documents and telegrams, felt refreshed and his breath flowed more freely as he sang. It seemed as though the weight of responsibility had been lifted from his shoulders until he came to the final refrain:

O Lord, have mercy upon us. Lord, let thy mercy lighten upon us as our trust is in thee. O Lord, in thee have I trusted: let me never be confounded."

He opened his eyes widely and the onerous burden of responsibility weighed on him more heavily than ever. Tsars and empires might pass, he thought, but their legacy continues for generations. Never before had he felt so acutely that the future of nations hung on his words, and the far-reaching implications of decisions he made at this crucial time would affect the lives of millions of people for decades to come. He had little doubt that he would be forgotten – just another name on the list of Romanov Tsars – and, after the relentless pressure of recent weeks, there was something attractive in the idea of lying forgotten in a cool tomb, unruffled by the cares of the world. But what he did now, the orders he gave and the decisions he made were more vital than anything he had ever said or done in the whole of his life.

"In thee, dear God, I put my trust," he prayed. "Even at this late hour, I cling to the hope that this war can be avoided...."

Perhaps Wilhelm would prevail on the Austrians to halt their bombardment of Belgrade; after all, his telegrams still spoke of his desire for peace. As an emperor, he was aware that no honourable country could abandon a smaller ally and he must have seen the ease with which Russia had persuaded to the Serbs to comply with virtually all the Austrian demands. It was surely possible then for Wilhelm to bring the same pressure to bear on Vienna. Why this intransigence? Why this reckless antagonism? And why would he speak of peace if in truth he was spoiling for war?

When the Vespers were complete, Nicholas turned to Alix who lingered in her prayers. Her lips were clenched so tightly that she might have been restraining a scream, and Nicholas had no doubt at all that her prayers for peace were even more fervent than his own. He smiled tenderly at his children whose faces, for all their youthful freshness, bore traces of the tension that had filled the whole country for days.

"Well," Alix sighed as they stepped out from the chapel, "let's trust that Willy will finally see sense."

"I have done all I can," Nicholas said sincerely. "I have urged him to persuade the Austrians to withdraw; I have done everything possible to make the Serbs' response to their demands acceptable; and I have presented so many offers of mediation, so I cannot understand how he can say that the outcome rests entirely in my hands."

Alix shook her head, "He has lost his head, I'm sure of it. I doubt that the poor old Austrian Emperor would have sent his troops into Serbia if Willy hadn't pressed him to do so."

"I still cannot believe that Willy would deliberately deceive me. His telegrams repeatedly stress that he has tried to restrain the Austrians but..."

"Oh Nicky," she gripped his hand, "it is because you are so honourable that you don't believe other men can be so treacherous."

"You think he has been lying to us all along?"

"Either that or he is quite mad. He says one thing and does another, and he leaps from one idea to the next with no reason or rationality whatsoever. He was always the same even when he was young. One minute he was elated, the next in the depths of depression. That's why he cannot be trusted."

The peace of the chapel had evaporated now and in its place came a despondent sense of imminent doom.

"Even Grandmama despaired of him," Alix said.

"I thought he was devoted to Queen Victoria."

Alix shrugged, "He was when the mood suited him, but she knew what he was like." She looked up thoughtfully, "How was it she described him? '...*Hotheaded, conceited, devoid of all feelings...with a very unhealthy and unnatural state of mind.*'"

Nicholas wearily dragged his feet, "I really hoped he would find a way to put a stop to this madness but the ministers think it's too late. They see war as inevitable."

She shook her head quickly, unwilling to listen, "I prayed so fervently for peace. Everything is in God's hands and he will not let us down."

They did not speak again until they reached the secluded villa in the grounds of the Peterhof Palace where Alix and the children made their way into the dining room for dinner. Nicholas, too anxious to eat, excused himself and hurried to his study to see if any dispatches had arrived during his absence. The usual piles of messages lay across his desk and he quickly flicked through them in the vain hope of finding a conciliatory telegram from the Kaiser.

The study was silent and calm: no frenzied activity, no sign of ministers or messengers dashing in with news. The steady ticking of the clock and the birdsong outside created so peaceful an atmosphere that it almost seemed as though the frenetic commotion of recent days had been little more than a nightmare. He sat down and exhaled loudly as the sound of soft footsteps approached. Moments later the Minister of the Imperial Court was standing in the doorway.

"Fredericks," Nicholas smiled, "any news?"

"Sazonov telephoned, Your Majesty."

"And?"

"I am so sorry, sir. Germany has issued an ultimatum. Unless you halt the mobilisation and withdraw our troops from the Austrian border, by this time tomorrow we will be at war."

Chapter 28 – Potsdam – 1ˢᵗ August 1914

Wilhelm paced the corridor, his thoughts raging like a battlefield in his head. In spite of the sunlight glistening through the windows, the palace seemed as dull and cold as a mausoleum. An ominous silence pervaded the place with such a sense of impending devastation that even the dogs seemed to sense the apprehension, and lay cowering and silent in corners. For the hundredth time he glanced at his watch and the lateness of the hour confirmed his deepest fear. Nicholas was not going to yield to the ultimatum. Within an hour Germany would be at war.

Shaking his head, he turned towards his study and with every step his anguish increased. Though tensions had been building for years, war with Russia had seemed unthinkable until a few days ago. Even when it had begun to dawn on him that Nicholas was not as pliant as he had imagined, there had been no reason to believe that he would hold out to the end.

He pushed open the door of his study and, snatching a photograph from his desk, stared at the image of himself with the Russian Imperial Family aboard their yacht, *Standardt.*

"For pity's sake, Nicky, see sense!" he whispered. "Does our friendship mean nothing to you?" He shook his head desperately and gazed at the Tsarina, "Alix, I'm pleading with you! Think of Grandmama – she would never have allowed this to happen. Think of our childhood; think of all that will be lost! You are a native German; you *cannot* allow him to provoke us into war. Tell him to withdraw his troops!"

A deep sense of betrayal turned his despair into anger and he dropped the photograph onto the floor with a loud clatter that brought his wife running into the room. For a moment, seeing her arrive so hastily, he hoped she might be bringing good news but, as she drew closer, it was clear from her anxious expression that such hope was in vain.

"No response from Nicky?" she asked.

He shook his head.

"What time is it?"

"Almost five o'clock."

"That's it then? It's all over?"

"So it would seem. I must sign the order for a general mobilisation and the declaration of war."

He picked up the papers already prepared on his desk and, with a trembling hand, added his signature, then, disgusted, he pushed the documents away as though they contained a contagion.

"Oh, Willy, how can it have come to this? So many of our relations and friends will suddenly become enemies. It's too unbearable."

His jaw clenched, "We must be strong now, Dona, and put all sentimentality aside. I did everything possible to prevent this but Nicky has thrown all my efforts back in my face. Come..."

He led her along the corridor to the magnificent Marble Hall where he gazed at the great copper dome rising over the gilded curve of the ceiling.

"It's fitting to be here this evening. This place was built to commemorate Frederick the Great's victory in the Seven Years War. Our time has come to emulate his courage."

Breathing deeply he sought to summon the strength of his ancestor and for a moment imagined himself being spoken of by future generations as 'Wilhelm the Great.'

"*Après nous, le Déluge,*" Dona murmured.

"Mm?"

"After us, the deluge. Isn't that what Madame de Pompadour said to the King of France, following his defeat by Prussia? Are we heading for another great Prussian victory or are we bequeathing a deluge to our children and grandchildren?"

Wilhelm shuddered and, determinedly sweeping away his fears, glanced once more at his watch. "Are our sons here?"

"All of them apart from Adalbert." Her eyes filled with tears, "He's still in Wilhelmshaven, preparing for his wedding. When I think how different that will be from this time last year and Viktoria Luise's wedding, when Nicky was our guest…"

"Nicky has betrayed us," he said firmly. "Now he must face the consequences."

As though summoned by a telepathic signal, ministers and attendants suddenly gathered on the corridors. Wilhelm, striding ahead of them, led the way to the front of the palace where the noise of the crowds outside rolled over the gilt panelling and electrically-lit chandeliers. For the past few evenings they had gathered, cheering and singing *Gott erhalte den Kaiser,* but tonight their voices were so much louder and more passionate as though stirred into some kind of satanic frenzy.

Wilhelm burst into a sitting room where five of his sons stood in their military uniforms like his own private army. The Crown Prince's eyes met his own with a confident expression bordering on arrogance and it occurred to Wilhelm that he and his eldest son had more in common than their name. He recalled the disdain in which he had held his parents' liberal views and the eagerness with which he had eyed the crown during the brief three months of his father's reign. Now, seeing the fire in his son's eyes, he could not help thinking that the Crown Prince was equally keen to assume the throne. Already, he feared that his heir's popularity exceeded his own and it troubled him that this younger man, who towered over him physically, had been blessed with physical perfection and a mother who adored him.

"I take it," the Crown Prince said, "that there has there been no response from Russia?"

Wilhelm shook his head.

"It's a great pity. I received such a wonderful welcome when I visited the Tsar a couple of years ago and, of course, since Cecile is half-Russian…"

"Oh Lord!" Dona gasped and pressed her hand to her forehead, "This news will be devastating for your poor wife."

The Crown Prince inhaled sharply and stood more determinedly erect, "Cecile is Crown Princess of Prussia now. She knows her duty and we are prepared to put personal feeling aside in defence of the Fatherland."

"Quite right," Wilhelm nodded. "We must set a good example to our people by playing our part with fortitude and conviction."

The Crown Prince smiled, "It would be un-German not to want to participate in this glorious conflict and I will be grateful for any command to which you might assign me."

Flattered by his compliance, Wilhelm rested his hand on his shoulder, "Spoken like a true son of the Kaiser! The Fifth Army would suit you well."

The Crown Prince's eyes shone with exhilaration, encouraging Wilhelm to say more.

"Since the French are almost certain to reject our ultimatum, they will undoubtedly take this opportunity to attempt to regain Alsace-Lorraine. I need strong commanders in the field who are willing to take whatever measures are necessary to hold them back. Are you prepared for that?"

"I would be honoured."

"I shall speak of it with Moltke as soon as possible."

Leaving the Crown Prince to revel in the glory of his new command, Wilhelm turned to his second son, Eitel-Frederick, whose doleful expression and stocky physique contrasted so sharply with the fiery erectness of his elder brother.

"Well, Fritz," Wilhelm raised his eyebrows, "are you not equally willing to serve your country?"

"Of course I am, father," he said quietly. "With your permission, I would like to take part in active service with my regiment of Foot Guards."

"You have my permission."

"Thank you," he murmured, "I am honoured."

"Then why the long face?"

He hesitated, "I cannot help thinking of the devastation this war will bring. Britain will not stand idly by if we march through Belgium so in no time at all, the whole of Europe will be at war."

Wilhelm, unwilling to consider the horror that lay ahead, murmured, "None of this is my doing," before moving on to his fourth son, August Wilhelm.

"Auwi," he sighed, acutely aware of the rumours of the boy's unnatural relationship with his adjutant. "I am sure that wherever you are posted, it will be more of a relief than a hardship for you to be separated from your wife."

Auwi flinched and cleared his throat, "It is my duty to place myself in the service of my country."

"Then perhaps this war will make a real man of you."

Auwi bit his lip but said nothing.

"For now you will continue with your duties as Staff Officer until I decide the best place for you."

Moving on to his youngest sons, he smiled with satisfaction, "Oskar you will remain with Guards; and you, Joachim with the Cavalry; and, since Adalbert will continue in the navy, we can face our subjects with our heads held high, knowing that there is no area of the military in which our family is not represented."

"And not only by your sons," Joachim said enthusiastically. "Our cousins are equally prepared to face any danger in the service of their Kaiser and country."

Wilhelm smiled, "It will be clear to everyone that we ask nothing of our people that we are not prepared to do ourselves. I trust that all of you will set a good example to your regiments and provide the inspiration necessary in the days ahead."

When the young men concurred with varying degrees of enthusiasm, Wilhelm turned to Dona, "You must be very proud of these boys, knowing that each of them is prepared to risk everything in defence of freedom and justice."

"*Dulce et decorum est pro patria mori!*" said the Crown Prince with gusto.

His mother's eyes filled with tears, "I pray with all my soul that that will not be necessary and you will all return safely to me."

Her distress wrung Wilhelm's heart so painfully that he could only respond with over-ebullient joviality. Slapping Joachim's back, he laughed loudly, "These are wonderful times for Germany! Never has there been such an opportunity to show the world what a united and powerful nation we are. In a matter of weeks this will all be over and by Christmas the Hohenzollern flag will be flying over the Arc de Triomphe and the Winter

Palace! Now, come, let's show ourselves to the people – a family united in the service of the empire!"

He pushed back the curtain and the roars of the crowd swelled in a great crescendo. A mass of flags bearing the Iron Cross and the Prussian Eagle swayed in the evening sunlight and a tide of people rolled like a river towards the window. Wilhelm stepped onto a balcony and raised his hand to acknowledge the cheers that resounded across the gardens and reverberated through the whole of Potsdam and beyond.

"I don't understand how they can find the prospect of war so uplifting," Dona said. "You would think that we were already celebrating victory. Are they too blind to see that so many are marching to their death?"

"No," Wilhelm said, reluctant to share her fears, "not to death but to victory."

After weeks of tension and uncertainty, like the onset of an illness the symptoms of which are debilitating but vague, the declaration of war brought the relief that comes with the eruption of a fever which, once and for all, clears the system of its sickness. Refusing to consider that this illness could prove fatal, Wilhelm basked instead in the certainty that God was on his side and that this would indeed be a war to end all wars. A great German victory would pave the way for German order and culture to be established throughout Europe. Then there would be no more need for wars; the adulterous alliance of Britain and France would be dissolved; Russia would come crawling for mercy, and the All-Highest Kaiser, loved by his people and revered throughout the world, would benevolently open his hand and grant them forgiveness.

Below the balcony, ranks of impeccably co-ordinated soldiers appeared. Their faces were eager and bright and their confident steps confirmed Wilhelm's certainty of the superiority of his army. The jingling of spurs and the click-clack of boots echoed like a well-orchestrated symphony and, as each line strutted by, turning their heads towards him in the march-past, he felt their eyes upon him like the eyes of musicians awaiting the guidance of an accomplished maestro to keep them in time. As though conducting a rousing anthem, he pulled a sword from his scabbard and raised it aloft to acknowledge their salutes. His heart swelled with pride until he caught sight of the tears streaming from Dona's eyes.

"They are so young," she murmured, "far too young to die."

His spirits plunged to the depths as again it occurred to him that for all his vast collection of uniforms and titles he had never captained a ship, commanded a regiment or seen active service. The pageantry and display he knew thoroughly but he had no experience of military strategy or the tactics of war. He recalled his father riding out to defeat the Austrians at Kőnnigratz and the rapturous acclaim that greeted his victorious return. Now it seemed that his sons would enjoy the same glory while he would remain, as always, watching from the side-lines. Even as he stood with his sword raised above the ranks of officers and conscripts, an even more daunting fear struck him. How could so inexperienced a conductor elicit from these young men the harmonious anthem of victory and peace? Would he not, instead, bring forth the cacophonous din of slaughter? And, should this war result in a German disaster, posterity would view him forever as an incompetent failure or worse – the Kaiser who led his country to its doom.

At length he withdrew from the balcony and, leaving Dona to the care of his sons, he returned to his study. He picked up the photograph of Nicholas and his family, "I didn't want this," he whispered. "This isn't my fault," and, pressing the photograph to his heart, he wept like a child.

By the same author:

The Fields Laid Waste

The Counting House

Most Beautiful Princess – A novel based on the life of Grand Duchess Elizabeth of Russia